About the Author

I was born and raised in Scotland, currently I live in Edinburgh with my partner. Half my time is spent working and the other half is split between writing, cooking, gaming and spending too much money on collectables and books.

I Am...

Gregor Macadam

I Am...

Olympia Publishers
London

www.olympiapublishers.com
OLYMPIA PAPERBACK EDITION

Copyright © Gregor Macadam 2024

The right of Gregor Macadam to be identified as author of
this work has been asserted in accordance with sections 77 and 78 of
the Copyright, Designs and Patents Act 1988.

All Rights Reserved

No reproduction, copy or transmission of this publication
may be made without written permission.
No paragraph of this publication may be reproduced,
copied or transmitted save with the written permission of the publisher,
or in accordance with the provisions
of the Copyright Act 1956 (as amended).

Any person who commits any unauthorised act in relation to
this publication may be liable to criminal
prosecution and civil claims for damage.

A CIP catalogue record for this title is
available from the British Library.

ISBN: 978-1-80074-935-1

This is a work of fiction.
Names, characters, places and incidents originate from the writer's
imagination. Any resemblance to actual persons, living or dead, is
purely coincidental.

First Published in 2024

Olympia Publishers
Tallis House
2 Tallis Street
London
EC4Y 0AB

Printed in Great Britain

Dedication

For George and Moira Macadam.
The greatest of inspiration and biggest supporters,
We all miss you.

Acknowledgements

Thank you to my partner Matt who, despite my being a pain in his ass, has never stopped believing in me.

Used

I feel the back of his hand connect with my face, throwing me to the ground. I'm not winded, but that doesn't mean I get a break. I hit the headboard, dazing me. He grabs me by the scruff of my neck then pins me onto the bed. I feel his breath on the back of my neck as he mumbles into my ear.

"What did you say to me, slut?" he mumbles, sending shivers down my spine.

"N-Nothing, s-sir," I strain out. Curse my damned stutter. He hits the back of my head.

"That's two. You must enjoy being punished." I feel the heavy pressure of his leg on my back as he continues pinning me to the bed.

"S-s…" I stop and try again. "Sorry."

"Sorry, what?" he says, increasing the pressure on my back. I take a deep breath and try again.

"Sorry, s-sir." Fuck.

"Five. You really are asking for it tonight, aren't you? I bet your hole is begging for my meat." I don't reply. "Isn't it!" he shouts, pushing on my spine with his bony knee.

"Yes, sir. P… Please." It's safe to say I haven't wanted his meat in years, not since this began, but he'll do a lot worse to me if I say no, or if I try and fight back. So it's safer for me to just… agree.

"That's seven now." I hear a click and know what is coming. I want to escape, but I know that struggling won't do anything, and he won't stop. I quickly lose my breath as he pulls on my T-shirt, dragging his favourite knife along it, exposing my back. He cuts away part of my sleeve and pulls it away from me. He runs a finger over my bare back and presses on my most recent scar. I wince at his touch. "You look so pretty with these scars. Good thing you're getting more tonight, isn't it?" I don't reply to that, but I do nod. Despite knowing all I do about him, this always surprises me. Not only does he like causing me harm, but he likes how I look with them. I feel him press the knife into my back, causing me to whimper. My pain doesn't stop him though, it only spurs him on.

"P-P... please s-stop." I can feel tears stinging my eyes, I never usually ask, but tonight I just wanted to be left alone with my book.

"Ten, no mercy now."

He starts slowly pulling his knife down my back. He then lifts it and makes another. And another. And another. And another. He only finishes when there are ten cuts down my back, the fresh blood running down my back and over the fresh bedsheets. I start seeing black spots; at this point, I have no clue what's happening. I think I feel him pulling at my trousers, and I'm too weak to fight back. The next thing I know is the familiar feeling of losing consciousness.

"Hey, get away from him!" someone yells... Wait, what is happening?

"Oh, look, it's your boyfriend!" another voice yells. What the fuck is going on? Suddenly, I hear punching and yelling and... "Let's get out of here, guys!"

Now I hear the sounds of footfalls on asphalt. This is... this is a memory. Not again. Why does this keep happening? I do not need to be reminded of what I've lost.

"Percival? You okay?" a familiar voice asks; I wish I could remember whose it was. Instead, I feel them tap my forehead twice, and I finally open my eyes to see my red-haired saviour.

"A... as good as s... someone who j-just got b-b-beat up can b-be," I stutter out. 'Red' helps me sit up and then plops down next to me, looking at my eye.

"Think you might have a bruise, but I'm not a doctor."

"That's for sure," I mumble.

"I heard that, Perry."

"You were meant to." I look up and see him smiling, then I feel a smile slowly emerge on my face, and we both start laughing. Red helps me up and walks us back to what used to be my family home; even in this distorted dream, I can tell that it's mine. Red pulls me into the back garden, and we both fall to the ground lying on the floor, basking in the awful Scottish weather. But, hey, at least it's not raining. After a few moments, Red sits up and looks at me; I turn my head and look back.

"We're always gonna be friends... right?" he asks me; I think his face is blushing. He was blushing?

"W-what kind of q-question is t-t... that? Course w-we are!" I reply. Red smiles then cross his legs.

"Okay, then let's make a promise." I sit up and face him.

"What kind of p-p-p... what kind?" He gently takes my hand; I feel my heartbeat increase. He takes my pinky then speaks.

"Percival. I will always be there for you."

"Promise?" I ask; he gives me that unforgettable smile once again.

"Promise."

When I wake up, I'm still in bed. Straight away, I can tell three things: first, my cuts have been bandaged expertly, second, I'm naked and third: my ass hurts like a bitch. Luckily, I'm not actually lying on my ass. Instead, I'm on my stomach. I bring my scar-riddled arm up to my face, rub my eye with the heel of my hand, and sigh. I turn my head to face the window in the room. The faded, bland curtains are still closed, meaning that he slept on the couch and bandaged me up at some point after he was done with me. One thing I know for sure about him is this: he never apologises, so I don't expect it. The one good thing about him is that he usually leaves me to sleep after a night like that. Usually, if he is unsatisfied, he stays and has seconds in the morning. Thus, rendering me pretty much inert for most of the day. Thank Apollo he was satisfied this time.

I hear the door creak open and shut my eyes, and I try to steady my breathing to make it seem like I am still asleep. I hear the bed creak and sink on my side. I feel him removing the covers that are protecting me, his hand starts running down my back. I instantly flinch at his touch, secretly hoping that he thinks I'm having a bad dream. They tend to happen… a lot. Unfortunately, he doesn't buy it, and he starts to prod my ass, forcing his sausage-like fingers into it, without any sort of lube. My eyes snap open, and I look up at him, waiting for him to talk.

"My co-worker is coming over in a few minutes, get dressed, or you'll be punished again." He starts to force another finger into my already sore ass, causing me to let out another whimper. "Wear the long stuff today." I nod at him. He removes his fingers, and I slowly let out a sigh before I wince at a pain in my leg. He's just cut me again. "That's for the lack of response, slut." He gets up and leaves, leaving the door open.

I sigh and suppress a cry and start to get up. I gently swing my legs over the side of the bed before leaning over to the bedside cabinet; I pull out a bandage to wrap my leg. Once that's done, I slowly get up and grab my clothes. After painfully pulling on my top, I'm forced to sit back on the bed; I'm just glad I've developed a high pain tolerance. I take a breath, and thankfully it's not that difficult to get my jammie trousers on. Once on, I start to walk towards the kitchen. I check the time and see that it's almost after eleven, meaning that he's gonna start drinking, and he'll want me to get a beer for him or… well, I don't want to think about what will happen if I don't. When I reach the living room, I see him sitting on the couch with another guy. This one is new. Most of his friends I've met, they're all as bad as him, especially when they get drunk. One of them even suggested using me as a cum dump; he was against it at first. His resolve lasted a week.

This might be a guy from work, but it's hard to know where he meets all these people. I give him a quick glance and see that he is shorter than my 'boyfriend' (I forgot to mention that, didn't I), but he is clearly stronger. Having said that, it doesn't mean I can trust him. Some of the people that I tried to get help from ended up on his side. Somehow, I ended up being the guy who lied to get away from people, oh and apparently, I have schizophrenia paranoia. Basically, it's all in my head that he's hurting me. The scars prove that it's not though. I may have autism, a touch of depression and self-destructive tendencies, but I am not a liar. The new man smiles at me and adjusts his glasses, probably to get a better view of me.

"Baby, this is Skye. He's the new guy at work."

"What do you mean, the new guy? I've been working there longer than you have!" he replies. I think he is a little annoyed. But, it… actually, it's tough to tell. I know I don't get many interactions with people, but still.

"Want a beer, love?" I ask, knowing full well that I couldn't love this asshole less. He grunts and nods, returning to his conversation with Skye. I walk to the fridge and grab a beer and a glass from the cupboard that are just too high for me. I hop up onto the counter to grab the glass. As I begin to come down, I slip and land on my ass; I wince and suppress my cry by biting down on the back of my hand.

"Everything okay?" a voice says. I quickly remove my hand, hoping that I'm not bleeding, and look to the door. I find Skye standing there looking down on me.

"W-why wouldn't they b-be?" I stand up and start to pour the beer.

I don't so much as barge past Skye, but I push him out of the way. If he finds out I was on the counter again, then he'll cut me. Or I'll do it for him; I deserve it, so why not save him the trouble? I hand the beer over and move away from him; he thanks me and doesn't ask any more of me. Skye walks past me, and I notice we are about the same height. But it's his eyes that get me. There is something in them that… you know I can't place it, but it feels like trust. But I can definitely see the sadness in there. His pale blue eyes remind me of someone; I'm probably looking too much into it, though.

"I'm gonna go clean the bathroom before I do some work," I tell him before I move away.

"What is it you do?" Skye asks me.

"He's a computer programmer. Means that he stays home all day while I go out to earn money," my oppressor replies in my stead.

"And make double the amount of money you make at the end of the month," I mumble quietly, making sure he can't hear me. I turn away from them and head towards the bathroom. To do exactly what I said I was going to do, clean. I usually do this after he... yeah. It makes me feel better. *I* may not be clean, but at least the house can be. Before I grab the cleaning supplies, I check my hand, and it seems okay, no blood, which is... I'll be honest, I was hoping for something, not that I bite myself all that much. I used to like hickeys, not sure that I'll ever enjoy getting them again. Instead, I just get cuts and bruises. This time I just wanted something different, I guess. I shake away my thoughts and grab the cleaning supplies. I start by cleaning the toilet scrubbing it more than once to make sure every inch is sparkling. I unconsciously roll up my sleeves, so I won't get them wet as I use the toilet brush. Next, I throw a loo flush into the cistern and move over to the bath shower.

There is always this ring around the bathtub that I just can't seem to get rid of no matter how much I scrub it. So, I clean as much as I can. Until I hear a cough from behind me, I pull my sleeves down and turn to face Skye, who looks a tad awkward. I look him up and down and wait for him to speak.

"Sorry, I know I'm interrupting, but your boyfriend said I could use the loo even though you are in here," he tells me. I don't respond, but I get up, walk outside, and tilt my head towards the toilet. He smiles again and shuts the door. A minute later, he comes out with wet hands and a grateful look on his face. I move back in and hover over the toilet. It's still clean. I look at it, confused. Why is it still so clean?

"Something wrong?"

"It's s-still clean," I reply. Three.

"Of course it is. Why wouldn't it be?"

"That's... Usually, w-when a guy uses it, t-t-there is s-splash back or even some h-hair on the seat, but... there's n-nothing," I respond. Nine.

"Well, you did just clean it; I didn't want to dirty it again. As for the hair, well… that's a private thing." He rubs the back of his neck; I wonder slightly if it is a nervous tick or something else. I don't respond to that, but I get on my knees and return to scrubbing the bath. After about a minute, I feel like someone is watching me. I turn around, and Skye is still standing there, watching me. I respray the ring and continue scrubbing. I can still feel him watching me, though. Okay, enough of this.

"What? Are you that interested in what I'm doing?" I snap at him. Oh, hey, I didn't stutter. I do seem to shock him, though. He thinks for a second before replying.

"If you make a paste with vinegar and baking soda, then you'll get rid of that stain much quicker."

I scoff at him, but he simply smiles and walks away. I stand up and move over to the sink. It's easier to clean since I can't clean the bath right now. I hear the two men laughing and decide I need something to take my edge off, and I… need to cut. I quietly close the door to the bathroom and lock it. I open up the mirror cabinet and pull out the razor blades that I hide in there. I roll up my sleeve and give myself nine quick swipes of the blade. I let out a sigh of relief as the blood flows out of my arm. After letting the euphoric pain dissipate, I drop the blade into the sink and start cleaning the blood off my arm. I grab a disinfected gauze and quickly wrap my arm, wincing in my blissful pain. I pull down my sleeve and notice that the cuff is wet slightly. I shake my head, clean the blade, and hide it back in the cabinet. I flush the loo and pretend that I was just using it. Once I've finished erasing my blood from the sink, I unlock the door. I'm always meticulous about cleaning, more so after I've cut. It doesn't mean I want to advertise that I do it to myself just because he does.

It doesn't take me too long to finish up the rest of the bathroom. I give my hands a quick wash and go to my small office. I turn on my computer to continue working on my latest project. The client I'm currently contracted to is a photographer, mainly family portraits. He has some really thoughtful shots that I like. I was almost tempted to ask for one as payment. But, I decided against it when I realised a physical copy might get destroyed. Thankfully the photographer offered one as payment and asked if there were any I liked. Then sent me a pdf file of the image to use as a screensaver on my computer. I always smile slightly when my computer turns on, and I get to see the picture. The photo is just two pairs of feet standing together, but one is on their toes, obviously stretching up to reach their partner. I asked about the gender of the two in the picture, and the artist simply replied, *'They are whatever gender you want them to be.'*

That's why I love it. It could be anyone. Not me, but I love the picture all the same. Since he gave me the shot mostly for free, I want his website to be perfect, so I've been taking longer to build the actual site. Thus far, I do really like it, but there are a few things that I don't quite like. I hope I'll get them done today; it shouldn't take more than an hour.

About ten minutes into my work, I get a ping on my screen and notice that I have a message from an online friend. He's called Atlas; well, his online name is Atlas03. He told me it was a joke, but I don't really get it. His username came up when we asked about our real names; we agreed not to tell each other our real names. In return for keeping our names a secret as a counter, we also decided to tell each other everything; I agreed until I let slip that my 'boyfriend' is abusive. Now he makes comments about saving me every time I bring it up. I know he cares for me;

we've been speaking for two years now, and it's so apparent it kinda hurts that he won't ever find me. So I bring up the chat and see what he's said.

Atlas03: Sorry for not messaging before now, I'm hanging out with my friend, and he just passed out on the couch, lol. 😆

Deathgrail38: Haha, dw about it. I've been… recovering since last night, and I didn't get up till 11. Did my usual tho.

Atlas03: Dude again? Didn't he get you a few nights ago?

Deathgrail38: Idk I don't really remember all that much about last night. All I know is that I was bandaged, and my ass was hella sore. Even Hades would wonder how I survived. 😆

Atlas03: How can you laugh at that? Seriously if it gets any worse, I may just have to come and save you.

Deathgrail38: I've lasted 6 years with the guy I think I can last longer.

Atlas03: You shouldn't have to 'last'. You should be trying to get out of there. I know you tried, but I promise that if you want I'll meet you wherever you want, and you can stay with me till this whole thing blows over.
Atlas03: Longer than that if you wanted. 😊

Deathgrail38: I know, Atlas. Maybe one day we'll meet but until then thank you for the offer. X

Atlas03: Okay. Oh shit, he's waking up. I better go; this guy is seriously annoying. I have no clue why I agreed to this. His bf is cute though. Bye Death. 😘

Deathgrail38: Dude, that's so gay. 🤭 Bye Atlas. 😘

I'm not sure how or why we ended up signing off our messages with kisses, but I really like it. Every time Atlas signs off, I always feel a little better and have a slight smile on my face. For the record, I don't really count this as cheating. If I could get out of this place and be with Atlas, I would already be there. We met about three years ago after I was finally allowed to start working. It got to the point where he was beating me for not. His fault, mind you. Once I started working, I had to set up a new email, and I ended up setting up a Discord account for fun.

Atlas emailed me a few days after I set up my web page. He approached me on behalf of his sister, so he was using her account. She has a small book store somewhere in Dumfries and Galloway. She wanted to set up an online store for her shop so that her books could reach more people around the UK. So Atlas talked to me on behalf of his sister because she was busy actually running her shop. It was pretty simple, and since they were one of my first clients, I had to make a good impression. Thankfully I did; Atlas' sister loved the design so much that she paid me a little extra for my work. During the time I was working, Atlas kept messaging me about changes that his sister wanted. Eventually, we talked so much and ended up on Discord; it was easier to get updates from his sister.

It wasn't until the following year that I accidentally let slip that I was in an abusive relationship. After that, Atlas was chill about my reasonings for not going to the police; it doesn't stop him from bringing it up all the time, though. It is shocking, but I trust him, though not as much as Elliot, my oldest and best friend. But I haven't seen him in years, and I doubt I'll see him anytime soon, so I trust Atlas to keep my secret; however annoyed he may be about keeping it. I close the chat and get back to work.

After another two hours of work, I am pleased with the layout of the website. I just need to get the file that contains all of my client's pictures. Which will take me another hour to arrange. After that, it's the simple case of making it live. And as I thought, it took me just over an hour. Once the site is live, I compose a quick email to the photographer and the link to the site and send it off to him. I'm about to start my next commission when I get a ping on hangouts from the photographer. It's three heart-eye faces, but at least I know he likes it.

I bring up my receipt template filling out the relevant information, minus the photo cost, thanking him for the praise and sent the email to him. He pays and even gave me a tip... the value of the picture. That's annoying, you try to do a nice thing, and someone repays it instantly. So... wait, why am I complaining about getting more money?

I shake my head and pull out my external hard drive; I like to save all my work onto an external source. Force of a habit, I guess it's as a precaution. If I ever get the chance to get out of here, then I just grab the hard drives and run. I thought it was clever. I stretch as the file downloads run, then crack my back, wincing at the pain I've caused myself. See, self-destructive.

"Something wrong with your shoulder?" Skye asks.

"H-how long h-h—" I take a breath "—have you been there?" I ask. Three, already?

"Not long, I was going to leave. That jackass you live with is asleep again."

"O-Oh." Four.

"So, your shoulder?"

"I-it's nothing. Just a t-tad tense after working so much. It'll p... pass." I force out that last part. I don't know why I find the letter P so hard to say. Six.

"What was that?" Skye asks; I just look up at him, confused. "You said six. Six what?" Oh fuck, I cannot believe he heard me saying that.

"Six new p-p..."

"Projects?"

"Yes. I would h-have gotten there you k-know." Ten, I'm in for it now.

"Sorry, I'm not sure about the protocol on stutterers. I kinda like helping them out with words." I look at him, tilting his head slightly. "What I mean is, if I know the word, they are going to say why not say it for them if they are struggling so much?"

"P... Personally, I don't mind. But other p... people may find it a-a-annoying. It's not like I'm always like this. Sometimes I get full sentences without o-one stutter." Unlike this one, ugh, I've lost count, great.

"Well, if I come over again, I'll try and remember not to correct you." He turns to leave.

"Just on P," I say suddenly, surprising myself.

"Sorry?" He comes back in.

"P. It's like the only l-letter I struggle w-with. The others I can... deal with."

"I'll keep that in mind. I didn't catch your name, by the way. He just referred to you as... well, it didn't seem very nice, to be honest." He gives me a soft smile, and I have to suppress my own smile.

"You don't want to know my n-name. Besides, I can't even say it." I turn back to my computer and open up a commission email. Improvements on a school's website, they've given me an administration login to make the alterations, I start work on it. *Good call turning away; we don't want pretty boy getting too close.* **I do! Please get closer to him.** <u>Focus, there are more important things right now.</u> Ugh, would you guys shut up!

"Peter? No, you don't look like a Peter." I sigh at his attempt and shake my head at him. "What about Paul?"

"Eww. Wh-who's even called P... that any more?"

"My step-dad was called Paul. What about Patrick?"

"As in the star f-fish? No, that's n-not it." I shake my head, but in reality, I'm trying hard not to react. Patrick is my dad's name, and it's been too long since I've seen him, not since the funeral.

"Paxton?"

"If I t-tell you my name, will you stop?" I say, spinning around to face him, only to find that he is way further into my office than I would like. I feel my breath start to quicken.

"Yes." He faces me and must see that I'm uncomfortable that he's in here, so he quickly steps out of the room. I start to calm down. I close my eyes and take a deep breath. I look at him then type it onto my computer screen.

"That's your name?" he asks. I nod. "As in..."

"Yes, as in the Arthur legends. Both my p... parents were o-obsessed."

"I like it, Percival. Got a nickname at all?"

"You a-ask toooo. Many questions." I face my computer. The truth is, it's been a long time since anyone thought of a nickname for me; it's hard enough to say without someone talking about Arthur legends. Yes, I like it, and I've seen practically every TV show and film to do with it. Personally, though, I much prefer Greek mythology, not that the media ever gets it right. There is always something that they get wrong, the biggest one being Hades. Although I think the TV show Atlantis did an… all right job with Greek mythology. Didn't actually have any of the gods in it; having said that, the worst film about mythology is Hercules. Now that is something you don't want to get me started on. I'll go on for hours. We both hear a giant snore from the other room; it causes me to flinch slightly. I don't think Skye noticed, though.

"Look, I've actually got to go. I said I'd help out at work today. Can I like get your number or something?" He wants what?

"Ummm. I don't actually h-have a p… one." I can see the surprise on his face. "I mainly stay in; I have no friends. And well, the people I talk to get to me through email, so I don't really see the p-p… point." I shrug and grab one of my note cards, writing my email down for him. I hold it out for him.

"So you only talk, through, like that hangouts things Google has?" he asks.

"That's my personal email, but yes. I have a w-w-work email, but Hangouts is the q-quickest way to get in c… contact with me." He smiles at me and thanks me before heading out.

As soon as he leaves, I feel… something, I'm not sure what it is, but he is the first person in a while who has actually wanted to get to know me. Other than Atlas, I don't count him since we've never actually met, as much as I'd like to see him. I'll think about it later. I should make some food, I'm hungry, and I know The Beast will be too when he wakes up.

Worthless

I am thankful that *he* doesn't wake up for the duration of my cooking; it was about five p.m. when I started cooking, and it's almost six now. I've made one of his favourite meals in the hopes that tonight he won't... Anyway, when I am done, I take a bowl of chicken stir-fry and head back to my office. That school website isn't going to improve itself, and it's already a huge mess. Before I got stuck here, I actually thought about being a teacher. I was pretty close to getting a job, but then I met him, and he... well, now he doesn't let me leave. To be fair, I did finish my teacher training, but then he stopped letting me go out, so I had to turn down the teaching job I applied for. When I do get to leave, it's because we need to make some kind of appearance. Usually at the hospital or he's taking me to his parents, that's really the only time I leave the house. His parents died last year, though, in some freak house fire.

I sit back in my chair and instantly lean forwards again. Guess I'm not relaxing today. I move my keyboard out of the way and place the bowl down. I start to eat it, gazing at my screen. I would love to use chopsticks to eat this, but I don't really have the patience to learn that particular skill. Suddenly there is a ping on my screen, and my chat with Atlas opens up.

Atlas03: Hey. You'll never guess what happened!

Deathgrail38: Did a crazy man chop off his leg with a chain saw? 😱

Atlas03: What? No…! I don't think so anyway. No, defo not. Anyway, I talked to the pretty boy that I mentioned before.

Deathgrail38: Really? Dude, that's so gay.

Atlas03: Ha, ha. How's your ass btw?

Deathgrail38: That was a low blow, Atlas. Tell me about this guy, then.

Atlas03: He is adorable and has an awesome name. I won't tell you because something tells me that I shouldn't. But I think he might be on the autistic spectrum.

Deathgrail38: What makes you think that?

Atlas03: Well, when I went to the toilet, he almost freaked that it was still clean and I stepped into his office, and I swear he was gonna have a panic attack.

Wait… what? That's what happened when Skye was over… could Skye be Atlas? No way, they are totally different. It's just my imagination, besides Skye… never told me what he does for work. Let's just assume they are the same person, meaning Skye already knows I am being abused but doesn't know he's met me. Hmm… I'm gonna try something.

Deathgrail38: Don't tell me you are looking for your next patient? I don't think this guy would want his faults advertised. I know I wouldn't. 😳

Atlas03: I'm not gonna look for a new patient. I'd ask him out, but he's in a relationship, and like I said before, his bf is crazy.

Deathgrail38: What does he do?

Atlas03: He is a nurse, not a very good one tbh. He thinks he's the best-damned nurse at the hospital.
Atlas03: He doesn't even hold that position; Lindsay does.

Yup, that is definitely my 'boyfriend' he's talking about. Meaning that this *is* Skye I'm talking to. Ugh, it's no wonder that we kind of slipped into a familiar rapport. So, do I tell him, or do I keep it to myself? I won't say anything to The Beast on the couch, that's for sure, but... I don't like the idea of lying to Atlas... Skye. Maybe I could make him realise who I am. Like, give him a little push. Yeah, that sounds food. Good. Oh, wait, I have food! I continue eating my dinner.

Deathgrail38: This is gonna sound out of the blue, but... What do you think of the letter P?

Atlas03: The letter P? That is really out of the blue. But it's not exactly a difficult letter. Weird tho, my new friend struggles with it, so I said I would help him out with it. What do u think about it?

Deathgrail38: I can't stand it. I mean, typing it is fine; it's not like I'm saying it. But saying it is problematic. 'Cause of my stutter.

Atlas03: …You never told me you had a stutter.

Deathgrail38: I just did, it's not that bad, it's worse when I'm nervous, or you know… he's… You get it, I don't need to say it.

Atlas03: I know we said that we would never meet or exchange our names, but… Can we meet? Like tomorrow?

Deathgrail38: You of all people know that I can't leave the house. I do want to meet you. But if there was something at *his* work that meant I had to attend, though, then I would be allowed out.

Atlas03: Well there is the Christmas party. I could send you an invite. It's not for a while, but still…

Deathgrail38: Shit! I've gotta go he's looking for me. Bye, Skye. Xx

Before bringing up the school's website, I quickly close the chat, opening up the admin alteration files. I inject my maintenance warning program then get to work on the changes. He enters my office as I start changing the code. He doesn't say anything, just looks at me while I eat and work. It's times like this that my anxiety spikes; I don't know what he's going to do. If anything. I hope that he'll just grunt and go off to find his food. I've got no luck this time. He whacks the back of my head and pulls my hair back, so I'm facing him. When he finally talks to me, I can smell the beer on his breath, and it almost makes me gag.

"You were very rude to Skye today. When he comes over

next week, you will apologise to him, and if he wants it, you'll let him take you." He pulls harder on my hair. "Right?"

"Y... yes sir," I reply, and he lets me go and leaves my office. I rub my eyes to stop the tears from falling. But they start running anyway. I sniff as quietly as I can; if he hears me crying, then he *will* hit me again. I take a deep breath and continue to work on the school's website. Still crying.

Took me three days to sort out that damned school website. Whoever programmed it did a shit job. They paid me a little more than I usually charge because I was so lovely about it, apparently. I open up my emails and see that I have two more requests for work from the photographer, something about finding the actual site. I do a quick google search and send over the correct address. He is swift to reply.

Xavier. K: Thanks so much for the address. My family were asking about it and couldn't find it.

Comp-geek: It's honestly no problem. However, you did give me that photo, so I feel like I owe you something.

Xavier. K: If you feel like you owe me, then you could take me out to dinner next week.

Comp-geek: I don't think my bf would like that very much.

Xavier. K: He wouldn't have to know. I know my wife won't know. 😉

Comp-geek: Then definitely not, I may not have standards, but

I'm not gonna do that.

I block the chat and close down the hangouts. I sigh, rubbing my face; there's always one, isn't there. Then I open up the following email and see that it's from the hospital. I skim through the email. It tells me that most of their systems are outdated, and they are in dire need of an upgrade. There's just one big problem, it's an on-site job. Now my bio says that I don't do on-site jobs, but looking at the money they are willing to pay… I think I have to. I'll have to talk him into it. I guess I have a few ideas on how to get him to agree.

I pick up my bowl and start to walk through to the kitchen, seeing him sitting eating his own dinner at the kitchen table. I silently wash my dish and put it on the rack to dry. I spin around and lean on the counter, looking at him as he enjoys the meal I made for him. He always enjoys the meals I make, yet another reason he thinks I shouldn't work. He wants me to be one of those stays at home partners. Don't get me wrong, I liked the idea of staying at home all the time. Before, I was forbidden to leave. I haven't left the house by myself for about four years. I got out once for my mum's funeral; he tried to stop me, so I snuck out that night, stayed on the street, and went to the funeral the next day. He was there when the funeral was over. I got to say goodbye this time. I shake my head and clear my throat.

"I. I got a job, and the client n-needs me to do it on-site." Fuck that. One.

"Nope. You have other work you can do. The house needs cleaning, and I still have pressure," he tells me, taking a bite out of his meal.

"It's a-at the hospital. You work there, so-oo. You could be there to p… p-pick me up after I'm done." Five, for fuck's sake,

I really hate this stutter. It wasn't nearly this bad before I met him. Just the occasional word; my parents and friends really didn't mind. They would help me get through the sentences that I couldn't quite get. W was always one I struggled with, not now, though.

"The answer is still—"

"They are p-paying me over double what I normally charge for a job like this. And it's not like I would be going anywhere else except the server room and possibly some of the op- operating rooms." I don't usually interrupt him, but this is important. I really want this job even if it means that I have to lose half of my pay to get him to agree. He looks over at me, and I can tell he's pissed that I interrupted him. He is about to talk again, but I get there before him. "You could give me a mobile and p... p-put a tracker on it, that way you would know where I w-was at all times. Or just text me, and I'll tell you where I am. This is rrr-really im-portant to me." My nerves must be through the roof; I haven't stuttered on a W in years. I can see him thinking over my proposition.

"I want seventy per cent of the pay."

"You'll get twenty-five per cent. For rent and food." The nerve of him sometimes. Like fuck am I handing over seventy per cent of *my* paycheck. He nods and tells me that I can buy a phone as long as I have it before starting the job. I smile and run over to him. I give him a hug and a kiss before running off to my office. I quietly shut the door and wipe my mouth with the back of my hand. I have to keep up the illusion that I actually love him. That should be enough. I jump onto my computer and compose a quick email to the hospital saying that I can start next week. My new phone should arrive before then.

I jump onto a phone company site and start looking at

phones. I would go for an older model, but it needs to be modern to get emails. Maybe even message Atlas. Skye did ask for my number, so I can give that to him now. At least I kinda get how his name is a joke now... Oh gods, I finally get it, heh that is funny. As I'm browsing, I see this really nice phone, a Samsung Galaxy S9. I check out its specs. It's not terrible, and I can just upgrade anything that stops working. I check out the available contracts, and all of them are for like two years. Guess I can't help that. I order it; a decent deal that means I can do my work pretty much anywhere. I smile to myself; maybe things will get better. I open up the chat between Atlas and me, and I realise I've made a colossal mistake.

I called him Skye.

Alone

My phone arrived two days later. The people at Vodafone are pretty awesome if this is all it takes for me to get a phone. Unfortunately, the first thing I have to do is activate the tracking system and tie it into my oppressor's phone. While I was doing that, I noticed that he got a message from one of his friends. In fact, it's the one who said I should be a cum dump, asking if they were still up for next week. That means more men attacking my ass. I wonder if I can stay late at the hospital and try to get work done overnight. No. They wouldn't let me do that; he certainly wouldn't. I hand his phone back to him and get up. Only to be pulled back down and come face to face with my boyfriend's wet dick. I look up at him before he forces my face into his hairy balls.

Okay, I hate hair. I honestly cannot stand it anywhere but on my head, and maybe my forearms, but anywhere else, I just can't. I shave the entirety of my body at least once a week, sometimes more if he's had his way with me or I need to clean out some cuts. I've asked him to shave, but he says it's unmanly to shave hair that isn't on your face. Having said that, he always says that he likes how smooth I am once I am clean. Hypocrite much. That is why I'm currently only wearing a jockstrap; he was feeling me up while I sorted out our phones. I shaved this morning, before my phone arrived, while I was in the shower. I really needed it; there was too much hair on my face, chest, legs and balls. The only hair I can't deal with is my head hair; he won't let me go out to get it cut. Once it was all gone, though, I did get to have a little bit of fun.

When he does stuff to me, he never asks. So, I don't see it as wrong to play with myself a little when I get some alone time. Like this morning, he'd left last night for an all-night shift. He's still up because I needed his phone. So, while he was away, I took my dildo and lube into the bathroom with me. I had to make sure I was clean; otherwise, this would be pointless. I was clean, thankfully. So while I was in the shower, I lubed up and well... there was a lot of bouncing involved. I don't usually do stuff in the shower, especially to the point where I cum, but I was grateful that it was all washed down the drain. I was a little breathless afterwards but partially satisfied. Suddenly he forces my head all the way down his length, and I feel him shoot down my throat.

When he lets go of my head, I cough a little and smile, wiping the cum off the side of my mouth. He tells me that I did an excellent job before he pushes me away and goes to bed. I sit on the floor for a moment before grabbing my phone and sending a message to Atlas. One message. My phone number. Skye and I started talking more after my blunder a few days ago. He quickly realised that it was me he'd been talking to for three years even though we had only met once. Enough to talk about what The Beast has been doing to me for the past six years. I gracefully collapse onto the sofa and wait for him to message me. But, instead, I get him calling me, I answer immediately.

"Hey, Atlas." I smile to myself and cough slightly.

"Hey, Percival, you doing okay?" he asks.

"Oh y-yeah, just had some meat c-caught in my throat." I hear him laugh on the other end of the phone, making me smile more.

"I guess he had some build-up of pressure today."

"I know t… t-that I did. Luckily *I* already took care of that." I snigger.

"I didn't think you bothered with that sort of stuff." Somehow, I'm now slightly pissed off.

"Just because he ab-abuses my body on a r… r-regular basis doesn't mean… Well, o-okay, I hate it, but I p… p… ugh, I like it when I do it to myself. It's p-probably the only reason he hasn't torn my ass yet," I tell him, taking a deep breath out to calm myself down.

"Sorry. I didn't mean to assume, but hey, you got a phone. That's awesome."

"Yeah, I told h-him about this j-job I have at the hospital. He was reluctant, but I think w-w-when he heard about the mm-money, he changed his mind about l-l-letting me out."

"What else did you have to agree to?"

"He'll be there to p-p… pi…"

"Pick you up?" he finishes for me.

"Yes, thank y-you. It's every day. You know t-to m-make sure I get home." I sigh and try to sink further into the couch.

"You okay? You sound, I don't know, a little on edge." He's right about that, but I think it's just 'cause I'm only wearing underwear.

"Well, you would be too if a-all you were wearing was a j-jockstrap."

"YOU OWN A JOCK!" he yells, then takes a breath. *"Sorry, that was too loud. Everything I know about you is wrong, isn't it?"*

"Oh, p-probably. I have three d-dildos and about ten jocks. I bought a few of them b-b…"

"Before?" he responds, and I mumble yes. *"The most I have is a fleshlight, a butt plug and a really crappy jock that… really*

doesn't deserve to be called one." I smile at his comment.

We talk for another hour and a half before he has to start a shift at the hospital. I think I'm gonna enjoy speaking with Skye. I guess I could consider him my friend. No. I can't; I don't have friends. If I did, they would try and get me out of this relationship and get hurt. I don't want that. After I end the call, I get up and make some food for myself. Something basic... so I pick up an apple; I'm not that hungry right now. I walk a short distance to my office. I shut the door and pull on my 'Believe in the Fireflies' T-shirt that I got last month, then jump into my computer chair. I boot up Minecraft and continue working on my megabase for this survival world I started last year.

I've been taking it slow in this world, making sure that I have plenty of resources and that I won't die unnecessarily. I've had one too many close calls with my best gear, so I decided to make a second and third set. When I travel to the other two dimensions, I'll use my second set. When I'm in the overworld, I use my first set. Currently, I'm in the nether looking for Ancient Debris to upgrade all my tools and armour. I knew it was gonna be challenging to find, but this is just ridiculous. The good thing is that I have a shit load of beds to blast my way through. I've barely gotten a stack of the stuff. I'd have more, but I had a lot of jobs come up when the new update came out, so I've really only just got to the latest items and blocks.

I'm playing for a good few hours when I hear The Beast roll out of bed. I relieve myself of my T-shirt, throwing it into the corner I got it from. The door swings open, and he stands and looks at me for a while. I pause the game and face him. He narrows his eyes at me and motions for me to stand up; I do. As I stand, he takes my hand, takes me into the bathroom, and tells me to sit on the toilet, facing away from him. Once again, I do what he asks. I hear him open and close the bathroom cabinet before I feel his hands on my back. Suddenly he rips off the bandage on my back, and I struggle to hold in my whimper of pain. Before I know it, I'm trying not to scream as he uses an alcoholic wipe to clean my cuts. Once he stops, I let out a sigh. I feel his finger trace over some of the older scars he has made. I jump slightly as his lips start tracing over them. Finally, he stops and covers up my most recent injuries with another gauze before grabbing my arm.

"I didn't do this to you." I don't look at him, but he grabs my chin and forces me to look at him. "Good, you know that you deserve it. Especially for that damned stutter that you have."

Still gripping my arm, he pulls out his knife; I make no attempt to pull away or stop him as he drags the blade diagonally across my arm, marking me six times. He rubs it with another wipe, deliberately putting too much pressure on it, I yelp. He increases his grip on my arm and keeps wiping. Then he wraps the entirety of my arm in a fresh gauze then leaves me in the bathroom. I sniff, then realise that I am crying. I bring my hand up to my face and see that I can't seem to stop crying. I rub my eyes with both hands.

I get up and run to my office and close the door as softly as I can. I lean against my door and cry quietly to myself. I haven't cried like this in years. It's always because of him when I've cried, but I haven't cried this much since the first time he cut me. I need something to calm myself down. I can't cut again… but I can do something else. I grab my arm and push down on my fresh cuts. I feel pain surge through me. Finally, I start to calm down; my breathing is ragged but slowing. There is a ping on my computer; I let go of my arm and sit down at my computer.

It's an email from the hospital asking if I can start the update a few days early. They have had an incident with their database and need help recovering the lost data. Primarily the data they lost is on upcoming major surgeries, chemotherapy patients and regulars. The information is vital to proceed with treatment. They even say that they will pay extra for the inconvenience. I think it over and reply to them. I tell them that I can start tomorrow, but I will charge one hundred and fifty pounds more for the data retrieval service. I ask them to write out two checks, one with twenty-five per cent of my pay, not including the one-fifty, and the other with the rest of the money. I also tell them that I may need a doctor's assistance with getting places, someone who really knows the patients and the building. I've added that deliberately as the only person I know that will fit that description is Skye. He's always talking about the hospital. I thought it would get annoying, but I just find it really sweet. So I send off the email and a text to Skye saying that I'd be starting tomorrow. He replies a few minutes later. I keep playing Minecraft while we talk. I'm not one of those sad losers who wait by their phone, waiting for someone to talk to them.

Skye: Glad to hear that you will be starting on the database from tomorrow, I've got surgery tomorrow, and I really need the patient data.

Me: Yeah, I was a little surprised that the data got lost. Especially on such essential files. You wouldn't happen to know anything about that, would you?

Skye: Are you insinuating something, Ser Percival?

Me: Not at all. I merely thought it was strange. Where are you, rn?

Skye: I'm at work, in the on-call room. I'm not expecting anything significant to happen, but I have time to talk to you.

Me: Good because when I come in tomorrow, I'm gonna have a bandage on my arm, and I don't want people asking questions about it. Skye?

Skye: Sorry, the chief just walked in and asked if I could show you around when you come in. Apparently, I fit your criteria. I'll make sure no one asks, dw buddy.

Me: Thanks, Skye. And I'll try not to disrupt your schedule too much.

Skye: I wouldn't worry. After this surgery on Monday, I'm actually on holiday, so I just told the chief that I could be at your disposal for that week. He was reluctant but agreed.

Me: Seems like I'm thanking you a lot today.

Skye: You are, but I don't mind. Damn, I gotta go; something just came but Bye Buddy. xx

I reply to his farewell, place my phone face down on my desk, and return to playing Minecraft. By the time it is ten o'clock, I've managed to collect a few more blocks of Ancient Debris. I have more than enough to upgrade my tools and armour… at least, I hope it is. As soon as I shut down Minecraft and my computer, I brush my teeth then head to bed. Once there, I am greeted by him, and of course, I feel I know what is about to happen. Whether my excuse will stop him is an entirely different scenario.

"You know the drill, bend over," he says gruffly.

"I have w-work tomorrow, s-so we can't," I reply. One.

"I thought you started on Monday?"

"They had a data cascade…"

"In English, nerd," he interrupts.

"They l-lost a lot of in-information regarding important p… p-patients." I stuttered on the damn P again. Three.

"You should have told me sooner; I was working out my shifts for next week."

"The chief has it s-sorted already. I am to h… have a guide." Five.

"WHO! I bet it's that dickwad from the maternity ward." I flinch at his yelling and back away from him. If he's angry, he'll hit me. <u>Explain who it is and quick.</u> Right.

"I don't k-know where the doctor works. It's some Dr Kearny, h-he has next w-week off. So, agreed to show m-me around." Thank the gods, I asked Skye his last name. Nine. Please no more.

"Hmm, well, at least it's only Skye. Fine, I'll be civil and not fuck you tonight, but don't be surprised if I can't keep it in." He hoists his bag up to his back. "I've got work till tomorrow night, so I'll walk you home then, at nine o'clock. Don't be late." He smacks my ass as he walks out of the bedroom. Once I hear the door close, and I'm sure he is away, I move into the bed. I was thinking about just going to bed, but it's rare that I'm alone in the house for so long, and having Skye call me buddy with the kiss. I think I'm developing a crush on him. He's probably not even interested in me the same way, so, for now, I'll stick to loving myself.

I carefully pull off my underwear and throw them into the hamper. I pull out my small box from under my bedside table and open it up. Inside are my three dildos and a bottle of lube. I don't do this very often, certainly not twice in one day, but… I don't know, but I want to be prepared for whatever *he* has in store. I grab my middle-sized dildo and the lube and jump onto my bed.

I squirt some of my lube onto my middle two fingers and gently start to rub my hole, slowly penetrating it. I start with one and manage to quickly slide two of my fingers inside myself. I remember when I first started thinking about doing anything with my ass, I was incredibly naïve. I used my spit to slide my fingers in and ended up hurting myself quite a bit. I was in high school at the time, and it's not like they teach you very much about the mechanics of gay sex. At least not when I was there. The only reason I started using lube was that I overheard someone talking about lube being good for something, probably wanking. But I went out and bought some and quickly realised it felt way better and was safer. Over time I got a little more confident, and by the time I was in fifth year, I was taking three fingers, but it didn't feel like enough. At the time, I was really only practising once a week. But then I managed to buy my first dildo. When I took it for the first time, I was in a lot of pain and didn't continue for another week. So, I worked up to get it in, and eventually, I got it in, and that's when the real fun began.

Once I've slid three of my fingers in, I start to prepare the dildo by coating it in some lube. I place it on the bed, positioning it right where it needs to be. I hold the dildo in place as I lower myself onto my sex toy. I let out a quiet moan and smile as I begin to bounce up and down. I'm in such pleasure that I begin to lean back. Suddenly I hit something I've never got before, and it feels… amazing! I keep trying to hit that spot and manage to get it into a rhythm of pressing it. I'm so engrossed in my pleasure that I forget that my dick needs attention too. I am bouncing for maybe ten minutes when I feel a build-up in my stomach. I know exactly what that means, I slowly increase my speed, and suddenly I release all over my bed. I sink down onto the dildo.

"Skye…" I moan out; I slap my hand over my mouth.

That has never happened before, I've never been able to cum hands-free, and I certainly haven't moaned out someone's name after I've finished. It's a fantastic accomplishment to cum hands-free, though. I know that there are guys online who can cum hands-free easily. I never thought that I would be able to do it. Something to tell Skye, I guess. Or maybe not, definitely not. I don't want him knowing I moaned his name after I came. It might slip out anyway; it's been three days since we first met. I definitely didn't think that the online friend I met almost three years ago would work at the same hospital as my boyfriend. Talk about luck; what's even luckier is that the hospital is about half an hour walk from here.

Oh shit… I have to clean up. I slowly take out my dildo, moaning once again and feeling a little empty now that it's no longer inside me. Before I start cleaning, I decide to grab my butt plug and slide it in, may as well. I pull off the bed cover and shove it into the hamper and replace it. I then take the basket to the kitchen, where I put on an overnight wash. I should be able to hang it up before I go to the hospital. I walk back to my bedroom, grab my dildo, and then run to the toilet to brush my teeth. I don't usually go to bed with a plug in, but since he's not here, nothing is stopping me.

I have done that before, and he took advantage of it. I manage to sort out the bed cover by myself, like usual, and throw it over the bed before hiding my dildo and lube back into their box. I slide the box away and jump into bed. As I fall asleep, though, my last thoughts aren't about my boyfriend.

They're about the red-haired boy I dreamt about a few days ago, and Skye.

Smart?

Waking up alone is one of the few things that I don't mind. Waking up screaming, on the other hand, is something I hate. It only happens when I'm alone too, why? I don't know. When he is here, I don't get many nightmares. I'll wake up shaking and sweating, but I manage to calm myself down. This morning is no different. I shoot up out of my bed with staggered breath and sweat trickling down my face and chest. I grab my arm and squeeze it, willing myself to calm down. It works. I have to shower and get to the hospital… and remove my plug; I forgot about that.

    I wasn't always this pathetic. I used to be reasonably confident and boisterous. But at the same time, I was a huge nerd; if I wasn't in the school's computer suite, I was on my phone doing something similar. I didn't have many friends, but the few I had were enough for me. I bet they wonder what happened to me. Last I checked, two of them decided to travel together while the other went to Dundee to teach. I wonder if they still… no. I hope that they have moved on with their lives and forgotten about me. I step under the warming shower and let out a soft sigh. I give myself a quick scrub, remove the plug with a quiet moan, replace the bandages on my arm and back before heading back to my bedroom.

    I pull on some smart clothes and make myself look somewhat presentable. I grab my bag and start to load it up with tools and computer programs I've made and been given. I pull the bag over my shoulder and get ready to step out of my flat. I pull the door shut and take deep breaths. It's been four years since I left the house; I really hope I don't have a panic attack. Dad always did think I would end up as an agoraphobic. I mean, I'm not, I used to love the outdoors, but my hay fever kind of discouraged me from going out and the last four years… well, it didn't seem essential to go out. Before I know it, I'm already outside the building, which way to the hospital? I pull out my phone and type in the address. As soon as it finds it, I start heading towards it. I don't pay much attention to my surroundings, but I am careful not to hit anyone. Having said that, it doesn't stop other people from bumping into me; it must be rush hour.

I finally reach the hospital and see someone waiting outside; I hope to all the gods that it isn't my boyfriend. As I get closer, I see him smile. *He* never smiles. *He* scowls at me. Finally, I make out the face; I need to put my glasses on; it's Skye. I smile as soon as I realise who it is. He gives me a gentle hug, which I return, before motioning me in and taking me to the server room. We don't talk on the way there, but I know what he will ask about, and I don't want to talk to him about it. I could. But it doesn't mean I want to. As I enter the server room, I cringe.

"What? What's wrong with it?" Skye asks, moving past me and into the server room.

"I-it's messy. Really m-mmmessy." Two.

"Yeah, that's why we contacted you. You came highly recommended."

"By whom?" I enquire.

"Me, and the chief. Apparently, he knows of your work. He would have been the one to greet you, but he said he would see you when you are ready."

"Bit cryp-p…"

"Cryptic, yeah, I thought that too," he finishes. I don't say anything, but I do head to the worst looking server. I should have brought my cable ties. I place my bag down and start to move wires around, bunching them up with one hand, then opening my backpack and taping them up. Not ideal, but all I can do for now. I'm there for what feels like an hour going around the servers, gathering various coloured wires and tying them together. I think Skye was called away to check on his patients. A nurse did come in and offer me a drink of something. I took some Pepsi Max and thanked the young nurse.

Now the wires are clean, I hook my phone to the closest server and scan through the files. Then my phone gets kicked out of the servers. I groan in frustration and disconnect it. I head out the door and find that the nurse's station isn't too far away, so I head towards it. When I arrive at the nurses station, the nurse who offers me the drink is behind the computer. I walk up to her and clear my throat, startling her slightly.

"Oh, hello again. Can I help you?"

"Y… yes. I was w-wondering if I could use your com… puter." Three in one sentence, and here I thought I was getting better.

"Of course, do you want to use this one or a more private one?" I shrug, and she gets up. "Why don't you use this one and I'll get Dr Kearny." She smiles softly at me and walks off. I sit down at the station and open up the file directory. I plug in my searcher program, and a warning bar pops up, telling me that it may disrupt some functions of all computers in the building. Lucky for me the program has its own warning informing people that's what's happening and disruptions may occur. I doubt it. It's a very sophisticated program. A progress bar appears on the screen, and I sit back and wait. I take a deep breath hoping that there weren't too many files lost to the data cascade. Suddenly someone comes up to the desks.

"I need the file on Mrs Jamison in room 3b, please. Now, it's imperative," a woman asks, my eyes open; I look around, hoping that someone else is around. Nope just me. Great. "Did you hear me? Get the file!" This woman is vulgar. I can't seem to make a sound. She moves in closer to me, and I get up and move away from her. What's she going to think? She's clearly pissed that I can't get the file she is asking for; what will she say when she sees the program running. I can feel my breath start to quicken. I know that she is still yelling at me; I don't know why. I look past her and see the program is still running… fuck it. I push past her and disconnect the hard drive, then run off back to the server room.

I slam the door shut and run to the back wall. I can hear that my breath is staggered, and… fuck is this a panic attack! I hit my head against the wall, and I sink to the floor; oh, shit, this is a fucking panic attack. It won't stop! Please, it has to stop. All of this has to stop. I grab my hair, hoping to stop the thoughts. I just want to go home. No, I have to do my work. *Oh, shut up, Percival, you can't do this; you're not smart enough.* I can do this; I've done it before. *Yeah, 'cause causing pain to yourself has worked so well.* I can calm down; I always do. *No, you can't.* Fuck, you're right. *Oh, great, and now you're crying.* Stop it. *You're so pathetic.* Stop it. *It's a wonder you get anything done at all.* STOP IT!

"STOP IT! SHUT UP, SHUT UP, SHUT UP!" I yell inadvertently. I go to grab my arm, but someone stops me, holding my arm lightly. I can't quite hear them, but they're telling me to follow their breathing. I have to focus on them. *You can't concentrate, idiot.* Ignoring my thoughts, I listen to them and track their breathing. In for three seconds, out for three. In for three seconds, out for three. In for four seconds, out for three. In for four seconds, out for four seconds. In for four seconds, out for four seconds. I finally hear my thoughts calm down and eventually open my eyes. I see Skye.

"Hey, you're okay. I'm here. Keep breathing," he tells me, his soothing voice calming me even further. He raises a tissue to my field of vision and starts to wipe away my tears, still telling me to breathe. I sniff and pull my knees up to my chest. I hold in my cries, that is, until I feel an arm wrap around my shoulder, I grab on to them and quietly cry into their shoulder. I feel a hand brush through my hair. Finally, I calm down.

When I lift myself up again, my eyes feel droopy, and I can feel the leftover tears in my eyes. I wipe them away with the heel of my hands. I sniff and rub my nose. I want to apologise to Skye 'cause I'm pretty sure that's who has helped me, but honestly, I really wish he hadn't seen me like this. Now he will want to protect me. I didn't want him to.

"Whoa there. Stay calm for me," Skye says, holding my undamaged shoulder. My breath must have been getting quicker again.

"W... why did you h-help me?" I ask.

"You needed it. You're not the first person I've talked down from a panic attack," he says, sitting cross-legged in front of me.

"I would have calmed myself down. I was fine." <u>No, you were not.</u> I get up. "I didn't need anyone's help." <u>Stop lying to yourself and to him.</u>

"Except you did," he says. I'm taken aback by his response. "You were screaming at the top of your lungs. I paged your partner; do you know what I got back?" I shake my head; he gets up and steps towards me. "He said to just leave you. Said that whatever was happening that it would resolve itself." I lower my head and sniff again. "Even if I wasn't a doctor, I wouldn't have left you in that state." He pulls me into his arms, and I start to cry again. *Pathetic.* He cares; let him in. *'Cause that will end well.*

"I'm, s… s…" I take a deep breath. "I'm sorry. I-I haven't h-had a p… p-panic attttack in a l-long time. B-but she was y… yelling at me and I j—I just." I break down again and start to cry heavily. I hear Skye shushing me. Why do people do that? What if I wanna cry loudly? *Yeah, get the whole hospital in here; that will be great.*

"You don't have to apologise." He lets me go and grabs my bag for me, slinging it over his shoulder. "Let's head somewhere quiet so you can calm down properly."

"And has a c-computer."

"Yes, that too." He smiles and holds out his hand. I don't take it, but I walk towards him, and we walk away from the server room. "It looks nice in there, by the way," he tells me. I feel my face heat up slightly.

"I t-think I've d… d… developed OCD. I had to f-fix it b… b-before I started," I respond; looking down at my fingers, I notice that I'm fidgeting with them.

"From what I saw there, I think I can concur. We can do tests after you've finished the computer work if you want to." I say nothing, but I do nod.

We stop outside an office that has Skye's name on it, and we go inside. He motions me to sit at his computer and sets my bag down next to me. I take a breath and reopen my bag looking through it to find the same program I used before… I growl suddenly, and Skye jumps.

"What's wrong?"

"I must have left my hard drive in the server room. I need it to find out what was lost in the data cascade. I can do it manually though it would take longer if I do. Might as well get started." I hear Skye snigger, and he tells me that he'll be back soon. But also, that he is locking the door so only he can get in, it means more privacy for me, so I wave my hand towards him, letting him know that it's okay.

It takes me three hours of searching, even with my program, to find just over half of the files. I groan after the fourth, having recovered three more huge files. I rub my eyes and look back at the screen. Oh, great, it's blurred. <u>Glasses.</u> Oh yeah, I reach into my bag and pull them out and put them on. <u>Better?</u> Better. I continue working until Skye comes back in with two trays of food balancing on top of each other. I didn't notice that he had left again.

He places the food next to me on the desk. From the corner of my eye, I can see another Diet Pepsi, a sandwich and... actually, that's it. I turn to look at the food. There is a banana, a sandwich, an apple, a drink, and some traybake dessert. But at the centre of it all is a little post-it note with a smile on it. I smile and look at Skye, who gives me a look of innocence. I notice that he is staring at me. I don't mind it, but all I keep thinking is 'don't ask about my glasses'.

"How's it going?" he asks. Thank the gods.

"O-okay. I g-guess there were a lot of llll-lost files," I reply, picking up the banana, only to have it taken away from me.

"That's good. Now eat your sandwich," he tells me, replacing the banana on the tray.

"B-but I want my banana," I say, reaching for it again. He takes it away.

"Sandwich first, then the fruit." I sigh, pick up the sandwich, and turn it over looking the ingredients. I know I'm not going to eat it for two reasons. One because I'm a pollotarian and this has ham in it, and second:

"You realise that I'm lactose intolerant, r-right?" I tell him, handing over the ham and cheese sandwich.

"You are?" I nod. "Fuck, I feel like an idiot right now."

"D-do… don't feel like that. You didn't know," I persuade him, but subtly holding out my hand for the banana, which he reluctantly hands over. I thank him and turn back to the computer.

"So, what was on that hard drive?" he asks. I take a bite out of the banana.

"It's a little h-h-hard to explain. Basically, I input the time where the files were lost, and it checks the saved files until it finds all the files bringing them back to the surface. From there, I have to sort the files and makes sure that they aren't corrupted. Then I just save it under a new name, not so different though that you wouldn't be able to find it," I explain to him.

"You are so smart, you know that?" That's wrong. Is it, though? "It sounds really complicated. But hey, I'm happy that you didn't stutter while you explained it."

"What a-are you talking ab… b… about?"

Before he gets a chance to respond, someone is banging on his office door. Skye sighs and gets up to open the door; I wouldn't mind knowing who is interrupting us. I turn back to the computer to try and get the last file, then I finally notice the time. It's half-past nine. I'm late. Very late. Why didn't I notice how much time had passed? I pack up my things and go to the door where Skye is arguing with The Beast about something. *It won't be you, don't get your hopes up.* I won't. With my head down, I mumble to my boyfriend that we can go now.

We leave the hospital in silence and for the duration of the walk home as well. When we get in, I drop my bag off in my office and strip instantly. Laying down on the bed, I wait for him to join me. I hope that he won't do anything, but I know I'm not so lucky. When he does join me, he cuffs my hands together, and I give no struggle as he does. I hear the flick of his knife, and I barely listen to him as he talks about how pretty my back looks with all my scars. Pretty soon, I feel him run his hands over my back and down to my ass. I cringe at what he might do to me.

When he did allow me out, I was mostly on time. I used to be excited to meet him. I was late a few times, and he got a little pissed at me but brushed it off. When I was late when we started to live together, that's when this started. The cuffs. The knife. Having his way with me. The first time I struggled against him. I tried to get out less and less until tonight, when I had no energy to try. I must have fallen asleep after my panic attack. I feel his knife dig into my back as he starts to giggle at the sight of my blood. I make no sounds, just hissing as the knife in my back causes me to blackout.

Nothing

I wake up to my phone ringing; all I can do is groan at the thought of getting up. He was at me all night; I woke up twice, and he was still going. I have no idea if it was all the same time, or it was... more than once. But my ass certainly feels like it's been abused more than once. All that work stretching, and it still hurts. I flop my hand over to my bedside table to find my phone, but it's not there.

Lucky for me, the ringing stops, so I'm gonna go back to sleep... ugh, who the fuck is calling me? I lift my head and see my phone peeking out of my trouser pockets. I carefully slip out of my bed and grab my phone. I shield my eyes when I turn the screen on, but I see that Skye is calling me. I go to answer the call, but it expires. My notification bar says that he's tried calling five times, talk about important. Maybe my luck is changing, HA! Like that will ever happen. The phone rings again seconds later. I answer the call and grovel out a hello.

"Hello to you too. Did you forget something?" Skye says on the other end of the phone.

"I forget a lot of things; you'll have to be more specific." I rub my eye, trying to force it to stay open.

"He was at you again last night, wasn't he." I don't respond. *"I guess that's my answer. When can I expect you at the hospital?"*

"Fuck!" When I realise that I've got work, I am up and

pulling on some underwear and a top... and some trousers all at the same time. Which results in me falling over. I hear Skye yelling over the phone, trying to get my attention. I take a breath and get dressed the correct way. Once I'm dressed, I pick up my phone and a pair of socks.

"What happened? I heard something fall over," Skye asks as I place the phone on speaker.

"I dropped some clothes," I say, grabbing my shoes and sitting down.

"That was some loud clothes."

"Well... I was in them." I hear Skye laugh over the phone as I get my socks on.

"Where are you?" he suddenly asks.

"Umm, I'm pulling on my shoes. Why?" Suddenly, Skye ends the call, and there is a knock at my door. I stand up and open the door. "Skye?"

"Well, come on then, I'm going to be late if you don't get your other shoe on." I look down and realise that I haven't put it on. So I grab it and pull it on. "Where's your bag?" I don't respond but grab my laptop inside my office, which I place into the bag. "Ready to go now?" I nod, grabbing my jacket.

We walk out of the flats quietly; I think Skye knows that I don't want to talk, but I also get the feeling that he wants to ask about it anyway. I don't want to talk to him about it because I know that he'll try and persuade me to leave him. I know how that will end. I tried it before; I got a black eye and a few broken ribs. No hospital for me though, I think he stole the supplies from them to use on me. I just can't understand why he beats me up and then patches me up afterwards. How about he doesn't beat me up or just beat me up and leave me to die. Gods know, I would prefer that to this... torture.

"Percival, can you tell me what happened last night?" Skye says.

"You know what hap-ppened." I rub my arm, squeezing it slightly. He carefully takes his hand off my arm and stops us in the middle of the street.

"I want you to do something for me. Every time he... hurts you. I want you to tell me how many times he does it, even if it's just hitting you. I..." He pauses, and for the first time since we met, I look him in the eyes. "I just want you to know that I can help you." I smile at him and rest my head onto his chest.

"Thank you, Skye, but I don't think anyone can help me now." I lift my head and continue towards the hospital, Skye trailing behind me.

When we arrive at the hospital, The Beast is there to greet me with a kiss. I reluctantly accept it and tell him I'll be in Skye's office continuing my work. He nods, and Skye escorts me to his office. On the way, we run into the doctor who was yelling at me yesterday. I suck in a breath and hide behind Skye... gods, I'm pathetic. I hope Skye notices my discomfort or maybe just doesn't do what he's doing right now, which is talking to her. Why is he talking to her? What could they possibly want to talk about? From the colour of her scrubs, I'd say she was possibly maternity... but I wasn't in the maternity ward yesterday. Also, who wears pink when you have that colour of hair? I mean, really. Yuck. I should probably pay attention to what they are saying.

"Do you know how long the servers will be down? I've got a patient having triplets within the next forty-eight hours, and I need to update her file," she asks Skye. Wait... since when were the servers down? <u>Did you do that?</u> I did not do that.

"What—"

"What do you mean the servers are d-down? The work has

only just started," I butt in, surprising Skye.

"They went down this morning. About seven a.m.," she tells Skye. **How fucking rude!** Yeah, maybe she just doesn't like me. Can't imagine why she is the... oh what if she feels guilty? *Do you really believe anyone would feel guilt for something they did to you?*

"We should go check the servers. Thanks, Doc." Skye turns around and walks me back to where I'm needed. I don't usually like being directed places, but this time I don't really mind. What I don't like is where Skye's hand is. I've got a fresh cut down the middle of my back. I'm worried that it'll open up. I was pretty rough this morning. I don't feel light-headed, so that is a good sign... should I get Skye to check it anyway? Maybe. I don't know—

"Ahh!" I hiss out and push Skye's hand off my back. He pressed on my back just a little too much, and... well, it hurt. Skye does look a bit confused, but then I can see the gears turning in his mind, so I quickly grab his arm and pull him into the server room. Which is entirely dark; that shouldn't be like that. I set down my bag, leaving Skye at the door; I start wandering around, looking for what's wrong. I wonder how much power is coming through the system. I go to my bag and grab my multipurpose digital voltmeter. Basically, it means I can check the voltage running through the system... which is none. I look over to where the power source is... okay, just why. I sigh and go over to the switch and turn it back on, and it comes back to life.

"Are you gonna explain what happened out there?" Skye asks as I sit down to do a diagnostic.

"Explain w-what?" I say, playing innocent.

"Well, one, what was wrong with the servers and two, you were in pain when I pushed your back." He crosses his arms.

Well, it's now or never.

"Fine." I stand up. "I'll show you why." I painfully pull off my tops and throw them on top of my bag. I sigh and turn around. For the record, I do have scars on my chest, but he usually leaves it alone. But there isn't much space left on my back for new wounds, so that might... will change. I hear Skye gasp and step towards me to get a better look. He's a doctor, so I can't blame him for wanting a closer look. I feel a cold finger trace some of my scars, and I shiver as his finger runs over them. I let out a silent whimper. Skye gently prods my shoulder where I was cut a few nights ago, causing me to hiss slightly. He apologises before he finally gets to my newest scars. He doesn't take the bandage off, but he can probably see a line of blood that most definitely covers it.

"I have to change this bandage; there is too much blood on the gauze. I'm surprised you haven't fainted yet," he says. He picks up my hoodie and gives it to me to put on. Which I do. I grab my bag, and we head over to his office. As we walk, I can see that some people seem to be a lot happier that the servers are working again. I don't understand why they had been turned off. It shouldn't really be possible, but that's what happened. I guess I fixed it, but really any idiot who has eyes could have seen that the entire system had been turned off at the wall. Someone really wants to keep me here, but who would want that? I'm nothing special, just a guy in an abusive relationship who's good with computers. Skye opens the door to his office and motions me in.

"Take off your top and lay down on the bed, please," he asks me; I blush slightly and oblige. Removing my top was just as painful as the first time. I lay down on the hospital bed on my stomach, not being in the mood to be funny... also, 'cause it hurts to be on my back. I hear a wheeled chair roll over to the bed, and

I feel myself drop slightly. I turn my head to look at Skye, who now has his glasses on and looks somehow even hotter than before. Which is just unfair.

He pulls on some latex gloves and carefully pulls off the bandage I was given last night. As he pulls it away, I hiss, and more so when he wipes away the blood on my back. He places a hand on my arm, telling me to take a deep breath and that he's sorry. Then he runs a wet cloth down my back; I suppress a scream brewing in the back of my throat, so I grip the bed hard, trying to keep it in. The wipe must have been covered in alcohol. That's the only reason it would have hurt so much. Once he's done, I let out a slow breath. I tell him that I hate him, but he doesn't respond; he just lowers his glasses and examines my back.

"How am I l... looking, Doc?" I ask.

"Well, he knows what he's doing. I'll give him that. The cut is to the right of your spine. Any closer, and well, it would hurt a lot more. There is a problem, though." He pauses. "You need stitches. This is too deep to heal without help."

"Y... you can't, though. He'll know I've had help and then I won't be able to finish my job. Then I'll n-n... never see you again."

"If I don't give you stitches, then the wound may get infected. I can't legally force you to get the stitches, but... as your friend, I cannot let you leave without them in good conscience. Plus, I am very good at my job. I don't think that he would notice them." I ponder over this and nod slightly. "I'll have to call in a nurse, not your boyfriend, obviously, but a nurse. One I trust too, so you can trust her also." I nod, and he gets up to leave. I'm waiting maybe three minutes before they come back. While they are away, I start feeling faint, so Skye can instantly tell something is wrong when he comes back into his office. He rushes over to me just as I pass out.

When I return to consciousness, I can hear two people talking; I know that one of the voices is Skye. The voice is… I can't recognise it; my head hurts. I just wanna sleep more, and I don't really get much sleep, usually insomnia. It can cause me to wake up during those… times, which causes me to pass out and then wake up again. Then when I am left alone, I do tend to wake up soaked in sweat. When he's home, and it happens, he tends to hit me and tell me to go back to sleep. He's said to me on multiple occasions that I'm just trying to get attention, that the dreams aren't real. They feel pretty fucking real when I get up and cut my arm to calm myself down.

"We *must* tell someone about this! I'm shocked he has this many fresh scars and is still living!" the other voice says.

"Yes, I know. It's Percival's wish that no one knows about any of this. If it gets out, then things could get worse for him, and I don't want that." That voice is definitely Skye's. I'm glad that he's sticking up for me… for whatever reason.

"Fine. But I am *not* happy about this, Doctor; I think that he should tell the police. Why doesn't he just leave the guy?"

"From what I understand, he—"

"He wouldn't let me," I mumble out, not really meaning to. Too late now. I open my eyes and see Skye and a nurse come over to the bed I am currently lying on.

"Hey Percival, how are you feeling?" Skye asks me.

"My head hurts, and I really want to sleep," I say, taking a deep breath and closing my eyes again.

"Percival, I need you to keep your eyes open for me. Can you do that?" Skye asks, shaking my shoulder.

"Hmmm, let me sleeeeep. Just 'cause you're hot doesn't mean I h-have to listen to you." Wait, what did I just say? **Hehehehe.**

"Horny comments aside, you do need to stay awake. And..." A hand comes up to my temple, I flinch away, but it returns, determined to press onto my forehead, I let it. "You are running a temperature."

"Who's the stranger touching my h-head?" I whisper to Skye.

"This is Lindsay. She's the nurse I trust; she helped me with your back. Although based on the dilation of your pupils and the fact you are slightly slurring your words and are acting a little drunk, I'm guessing you have a lack of blood in your system. So, Lindsay is gonna go run a blood test and get me a blood packet so we can do a blood transfusion that we can put into your system."

"Sounds like a p... p-plan, I think. Can I go to sleep now?"

"Absolutely not. You're going to sit up and continue your work." I groan and start to sit up. Skye is quick to help me, giving me an angled pillow for my back and handing me a laptop... I think it's mine... but I don't remember... no, wait, yes, I did bring mine. So I open it up and accidentally hack into the hospital servers without really trying.

What was I working on yesterday? Oh yeah, file recovery, now I need to update the system, which means a systematic rundown of all the computers in the hospital to see what needs to be upgraded and what doesn't. I'm gonna do it alphabetically; it makes things so much easier. Also, I prefer alphabetical to all the randomness, I hate that; I can't focus when it's like that. It pisses me off. Why? I don't know. It does. I should probably have been tested for it. Oh well. Need to focus, I wonder what I could have for dinner, and now there's a straw in my face.

"Drink," Skye says; I flinch back slightly then start to suck on the straw cautiously.

"What is this? It tastes g-good," I tell him because it really does.

"It's gonna help level out your blood sugar. Until we get the transfusion underway. What are you doing?"

"I'm doing a systematic check of all the computers in the hospital to see which ones need an upgrade. It is all of them so far, but I'm only twenty per cent through the checks, and there is a lot, so who knows if it's gonna be all of them or half. I am not that optimistic." I turn to look at Skye, who looks dumbfounded and confused; it's actually a little hot. <u>Focus, Percival, do not go falling for him.</u>

"Your stutter," he says.

"W-what?"

"When you were speaking just now. You didn't stutter once, not even one per cent."

"W-what are you t-talking about? I always stutter." I am so confused I have not stuttered. I always stutter, even when I explain… Things. "No, I don't, I've just never finished an ex-p… explanation."

"He stops you, telling you to dumb it down. So, he can understand you." I nod. "How are you with him?"

"It's not like if I went back k-knowing what I know now that I would ch-choose him." Skye nods, telling me that I can keep going. "We met six years ago; I was nineteen. I was almost finished with my degree. My dad had an arrangement with the dean to do the course in two years. D-Dad always did think I could do way better than I was letting on." I take a sip from my drink and continue. "I went out with my mates to a gay bar, yeah

I know, it wasn't mm-my idea. Anyway, I don't really like drinking, but h… h-he does, so when we met, he was totally hammered, and I was… really horny, so I wasn't really thinking, just thought about a o-one-night stand. Wouldn't that have been nice?"

"So, he was supposed to be a one-night stand?"

"Yes." I start explaining what happened six years ago.

Not a One-Night Stand

Six years ago, I met him in a gay bar. He was there to get piss ass drunk and maybe get his dick wet. The problem was he wasn't gay, not even bisexual or pansexual. He was straight and very straight; I have no idea why he was even there. I was sitting at the bar; my two best friends were fending off other drunk men who thought they were both cute. Of course, they were trying to hit on lesbians, although it seems like Elliot had found a willing girl to make out with; maybe she was bi. I know that Elliot is bisexual, even suggested that we should be a couple. He's usually drunk, so I gently tell him no. I love him but just not in that way; I've known him practically all my life. We've had birthdays together, went to the same school, he came on holiday with me, and even found him wanking once. That resulted in many questions and a few days of questioning my sexuality before I realised I was gay – what a fun week.

My future abuser came stumbling over to me, startling me a little, but I just sighed and sipped at my soft drink. *He* asked the bartender for another pint of beer which he was refused. Then he had to start kicking up a fuss saying that he 'hasn't even had that much.' I snorted at his comment and downed the last of my drink, and was about to walk over to Elliot to see if he wanted to go home and play video games. I was suddenly pulled back down onto my seat by the same guy that sat next to me. I feel his hand run up my thigh, which I grab and pull away from me.

"I don't like it when people p... p... molest me." I flick his hand away, still stuttering on that damned P. Dad said that if I couldn't say the word to think of a workaround, I did get quite good at it.

"What is someone as hot as you doing in a place like this?" he asked me.

"What makes y-you think that I'm here w... w-willingly?" I say back.

"You're not alone then? Can't take you away from your partner then."

"Who says I'm in a relationship?"

"Cute guy like yourself, I can't believe that."

"Believe it," I respond and get up to leave, only to be pulled down again. "Look, you seem nice, but I am not looking f-for anything. Maybe when you sss-stop looking at all the girls that go past, you can call me."

"I thought we were having a conversation."

"Yeah, and I ended it."

"Well, I didn't. I wanna show you a good time."

"Do any of these lines ever w-work?"

"Never fails."

"Really? Never fails?" He nodded, and I beaconed him in closer to whisper in his ear, "That record is no longer as flawless as you think." I pushed him away and finally got up to go across the room. In retrospect, that entire conversation had red flags all over it. Elliot was still sucking face with a girl, and Sammy looked upset that he didn't score. I sat next to him and nudged him, causing him to laugh. I hadn't known Sammy all that long, but I considered him an excellent friend.

"Who's the guy?" Sammy asked.

"Some horny idiot."

"Sounds like your type." I hit him with my elbow.

"He's straight. I've been keeping my eye on him." I looked at Sammy. "Don't give me that look. The bartender asked me to watch him. I did w-w... w... w."

"You worked here, I remember." I mumbled my thanks. "You okay? It's been a while since you've stuttered like that."

"Not the b... biggest fan of c... clubs. Or d... d-drunk guys w... who try to h... hit on me. On an unrelated note. Here he comes totally uninvited." Sammy's head snapped around to the drunk man that was fumbling our way. He's persistent; I had to give him that. I remember thinking that if he wasn't straight, I might have thought he was hot, but not while he was drunk.

He plopped down in front of us and looked right at us, specifically me. He placed a drink in front of me. It was a shot of tequila, he nodded at me, and I grabbed the glass. I made it seem like I would drink it before I handed it to Sammy, who downed it and shouted 'whoo'. Usually a good thing. The idiot across from me looks confused. I didn't say anything, but Sammy looked happy, and that was more important to me.

"That was meant for you," he told me.

"I know, and I gave it to h-him. If you're gonna b-buy me a drink, at least ask me what I like." I sat back in the, frankly, uncomfortable chairs and placed my arm around Sammy, who sat a bit closer. It was an unspoken rule between the three of us. When we got uncomfortable, we would put our arms around one of the others, and they'd get closer. It created the illusion that we were a couple or at least very close friends. I did it with Elliot more than with Sammy because it used to make him uncomfortable. He was drunk, though, so I didn't think he'd mind.

"I thought you didn't have a bf?" the man asked.

"You're r... r-right, I have two... although one of them is currently m-making out with someone else, we don't mind, though."

"So, I still have a shot." I snorted at his comment and got back up to get a drink; of course, he followed me. I ordered a Diet Coke and stood at the bar with him beside me. "Come on, I know you want me. I can see it in your eyes."

"What you see is exasp... exasperation." He didn't accept that. "Look, I'll ad-admit this; I am crazy horny and w... wouldn't mind having sex with someone. Just not a straight man w... who will most definitely regret it in the morning."

"Who's says I'd regret doing anything with you?" I pondered for a second before I grabbed the side of his head and kissed him hard. I deliberately started messing with his hair, and as I began to feel his hands wander up to my ass, I broke the kiss. Pushed him onto a bar stool, slid my drink over to him and made my way over to my friends. One of whom passed out. Elliot. It was always Elliot. I told Sammy to help me take him home. Sammy obliged and lifted him over his shoulder.

I quickly finished my drink and followed them out of the door with someone on my tail. When we got out into the cold air, I told Sammy that I'd be home tomorrow. I wasn't one for one-night stands, but at the time, I managed to get myself all hot after that kiss. We embraced quickly, and he headed home. I grabbed the idiot and called over a taxi to take us to his place. From there, you can guess what happened.

I woke up first in the morning; not getting drunk has its advantages. Especially, as I would learn, he tends to fall asleep after ten bottles of beer. I was quiet and managed to slip out of bed and pull on my clothes before he got up. He was still snoring like a train as I left his flat. I practically ran down the stairs and out the front door. I wasn't feeling all that clean that day, and I remember feeling like I shouldn't have had sex with him. Too late now, I suppose. I decided to walk back to my place and grab a hot chocolate on the way.

The morning was pretty bleak, the sun wasn't out, but it was still warm enough that I didn't need my jacket. As I got closer to my flat, I grabbed a watermelon and an Oreo chocolate bar from the corner shop. When the boys got drunk, these were the things that made them feel better; Sammy likes melon, which somehow makes him feel better. Something about his grandmother giving it to him when he was ill, I'm not really sure. Elliot just likes chocolate, especially Oreos.

When I finally got home, I heard the two men groaning on the couch. I sighed and deliberately shut the door loudly, causing them to groan more. I threw the Oreo bar at Elliot and then started to cut up the watermelon for the rest of us. Sammy moved to sit at the table and watched me as I cut the watermelon. I grabbed a plate, placed a slice of melon on it and slid it over to Sammy, who carefully started eating it. I smiled again and turned the kettle on.

The next few days were pretty quiet and mainly included Sammy and Elliot getting on at me for the one-night stand, Elliot especially. He was complaining that we never had a one-night stand. So, I jokingly told him that we could have a one-night stand if he got a full-time job. He was annoyed, but I think he ended up getting a job that he really loves. Of course, at the time, I was dating my first one-night stand.

I saw *him* again about a week later in a coffee shop. I was supposed to be meeting Elliot after an interview he was having, but he was running late. My future abuser sauntered over and sat across from me. I ignored him at first but eventually, I couldn't. He wouldn't stop trying to talk to me.

"W-what are you doing here?" I asked him finally.

"I'm trying to have a conversation with a cute boy." I felt my face start to heat up, so I tried to stay calm. I could smell the alcohol on his breath, so I knew that something was bothering him.

"You're still drunk, and if you were sober, I'd think about talking to you."

"Let me take you on one date, and I promise I'll be sober." I couldn't tell if he was sincere or not, so I asked for his phone. I put my number in and a reminder of a date for two days later. Once I gave him back his phone, he smiled and left. After that, I never received a message from him. Not once.

He was actually sober on the day of our date, and it seemed like he didn't regret sleeping with me. I took him to the cinema to a film I knew would be very quiet, as kind of a test. Sometimes people do... things in the seats. I'd never done it myself; public displays of affection really aren't my thing. Surprisingly he was a complete gentleman, only placing his hand on my leg when it wouldn't stop bouncing. I was nervous, sue me. We held hands as we left the theatre, and he treated me to dinner. We started dating from the end of the date; he gave me a kiss goodnight and asked me to be his boyfriend. I was going to say no, but... after that date, I couldn't help but say yes.

"S-so that's it. T-that's the story," I tell Skye. I've never actually told anyone that story, but I'm glad I told Skye.

"What happened to them? Sammy and Elliot?" he asks.

"I... I think they still l-live together. I'm n-n-not sure it *has* been six years." I lower my head. I hate myself because I lost touch with my two best friends because of an idiot who hasn't ever told me his sexuality. "Besides... I doubt th... they would want to talk to me again…"

"How long had you known them?"

"I met Elliot w-when I was… about six or eight months old. He's two years o-o-older than me; I was ten when I caught him… p…"

"Pleasuring himself. I wasn't going to ask about that; how old were you?"

"B-bit personal that," I tell him, he goes to talk, but I stop him. "Old enough. Sammy, I met j-just before I started uni. He mm-met Elliot the year before. Elliot th… th-thought we would get along great; he was right. Even ab …about the idiot nurse I'm 'dating'." Talking about this is gonna make me cry. In fact, I can feel a tear sliding down my face, wipe it away before Skye can notice.

"Are you okay? It's probably hard for you to talk about your past." I sniff and rub my nose with the back of my hand. I nod at Skye and try and focus on my work, thirty per cent though. Too distracted, too caught up, too… *forgettable*. Fuck, and here come the tears. Ugh, I hate crying. "Whoa, okay crying person in my office, let's just…" He grabs my laptop and places it on his desk, then sits on the edge of the bed where I practically dive into his arms.

"Why did—it have to—be me?" I say between sniffs; Skye gently rubs my back, avoiding my new bandage.

"You made some bad decisions. Unfortunately, it was him that caused all of your pain." I feel him kiss my forehead. "You deserve so much more than this." Another kiss. "I wish I could help you more…"

"You have!" I move out of the hug but keep my arms around him; I'm not sure why. "You fixed up my back and talked me down from a panic attack. Not even he has thought to do that; he just lets me ride them out." His hands run-up to my face, and he kisses my forehead. It's so gentle I almost don't want him to stop. But I know he has to; I lean my head onto his chest. He kisses my head one more time, and we finally break the hug; he gets up and passes me back my laptop. I flip it open and continue working through the list of systems.

Two hours and one blood transfusion later, I'm struggling to get off the hospital bed after finishing my diagnostic of the hospital. Skye fell asleep on his desk chair, and I didn't want to wake him to disconnect me... wait, how am I gonna get my shirt on? Where am I gonna go? If he sees me walking around with a blood bag attached to me, then he'll know someone else knows. I have to wake Skye up. Okay, here goes. I hop back up onto the bed and call out his name a few times. Eventually, he starts to stir, and when he sees me, he sits up.

"How long was I sleeping?"

"Nnn... not long at all." He lets out a sigh of relief and stands up and stretches. He looks around the room and grabs a biohazard bin, a plaster and a cotton wool ball. He brings them over, placing them on the bed.

"Oh, good, the transfusion is done. This may hurt a bit." He carefully peels off the sticker that was keeping the needle in place on my wrist. I hiss, a little bit more so when he finally pulls out the needle. He places the cotton wool ball on my wrist and places the needle into the bin. He then throws away the cotton and puts a small circular plaster where the needle penetrated my skin. I roll my wrist and crack my knuckles before grabbing my hoodie and pulling it and my T-shirt back on. I turn to face my laptop and check where I need to go first. Ah, that's right...

"We need to head to your CT scanners; there is a fault in the system that is causing false readings. It's probably not enough to affect any diagnostics, but it needs sorting first." Okay, that time I heard it, no stutter. That's... kinda cool. I think I'm smiling to myself, and I think Skye can tell I've noticed too. I kneel down and open up my bag. I pull out a tool belt that includes some screw heads and an assortment of different cable heads. I throw the belt around my waist and fasten it up and face Skye. "Let's g-go." Damn it. Skye opens the door, and we walk to the CT scanners.

"So, we have two CT scanners, is the problem with both of them?" he asks.

"No, it's j-just the one on the first floor."

"They're both on the first floor." I don't respond. I'm an idiot. This could be harder, except that I remember its serial number, so all I need to do is check it... or ask.

"Wh... which one has the sssss... service number six-five-six-six-seven-two?"

"That would be the second one, it's further along, and we'll have to check and see if it is in use at the moment." I nod, and we walk the rest of the way in comfortable silence. Which I like.

When we arrive, the first thing Skye does is check the schedule for the scanner. I quickly connect up my laptop and start running through the codes. It all looks normal; it's hard to say, I don't know what they should look like, and the internet will be no help. Unfortunately, I have twenty minutes before the next patient comes for their scan. After that, I'd have to check the other CT scanner and have it running.

"Ugggghhhhh," I groan out.

"What's wrong?"

"I d... don't know what's wrong w-w-with the codes, I can do t-two things. Either I can run one of the programs or go to the other scanner and check its base code, although I may have to do that anyway."

"Can I help?" Skye asks.

I am about to respond when someone else answers for me.

"No, you cannot!"

We both turn around and see *him* standing in the doorway, and he doesn't look happy.

Busy

Skye spins and faces him; I try to make it look like I am busy... because I am. Well, sort of, I'm just trying to avoid looking at my current boyfriend. So, I'm running through the codes to see if I can find out what's wrong without turning the damned thing on, which at the moment doesn't look likely.

"What the fuck are you doing in here?" he asks. Even from here, I can feel the anger radiating from Skye. <u>You could ask him to calm down.</u> Are you kidding?

"Working on the CT scanner. Unfortunately, it has a fault, and I'm trying to be of some help to Percival," Skye replies. Don't get me wrong; I like that Skye is helping me so much, but I don't understand why he is helping me. I'm not that useful or interesting or anything, really.

"I have a patient who has an appointment, so leave now." He moves over to where I'm sitting and waits. I know he wants me to stand up, but Skye sits me back down as I start getting up. He pushes me and the wheely chair over to my laptop. I continue my work from there. I am not getting in the middle of... testosterone. (Yes, I know, okay. The irony isn't lost on me.)

"I think you are intelligent enough to work standing up while Percival works his magic. In fact, he was just saying that he needed to run one of the programs we use, so this will help everyone," Skye tells him. I'm smiling again; not many people stand up to The Beast; those who do usually end up hurt. Having said that, it's usually me that gets hurt. It would happen more after I moved in with him. He huffs and starts to boot up the system in time for the patient he was talking about. Skye comes over to me, crouches next to me.

"So, what do I need to do next door?" Skye asks.

"Wait. Y-you were serious?" Skye nods at me. "Oh… okay, t… t-take this and plug it into the system. When it starts to run, it'll a-a-ask you if you want to record the pr… pr-procedure say yes and the hard drive will d-d-do the rest." He smiles and is about to leave, but he seems hesitant. I nod at him, letting him know that I'll be okay. Now I am alone with my abuser, never good, but I'm working. He should leave me alone. I keep running through the code, doing the same as what Skye is doing. Recording the program to find the fault.

"You two seem… close," he says, breaking my concentration. I nod; I don't think anything more is needed to be said. "What happened to your arm?" Fuck… Play innocent? It will *not* work. Oh! I know.

"I self h… harm you'll have to be mm-m-more specific." I really wish I didn't stutter sometimes. So, that is the lie you decided to go for? Enough of your sarcasm.

"This one." He grabs my arm and holds the small plaster to his face. "You didn't have that last night."

"I… Ummm." Think quicker damn it. "I was g… gonna cut this morning, then Skye knocked on the d-d-door, and I couldn't ff-finish." Great lying, Percival. I'm an utter, utter idiot he's never gonna—

"Hmm, fine. You'll finish it tonight, of course." I nod, he hits my head. "Right!"

"Yes. I'll f-f-finish it tonight."

"That's better." He moves away from me and continues his

procedures. I keep my head down, trying to stop myself from having a panic attack. I cannot believe he bought that. Yeah, me either, help me with my breathing? Of course, in and… Out.

Skye comes back through just as *he* finishes up with the patient, so he's leaving as Skye comes in. I think words were exchanged, but I couldn't hear them. Having said that, Skye seems angrier, so I'm guessing it wasn't anything good. He places the hard drive next to me, and I plug it into my laptop. Once the program has finished downloading, I set the two side by side and run a simulation of the CT scanner doing its work. This can take some time, so I can just check for updates on the other computers. I slide over and start to check all its vital and secondary systems. I can feel Skye hovering around me, and he's… is he pacing? I listen for his footfalls and hear him turn on his heels before walking again. Yup, he is definitely pacing.

"Skye, stop." He stops. "W… w-what's wrong?" I stutter out.

"Your boyfriend thinks that I'm hitting on you and even told me to back off, or he'd get me fired."

"Can he d-do that?" Ignoring the flirting comment 'cause he could just be being charming. People are like that.

"HELL NO!" I flinch at his sudden yell and cower away slightly. "He has fuck all on me, and I have more on him than he will *ever* be aware of! I could get him fired so quickly the police will have to be here an hour before!" I'm used to people being angry. Usually, it's directed at me. It doesn't mean I'm any less afraid; I don't naturally flinch like this either. I think because I'm used to *him* shouting when others shout at me, I start to freak. I don't know. I'm not a fucking therapist. Finally, Skye seems to notice how uncomfortable I am. Tears are threatening to fall, but I will not let them. I see him crouch next to me out of the corner of my eye, then the tears fall. "I'm sorry. I didn't mean to yell," he says softly, so soft I'm surprised I even heard it. His hand comes up to my face and wipes away my tears. I shake my head; it's not his fault that he got angry. "Don't do that, Percival. Don't invalidate your feelings. They are important. If I've upset you, just say."

"Yelling. You…" I clear my throat. "I've never heard you s… s-so angry before. Of c-course, when h… h-he yells at me, I deal with it, I'm used to it, but it doesn't mean I don't flinch when people yell. But, it's my fault, I shouldn't have asked such a stupid question; I knew what would happen." I am still crying, so I rub away some of the tears.

"It's not your fault at all. I should have controlled my emotions better, and I'm glad you told me." He smiles at me; I glance down and see the smile. Fuck me, it's incredible! Like empires would fight over that smile, fucking hell it makes him so hot, fuck. I'd ask him to take me right here and now if we weren't in public.

Also, if you were sure that you actually could.

Yeah, I have no idea what state my ass is in. But, now that I've seen his smile, I can't help but smile back. "Hey… you have a really nice smile. It suits you." Great, now I'm blushing, I face away from him.

"T… t-thanks." He needs to just stop complimenting me. I have to focus on my work, **trying to find out what kind of underwear Skye wears.** What! No, I do not need to know that. Although… no, I need to fix the scanner **and get Skye naked.** NO! I do not need to do that; shut up, brain.

Fine, I will.

I don't need to work here, though; I grab my laptop, stand up, and ask Skye to take me back to his office.

So, you can fuck?

I thought we agreed you shut up.

Nah, I'd rather keep annoying you with horny thoughts because you need it bad.

I have a boyfriend he does—

Don't lie; he does *not* satisfy you.

Okay, fine, it's terrible, always has been, but I cannot just let Skye have sex with me; maybe someone will have sex with me one day. Maybe even Skye, but not today.

Hate to tell you this, and the tent in your underwear may help my point; you are still hella horny.

Fine, if *he* isn't here tonight, then we can try hands-free again; Deal?

…Deal.

"Would you mind if I asked you a few questions?" he suddenly asks after a few minutes of silence in his office. I look at him suspiciously but nod.

"I noticed before that—"

"HA! I fucking found it!" I accidentally interrupt him. "S… Sorry."

"It's fine, what did you find?" He gets up and comes over to me; he was sitting on the bed.

"Someone changed the codes, so see this one." He nods. "Well, this is the working scanner, now look at the same line of code but on the faulty one." I slide the mouse over so Skye knows where to look. "Do you s-see it?" He shakes his head. "It's been changed from a one to a zero, so literally when the scanner got to this point in the program, nothing would happen."

"That is… is…" He stands up. "We had a worker in there the other day looking at the magnets, would it be possible to change the codes from the scanner itself?"

"Possibly, if they connected their phone. You would need some very specialist equipment to even get to this point. You saw h-how long it took me to g... g-get here."

"Someone could have done it if they knew where they were going?" I nod. "Seems strange, though; why sabotage medical equipment?"

"This morning... the servers were t-t-turned off. What if s-someone wants to keep me here?"

"That doesn't make sense. Your own boyfriend doesn't want you here." I look at him slightly hurt. "Sorry, but it is true."

"Yeah, I k-know, it doesn't make sense. Also, w-why now? W-why not before? It's n-n-not like all of your stuff is ou... outdated, you're actually pretty up to date computer-wise just a few minor..." I sigh, "A few minor faults like with the CT scanner."

"Okay, so I'm with you now. Someone definitely wants you here. You wouldn't happen to have some kind of tracker program in that bag of yours."

"I left it at home." Skye looks at me with this slightly horrified look. "I'm kidding. No, I don't have one of those; no one does; this isn't the movies. But, even so, we would both have to be on the system for me to actually get them."

"What about like... what do you call it." Skye scratches his stubble-covered cheek while he thinks of the word. "Got it, like a system echo."

"Oh... oh, that's good." I turn to face my laptop, oh I... I should tell him. "Okay, so w-what I'm about to do is a little b-bit illegal, but since I'm being paid, it's kinda fine. I still shouldn't."

"But you're gonna do it anyway." He finishes for me, and I nod.

I open up the program I used earlier today, hack my way into the hospital servers, and start looking for server ghosts. It's like what Skye said. Everyone has a virtual presence online. Even if someone is hacking, or has hacked into something. Even changed the codes on anything. Then I can track it back to the source, well, not really. Basically, I can see what was connected, and from there, I can... well, I can hack the phone. I never do this, for the record, it's very illegal and a breach of privacy, not to mention that if they know what they are doing, they can just erase their presence. It's not easy, though. After an hour of searching and Skye pacing again, I start to track a specific phone that might have been connected to the CT scanner; it's hard to tell. From what I can tell, they have been here a lot. Their phone connects every day simultaneously, but it constantly changes when the phone disconnects from the servers. I check the time; I've been here for seven hours. Gods, no wonder I'm tired.

And horny, don't forget that.

I can't; you won't let me. I'm gonna have to try again tomorrow. Hopefully, whoever is doing this will connect to the server while I'm here. I stop typing and place my head on my desk, close my eyes, then I hear a heavy tapping on the window. I lift my head and see that it's raining. Great. I'm gonna get wet; lucky I am prepared for this. I disconnect my laptop and shut it down, placing it in my bag. I stand up to find a napping Skye on his own bed; I smile at the sleeping man before me. I go over and shake his shoulder gently so he will wake up. Slowly he starts to come back to reality, just in time, too, as someone starts to knock on his door. His eyes widen when they do, and he runs over to the door and opens it up.

"Ah, Doctor Kearny. I'm glad you're here, but I thought you were on holiday."

"I am, but the chief asked me to help someone out with the

computer upgrade we are getting. What's happening?" Skye asks them.

"There has been an accident in Leith. Three males and two females have been seriously hurt by a third drunk driver. Unfortunately, he was pronounced dead at the scene. Anyway, one of the men is asking for you specifically; apparently, you've worked with him before." A nurse, I think, tells him. Skye nods and lets the nurse know that he'll be along shortly.

Suddenly, Skye is stripping in front of me. I blush and turn around; I'm assuming that he is pulling on some scrubs. I hear a rattling and see him pulling on a lab coat. He doesn't apologise or say anything as he leaves. I do get the feeling that I shouldn't follow him. But I'm curious, Leith is close to where I used to live, so I follow him quickly. The dude can walk fast; let me tell you that. I follow him at a distance, I feel that I shouldn't be following him, but my curiosity has always gotten the best of me.

He enters A&E and walks over to the end of the room; I intend to follow him, but I wait and look around instead. Scottish ER departments are very different from what I would expect. Each patient has a small alcove where they are treated and taken away, if necessary, there are two beds per alcove, and by each bed, there is a heart monitor and a chair. Above them are some curtain rails and curtains. I always thought the colour was a bit… bland, I guess that's the point. A nurse brushes past my arm; I definitely shouldn't be here. Maybe finding Skye is a good idea.

I walk down to where I last saw Skye. On my way, I see the two females. When the nurse told Skye about them, I assumed two older women. They can't be any older than twelve or thirteen. They look so much alike that I think they're twins. So that makes the man their father. If I could call my dad, I would. I wonder if I faked an injury, if he'd examine me…? I doubt that he would, though. He was always swamped when I was a kid, so I don't think that's changed. He would be about fifty-five by now, so many birthdays that I've missed. I doubt anyone would forgive me for practically disappearing for six years.

I find Skye, and I watch as he examines the unconscious man. I step further into the room. The man on the bed looks familiar, but I can't place him. He has head trauma, so his face is covered. Seems like his arm is broken, and there is something wrong with his leg too. The man on the bed is alone, but there are two bags by his bed. <u>Someone else is here</u>. Agreed. Hades, I really shouldn't be here. I should go; I don't even know why I came. Did I think that I would see someone I knew? I disappeared like they would understand why I suddenly—

"Percival?" someone says; I spin around and see someone I never thought I'd see again. I swear I'm gonna be out of tears by the end of this day. I start to cry as he runs over to me and hugs me. I can't help but bury my head into the crook of his neck.

It's Elliot.

Missed?

"Where have you been?" Elliot says, his arms are around my neck and stroking my head as I cry. I just shake my head, apologising softly over and over again. "Shhhh, baby, it's okay. I'm sorry, it's been a rough day." I forgot how intimate we used to be.

"Percival? Are you okay?" I hear Skye's voice behind me, so I reluctantly get out of Elliot's embrace and face Skye.

"S-Skye, this is Elliot. My…" I want to say best friend, but I'm not sure I can even call myself that any more.

"I'm his oldest and best friend. You… you're Doctor Kearny, aren't you?" Elliot confirms for me; Skye smiles. I'm not sure I can tell you why.

"Yes, that's me; you must be Sammy's best man." They shake hands. Hang on, best man?

Finally, I look at my old friend and see that he is wearing a dirty, soaked wedding suit and a red tie. His waistcoat is a soft cream colour with a flowery pattern over it. Elliot always did like flowers; he's even got his natural hair colour back! What the heck happened in the last five years. I rub the tears away from my eyes. Other than the lack of colour in his hair, he's the same person I've always known. The redhead from my dream.

"Yeah, I know; I scrub up well." He escorts me over to where Sammy is lying. I see that he, too, is wearing a tux. I need to start paying attention to my surroundings. **Like that is gonna**

happen. Hey! Shut up.

"Yeah, you both d-do. B-b-best man. Quite an honour. When did t-this h-happen?"

"Oh, you remember that bar that you hated up on the mile." I nod. "Well, four years ago, we were looking for you and figured that you may go to bars. We didn't find you, but Sammy did find the love of his life. But now I found you, in a hospital of all places." He hugs me again; I flinch slightly as he touches my back, but I return the hug. I will not cry again. **Yeah, you will.** I hate it when you're right!

"Elliot, we have to give you a check-up. Do you mind?" Skye tells him, we break our hug.

"Oh, dude, I'm good now that my best man is here." Nothing is said for a second, but Skye does look confused. "That's you, Perry." Wait, I'm his best man? Isn't he the best man? Not what he means… are you going to let him get away with calling you, Perry? No!

"I t-t-told you not to c-c-call me that," I tell him; he gives me that cheeky smile he always gives me when he calls me Perry. "I t-trust Skye, so you w-w-will get the check-up. Please?"

"Back in my life for less than five minutes and already telling me what to do. Fine, but can you stay with Sammy? If his fiancé comes in and sees him alone, she'll kill me." I nod and give him another hug, surprising both the men in front of me. I break the hug and sit down. Elliot laughs and walks off with Skye.

I stare at Sammy for a good half hour before someone shows up… a woman in a wedding dress. She looks like she is about to cry. I get up and stand awkwardly. Her dress is beautiful, the typical wedding dress, big and puffy. Her veil seems to be missing though, I wonder what happened.

<u>Percival, there is a crying woman. Go help her.</u>

Right, sorry. Not the time to focus on her dress.

"Hi, sorry. I'm p… p-p." Fucking stutter.

"You're Percival. Aren't you?" I nod. "Sammy and Elliot always talked about you. Who found you?"

"Your doctor," Skye says. "Hello, Abigail." They hug quickly, and she takes him by the shoulders.

"Doctor Kearny, how is he? Tell me that he is okay." Her hands drop, and she stares at Sammy.

"Your fiancé is fine; unfortunately, I'll have to keep him here for observation for at least twenty-four hours. He had a lot of pressure on his spine, and he's broken his arm, and his leg is fractured in three places. He's lucky to be alive; someone still wants him around," Skye jokes.

"Oh, Sam would never die without asking me first."

"Really? I can't die without asking?" a voice croaks out. I spin around and see Sammy looking at his future wife. She runs over to the other side of his bed and starts kissing him, telling him how much of an idiot he is. "Honey. I'm fine, see I'm still alive."

"Right, we're just gonna take you to a semi-private room now. Don't worry, Abigail, you can follow," Skye says. Nurses walk over to his bed and take him off the bed and onto another, one then he's being rolled away. "Oh, Elliot is in the room too, so you will have someone you know at least." I see Sammy's free hand lift up with his thumb in the air.

The hospital bed is wheeled away, so I sit down on the chair again. I rub my hand over my eyes and sniff. I get up and start to leave the hospital. I lost track of Skye once he'd left, but I think he thanked me for staying with Sammy. If I'm honest, part of me doesn't want to leave. <u>No, it is all of you.</u> Shut up, we have to go… I reach the doors and see *him* waiting outside for me. No. Not tonight, you know what? Never again, you were right. Thank you. Right now, my friends need me, and I am staying with them.

I turn around and head to the reception, asking for Elliot's room, and I'm given the answer straight away. I head up without a second thought. I jump in the elevator just before *he* can see me. As I'm walking, I can feel my breath start to quicken. **Fuck we have a panic attack incoming!** No, we don't. We're fine, we got this… right? I… I think we are going to pass out. Not yet we are so close. I stumble into the door, open it and see Elliot, and he smiles at me. Then I pass out. I really hate it when you two are right.

Someone is stroking my head. Who is stroking…? Actually, it feels really nice. I lean into the hand a little, and I hear them let out a giggle. One I remember all too well. I open my eyes and see Elliot looking at me with the cheeky smile I remember.

"Hey, there, sleepyhead," he says, flashing a huge grin. I blush at the cute nickname; he's always doing that.

"H-how long was I out?" I ask, why is that the first thing I care about.

"Not long, maybe a day, Sammy is getting released later. I watched you pass out yesterday and decided to stay. It doesn't feel that long, though, too busy keeping you calm to notice." What does that mean? "When did the nightmares start? I know for sure you didn't have them when you lived with us." Wait… I've been asleep for a day! He's gonna kill me. I sit up slowly, crossing my legs.

"Three years ago. A little a-after Mum's death." I sniff. I haven't actually thought about her since the funeral.

"I'm sorry, I wasn't there. I didn't find out until I ran into your dad last year." I shake my head. "You got thinner too, Percival, and I don't think these were there six years ago." He pulls up my sleeve, revealing my cuts; I instantly cover them up, pulling my hand away. He sighs. "What happened?"

"Nothing happened…" He gives me a look, and it breaks me. "Except the b-biggest m-mm-mistake of my ll-l-life. That's w-w-what h-happened." Elliot starts to run his hands through my hair again and gently rubs my arm. I lean into his side as I cry.

"Come back with me; I can get you away from him."

"He'll find me. I t-t-tried to a few months a-after I moved in. I ll-left with my bag and came home; I was about to kn-kn-knock when he grabbed me and… yeah."

"That was you? I thought it was one of the kids on the floor above us. I knew I should have gone out further. Where is this fucker? I'll kill him myself."

"Get in line." My head shoots to the end of the bed where Skye is standing with his arms crossed. "Your partner thought you were working all last night but is going to be here any second, so you have a choice. You can hide, with my help, of course. Or go with him. I'm going to get him fired either way." I sit up, swinging my legs over the side of the bed. An idea comes into my mind. **It's a bad idea.** <u>Only if it does not work.</u> **Still makes it a horrible idea, ya know.**

"H-hold off, for now. I have an idea."

"If it involves you getting hurt more, then I am not behind it."

"T-three h-hours. Then c-come over. I'll be out b-before then." With that, I grab my bag and meet my oppressor in the hallway, passing him deliberately, pretending I didn't notice him. I know he'll catch me. I just need to make sure it's in a camera's field of view. <u>End of the hallway, to the right.</u> Thanks. If someone really does want me here, then they should be watching. I feel him grip my arm and pull me to face him.

"Where were you?" he growls. I notice the steady red light of the camera in the corner of my eye.

"Skye n-noticed I was t-t-too thin for my age and was mm-making sure I'm h-healthy."

"Five. Get your ass home now. You have cuts to give yourself and my pressure to relieve." I don't reply, but I keep walking, his hand still gripping my arm. I know my arm will bruise. But, you have us; we can get through this. Yeah, I sure hope so.

I'm surprised that despite my weakened state, I manage to keep up with him. When we get in the door, I place my bag in my office, and he grabs me and slaps my face, then he hits my stomach a few times until he hears something crack. I yelp at the pain. Next, he throws my head against the wall causing me to get very disoriented. Finally, he steps on my leg; I can feel the tendons crunching underneath his foot.

I keep suppressing my screams as he says something. I'm not sure what, I can't really hear, but I have a feeling I already know what it is. He gets off me, and I'm about to get up when he helps me instead. He slams me against the wall again and removes my trousers with his knife. I feel the pressure on my back, and I know what is about to happen.

You said hands-free, not this.

Yeah, I know; I wasn't exactly expecting it either. I can hear myself screaming in pain until he covers my mouth.

You deserve this; you know that, right? But, thinking you could escape, it was never going to happen.

No, I don't. No one deserves this kind of pain.

Three hours that's how long I gave them. All I have to do is hold out for that long, that's if I don't get to my side of the plan first. <u>You will need something to use, you realise.</u> *There is an old snow globe in your office.* I could use that on him... no, it's not strong enough and would break on impact. *What else can you use? That is easy to hide also?* What about the lamp beside the bed? I can grab that instead. Easy enough to grab it and hit him with it in one movement. No need to hide it. <u>Yes, that could work.</u>

Suddenly I am dropped to the ground. My vision starts to fade in and out, I watch him strip and go into the bedroom, so I crawl into my office and grab my knife. I pull off my shirt and slice my upper belly six times on the left side. The cuts aren't deep but enough that he'll be happy. I know I'm going to find him naked on his bed. I stand up and shake my head slightly. I need to have some sort of vision for this to work. <u>Wait, start downloading all your files.</u> Good call; I didn't turn it off, so it's easy to start downloading everything off it. I won't start from scratch if I get a new one.

I walk to the bedroom using the wall to guide me where he is waiting, and he is already at full mast again. I climb onto him, feeling his rock-hard member pressing against my ass. His hands run over my body and rub the blood over my chest. I lean down and kiss his neck and work my way down and back up. Then, using myself as a distraction, I grab the lamp, sit up and hit him across the side of his head. The light smashes, and he is knocked out. I jump off him and throw what's left of the lamp onto the bed. But I miss it, and it hits his head again.

I have to work quickly. I reach under the bed and grab his handcuffs and rope. I not only tie him to the bed, but I handcuff him to it. I take the handcuff keys and flush them down the toilet, after which I start to pack my things. I check the download of my files, it's almost done. <u>Get your clothes packed.</u> I throw some clothes into my bag along with my entire hard drive collection once it finishes. I am leaving six years of my life behind, but hopefully, I can get some of my things back. Although a lot of it is terrible memories. I pull on some clothes that aren't ruined, including the only underwear I have which is a pair of pink jocks.

<u>Now isn't the time to be picky, Percival.</u>

I nod at myself and pull on the rest of my clothes; I throw my bag over my back and head to the door. I am about to leave when I realise I could lock him out. He always keeps his keys in the same place. I find his trousers on the floor and his keys in the back pocket, the problem is that it's taken me two hours to get to this point and his jeans are in the bedroom. So, he's coming back into consciousness. I quietly get out of the room and lock it behind me; he locked me in there once with him. He said he wanted to use me when he wanted. He didn't do it again when I almost killed myself. Let's see how he likes it. With both sets of keys, I run out the door and lock it behind me. I run down the stairs and throw both sets into the trash and run to the hospital.

I see myself getting strange looks as I'm running. Usually, I would mind a lot, but I have to keep my mind occupied right now. The adrenaline running through my system will only last so long. I'm shocked it's lasted this long… wait. I can feel myself start to slip now. OUCH! What the fuck is that? Oh, shit, my ankle, it's really fucking sore. Great, just great. Oh, and my ribs hurt, and now I see spots – more blood loss, probably low blood sugar as well. I am still five minutes away from the hospital. <u>*Come on, Percival, just a little longer.*</u>

When I get there, Skye and Elliot are outside waiting for me. I run into Elliot's arms, who quickly notices the blood and picks me up before I faint again. I lean my head onto his chest and try to even out my breathing. I think I pass out because the next thing I know, I'm on a bed with Elliot trying to get me to talk.

"Come on, Percival, I just got you back. Don't go running out on me now," Elliot tells me.

"C-can..." Oh, come on, <u>Percival, you can speak</u>. I've got this.

"Yeah, buddy?"

"Can I h-have my old r-room back?" I stare at Elliot as he starts to laugh at me.

"Of course, you can. I never did get another roommate." I start to groan as they put needles into my arm. "Tell me what hurts, baby, they'll help, I promise."

"My head, my belly. My arms, my ankle and my... Fuck! All of me, Elli, make it stop, please!" I scream, feeling the tears stain my vision.

"He's been running on adrenaline for at least an hour. I can see the bruise forming on his chest, and these cuts are self-inflicted. His ankle is sprained, and he most definitely has a concussion. Elliot, are you okay being his guardian in the meantime? There is a lot we have to do." Elliot looks at me, and I nod, I was gonna say something else, but I can feel myself slipping. Already? No, I have to have more time!

"Baby, you gotta stay awake. Please."

"I just want ss-sleep, Elli," I mumble out.

"Come on, remember what you told me all those years ago. If I get a good job, you and I will go on a date, right." I nod, know what he's doing, and if it helps, I'm all for it. "Where would you take me? huh?"

"I... I don't knowwwww. I haven't been out in f-f-five years. W-What's still cool?" I can hear myself slurring my words; it makes me sound funny. So, I start giggling.

"What's happening?"

"Possibly hysteria? He has to stay calm."

"B-but I sound sooooo funny." Hehehe, I sound hilarious.

"Yeah, you do, Percival, you know what else is funny? Minecraft fails." That really sets me off. I can't help but giggle… then something happens; I feel something start to run out of my mouth; I already know what it is before I see it.

"Get him under now!" Skye yells, and then the world goes black.

Broken

Someone is holding my hand. Who's holding my hand? Why is it so dark? Oh right, I fainted, again, didn't I? Just what I needed today. I haven't even finished the job I was given at the hospital. I bet I didn't even get out of the flat. I bet I'm still there... but he never holds my hand. I try to open my eyes and groan at the light. So I snap my eyes shut.

Oh... the hand is gone. I need to know who was there; I open my eyes again, and the light has pretty much gone. Is it night-time now? It must be, although there is a small lamp on a low setting. So I'm not in the flat? I'm in a hospital bed. Why am I in a hospital? Oh, fuck, I remember what happened now; oh shit, is that my breathing?

Why is it so fast?

Why am I even...

Ugh, my head hurts. Why does my head hurt? And what is with the pressure on my arm? Okay, let's try opening my eyes again. There is that damned light again; who puts a light on that bright? Finally, my eyes open... oh... that light was the sun; I guess that can't be turned down. I lift my arm to rub my eyes, only one responds. When I look down, I see a green-haired person lying on my arm. Elliot. Only he would be mad enough to dye his hair green, my favourite colour, I might add. I reach my hand over and run my fingers through his hair. I feel him lean into my touch and give off a small moan. He always enjoys it when someone plays with his hair. So do I, for the record. I hear him start to moan again until he cuts himself off; he must have realised. He slowly sits up and looks at me. Is he gonna cry? I was only out for a few days.

He jumps up and hugs me. I groan at how tight he grabbed me; I rub his back in the hopes he might calm down, but I don't think he will. He breaks the hug, grabs my face gently, and places our foreheads together; I put my hands on his. Why does it feel like I haven't been hugged in a while? I know that I haven't been embraced like this since I started dating... him... Breathing again. It's picking up. Why? This cannot happen again.

"Focus on me, Percival. Listen to my breathing," someone says, I listen to their breathing and try and match them. I'm not sure how long it takes, but I calm down, and I lean onto Elliot's chest. Am I crying again? Yes, I am. "Lay back, baby. I'll get you something to drink." I obey him, laying back, getting a good look at the man in front of me.

There are bags under his eyes, his hair is unkempt, almost like he hasn't washed it and his clothes are. Well, they look well worn. I watch him as he walks over to a water station and notice his walking is a little sluggish. He cracks his back, an annoying habit that he won't ever stop; believe me, I've tried. I have missed it, though; I can't help but smile. I can't believe after all this time, he still wants me. I feel like I betrayed him, chose an idiot partner over him. My best friend, most outstanding support and I can't deny that he is my brother. No blood relation, but I still consider him that.

I continue to sniff and rub the tears away from my eyes, fucking hell, I am an emotional wreck today. Elliot notices my distress and runs back over with a cup of water and a straw. He sits back where he was and holds the straw out for me. I sip on the water as he wipes away my tears. I finish the drink and sniff again.

"I'm s-s-sorry," I say, my voice is a bit groggy. I suppose since I haven't talked in a few days, it may be difficult.

"Why would you think I needed an apology? I didn't find you; I should be saying sorry," he tells me. I shake my head, and he hugs me again.

"Let's ag... agree to disagree t-there," I mumble into him; he nods and kisses my head.

"Okay, but..." He takes my free pinky. "Keep me in the loop with everything. Promise?"

"P-Promise." I forgot we did that.

"Hey! My favourite gay is awake!" I know that voice; Elliot lets me go, and Sammy enters my room and gives me a soft hug. What's with all the hugs? And what does he mean, favourite gay? I'm the *only* gay he knows. Elliot doesn't count; he's bi.

"How is your l... l-leg and arm?" I grovel out, rubbing my nose and trying to look somewhat presentable.

"A right sight better than you, I'm betting." He settles down in the chair next to my bed. His future wife stands behind him. A deafening silence falls over us; I can't stand the quiet any more. It usually means something is wrong.

"W-well. You two certainly s-s-seem to have had a f-f-fun five years," I tell them all.

"Some of us, anyway. Elliot here did become a teacher, so I don't know how much fun that would be," Abigail says. Sammy laughs, and I smile; I have to stop myself laughing. My chest hurts for some reason.

"I like her, S-Sammy. She can ss-stay," I tell him.

"Hey, I enjoy teaching kids. I find it fulfilling," he replies, crossing his arms and pouting. It's cute.

"Nice to know I have your seal of approval. It means nothing to me, but thank you anyway." Seeing Abigail out of her wedding dress is interesting. She is wearing a leather jacket and skinny jeans. She definitely has that 'do not mess with me' look. Especially with her messy blond hair flowing over one shoulder. How the hell did Sammy end up with her?

Before anything else is said, a nurse walks in and notices that I'm awake. She comes over all smiles. My breath increases sightly, but it's only enough that I'd be the only one who notices. She raises a light up to my eyes, and I flinch away; she huffs and tries again. This time I bat her hand away, hard enough to knock the light out of her hand. Why did I do that? I look closely at the nurse; I feel my breath increase again. This time everyone notices it.

"Get out," Elliot says to the nurse, moving her out the way and sitting on my bed again. "Calm down, buddy, okay, just breath." I watch the nurse leave, clearly unhappy, and I start to calm down. Elliot continues to hold me, and I focus a lot more on my breathing. Then, after a moment, the conversation picks up again.

"Well, I, for one, am glad you are awake again. Maybe you can convince greenie here to take a shower," Abigail says. I can't help but laugh.

"I do *not* smell that bad."

"Yeah, you do," I mumble 'cause it's true. But if I'm honest, it is strangely comforting.

"Do you guys always have to insult my choices? Percival needed me, and I wasn't going to leave his side, if that meant no showers, so be it."

"I n-n-never said I minded." I place my head on his chest again and try to keep my breathing as steady as his. His arms wrap around my back and… No pain. Why is there no pain? The only way there would be no pain would be if I had been out for longer than a day or my medication is incredibly high. I lift my head back up. "W-what have I missed? It c-can't be much… Right?" No one responds. "Right?"

"Percival, how long do you think you've been here for?" Sammy asks. I can see all of their faces are different. They were happy before, now they look… worried.

"A few d-d-days right. Three tops." I look at Elliot.

"Percival." Oh no, he only calls me that when the news is terrible. "You were out a lot longer than a few days. After you got to the hospital, you…" He takes a deep breath. "You started coughing up blood. The doctors and nurses were amazing and put you under immediately, and took you for surgery. Thirteen hours. Worst of my life, they told me that one of your ribs punctured your lung and, making you laugh, dislodged it. I suppose that's better than it happening after they thought you were fine." Elliot tells me, and I know there is more. Before I can say anything, Sammy takes over.

"After they sorted out your ribs, they found scarring on your lung. From what they said, you'd broken your rib before, and it had weakened the lining." I face him.

"I remember," I interrupt. "The f-f-first time it ha… happened, my chest hurt a lot like sss-something was rubbing something t-t-that it shouldn't."

"Basically, the lining on your lung was so weak that when your rib broke again, it went right through you. Then there is your leg, arms and your back," Sammy said.

"How long, Percival?" I face Elliot again. "How long was he abusing you?" I don't respond. "Some of the cuts are self-inflicted. How long?" I don't respond. I just look at my bedsheet.

I can feel myself shaking. I have to tell them; I start to talk, but nothing comes out. I can feel the tears falling onto my hands. Hands? I grab Elliot's hand and take it in mine. If my body doesn't let me talk, then I'll find a way to make them hear me. I open up his hand, palm up, and run a finger over each of the five digits, then I run the same finger halfway up his index finger before drawing a Y on his palm.

"Five and a half years?" Abigail says, I flinch slightly, not realising how close she had gotten. I nod at her answer. "Fucking hell." I take a breath and manage to calm myself down, enough to talk anyway.

"That's… one w-w-way to p-p-p-p… put it." Fuck you letter P. Once again, Elliot hugs me, and I, him. "B-but I'd I… imagine hh-hell is a b-bit nicer." Elli sighs at my joke, but I can tell he liked it.

"Okay, baby, you are never leaving my sight again. We'll get you moved into your old room as soon as possible." I nod into his chest. "There are two more things, the tendons in your leg snapped, so you may find it difficult to walk on it. But I'll be right here to help. Now to finally answer your question. You were out for a month. You woke up twice during it, but you passed out, panic attacks both times. Somehow I managed to calm you down and decided I wasn't going anywhere."

Fuck. I was in a coma. FOR A MONTH! My breathing picks up, but I close my eyes and grab my wrist. There is no pain, but if I can squeeze it enough, Elliot starts to scooch me over, and now we are both lying on the hospital bed, in relative comfort. I can't get to my wrist. At first, my breath is still incredibly ragged, but it starts to slow; Elliot was holding onto my arms to stop me from harming myself. This is where I'm going to start struggling. Eventually, I do begin to relax in Elliot's embrace.

Abigail and Sammy start talking about their wedding. Since they lost their deposit on the venue, they have to look for new places, but it seems they can book the same place again. It's annoying, though, because they don't think they'll get the money for a second deposit on the wedding and need it by at least next week. However, I do compliment her on her dress.

"Hey, this time, you can be there, Percival!" Sammy says. I see his face light up at the idea.

"Percival never did well in a crowd before we lost him. Do you really think it's a good idea now?" Elliot tells him, his hope dies. Nope. I have an idea. **Your last one landed us up in hospital.** Shut up; this is a good one.

"W... what if it was small?" They all look at me, confusion etched over their faces. "If it was just sss-say, family and friends, then it wouldn't be b-bad. No... p... p..."

"Panic attacks?" Elliot finishes for me, and I nod.

"I know it's not what you wanted, honey, but what do you think?" Sammy says.

"Hmmm. I can get behind this, but the venue we booked is for one hundred people."

"Honeymoon?" Confused looks again. Come on, brain catch up. "Where w-w-were you going?"

"Oh, south of France to a region called, Juan-Les-Pins. It looks amazing on the website, right near the beach too," Sammy says.

"When are you going?" Oh, hey, no stutter.

"We had to rearrange the last flight, and it's in two weeks. The venue date is in three weeks. I'm not sure what we're going to do. This is the only date we can get," Abigail explains.

"The reverend? Is it someone you absolutely w-w-want?"

"Yes, it's my mother. You've met; she didn't like you guys

much," Sammy says. Oh, I remember her. She told me that the next time she caught Elliot and me messing around in her church, she'd make sure our parents would know what we did. No, I do not care to explain.

"Oh yeah, I remember that!" Elliot says. Please don't. "That was when she caught us kissing in the confession booth." I hit him. "Ouch, hey, I enjoyed it."

"Why is this the first time I've heard about you two kissing?"

"Is it really a-allll that sup… surprising?" I say.

"It's not like we did anything bad. I was teasing him because he hadn't had his first kiss. He grabbed me, pulled me into the booth and kissed me. Well, it was a little more than a kiss. We made out a little bit. I had fun." And now you understand. I have to go die from embarrassment now. I can feel my face heating up; I can hear Sammy and Abigail laughing.

"I really wish you hadn't," I mumble into Elliot, trying to hide my overly red face… Suddenly I am very aware of how close Elliot and I are. Normal friendships aren't like this? Are they? **No.** Hold on, what is in my dick right now? I re-position myself on the bed and slide my hand under the covers to check. I really should have realised they'd do that sooner. I remove my hand and sink back into Elliot's arms, trying to ignore my little revelation. I do feel really safe here.

"So why do you ask?" Abigail asks after they finish laughing.

"Hmm? Oh r-r-right. Have the w-w-wedding in France. P… p… fly everyone out and have it on the beach. No need to p… pay for a v-v-venue." Oh wow. V, that's a new one. Abigail's face lights up, and it seems like she likes my idea. Sammy, however, doesn't look happy.

"There is no way they could afford that, baby," he tells her.

I watch as her face slowly changes.

"Find out how much. I'll p… p… give you the difference." Of course, everyone blows up at that. "W-what? It's my money. I make a lot of money, you know."

"Oh yeah? How much money have you saved up?" Sammy says, exasperated.

"Half a million." All of their mouths drop.

"What the fuck, Percival?" Sammy says.

"Have I ever told you how hot you are?" I hit Elliot lightly, telling him to shut up.

"Consider it my w-w-wedding gift." I smile, and the happy couple starts to laugh. Sammy gives me a hug, as does Abigail. After that they decide to go, they have lots to do, I suppose. Once they are gone Elliot, and I fall into a comfortable silence… no, wait. He's snoring. He's asleep. I snuggle into his chest and close my eyes; I feel myself drifting off when someone clears their throat. I turn to the source and see Skye standing at the end of my bed.

"Hey," he whispers. I give a small wave. "How are you doing?" He moves the chair where Sammy was, closer to the bed, and sits.

"I've been b-better. The n-nurse seem to t-t-trigger something. Also… could you… umm." I blush at what I'm asking.

"What?" Skye asks, and I nod my head down. "Oh! Yeah, I can deal with that."

Carefully Skye removes the catheter that is inside me. It is really uncomfortable getting it removed. But, I'm not gonna lie; I was struggling to keep my hard-on down while he was taking it out. Lucky for me, my dick only started getting hard after I was covered back up. Making up for the month it missed, I suppose.

Oh yeah, you are gonna be horny for a while. So have fun with that. Fantastic.

"Other than your leg and the bandage on your chest, which I'll change tomorrow, Elliot is free to take you home as soon as you feel ready." I nod and try to settle back down. "Did he tell you how long you were out for?" Once again, I nod. "He stayed. The entire time. Despite all of my arguing and my staff telling him you would be fine. I got the feeling he didn't trust us; I wouldn't trust us either. Our entire staff is under review."

"Why?"

"Oh ya know, someone let slip what happened to you and that it was one of our nurses that was the cause, so the chief had the police interview everyone. Very detailed too, I had to show them our chat. To show that I only met you properly last month. Oh, the police will want to talk to you. I'm keeping them away for now." He starts to get up, other patients to see.

"Thank you, Skye. F-for everything. You're a good friend." He smiles and leaves, and I close my eyes and fall asleep.

Tricked

The best feeling in the world is waking up having your hair stroked; I've noticed mine is longer than it was. That's what I get for being in a coma for a month. I know it's Elliot's fingers running through my hair because I honestly think he is the only one I would let near me at this point. Sammy is different, I trust him, but it's not like he won't raise his voice at me. Or stroke my hair. Elliot works with kids, so he knows how to be gentle. I would assume more so with abused kids. I'm not saying that I am a kid, but I think it's a fair comparison in my state. Honestly, I could stay here forever. Unfortunately, nature is calling me. I groan and try to sit up.

"Noooo, stay here," Elliot says; gods, he's a child.

"I have to p... p... pee," I tell him. He understands and lets me go. I realise I'm still connected to the drip, and apparently, my ankle won't support my weight any more, so... how the fuck am I supposed to do this? My ankle is in a brace, so I guess that will help me, just not a lot, and one month without walking is a long time. Suddenly a pair of arms scoop me up. I grab the drip, and I'm walked to the bathroom. It's Elliot. When did he get so strong? Or did I—

"You have lost a lot of weight, Percival. I feel like I'm holding a couple of grapes," he tells me. I huff.

"You've been watching t... too mmmuch Brooklyn 99," I tell him. He laughs and sets me down on the toilet.

"Just call when you're done." He smiles and shuts the door for me; I pull up my... robe and get to my business. I haven't really drunk anything for the past month. I guess that's what the drip is. They'll probably take it out soon. Good, because I really don't like having it in. Using pain to calm me down has to stop. As much as I may not want to, I'm going to have to rely on Elliot more now. I doubt he is ready for that, but his load will lessen as soon as I can walk again. I gently tap my foot on the floor and hiss as pain shoots up my leg; I guess that's a no to standing up. How am I meant to flush this?

Well, I do have one good leg. <u>This is a bad idea, but you are *not* going to listen to me, so go right ahead</u>. I scoff at logic, and I stand up using my one good leg and the drip. Shockingly it holds my weight. I manage to flush the toilet; I pull down my robe as Elliot comes in to see me standing on one leg, gripping onto the drip stand to dear life. He sighs and comes over to help me. I wrap my free arm around his neck and start to hop out. Apparently, he's not letting me get away without help, though. I am in the air and back in his arms, being carried like a bride. The only bride here should be Abigail.

"I could h... have handled t-t-that," I tell him as he lays me on the bed. He stays quiet and sits by my bed. "I still w-w-worry you. Don't I?" He shakes his head. "Then w-what?"

"It took the police two weeks to find your ex; he was waiting for me to step out so he could steal you away again. When they finally caught him, he claimed you were his property, and he wanted what was his. So yeah, I'm worried for you." He doesn't sound happy, but two weeks. How long did it take for him to get out of those restraints?

"You'd think after hh-hitting him w-with a ll-lamp he'd get that I'm finished w-with him." Got him; Elliot is smiling now.

"You hit him with a lamp?" I nod; he bursts out laughing. "Okay newfound respect for you. I think that I should tell you that I have moved out of our old place, it's Sammy and Abigail's, for now. But, lucky for us, I did get a two-bedroom flat in Musselburgh. It's close to work, so if you're okay moving there, then we can move you in tomorrow." I smile and nod at him.

I start hearing a commotion outside my room and turn my head to the door. I see Skye backing into the door, holding off a man in black, the door is opened, and I notice the black uniform; it's a police officer. I turn to Elliot, who grabs my hand for reassurance. I really am not ready to talk about what happened. <u>Better to get this done, though</u>. The police officer starts to threaten Skye, so I yell at them to stop.

"STOP!" That shuts everyone up, shocks the hell out of Elliot too. "Skye, it's f-f-fine. Let him in." Skye leaves the room, and the detective stands facing me at the end of the bed.

"Can we have some privacy?" the officer asks, Elliot gets up to go, but I grab his hand tighter and pull him back down.

"He stays. Or y-y-you go," I tell him; he doesn't like it but agrees. The truth is that I feel like I'm suppressing a panic attack, and Elliot is the only reason it hasn't become a full-blown attack yet. I really get the feeling that I should be in a psych ward or something.

"Just before you start asking your questions. I would recommend not mentioning Percival's ex's name. It may trigger a panic attack, and you don't want to be around when that happens," Elliot tells the officer who takes it under advisement. I thank him under my breath, and he gives my hand a gentle squeeze.

"Can you tell me your relation to… to the person in question?" the officer asks.

"He was my b-b-boyfriend. For six y-years." He writes that down.

"How soon did the abuse start?" I tense at the question, and I feel Elliot start to stroke my hand; it's helping, not by much, though.

"End of the t-the f-first year, I h-had mmoved out to live w-w-with him then it started."

"Why didn't you leave?"

"W-what makes you think I d-d-didn't try?" I tell him, how fucking dare he.

"There is no need to get defensive or nervous. Now, how soon after moving in did you try to get away?" the officer asks me. I can tell he doesn't really believe that I tried to get away. Looking at him, I get the feeling that he is very… old fashioned.

"I tried to get out a w-w-week after I moved in with him, he suggested tying me up. Of course, I am not into that. He t-t-tried to anyway, and when I told him no by p… p… pushing him away, he hit me twice. Then I p… p-p… grabbed a bag and left. He found me outside my old apartment, knocked mmme out. When I came too, I w-was tied up, and he was…" Fuck you, I am not finishing that sentence. I shut my mouth, if he can't—

"Go on, what was he doing?" He motions.

"How can you be so dense? Percival was being raped!" Elliot yells at him. The officer seems shocked at Elliot's reaction. I'm not. It was pretty obvious where I was going with that sentence.

"Sorry, that was not my intention to anger you. How often did that happen?" the officer continued.

"Too much," I reply. I am no longer in the mood for long-winded answers.

"Did you fight back?"

"At first, it got harder and harder to find a reason to."

"Did you ever hurt him?"

"Once. When I left last month." The officer seems shocked by that. "Surprised?"

"Very, gay men are known for being squeamish and poor fighters."

"Take your fucking stereotypes and shove them up your—" I start, but Elliot cuts me off.

"Percival clearly tried to run away. Stereotypes aside, he did hit that asshole with a lamp just to get out, and he still tried to get him back." Elliot cuts me off.

"From my perspective, Mr Grace hit his ex after receiving unexplained injuries."

"They w-were him," I explain. "I don't r-remember exactly w-what happened, but I remember him kk-kicking and punching my chest a few times. Throwing me against a w-wall and standing on my ankle. I think that is enough proof." I am getting really sick of this guy.

"The only other person that confirms your injuries is Dr Kearny, but since this entire hospital is under police investigation, it's unlikely anyone will believe them."

"So, you're telling us that bastard may not even go to jail for domestic abuse or rape?" Elliot asks.

"No. I'm saying that there is a higher chance that Percival will go to jail for the assault than the other guy will for domestic abuse."

"You don't believe me." I lower my head.

"I'm sorry, son. You had—"

"I'm not your fucking son." I take a breath. "I want you to get the fuck out of this room."

"I hardly think the swearing is necessary."

"Get. The fuck. Out. You don't believe a word I've said, so why should I tell you any more? If you are going to side with the asshole who caused this!" I spin around and expose my back to the officer. "Then get the fuck out!" I think I showed a bit too much, though, because Elliot moved the sheets a bit. After a minute, I pull my robe back around my shoulders and sit down, pulling my knees up to my chest and rubbing my ankle. Jumping up like that was not my best idea. Nothing is said for a while. I assumed that the officer left because Elliot was on the bed, holding me close as soon as I curled up. I hear a cough and look up at the officer who is still there.

"I would like to apologise for my behaviour. It's not the best technique to get answers, but I see now that you truly weren't lying. As for your ex, I can assure you that he is going away for a long time." Wait... what? He was tricking me? To get me to show my scars? "You are probably very upset right now, and you have every right to be, but I'm on your side."

"You really need to stop using that technique," Elliot tells him. I can hear the anger in his voice.

"Yeah, I'll let my partner know that it does more bad than good."

"Y-y-ya t-think?" I stutter out. After that, he does leave as requested but tells me that I don't have to attend the trial if I don't want to, which I'm grateful for. However, that doesn't mean I like the officer any more than when he came in. Elliot is still holding me for a good hour before Skye comes in with some of my clothes. Immediately I see the underwear I was wearing when I ran out. Elliot giggles at the colour and tells me that he didn't expect this sort of thing from me. I don't say anything, but I hide them under my other clothes. Skye tells me he has to check my stitches, so Elliot gets off my bed, and I lay down, covering up my privates. My chest was in a bit of pain when he started prodding me and changing the bandage, but he told me it was safe for me to leave. Skye carefully removes the drip from my wrist without any pain. Or so he said; it hurt. Never believe doctors when they say it won't hurt.

Once he leaves, Elliot hands me my underwear, making me blush and call him an ass. Thankfully he turns his back as I pull them on. I still do it under the covers, though. 'The hero always looks', Elliot may not be my hero, but I've seen him naked, so I think he'll want to return the favour. Once my underwear is on, he, unfortunately, has to help me with my trousers. It's not as awkward as I thought it would be... until Elliot comes to my crotch and blushes. He is quick to push away and leave me to finish off while he signs my discharge papers. I forgot that he is my guardian because... I forget why but legally, he is responsible for me until... okay, I don't know when. The point is that he's looking after me. I guess it would be until I can look after myself.

Elliot comes back as I am struggling to put on my hoodie. It's hard to lift my arm up to put it on, but he manages to get it over my head before he gets to my socks and shoes. I feel like an idiot. I can do all this myself; I shouldn't need help to put my god's damned shoes on. Lucky for me, I started buying elastic laces, so my boots are basically slip-on now.

"Hmm, that's really cool," Elliot says, examining my red shoes.

"Elastic laces. I'll sh-show you the link o-one day," I reply as I jump up onto my one good leg. Elliot wraps his arm around my waist and helps me... hop. We manage to get all the way to the door, where Skye opens it and is standing; a wheelchair is beside him. "No. Absolutely not," I say, hopping back slightly.

"You can barely walk. This will at least ease the pressure on

Elliot," Skye tells me. I'm still not convinced.

"Come on, Percival," Elliot starts. "Doctor's orders." I hate it when he does that.

"Just b-because you can quote Rick R-r-Riordan novels to me doesn't m-mean I'll listen... fine." I reluctantly sit in the wheelchair crossing my arms. Elliot smiles and starts to push me out of the hospital. I should probably explain the Rick Riordan thing; Elliot was reading Heroes of Olympus when I was just starting the series, per his request. Once he finished the series, he would quote his favourite character, Will Solace. Personally, I always liked Nico, but that's just me. Then I read Magnus Chase, and, well, Alex is just incredible. Anyway, 'Doctor's orders' became his favourite phrase, and he says it to me to piss me off. He's not even a doctor.

I love this hoodie, mainly 'cause it's like three sizes too big for me and has a huge hood. With everyone staring at me too, I'm quick to pull it up to cover my face. Spending five years indoors does tend to bring out the paranoia about who you can actually trust.

Which is no one.

I trust Elliot, don't try it. I've known him my whole life, and I don't think anything could break my trust in him. So, when he pulls my hood down and tells me that no one is staring at me. I listen to him without question. I'm still incredibly anxious about being seen, but I trust him; I'm still playing with my sleeves, though. When we finally get out of the hospital, Elliot walks us into the car park, and I get outside for the first time in a month. We stop in front of his new car. I say new because I've never seen it before. It's a lovely, dark green that reminds me of the dark prismarine block from Minecraft. Elliot opens the car door for me, and I manage to hop up and in before he can help me. There are some things I don't want help to do. Skye also places my bag in the back of the car behind my seat. I didn't even notice that he was following us. He crouches down by the door and holds my hand; I feel the blush come to my face.

"I know you probably won't trust doctors, or nurses, again, so when you next come in, I'll make sure that you *can* trust us. If not, well, I guess I'll be making more house calls," Skye tells me, smiling. Not sure what to do. I just smile back at him and nod. Elliot joins me in the car and leans to face Skye.

"Thank you, Doc. I'm sure our Percival will let you know where I live." When he says that, I feel... weird. I think I'm shaking, yup. "Woah, not in that sense, Percival. More in a friendship way, you know a term of endearment." He starts to stroke my arms, and it calms me down. But I definitely don't like the idea of being owned; *he* said it enough. "Let's get you home; some decent food and sleep will do you some good." With that, Skye gives me a quick hug, shuts the door for me and waves us off.

The drive back is quiet, just listening to Elliot's music. Sabaton, fucking fantastic music. I can feel my head nod softly to the beat. I was pretty against heavy metal in my high school years. After I moved out and he... after everything that has happened, I started getting into it more. Sabaton was one I knew, so I checked them out first. I would not mind going to one of their concerts. I think Elliot went once; I'd said no at the time, I slightly regret it now. How was I to know that I'd end up really liking their music? Slowly the car comes to a stop in front of a flat building. Elliot unbuckles his seat belt and leaves his car; I open the door and get ready to step out when Elliot appears and goes to pick me up.

"No. No w-way." I push him back. "I'm not b-b-being c-carried like a b-baby again."

"What would you suggest then?" he says, sounding exasperated. I ponder that thought for a second.

"TT-turn around and crouch." Confused, he gives me a strange look but agrees. I then surprise him by climbing onto his back and wrapping my arms around his neck. He catches on quickly, grabbing my legs and hoisting me up to keep me comfortable. He shuts the car door with his foot and starts to walk me up to his flat. He manages to pass me the key to open the front door, which is just the first hurdle. The stairs are where I thought Elliot would struggle, but I forgot to consider my new weight. Elliot will have me eating more to compensate for that. When we make it to the top floor, only three flights, Elliot bends down so I can reach the lock, and he opens the door and walks in. I notice that I am starting to get a bit sleepy. My body won't be used to moving so much. Elliot, I think, puts me down on his bed, carefully pulling off my shoes. I hiss when he pulls the shoe off my right foot. He apologises and takes it away, letting me slide out of my trousers. Once I'm free I quickly climb into the bed and bury my face into the pillow when he isn't in his room. It smells like Elliot. I make some sort of sound of contentment and smile before sleep takes over me.

Left Alone

I have no idea how long I was sleeping, but the flat is quiet when I finally get up. It's unsettling. I remember falling asleep on Elliot's bed, but I'm not sure what time it was… come to think of it. I'm not even sure I know what day it is. I don't have my phone to check, and who knows where Elliot is right now. I turn over in the bed and see that I have a lime green blanket covering me. I throw it off and sit up in the bed, rubbing the sleep from my eyes. I see a digital clock on the other side of the bed that reads 10.37, oh… I slept the night. Oh! I slept the night in Elliot's bed. Where did he sleep? The other room? On the sofa?

I remember he's the type to do that. That dummy, I swing my legs over the side of the bed and carefully test my legs. They seem fine; I try the weight on my right leg; it hurts, but the brace is helping a little. I pick up my feet and tighten the straps. Again, it hurts but not as much as it did. I place my left foot down first and hop slightly, testing the weight again as I walk. Finally, I make it to the bedroom door, which I open and walk towards what I can assume is the living room or a kitchen.

There's no sign of Elliot on the sofa or any snoring coming from the other bedroom. So, he isn't in the house at all. I'm alone again. I'm not sure how to feel about this. Being alone was always a good thing when I lived… away from Elliot; it meant I wouldn't be used for a few hours. A day if I was lucky. I fall onto the couch and take a few breaths, I pick up the TV remote and find that *Friends* is on, but I skip past it. I like that show, but there is only so much of it that I can stand. Lucky for me, I find something good to watch – an old film from the '90s.

I throw the remote onto the table in front of me and see a note on the table. I pick it up; it's from Elliot. I smile involuntarily.

>*Hey, Percival,*
>
>*Congratulations, you made it to the couch. I would have been there to see you wake up this morning, only I had to get to work. They were lenient about me missing a few weeks, but now I really have to get back. I'll be back at around five o'clock. I assume you can stay busy until then. Sammy may be over at some point after lunch. I'm not sure if Abigail will be coming or not, and they might bring lunch. If not, then there's stuff in the fridge you can have. Oh, and your phone was in your bag, which is by the door, sorry, you'll probably try walking again. See you after work,*
>
>*Elliot.*

After finishing the message, I place it back on the desk and see my bag chilling by the door. I take a breath and stand up. I carefully walk towards my bag and decide to sit on the floor to look through it. I find my phone, and it's turned off. Good. The longer it is turned off then, the less chance there is that *he* will find me. I place it back in the bag and look through it. Mostly it's just my work equipment, a few spare parts from old jobs but nothing that will keep me busy… oh, now there is an idea. I slide the bag back over to the sofa, then I slide myself over too. I manage to get onto the couch, where I pull out a small tripod and magnifying glass. I grab my own glasses from the side pocket and put them on; next is my phone. I take the back off of it, easily let me tell you. Once it is off, I start moving the magnifying glass around, looking for the tracker. Most phones have a tracker, mainly to find them or for parents to keep an eye on their kids. I don't think many people actually pay attention to it. But, I don't have a choice.

I find the tracker behind the battery, which makes it awkward to actually get to. That doesn't mean that things aren't simple. I disconnect the battery and place it out of the way. Now it's easy to get to. If I had my computer and all of my equipment, I would wipe and rewrite the tracker. However, I don't have all my stuff. For now, I'll have to think of another way to track my phone, as much as I may not want to. Ringing… what's ringing? I lift my head and see that it's the landline, thank the gods that Elliot has it close to his sofa. Sammy is calling. I mute the TV and pick up.

"Hey, Sammy," I say.

"Percival, hey. Good to hear that you're awake. Abi and I are coming over soon. Is there anything you want?" he asks; I have to think about this for a second.

"Honestly, I could r-r-really do with my com… puter and some food. But I'd settle for a new p-p-phone tracker."

"Can't you just buy a new phone?" Now there is a point. Feels like a waste; I have an excellent phone right here.

"My… p… cell is just as good. I j-just need to w-wipe the tracker so that… so I can't be ff-found." I hate using the American name, but sometimes it's all I can use.

"Well, I think I can get some of your stuff into my car. What would you need?" Wait… are you serious? Is he gonna get me all my stuff?

"W-well I… Ummm… everything I'd n-need is in or on my d-d-desk. But you'll have to take apart the desk for some of it."

"I'm sure Abi can deal with that. She's stronger than she looks." I can hear he says something along the lines of: 'Fuck yeah, I get to break shit'. Which really fills me with hope... sarcasm. "So, what is this thing we are looking for?"

"You'll know it w-w-when you see it. It's hidden *in* the top d-drawer, take everything out, and... w-well let Abigail break it to p... p-p..." I pause. "Destroy the desk."

"*She is pleased about that. You sure you don't want the desk? I'm happy to come back for it; I can probably get it in the car if I break it down a bit.*"

"Every t-t-thing *in* the desk w-will be fine. I n-never liked the desk." I assure him. He proceeds to tell me they'll be over in an hour and hangs up. I then return the phone to its place by the sofa and return to my disassembled phone. I unmute the TV just as the adverts finish and *Sleeping with the Enemy* comes back on.

Sammy and Abigail are true to their word when they arrive at the house pretty much bang on an hour later. Either they planned that, or it was pure luck. Abigail starts to take my things into the second bedroom while Sammy cooks some food. I think he is making... okay, I have no idea what he is making; it smells like chicken, which I love. He even remembered that I'm allergic to milk, which was awesome, so I'm getting chips too. I feel like a little kid with them, to be honest. They are all helping me so much. Elliot put me to bed last night, Sammy is cooking me lunch, and Abigail hasn't done anything yet, but I feel she will try. I'm not sure what she does for a job, I should ask. When it came to what was hidden in my desk drawer, Sammy immediately brought it to me. It's just a brown envelope, but I know what's in it. It is evidence. Evidence of what he did to me at the start of our relationship. I figured that it might come in handy one day; I guess today is that day. I see Abigail start bringing in the main bulk of the computer. I call out to her, motioning her to bring it to me.

"W-wait. I n-n-need that!" I stutter out, flailing my arms. She looks at me confused but brings it over. I clear a space, and she sets it down on the table. I fish my pocket drill out of my bag and attach the right head before removing the side of the CPU. I don't let it get dirty, so the inside is clean, and I pull out a small heatproof wooden box. The box is nothing special, just some novelty I bought online. I was tempted to get a Japanese puzzle box. However, I knew I wouldn't have the temperament to memorise how many moves it would take to open it. Inside is a red hard drive marked with a black pen and my credit card. I have the numbers memorised and use online stuff more than anything. I place the hard drive on the envelope and place the card, still in the box, on the table.

"What is all this?" Abigail asks.

"Evidence," I tell her, she picks up the hard drive and turns it over, gasping as I start to put the side back on the CPU. "I can guarantee y-y-you don't w-w-want to see that."

"How did you know you would need this?" Sammy asks; coming over, he hands me some food, chicken and chips. For the record, what I wrote on the Pen drive was 'Rape vid'. That's why I hid it, I wasn't proud that I had filmed it, and I was going to send it to the police. Something stopped me; I guess I didn't want my rape video out in the world. Not then anyway.

"I didn't. I'd all b-but given up that I w-would ever get out, I was half t-tempted to just throw it out. Glad I didn't." I start eating my food, fantastic, way better than that hospital shit.

"I can take it to the lawyers tonight," Sammy tells me; I just nod and keep eating. I can feel both of them staring at me as I do.

Eventually, Abigail just starts to get what's left of my equipment from the car. Sammy is the one who takes the tower into the next room. Watching him struggle to do so is funny. Turns out there wasn't that much more stuff to come in from the car. Once it's all in, I literally hop into the other room and find a desk in the room. I miss my chair, but there is one in this room. I manage to pick up the CPU and place it on top of the desk. I connect it up to the monitor; next is the speaker, and then it's just plugging it in. I turn it on, and everything works perfectly. Well, almost, I connected the speakers incorrectly, and the monitor has smudge marks all over it, but I can deal with them both. Oh, and I have no keyboard... or mouse.

"Here you go, the last from the car, forgot they were in there, sorry," Abigail tells me, placing them on the desk. I thank her and connect them up and log in. I reach into one of the drawers only to remember they are empty. I grab the small box on the desk and place it in. The new drawer is smaller than my last desk, but the box was always smaller than the drawer. Now it fits perfectly, very satisfying. "What does all that do?" I jump slightly, realising Abigail didn't leave the room like I thought.

"It varies. Some are just m-motherboard p-parts. This is the one I w-want thought. W-was there any t-trouble?" I question.

"None; the police officially released the flat a week after you were admitted. No one has been in there since. It's yours, by the way, since you know. The whole jail thing."

"Sell it. Rent it. I don't care; you have it." I don't want to go there ever again.

"Can I ask you something?" she asks, sitting on the unmade bed. I guess Elliot did sleep on the couch. I spin my chair to face her and nod. "When did you know you were gay?" Woah, where did that come from? I thought she was going to ask about the flat.

"Oh... umm. I w-was ten, caught Elli n-naked in his room, started the whole p... p... my questioning. Took about a w-week for me to admit it to m-myself, then I was thirteen when I told Elli."

"Wait... so are you actually out?" she asks; I shrug.

"It kinda just got... lost, I guess. The only reason we w-went out that night was 'cause Elliot let ss-slip that I was gay in front of Sammy a few n-n-nights p... before." She laughs.

"Yeah, that sounds like something Elliot would do; I take it you forgave him."

"Hard to stay m-mad at him. Even now." I feel a slight blush creep onto my face, but it fades fast.

"So, do your parents know?"

"Oh yeah, I t-told them at the same t-time as Elliot. Very supportive, even got me a p-p-... a flag, for LGBTQ p... plus." There is a pause, "No, I don't s-still have it. Thrown out y-years ago by... him."

"Well." She pauses. "You'll just have to have a proper coming-out party then!" She smiles.

"Thanks, it's a n-nice thought. But everyone that n-needs to know knows. Except for Skye, I'm p... p... I'm sure he c-can guess, though." She rests her hand on my shoulder and squeezes it gently, then gets up and leaves me in the room to find Sammy.

They leave twenty minutes later with some dinner for Elliot and me. After they are gone, I use my chair to roll out and grab my broken phone. Wheeling out there was easy; getting back was difficult. I almost dropped my phone twice while I was trying to get into the room. Once I get back, I manage to wipe the tracker completely and change everything on it, so there is no way he will find me again. I was quicker putting my phone back together than taking it apart. Take from that what you will. Once it's back together, I put it on charge and open up Minecraft.

Thankfully everything is still where it's supposed to be, and nothing was lost in translation. Once the game is open, I continue working on a massive storage system for all of my items, fun times. It's probably weird that I am a whizz with computers, but I cannot do any sort of Redstone for the life of me. I am way better at landscaping and house building. While playing, I check my phone's charge, getting up there, only fifty per cent now, but enough to turn it on. It's about five minutes after I've unlocked the phone that all the messages I missed over the last month start to come through. Emails about jobs needing doing. Stuff about my flat, emails from the police mainly. I swipe them away instantly; I've had just about enough of them. There is one message that freaks me out, though, from him.

Him: *When I find you, faggot, I will kill you. Not even jail will keep me from what is mine.*

I lock my phone and push away from my desk, calm down, Percival, you're okay, he can't... he's in jail. No one will hurt you. Skye will protect you; you know he will, and the evidence that you've just given the police will be more than enough to send him away for a very long time.

Calm down.

I'm trying. It's very hard. I start to tug on my hair; it's sore but not life-threatening. I hit my head a few times to see if that would help, and it doesn't.

You know how you can calm down. It just takes one little—
Fuck off.

It's not so bad; you deserve it. And if you die, who's left to care about you?

Elliot cares; just try and breathe. Just like he tells you to.

Breathing might help, steady breathing. In and out in and...

in? Out and out? Fuck. Fuck.

"FUCK!" I yell accidentally.

One little cut, then maybe a few more. You can do it.

Somehow, I'm up and running towards the kitchen; I grab Elliot's smallest knife and place it on my wrist. I drag it across my forearm, slicing deep into my arm. I let out a sigh of relief. I make another just below it, and another, and another. After seven cuts, I start calming down. I feel all sleepy now. I hit the side of the kitchen bunker with my hip and slide down until I hit the floor; I can feel myself falling asleep again. Falling onto my side. Sleep is good. I don't want to go to the hospital. I just don't want to… I don't… I…

I see a blob of green running towards me as I pass out.

A Mistake

Ugh, my head, my arm. Elliot!

My eyes shoot open to see Elliot sitting at the desk chair in the room he's given me. He's not asleep, and he definitely doesn't look happy. I sigh, my arm is wrapped up, and I'm... I'm topless. I cover my body with my arms. I don't need to see my scars. I look at Elliot again. He clearly knows I'm awake, so why isn't he saying anything? I'd rather he said something; it's increasing my anxiety way too much. I sit up; Elliot seems shocked. Okay, maybe he didn't know I was up. He picks up a hoodie and throws it at me. I quickly pull it on and wrap myself in it as much as I can... why is he smiling? I carefully give the hoodie a sniff; it's one of Elliot's. He's giving me his hoodie? Why?

"You scared me, Percival," he says, coming over and sitting on the bed. He keeps his distance, but I still scoot away on instinct. I nod as he sits. "Why? What caused this?" I clear my throat; I can feel the tears falling already as I remember what happened.

"M... m-message. On p... p-phone." He looks confused and looks behind him at the desk where my phone is still sitting. He unlocks it, no password, and I can tell the message is still up. Just typical that the first message *he* ever sends me is a threat. Elliot locks the phone, sighs and comes back over.

"Do you need something?" he asks... what? I don't know what I want? I... I...

I grab him and hug him, finally letting my tears fall. I sound awful; I hate crying. I haven't actually cried like this since mum died. When I did, I was entirely alone, but it wasn't like this. This time, someone is here. Elliot's arms wrap around me, and he strokes my back. He doesn't say anything, just lets me cry. I'm still crying when he picks me up and takes us into the living room. I am carefully deposited on the sofa, still sniffing like a baby; Elliot is hugging me. I'm sitting in his lap, clutching to him for dear life. My life isn't really on the line currently, but there's no way I'm letting go.

Eventually, my breathing steadies, and I start to calm down. Enough that I can release Elliot from my killer grip. He slides me off his lap and goes into the kitchen. Probably to make the dinner Abigail and Sammy left for us; it smells like tomato pasta. I rub my eye with the sleeve of Elliot's hoodie. I really shouldn't; this is a nice hoodie. I definitely don't want to get snot on it. Big mistake. Like me.

Elliot sits on the table and hands me my dinner and a spoon, then sits next to me with his own dinner. I eat slowly, and he practically inhales his food. It's weird, but I am not that hungry, even though I know I should be. I take another spoonful of the pasta and place the bowl on the table while I chew. I reluctantly swallow the pasta and rub the tear stains off my cheeks. Elliot pulls me into his lap again; I don't object. I curl into him and sniff silently until he hands me a tissue. I blow my nose and lean my head back on his shoulder. His arms are wrapped around me and clasped together, so I'm not going anywhere. Elliot turns on the TV and starts to watch a baking show. I'm not sure what it is, but it looks interesting enough, so I watch it with him.

"Sorry I took your hoodie off," Elliot suddenly says after about twenty minutes of silence.

"It's… it's fine," I reply.

"I was checking for any other cuts; I didn't need you bleeding out on my spare bed." He laughs slightly. I hit him gently with my head. "Okay, I get the point. Sorry. Promise you won't do it again."

I don't respond. I can't promise that I won't cut myself again, even *I* don't know if I'll do it again. I keep saying that I won't use pain to calm myself down, but then this happens, and I'm back to square one. The pen Skye gave me was an all right way to get past it. It was something to focus on, I guess, like… you know what? I really should stop analysing myself. I'm not a therapist; I work with computers, not people. Although I theorise that we aren't wired all that differently.

He's waiting on a response, Percival.

Oh yeah, I should reply. I shrug.

Well done, you have successfully worried him even more.

"Shut up," I mumble out.

"What?" Elliot asks, fuck did I say that out loud?

"Oh… umm. N-not you," I tell him.

You are going to look crazy.

Gee, thanks.

"Who then? I'm the only one here? What aren't you telling me?"

"I… ugh, you'll think I'm crazy." I try to get up, but Elliot stops me and gives me a look. My resolve cracks immediately. "Fine. I… I hear voices. In my head. They whisper things, remind me to respond, how horny I am or how much of a mistake I am."

Because you are and don't forget it. Worthless too, can't even kill yourself correctly.

I shake my head and continue. "It's usually only t-t-three voices. Logic, horny and… w-w-well, I'm n-not sure w-what to call the other one. B-but she is the one that tells me to…" I can't finish the sentence.

How pathetic.

"To cut yourself?" he asks, and I nod. "When did they start? I don't think I remember you ever talking about them." I shrug again.

"Not sure, logic w… was always kind of th-there. Horny came along w-when I was fourteen, and the other one is the n-newest. I have a h-handle on them and ignore t-them, so they d-don't usually g-get to me."

"Who were you telling to shut up?"

"Logic, they told m-me I'd worried you after I sh-shrugged. Which I already knew." I cross my arms; I feel like a little kid again.

Now watch as he leaves you. I scrunch up my face.

"That…" *Here it comes.* "…makes total sense to me."

What? What?

"What?"

"When you were seven, we were playing that card game, do you remember? You were talking to me, but you weren't."

"Oh… yeah. I b-b-beat you that t-time."

"No, you didn't. You cheated."

"I did not!" <u>You definitely did not.</u> "Logic agrees with me, so ha!"

"Cheater." He laughs at me, and I hit him with my head again. He fakes pain but cuddles into me more. I cuddle back, feeling much safer than before. We watch more of the show until the adverts come on and Elliot talks again.

"So, if you can't promise, you won't cut again. Tell me when the bad one is talking… maybe horny too. Not so you can do stuff about it, just to keep me in the loop." I laugh slightly at him, trying to find out how horny I am.

"I'll try. No p... p... promises about horny though," I tell him.

Oh, dude, by the way, you are in a very compromising position. You're totally gonna get hard.

Go fuck you. I can feel myself getting hard now, and my face is heating up. Fantastic. I have to readjust myself, fuck, Elliot's totally gonna see it.

"Something wrong?" he asks.

"Umm... j-just got r-reminded of something."

"Would that be something to do with the tent in your underwear?" Now I am very red, and I have to get off his lap. I try to scramble away and get about... nowhere before I am pulled back onto his lap. "Do you want to go deal with it or just ignore it?" Why are you doing this, you arsehole? Just let it go away; you are so not helping. Just thinking about it...

And now you're having a panic attack. Just pathetic. I bet you can't even wank without panicking.

<u>Shut up, you are not helping.</u>

To be fair, that's his job; I just need some release.

"All of you shut up!" I yell and jump out of Elliot's arms, he looks shocked, but then I think he realises that he's gone too far. I can hear my heavy breathing. Elliot takes my arms and hugs me, and I'm crying again.

"W-what's w-wrong w-w-with me?" I cry out.

"I don't know, baby." I flinch at the name. "Okay, not baby, buddy?" I nod. "Good. Look, we'll get Skye or some kind of mental expert over tomorrow, and they'll be able to help you. But remember, I'm not going anywhere."

"Promise?" I say, shocking myself that I didn't even stutter on the P.

"Promise." Once again, he lifts me up, and I'm in his lap. We continue watching that baking show until I fall asleep in Elliot's arms.

I wake up in Elliot's bed again; why does he keep doing this to me? He should take his damned bed. <u>He is worried about you. Cut him some slack.</u> Yeah, well, I wouldn't care if he slept in the—what the fuck he is in the bed with me! Oh... Where are my trousers? Don't get me wrong, I'm glad to have them off, but... it would be nice if I had been asked, you know. Suddenly Elliot is facing me. He has the cutest face ever. <u>What?</u> **What?** What? He's asleep; it's not like he's gonna hear me, besides the way his hair is and his resting face. You can't deny that he looks good. **I agree, also good morning.** Ugh, morning, you are too cheery in the morning. **That's not the only thing I am.** I lift my head and see that it's just before six, and it looks like an alarm is about to go off. I lay back down and just look at Elliot. After ten minutes, I think, the alarm goes off, and he stretches over and turns it off. He turns over and finally looks at me.

"Morning," I tell him.

"How are you and the others?" he asks.

"We are good; only t-two of them are up. I'd like to k-keep it that w-way." He nods and gets up. I blush instantly when I see that he is just in his underwear. I hide my face with the covers.

"Woah... seen me naked but can't handle me in my underwear?"

"Y-you were twelve at the t-time. T-this is v-v-very... different." I hear him laugh at my response; I stay hidden. **You are a sexual mess, you know that?** You don't say, never would have guessed that, not after how I got hard with Skye, and now Elliot has practically stripped me. I was even hard when I was sitting in his lap yesterday. Yeah, I'm a huge mess. I feel the bed sink, and Elliot taps my head a few times. I pull the covers down, exposing my eyes. Thankfully he is dressed.

"I'm going to work now; I've given Skye a call, and he'll be here after ten. Don't fall asleep and yes you can borrow my clothes. They should… yeah, they should fit you." I nod, and he kisses my head. "Be good; I'll see you at five." I grab his shirt and kiss his cheek. We both blush, and I cover my face again. I hear Elliot huff and get off the bed. "Goodbye, Percy." I shoot up.

"What did I fucking tell you about calling me that?" I glare at him, and he runs off, I get up and chase him, but he is out the door before I can get him.

You realise that ordinary people don't do that… right? Shut up, horny.

There is no need to be rude, Percival.

"Yes, there is; making me hard last night was not a good idea!" I say aloud, not thinking about it.

Not sorry.

It's probably a bad thing that I am encouraging myself to talk to the voices, but what's the worst that could happen? It's not like I have MPD. I'm glaring at the door. I should stop, but what to do… Bed? Going to bed sounds good. I limp my way back to Elliot's bed, strip off the hoodie, and jump into the bed. **You know you're—** Yes, I know I'm only in my pink underwear. I'll take them off later once I raid Elliot's drawers for clothes. I pull the covers over myself and close my eyes. I don't think I'll fall asleep, and I don't want to, but this bed is just so comfortable.

I'm in bed for a few hours, not really doing anything, just lying in bed. I am very aware that my ass is sticking out of bed, and being that I'm only wearing my pink jockstrap, I'm starting to get the feeling that I should get up. I might have work, and more money can never go amiss. So, it's now just before ten o'clock; I've been relaxing for three hours, what a waste. I strip myself of the jocks and throw them into Elliot's wash basket in his room. I hobble to Elliot's chest of drawers and open them, searching for something to wear. Feels weird to be naked and not be… touched. I shiver and grab a pair of red shorts that look like they will fit me; I pull them on immediately. I open another drawer and see that they are filled with T-shirts and… hey! This is my shirt!

I pull out the T-shirt and hold it in front of me. It's my Camp Half-Blood shirt that I bought; I thought I'd lost it when I moved out. I wonder… I bring the shirt to my face and take in a breath; it does smell like Elliot. I smile and pull it on. I wonder how he ended up with it? I can't believe I would forget something like this. Looking in the drawer again, I see that the next T-shirt is a purple Camp Jupiter shirt. He always did prefer the Heroes of Olympus series. The smile doesn't leave my face as I close the drawer and limp my way to the other room. I manage to get all the way to the kitchen before I start struggling to walk. I sit down on the sofa, placing my drink and snack on the table.

I lift my leg up and remove the brace from my leg and not only let out a sigh of relief, but a hiss of pain soon follows. It looks so swollen. Is that a good thing or not? I'd guess not; I'm no doctor, though. Do you know who is a doctor? Skye, and I think he's at the door. Elliot most definitely locked the door when he left this morning, so I'm gonna have to open it. I get up and hop over to the door and open it. When Skye sees me, he smiles and then realises that I am standing on one leg and is very quick to help me. He wraps his arm around my waist; I put an arm around his shoulder. Skye then escorts me to the sofa. I sit down, and he starts to examine my leg.

"It's swollen," he tells me. <u>You could have said that to him.</u> "But it's set correctly. I'd like you to keep the brace on for a while longer just to make sure you don't have to have surgery again."

He glances to where I threw the brace onto the floor. He picks it up and proceeds to carefully put it onto my foot; it still hurts. "Take off your shirt." Once again, I blush but obey and carefully take off my shirt. I'm not going to lie, I completely forgot that I had stitches in, but I suppose that's what happens when you're asleep for a month. You miss things. I decide it's best to lay down on the sofa; the gauze is on my left side. I make sure that I'm facing a way that makes it easy for him to access. I can tell he noticed my bandaged arm, and I'm not going to talk about it. He starts his work checking my stitches, and he seems happy.

"All g-good?" I ask.

"Yeah, you'll probably have to wear it for another week. Mind if I check your arm too?" I sigh and hold it out for him to examine. He carefully unwraps my arm and starts his examination; he prods the skin around my cuts and then pulls a new gauze out of his bag and wraps it up again. Then sighs, throwing the old bandage out. "What happened?"

"Nothing happened," I say. <u>That is a lie.</u>

"Percival, you told me what was happening before. This is no different... Did Elliot do this?"

"Why the fuck would he do that? He's my best friend; he's the one who bandaged me up!" ***<u>How dare he accuse my best friend.</u>***

"It was just a question."

"Yeah, and there's the bloody door," I say, pointing towards it.

"Percival, come on, that's not—"

"Leave!" I shout, he raises his hands in defeat, and I pull on my T-shirt and hoodie, wrapping myself up in it. I hear the door close. I turn the TV on to a musical and watch that for the rest of the day.

Unclean

I tried to watch TV, I really did, but the flat is just… so unclean! Clean. Everything *has* to be clean. Who cares if my leg is killing me, this bathroom is a state. You'd think that Elliot hadn't even used it, cleaning products have no organisation, and you don't even want to know about the shower. Ugh, the limescale I'll have to let the shower head sit in… well, at least he has the proper cleaning equipment. If I'm going to be staying here, then I will not be living in a pigsty.

Only took me three hours to clean the bathroom; the bedroom was simple, seems like he keeps it in good condition. The kitchen was next, and Elliot definitely doesn't use it very often, and it's clear that he doesn't clean up after himself when he does. So I'm still cleaning when Elliot comes home. Of course, I'm on the floor cleaning it, with my ass facing him when he arrives, so when I finally notice that he is here, he makes his usual comments.

"What are you and your bubble butt doing?" he asks, taking off his jacket.

"Cleaning," I say, continuing to scrub the laminated floor.

"You don't have to." I ignore him and continue. "Percival, stop." He crouches next to me and gently takes my hand, telling me to stop.

"It's not clean, Elliot. Let me finish." He grabs both my hands and forces me to look at him. "Let me finish!"

"Look at the floor; it *is* clean. But you are sweaty and have dirt all over your hands. Maybe you should have a shower, clean yourself." I look at him properly this time and see that his hair is greasy; there are still bags under his eyes. He looks even worse than the day that I woke up. Has he not been sleeping? What am I doing to him? I finally drop the brush and hug him.

"You ss-smell," I mumble.

"Gee, thanks bud." He hugs back.

"It's… I m-mean it's awful, but actually k-kinda nice. Comforting." He lifts me up and takes me into the bathroom; he deposits me on the toilet seat. He looks around.

"Did you clean in here too?" I nod, and he shakes his head before starting up the shower. He pulls off his tie and throws it out the door; he kneels in front of me and picks up my leg. He carefully takes off the brace and lays it on the floor, he looks at me, but I'm not really registering anything. I know that Elliot is speaking, but I can't really hear him. I do hear the shower stop and the bath start running.

"Why?" I suddenly say. I surprised myself with that one.

"Why what?" he responds, taking my hands.

"Why do I feel so unclean? Why did I have to be an idiot?" I start crying again, and he pulls me into another hug.

"He did this to you. It's not your fault. This may make things awkward, but do you want a hand in the bath? I remember how much you like them." I sniff slightly and nod. I know he could be using this as an excuse to see me naked, but I really don't care at this point. I pull off my top and shorts then step into the bath that has been drawn for me. Pulling my knees up to my chest, keeping everything covered. "The bath wasn't done."

"Y-you should rr-remember that I always do th-this," I tell him; I like sitting in the bath as it fills; I'm not sure why but yeah.

I hear Elliot sigh. He pulls a stool out from somewhere and sits on it, facing me. He then grabs some of the bubble baths and pours the liquid in by the taps. I sit there watching the bubbles expand, and Elliot sits quietly; he's watching me. I can tell.

"The flat looks perfect, by the way," he tells me; I thank him and look down. I then see the big plaster that Skye put on a few hours ago. I go to take it off, but my hands are wet, and I know that Elliot doesn't have anything close to this in his flat. Oh, and there is the bandage on my arm too, that I've gotten wet. Good going, Percival.

"Elli, could… could you… could you take my bandages off?" I ask him; he smiles and tells me to stand up, I don't. I carefully go up onto my knees, keeping my dick covered. I'm trying really hard not to blush. Elliot does an excellent job taking off the bandage so much so I can use it again. There is, thankfully, no blood on it either, which is good. The dressing on my arm is a different story; it's entirely soaked through, and even if we dry it off, it's not sanitary any more. Thankfully it was one of Elliot's, so I assume he has more. No harm there. I sit back down and sigh as the warm water soothes my body. I hiss when it hits the edge of my stitches. Elliot jumps, ready to help me, but I motion that it's okay. He sighs and asks if it's okay to clean my back. I have no idea what it looks like, but I know for sure I don't want to clean it; I tell him it's okay. Plus, he has really soft hands, so it'll be nice for me, and I can do the rest of my ugly body.

"I have a confession to make," he says after he finishes washing my back and my 'cleaner' arm. I look over at him. "I've seen you naked before." My eyes widen, and I drop my legs into the water.

"Wh… what? When?"

"You remember the time our families went on holiday

together; you were eleven?" I nod. "Well, the day we decided to go swimming in the sea with our wetsuits and afterwards we had to use the public shower. Well, I didn't get into the shower as quickly as I let on. Some older asshole wanted me to shower with him, but I told him no and 'left'. So, when I came back to check on you, I may have peeked through the gap in the door... and..." I splash him with some water.

"You jack ass!" I laugh.

"Hey, I think I've done well to keep this to myself for so long." He wipes the water off his face. "For the record, you have a very nice butt; that was really all I saw." I roll my eyes at that comment.

"S-so we've been even f-for thirteen-ish y-years." He nods. "So this is a-also the s-second time y-you're seeing me n-naked."

"Oh, no. I know what you're thinking. I am not getting naked for you; I don't care what you've been through," he says, crossing his arms.

"I was n-not gonna say that." I lean back in the bath. I was totally gonna suggest that. But, it seems fair that I see him naked again since he has seen me naked twice... although... I could just be really horny.

Oh, you definitely are.

Lovely, thank you for the confirmation... oh no. I've had an excellent idea, but Elli will catch on quick if I do it, and there is a huge chance it will piss him off. Guess I'll just have to risk it. I pool a bit of the water in my hands and then deliberately flick it at Elliot's shirt. He jumps up and yelps. I can't help but laugh at him so much, so I slip in the bath slightly. I manage to grab the sides of the tub and stop myself from submerging. Elli sees, though, and he starts to laugh too. Suddenly we are both having a laughing fit in the bathroom.

We finally stop laughing, and Elliot removes his shirt, so I get to see him half-naked. His trousers are wet too, and as he starts to take them off, he catches on to my not so subtle plan.

"Ah. So that was your plan. Nice try, Percival, I'm going to my bedroom to change, and you are gonna finish washing."

"What p... plan? I don't k-know what you're t-t-talking about."

"Sure, you don't." With that, he steps out of the misty bathroom and closes the door behind him. I grab the body wash and start to gently wash my arms and my chest. I clean around each of them and pour some water over them to remove the soap. Next is my hair which is more accessible than my body... I'm gonna need to get a razor. Hair... wow! Why is my hair so long? I do not remember it being this long. Ugh, there is so much of it. I miss my undercut. A hairdresser is something that I will have to deal with now, and they like to talk. Oh boy, that is gonna be fun. <u>Focus up, Percival, you need to wash your hair, not complain about it.</u> Right. I grab the shampoo and start running it through my semi-wet hair before dunking my head in the water to clean it out.

I realise now that I complained about my hair but haven't really had a haircut in about four years. *He* decided that he didn't like me going out to get them, said it was a waste of his time, he'd always come with me. Because of my month-long nap, I have enough hair for pigtails, which I don't want. I bunch up my hair and ring out the water before exiting the bath. I grab the towel I put on the railing and dry myself off before wrapping it around my waist.

I look into the mirror and look at my hair and my face. I look like shit. I feel like shit too. I'm too hairy, and I don't have a razor to fix that. *Or fix that clean arm of yours. You know Elliot's gonna be watching you with knives from now on.* Well... yeah, as soon as I woke up yesterday, I knew that. But I do want to shave one way or another. I shake my head of as much water as I can, then dry my hair again with my towel. Of course, when I turn to leave, Elli is standing in the doorway with a freshly wet shirt caused by me. Oh, fuck, he looks pissed; I start to back off when he starts to laugh. I stare at him. Why is he laughing? <u>I would think he is laughing at the unexpected nature of what you just did.</u> Oh... yeah, that makes sense.

"What are you some kind of wet dog?" he asks when he finally calms down. I shake my head; I'm still scared he's gonna hit me or something. "Well, from now on, I won't disturb you when you are drying yourself." Why is he so confusing? He should be screaming at me; I ruined his T-shirt. Why isn't he normal? I think my breath is quickening again. I can't tell, but I know Elli sits me down on the toilet and tells me to breathe. It doesn't really work, so I grab my arm and push down. I hiss before Elliot pulls my arm away from my scars. That's when I start to focus on him. "Are you with me, Percival?" he asks, and once again, I nod. "Oh, thank the gods," he hugs me gently. I don't flinch. I was expecting it. "You really scared me there, hun." I smile.

"Hun. T-that's a new one," I mumble out, wrapping my arms around Elli; I really have missed his hugs. It might be that I'm smaller, or he's gotten buffer, but I feel engulfed by his arms. Definitely makes me feel safe.

"Do you mind it?" he asks, and I shake my head. "Good, because I've been trying to think of something non-generic to call you that isn't Perry; I know you hate that." He lets me go; I silently whine to myself now that his warmth is gone. He runs his hands over my shoulders and down to my upper arms before stopping. "I'll get you some clothes." He gets up and leaves the bathroom. I grab the first aid kit, bandage and brace before following him into his bedroom. I sit on his bed and wait patiently.

In all my years of knowing Elli, I've never known him to be so gentle. Don't get me wrong, he's not a pushover or an asshole, but his parents were pretty bad to him, so he got tough. They weren't abusive, at least not the kind that I went through, but they were picky. When Elli made something, they would criticise it to high hell; they were like that with me too. Of course, they had no idea what I did, so I knew everything they said to me was basically speculation. I think the only thing they never got on at him for was being my friend. I remember overhearing them, saying how proud they were that he befriended 'someone like me'. Whatever that means.

My point is that Elli is actually one of the nicest people, but if he has a problem with you, you'll be hearing about it. You'll again hear about me if I've done something really cool. I remember him telling his parents once that I hacked the school – accidentally, in my defence – and there was this sparkle in his eyes now that I think about it. He's just finished wrapping up my arm when I realise he is asking me something. Fuck, I got distracted thinking about him.

"Did you hear me, hun?" he asks.

"Hmm? No… s-sorry. Spaced out th-there," I respond.

"I was saying that at some point we should go to your place and get some of your clothes and anything else you want. I know you got Sammy and Abi to grab a few things, but with two cars, we could probably get the rest of it."

"I… um…"

"Oh, shit. Idiot Elliot. You don't have to go in at all if you don't want to. Even if you came along and waited outside, that would help us."

"When?"

"Well, it's Thursday tomorrow, so maybe four or five o'clock ish? Or wait till Saturday?"

"T-t-tomorrow sounds g-good to me. Plenty t-time to ss-sleep." I smile at him.

"Oh, really? You're gonna sleep that long?"

"Why, n-not? You used to do that."

"That was different. I stayed up till four a.m. most nights."

"And now y-you're a teacher."

"I know. Shocking isn't it." He smiles and hands me the shorts and T-shirt I was wearing earlier. He then steps out of the room for me to pull them on. I pull the shorts on quite quickly, and I'm about to do the same with the T-shirt, but I change my mind. I call Elliot back in and ask him if he has a long-sleeved jumper I can borrow; I totally don't mean steal. He says yes and pulls one out of another drawer. I turn around and pull it on, then my Camp Half-Blood T-shirt; I spin around and face a gaping Elli. I snap my fingers in front of his face, and he snaps out of whatever daze he is in. He then claps his hands and starts talking about dinner.

Abigail and Sammy turn up with dinner. Apparently, they wanted to talk more to me about my offer, and since Elli is my guardian right now, he gets involved. Dinner was good. I haven't had a takeaway for ages. They got me a fish supper; they even made sure that milk wasn't used in the recipe, which is better than me making my own batter, done that, though. It was a fun day, not a fun night. Anyway, turns out that the hotel that Abigail and Sammy were going to stay at owns the beach, and you need to have their permission to hold public events on the sands. Easy enough to arrange through hacking, but Sammy and Elli told me not to, I called them spoilsports in return. It didn't matter in the long run. The hotel was happy to arrange it and even gave a ten per cent discount because there were only ten-ish people coming. Which is a manageable amount for me. I've met most of them anyway, just Abigail's family that I haven't met.

"So, this is the difference you want to pay, Percival," Sammy says, handing over a bit of paper; it's more than I thought. Luckily, I have savings that will remain unaffected by this. I was eating the moment he slid over the paper, so I finished my bite before responding.

"More th-than, I thought. But still not an is… issue," I tell Sammy.

"Are you sure, Percival? That's a lot of money, and everyone has agreed to get their own tickets."

"Is this the price, with everyone buying their tickets or with Percival buying them?" Elli asks.

"It's the price for his and your tickets because I doubt he'll let you buy your own ticket," Abigail tells him.

"I can buy my own ticket!" Elli argues.

"Yes. But I already b-bought it. You'll get the money s-soon," I tell them, then Sammy's phone vibrates. "Or right, n-now." I dip one of my chips into some sauce and continue eating my meal. Best I've had in a long time. I can hear Elli stewing beside me, so I nudge him. "Consider it my g-gift to you for all th-those birthdays I m-missed," I whisper to him. I watch him ponder my response before he nods and continues eating his pizza, less angry than before.

"So, how is living with Elliot, Percival?" Abigail asks.

"I'll tell you wh-when he's around ff-for more than a few

hours," I tell her. My comment was apparently funny because Sammy starts to choke on his drink before laughing his head off. Elli just shakes his head at my comment, and I look at him a little confused; that's when he starts laughing. I still don't get it. I think Abigail notices my confusion more than the other two idiots in the room, so she isn't laughing but nods at me. I return the nod knowing that she is asking if I'm okay.

"I would like to propose a toast." Sammy stands, we all groan. He always does this, has to announce stuff and raise a glass; I hated it before. I tolerate it now. "It's not every day that your best friend disappears from your life and comes back into it through a car accident. I think I speak for both of us when I say that we have missed you, Percival. Now we'll just miss your money." We all laugh. That joke I understood. "I can guarantee that none of us will let you go again, and please, no more idiots. The craziest thing I wanna hear about you doing is falling in love with Elliot." Sammy slaps his shoulder, and I watch Elli blush. "But in all seriousness, Percival, I wish you all the happiness that you have missed out on these last five years. I hope that we are there to share the happy moments with you too. I couldn't ask for a better friend or a better family, cheers." He raises his glass and takes a drink; we all do the same.

As speeches go, that wasn't the worst he's done. It was actually charming; I think I can feel some tears slipping down my face and a thumb wiping them away. I look up and see Elli smiling at me. I smile back at him, and not just any smile. A smile filled with pure happiness; I haven't smiled like that since I lost them all. I hug Elli and mumble that it's good to have him back. Finally, I have my family back.

I am never losing them again.

Strong

True to his word, when Elli came home today, he told me to get my shoes on and that we were going to my old place. I call it mine, but it never really felt like home. So, I reluctantly pulled on some of Elli's clothes, my shoes, then made my way out to his car. Elliot tells me that Abigail, Sammy, and Skye are also coming to help as we drive. I sigh at the thought; I know it's only been a day, and I should probably get over myself, but Skye really hurt me. I know he just wants to look out for me, but I trust Elli more than anyone else. I'd trust my dad, but I haven't seen him properly for about ten years. We talked briefly at the funeral, but I was dragged away before I got to say goodbye.

    I miss him. He seemed so sad when I saw him at the funeral, and I wasn't even there to help him through Mum's death. Any normal boyfriend would have let me go back with my dad, but no, he barely let me out for an hour to see him without dragging me away. What's worse is… I don't know where she is, I didn't get a chance to see her before she died, and I don't even know where she is buried. If she was buried! For all, I know she could be ash in an urn on Dad's mantel. It hurts to know that one of my last memories is when we met for coffee before moving in with *him*. That's it, I didn't see her again because she wanted me to focus on my studies, then I stopped contact because my phone was taken away from me. I don't want to know what was going through her head when I didn't come and visit her in hospital. Or even Dad's when I almost didn't turn up for the funeral.

"So, what happened with Skye?" Elli asks, breaking me from my thoughts. I rub my eye before answering.

"W-who says anything ha... happened?" I reply, scratching my arm lightly. *At least get a knife or something.* Shut up, you.

"Look, I know something happened between you two, and you know I'll be on your side no matter what."

"I g-guess." I take a deep breath. "Skye saw the cuts on my arm and thought you caused them."

"HE WHAT!" I flinch. Stay calm; tell him what you want him to do.

"Elli, please, calm down." Thank you, Logic.

"Sorry." Elli pauses to take a breath. "Ugh, I cannot believe that guy. I've known you for ages, and I stayed at the hospital for two weeks to make sure you were okay."

"I agree, that's w-why I asked h-him to leave yesterday."

"Did he finish his check-up?" I nod. "Good, so I can punch him, right?"

"What, no!"

"What if he doesn't apologise?" I go to reply, then think about what Elli is saying.

"Only if it's not the face and I can't see it."

Elli whispers yes and continues to drive us. I really have missed Elli; our conversations may not be intellectual, but they are never dull. Conversations with the other guy mainly consisted of him telling me to do something or dumb it down so he could understand it. Before I lost Elli, he never asked me to do that; Elli was—no—*is* curious, so he asked me to explain it to the best of my ability. It's probably one reason he went into teaching, to help explain things to the kids who don't understand.

If I remember correctly, he was one of those kids who always struggled with maths and spelling. I tried to help the best I could, but being two years younger meant that there was only so much help I could give. He always said that if he ever became a teacher, he would make sure every child understood what to do, even if it meant explaining it a few times. Personally, I thought he would stop doing it after a year because it was too tedious. Having said that, I have no idea what his teaching style is like. I know for sure I couldn't do teaching any more.

Abigail, Skye and Sammy are waiting outside the flat complex when Elli and I arrive. Skye looks a little uncomfortable, and he's rubbing his arm, but Abigail looks happy… she hit him already… good. Elli parks right outside the door, and Sammy is there to help me get out. My leg has been getting more comfortable to stand on as of late, so I should be able to walk for a few hours before it gets too tricky. Feel strange being back here; last time, I was running away. Really hope that I don't have a panic attack. Just have to stay focused on the here and now… although the here and now has a lot of trauma and will most definitely cause a panic attack.

"Here, you might need these," Sammy says, holding out the key; I take a breath and grab the keys. I unlock the front door, and the others follow me in. I hold the door for everyone and look for an elevator. Oh, wait. Is there one? No, there is not. Cut me some slack, and I haven't seen the lobby in six years. I sigh yet again and start to walk up the stairs. The one thing I do remember is that I lived on the top floor. It's a lot quieter, one of the perks about the flat. There weren't many. We reach the top floor, and I can feel everyone's eyes on me, mainly 'cause I'm standing outside the door. I know it's the right one because it has *his* name on the letterbox. I feel a hand slip into mine and give it a light squeeze. Yet again, I take a breath and open the door.

"Welcome to my life," I say as I open the door. I walk straight into what used to be my office and start to look for anything left. I crouch to pick up my Fireflies T-shirt then slip onto the floor. Looking around, I see almost all of my shirts and a few pairs of underwear. Feels a bit empty without my computer… or the desk; Abigail really went to town on it. At least something about this place makes me smile. I feel a hand slide onto my shoulder, and I instinctively flinch away; I turn and see that it's just Elli. He smiles at me and places a box next to me. I smile back and start folding and putting the clothes that are in here into the box. Once I'm done, I pick up the box and go to the bedroom, where I find the door is broken down and Abigail inside throwing clothes out of the dressers.

"We should b-b-burn it all," I tell her. She faces me and smiles.

"I agree. As an apology, Skye's boss said we could use his house for that." Wait…

"Did he say sp… specifically burning clothes?"

"Probably. Skye is the one that told me. Where's your stuff?"

"All my s-s-s-stuff is in that," I tell her, pointing to the bedside cabinet. I move over to it and see a mess of rubber all over the floor along with some shards of the lamp I used to hit *him* with; at least I'm wearing shoes. I pull out the drawers and dump them into the box, I can tell Abigail is watching me, but I don't mind. It doesn't feel that long ago that we first met; technically, it's not for me.

Wait, where did all the rubber come from? I drop the drawer on the bed and kneel down to look under the bed. I feel around for the box where I hid all my toys. Yup, they are all over the floor destroyed; that's at least a hundred quid down the drain. Not that I've got the energy to be using them anytime soon. Anything else that was in the box is gone too. I scoop up as much of the rubber as I can and place it into the container. I ask Abigail for a pen, she passes one over to me. I write on the box that it needs to go into the bin and leave it on the bed. Then close it as that is all my stuff.

<u>I know this place is not great, but perhaps renting it would be the better option?</u>

That's not a bad idea, it's a steady income, and I don't have to tell them that I was abused in here. That's a lot of cleaning. But I own everything in the flat, so I can rent it out as a furnished flat. So, yeah, this is the best idea for it.

"You okay?" a voice asks me; I turn and see that it's Skye. I grunt at him and pick up the box, then my leg decides to give way, and I yelp in pain. "Woah there. I got ya." He catches me as I fall; I shake him off and limp away. "You have to talk to me at some point, you know." I stop at the door.

"Everything okay?" Elli asks; I nod and hand him the box, then ask for a second, he agrees, and I shut the door on myself and Skye.

"Per—" he starts.

"No. You don't talk. I do." He closes his mouth. "Do you have any idea how hard it will be for me to trust people? Because clearly, you don't. I trust Elliot with anything and everything, including my care. I had cuts on my arms because I found a text that scared me so much that I had a panic attack and cutting was the only way I knew how to calm myself down. What's worse is that someone I considered my best friend then has the balls to ask if it was the person who agreed to take care of me. Elliot was always there for me, no matter what. It may have been a while, but I trusted him when we were kids, and I still trust him now. Do you have anything to say?" He says nothing. "Talk. NOW!"

I yell.

"Sorry, I was just... look, I wasn't thinking. I'm sorry, Abigail already made me swear to apologise. I was going to apologise anyway. I'll admit I was angry that you sent me away, but I realised that I had crossed a line."

"You're damned right you crossed the line. Hmm. Fine, I'll forgive you under one condition."

"Anything."

"You b-buy us all p... pizzas. Tonight." He smiles and agrees. I open the door and leave the bedroom, and head towards the living room. I realise now that most of my DVDs and comics are still at my dad's, so we are basically done here. The place just needs a good clean. Especially since there is blood everywhere, on the wall and in the bedroom. Easy enough to clean.

Everyone gathers in the living room, once again watching me. So, I tell them that we can go and that Skye is going to buy us pizzas. They ask me if there is anything else, and I tell them the place needs a clean, but that's it. Skye must be incredibly sorry that he hurt my feelings because he offered to pay for a cleaning service. I don't say no. Would you? I lock the door behind me and hand the keys to Skye. He says nothing but tells me that he'll get it done. I think I might have run out of the building because my foot is sore, and I am out of breath when I arrive at the car. Elli appears soon after, opening the door for me, and I practically dive into the seat.

The door doesn't close, but I hear Elli tell the others something about seeing them at the flat. I listen to them drive off, and Elli's face appears in my peripheral vision; I turn to face him. I slip my arms around him and start to cry; I'm not even sure why. <u>You know why.</u> That doesn't mean I want to think about it. Elli doesn't care that I'm crying; he returns the hug and rubs my back in small circles. I sniff and break the hug rubbing my nose with the back of my hand. He gently stops me and hands me a tissue.

"P... p... pathetic. Am I r-right?" I say, blowing my nose.

"Nope. I think it's perfectly normal. You've been through a lot of trauma, buddy. If you wanna sit and cry into my shoulder for half an hour, just tell me. Or any of us, for that matter, we'll be there for you," he tells me; I wipe yet another tear away from my eyes and nod. He gets up and shuts the car door for me.

"W-when did you g-get so g-good at this?" I ask him when he sits in the driver's seat.

"It's what I do." I look at him and cock my head; he starts to drive.

"What? I th-thought you w-were a teacher?"

"I am." I start to say something when he interrupts me. "I'm an additional needs teacher, so I help kids who have a stutter, ADHD, dyslexia, stuff like that. Kids that struggle to understand the topic and disrupt class lessons. I show them how to understand it and give them the tools to do it without my help in class. I also help parents understand what their child needs when they're at home. Not many of them like hearing it, though."

I stare at my friend in shock. He's not only helping kids like himself but kids who are like me. Now I don't have ADHD or dyslexia, but I know how it is when you stutter and try to answer a question. I got better, thanks to my parents and Elli, but eventually, in school, I just tried to avoid answering questions unless I knew I wasn't going to stutter. Even then, it was rare. Dad always said I had to push myself if I wanted to get a handle on my stutter. That makes him sound like he was an asshole; he wasn't. All my parents' memories are good ones; they were so accepting of me in every way.

"Percival, you're crying again," Elli says; I can hear the

worry behind it.

"S-sorry, I was just thinking."

"Don't be sorry." He rubs my shoulder. "What were you thinking about?"

"Mum and Dad. Remember w-when I came out to them?"

"And they took us both to dinner?" I nod. "You know, I think they thought that we'd end up together."

"Yeah, I overheard Mum s-say that once that she thought w-w-w-we would end up as more than f-friends."

"Was that the time when we went to the swimming pool party, and you didn't want to get in?" I nod. "We sat by the pool with our feet in the water and just talked, right?"

"Yeah, didn't someone t-try to pull m... me under?"

"Oh, fuck, that's right! What was his name? It was something idiotic." We both go quiet as we think about his name. Strangely enough, I can picture his face clearly and what he looked like in our primary school days. Elli and I had a similar group of friends; we were so close that we tended to share any friends we had in classes. Of course, this time was during the summer before I started high school, I think it was about a week before school started, and I'd told Elli that I didn't want to go to the party. So, he said he'd come with me.

"Deacon," I say suddenly.

"Yes! That was the fucker's name. What happened after he tried to pull you under? I can't remember."

"I'm n... n-not surprised. You basically b-blacked out."

"Oh, gods. What did I do?"

"You punched h-him and pushed him under the w... w-water. You only stopped because I told you to, which ended in you g-g-getting a weak right hook, b-but it was enough to knock you out. I had to p... p... drag you out." Elli starts to laugh, and

I can't help but join in.

That's one of my favourite memories from our childhood; I remember Mum talking to another parent while he was out. She called him my own personal knight in rainbow armour. He dyed his hair a lot of different colours with Mum's help, so it's funny. That's when she said she wouldn't be surprised if we became a couple. I was going to tell Mum, Dad and Elli about my sexuality when we got home, but then the parent she was talking to said some homophobic stuff which sent me into a minor panic attack. Mum took us both home after that. It was almost another year before I had the confidence to come out to them all.

We are still laughing as Elli carries me into his flat. I don't actually remember him picking me up, but I don't mind. When Sammy, Abigail and Skye try to ask us why we are laughing, it just ends in us laughing even more. Eventually, Elli manages to tell them the story; Abigail loves it and starts laughing with us. Sammy is a little confused, and Skye doesn't laugh because he disagrees with violence. Then, of course, Abigail wanted to hear more stories from our younger years.

"Oh, what about the one where your dad caught you with a boy?" Elli says.

"Ummm, h-how about n-no." I sink into the couch, hoping that I won't have to tell the story.

"Oh, come on, Percival, tell us the story!" Abigail starts, and suddenly they are all encouraging me.

"F-fine, but it's n-not as bad as you think," I tell them, and I start to tell the story…

Caught

The story is nowhere near as bad as Elli has made it out to be, but here's the whole story. I think I was in my fourth or fifth year in high school, and, well, I had a crush on my friend. He was blond and from South Africa, but he had this heavy English accent. I don't remember his name, but I think it began with a J; I'm not sure. I'm just gonna call him J for the remainder of the story since I can't remember. I was also convinced he was straight since he'd never shown any interest in guys.

Anyway, we were pretty close, and I really didn't like him when we first met because well... I don't know why; I guess I just found him annoying. But I got over myself eventually, and it turned out he was pretty awesome. He was a total computer geek like me, so we challenged each other in the computer lab to see who could code faster. Usually, it was me, but he won once or twice; he'll probably tell it differently.

One day we were in the computer lab, sitting next to each other, doing some homework for computing class. We were chatting about nerd stuff like we always do, and he remembered that he had something to show me, so I stopped working to focus on what it was. He then proceeded to bend over to get the thing out of his bag. As he did, his shirt came undone at the back and exposed his red underwear, with a convenient hole under the waistband, and I saw the start of his ass. I'll be the first to admit that I had checked him out a few times, and I was curious about what his dick looked like. But we were terrific friends, and he had shown no interest in being with me, so I ignored my thoughts, primarily the horny ones.

After seeing his ass, I flushed and looked away… okay, I kept looking. It's not often that you get to look at a guy's ass in school. When he came back up, I was still looking in that general area, but he didn't seem to notice, and he shoved a comic in my face. I shook myself out of my daze and looked at the comic, it was one we both really liked, and I couldn't believe he'd gotten it. Causing me to forget about what had just happened. I browsed through the comic, commenting on how cool it was, and when I tried to 'steal' it, he took it off me and put it next to the computer he was on.

I didn't think about it again until I got home that night before I went to bed. So you can imagine what happened next. After I… finished, I got so embarrassed; I'd never thought of a friend when I was wanking; I mainly just read porn. Watching it is too much of a hassle, so is reading, mind you. After I cleaned up, I went to bed and tried to ignore the feeling of guilt brewing in my stomach. When I saw him the next day, I was going to avoid him, but of course, he brought something else to show me. Unfortunately, he didn't get the chance to.

"J, what are you doing? We said we were gonna meet before school started!" his girlfriend shouted at him. Don't get me wrong, she was actually lovely, but, at this moment, she was a complete bitch.

"I just got in the door, honey bun," he said; I internally gaged, hetero pet names can be so… ugh. No offence. "This is only going take a minute. I know that Percival will love this," he told her, turning back to me.

"Why is it that he comes first? I'm your girlfriend; I should be first!"

"He's my best friend! And you never put me first, so I get to hang out with him while you go off and talk about me, behind my back, to your friends."

"Ugh, I don't remember what I saw in you 'cause all I see now is a fag."

"Is there a p… problem with that?" I speak up. Like hell was I gonna let her get away with calling him a fag.

"You have to see it too, Perry." She starts acting like she knows me. "His hair is always pristine, and he admitted to getting a manicure."

"So that's you're b-basis for calling him a fag. I can't imagine what you'd d-do if you were actually face to face with a gay man."

"My parents say it's wrong, so…"

"Oh, your parents say it's wrong! They are never wrong, are they? So that must be the prevailing opinion of gay people. You wouldn't be able to tell if someone was gay if they were standing right in front of you. Come on, J, let's get out of here." I admit that I was a tad melodramatic, but she was wrong and needed to be sorted out, and I definitely didn't want to come out to the entire school. So I took J to his first class and then left for my own. We didn't see each other again until the next day. I was busy that lunchtime playing the ukulele; yes, I can play. I just don't have one any more.

When I did see J again the next day, he thanked me and gave me a hug. He was a little bit weird about touching people so getting a hug from him was huge. I invited him over that night to read some of my comics and play some of my games. His face lit up, and he went to text his parents right away, so did I, but I wasn't so active about it. My dad's rule was that he had to be told someone was coming over, but he'd leave me alone other than that. Elli was the only exception since he was around constantly, he practically lived with us. He moved out by this point, and my dad could tell that I was getting lonely, so he was very supportive of having J over.

The rest of that school day was pretty dull; the walk home was enjoyable, J wouldn't stop talking. On the way, I stopped off at Mum's hairdressers to say hi and ask her when she would be home; it was the usual time. She would inquire about my day and tell me to tell Dad to go easy on the spice; inside joke between us all.

When we arrived home, I said hi to Dad but dragged J up the stairs so that Dad wouldn't grill him with questions. At this point, I should mention that I had a routine when I got home that involved me removing my school clothes and pulling on some lounging shorts and a baggy T-shirt... I also forgot that J was here with me, so he saw me half-naked. Not my intention. When I turned around and saw him so red in the face, my face went red too. I quickly apologised and left the room to finish changing.

When I returned to my room, I put my school clothes at the end of my bed. We both seemed to shake off the embarrassment quite speedily and fall back into our usual rapport. After about three hours of gaming and reading comics, J's mum texted him, telling him she was coming to pick him up. I was a bit upset and so was he, but I gave him my address so she could pick him up. About twenty minutes later, a car horn sounded from outside, and we both knew that it was J's mum; we both got up and walked downstairs to the door. He gave me a quick hug and left.

The next couple of weeks at school were... interesting. There seemed to be this tension between us; I wasn't sure if it was a good, bad, or sexual kind. But I did catch J checking me out a few times. Then after another week, something finally happened. We were in the computer lab during lunch, as usual, when he remembered something he wanted to show me, and he did it again. He bent over to get it out of his bag, and I was looking at his ass too. Only this time, I don't see any underwear; when he comes back up... well, it slipped out okay.

"Where's your underwear?" I asked; I slapped a hand over my mouth and cursed myself under my breath.

"Oh... yeah, they kind of got ripped this morning on the bus and well. I was uncomfortable wearing ripped underwear, so I took them off. Why were you looking?"

"Hard not to w-with an ass like that," I said. "Wait... what I mean is that... I was f-facing you anyway, and there it was, h-hard not to look." I pause. "I'm not coming off as straight any more, am I?"

"No, you're not." He smiles at me. "Don't worry, I figured someone would notice. I'm glad it's you, though. By the way, wanna hang out tomorrow?"

"Sure!" I was so glad that he didn't freak out on me. "My place or yours?"

"Is it okay if I come to yours? My mum doesn't really like having visitors over." I nodded, and we went back to work. But, for the record, it wasn't always like that. After that week it happened every so often but the furthest... Well, just wait and find out. His bending over happened a few more times, and I'd make very gay comments on it; he laughed, then we'd try and sneak a kiss.

We met the next day, and it was more of the usual, although the only difference was that he was talking about coming over to mine. He was really excited about coming over. At the time, I didn't care for the reason; I was excited too. It wasn't often that I had someone over who wasn't Elli. At the end of the day, we walked back to mine, and a few times, our hands brushed past each other, and I'm pretty sure I saw him blush; I can't blame him. I was trying not to blush. When we got in, he went to the toilet to change, meaning I could change privately. I was happy that I didn't want to repeat last time... okay, maybe I did wanna repeat. But I didn't want to ruin our friendship. When he returned, we started reading more of his comics, and I showed him a few of the new ones I got; he usually liked what I had.

After about an hour, he put his comic down and looked at me. I had been scrolling through my phone, so I knew that he was watching me. When I put my phone down, I noticed that he was really nervous, so I sat up, crossed my legs and gave him my full attention.

"What's up, J?" I asked. For a moment, he didn't say anything; it just looked like he was working himself up to say something. So, I took the leap for him. "You kn-know the other d-day when you caught me staring at y-y-your ass?" He finally looks up at me, confused.

"And you said that you're not coming off as straight?" he asked, and I nodded.

"Well... that's b-because I'm n-not straight. I'm gay." When he heard that, his face seemed to lighten a little. Something told me that it was what he needed to hear.

"I'm happy that you told me. I'm glad you told me, although I had my suspicions." I could tell J was nervous. It was kinda cute.

"Well... its n-not like I really h-hide it." I smiled at him.

"How did you know that you liked guys?" he asked, and I laughed.

"You don't want to hear that st... st... story, trust me. I've known since I w-was ten, so really I've known f... f-for a while."

"Percival."

"Yes, J?"

"I think I'm bisexual."

"Thank you for t-telling me," I tell him, and I give him a hug. "I accept you for you." That's when he started to cry. I rubbed his back and carefully pulled him into my lap to make him comfortable. He didn't object, and he seemed to enjoy it. After a while, he pulled away from me and rubbed out the remaining tears from under his eyes. Then he looked at me like he was going to say something but didn't. Instead, he kissed me. I sat there very stunned for a moment; I quickly noticed that he had said something, and he was freaking out about it, so I shut him up by kissing him back. He broke the kiss again and held me away slightly.

"Wait, are you sure you—" he started.

"Shut up," I told him, and I started to kiss him again. We were making out for a good few minutes when my dad walked in on us just as we lay on my bed. I was on top, about to slip my hand into his underwear. But, instead, I stopped and faced my dad.

"Dinner in half an hour, son. Is your... friend stayin'?" he asked.

"I'll check, Dad," I told him. I tried really hard not to blush and managed to cover up my very obvious hard-on. He shut the door, and I listened to him going down the stairs. I turned to face J, who was very flushed and even more embarrassed that he had just got caught. "I'm sorry, u-usually he knocks." I lean my head on his chest, then he starts to laugh.

"I don't mind." He sat up. "I've wanted to kiss you for ages, and now that it's finally happened, I can't quite believe it." I gave him a peck on the cheek.

"Better believe it. Oth... otherwise things might g-get awkward." He kissed me again, then started to get up. I fell onto my bed in frustration. "What h-happens now? I don't w-wanna do fuck b-b-buddies."

"Neither do I, but I don't want everyone to know, so... can we keep this between us?"

"Yeah, of course. Meet in s-s-s-secret to make out sounds great to me."

"Are you thinking about us making out in school too?" I gave him an inviting smile. "Oh, wow, okay. Maybe we could make out in the computer lab tomorrow then?" he suggested. I stood up and kissed him lightly.

"Of course."

We started dating in secret after that. It was not my best idea; I began to hate it honestly, but I managed to have fun. Felt like I was a secret Gay-gent. No, I've never said that before. Hopefully, I never will again. My dad never interrupted us again, and he started knocking every time he came into my room. Which got less and less often anyway due to his job. We got as far as seeing each other's asses, but then he freaked one day, and we went to just making out and feeling up. It was fun till we decided to break up about a month after we finished high school. I don't regret dating him.

"Wow... you were so confident back in the day," Skye tells me. I shrug.

"Wait a minute. I thought Elliot was your first kiss. You didn't tell us you were dating anyone when we met," Sammy butts in.

"Me and Elli m-making out h-h-happened b-before J and I st-started dating."

"I'd say about a year, year and a half?" Elli tells him, and I nod.

"Do you know what happened to him?" Abigail asks.

"He went to do animation at Dundee Uni. Lost t-touch with him after a wh-while, he had j-just started dating someone else I knew in s... sss... school, she was nice. Apparently."

"Maybe you could try to talk to this J again," she suggests.

"Nah. We d... d-drifted apart before I mm-met *him*." I shudder at the thought, thankfully Elli is there to comfort me.

"No harm in trying, though," Skye suggests.

"Hang on, wasn't his mother the one that gave you that panic attack at the pool?"

"I... I think s-so. Maybe?"

The room goes quiet, and all I can hear is everyone's breathing. Until the buzzer on the flat phone goes off, making us all jump, I can't help but giggle at that. Sammy is the one to get up and open the door for whoever it is. Turns out it was the pizza guy. When Skye had time to order them, I'm not sure, but he even remembers to order a pizza with lactose-free cheese. It didn't taste great, but still, it's the thought that counts.

Once the pizzas arrive, everyone settles into a sort of hunger silence as we eat, which is really awesome, and I enjoy it. I was finished first; granted, I didn't actually finish the pizza, but that might be because of my body weight. While everyone else eats, I decide to try and find J. Probably doesn't help that all I remember of his name is the first letter. I mean, I could look up old schoolmates to see which ones still have him as a friend, I could also—

"Hey, Percival, do you not have Facebook?" Abigail asks me, interrupting my train of thought.

"Ummm..."

"I'm guessing that's a no. *He* didn't let Percival have a phone. I'd be surprised if his account is still active," Elli answers for me, which I'm grateful for, but I think they need a little more in-depth.

"Elli's right. I h-had to get creative w-with where I wo-would 'socialise'. Skye knows about it. I d-d-deleted the account, with h... he watched," I tell them.

"Ahh... so are you gonna set up a new one?" Sammy asks.

"Do I r-r-really need one?" I probably do if I want to reconnect with people, but part of me really doesn't want to. Mainly because of all the questions I'll get asked, like what I've been up to since high school finished, or 'are you still friends with Elliot', or even 'are you seeing anyone right now'. I'm not dealing with them. Not while I am so unstable. <u>At least you admit *something* to yourself.</u> What's that supposed to mean? <u>You will find out eventually.</u>

"No, you don't need one, but it'll help you expand your social circle," Abigail suggests.

"I l... like this circle." She doesn't push it any further, but I get the feeling that she doesn't want me to find someone to 'share my pain with'. No thanks, I'll stick with Elli. He doesn't have to understand my pain, just know how to talk me down from panic attacks, anxiety attacks, and general depression that I'm sure will worsen any day now... "Fine, I'll g-get Facebook."

They all start laughing while I download the app onto my phone. Once it's set up, it is a mad scramble to get the position as the first friend on Facebook, which I make sure is Elli. They should have seen that coming. After that fiasco, it wasn't too difficult to remember the name of at least one of my year mates, and I found my ex. Ironically his name was Jay; I smile slightly when I see his profile picture. I send him a friend request and leave it at that. Right now, I'm exhausted. I feel myself slip onto Elli's shoulder, and the world fades from view.

Saved

I'm surrounded by darkness; I already don't like where this is going.

The floor is slightly wet; I can tell because my bare feet are cold. This feels so much like a movie. I'm not freaked out; I come here a lot when I know I'm about to have a nightmare. Or would they be night terrors? Not sure. *He* should show up any second and start his usual; no matter how hard I try and block it out, it always gets to me. What's that? There is something over there; what is that? I'll have to get closer, definitely not liking this.

As I get closer, the object becomes more apparent; it looks like a glass box. There is someone inside it. I begin to run because the person inside the glass box has green hair. I finally make it to the cage and start banging on the glass to get Elli's attention. But he doesn't seem to notice me or hear me. Suddenly, I hear a loud 'thunk'. Slowly the container starts to fill with water. Elli reacts to the water and springs up. I bang on the glass chamber harder in an attempt to get his attention. He turns around and finally sees me. He smiles and places his hand on the glass over mine. I smile back at him then start banging again as the water rises.

I start to punch the glass when someone grabs my hand. It's *Him*. I'm dragged away from the glass chamber; I struggle in his grip, trying desperately to get back to Elliot. I watch Elli start to shout and bang harder in the cage as he takes me away.

'Weakling.' The voices are starting again. He grabs my face, so I am forced to look at him.

"You are nothing but a waste of space. I am the only one who tolerated you," he says. *"You can't trust anyone. I will kill anyone who will keep you away from me."*

I manage to look back and see that the tank is almost completely full. That's when I hear his zipper get lower.

"Now be a good little slut and bend over for your master." I start struggling more. I will not be abused again. I don't want this! Who would ever want to be used and raped and belittled? I want Elli! I have to save him.

"Let him go!" I manage to shout.

"I see. If you're not going to show me respect, then this will get... sore."

"N-no! P-p-p-p-please just l-l-let Elliot g-g-g-go!" My pleas fall on deaf ears as my clothes are removed, I continue to struggle. I watch my best friend drown as I am raped.

I wake up screaming, panting and sweating. Elli swiftly starts rubbing my back and trying to calm me down. I must have woken him up, but I can't focus on him. I'm just trying to get the image of him being dead out of my head. It felt too real; I've lost Elli once; I will not lose him again. I've lost Elli once; I will *not* lose him again. I take a breath and wipe my forehead and notice how much I am sweating. So, it's not a surprise when Elli comes back through the bedroom door carrying a towel and a glass of water. He gently wipes my forehead with the towel, then hands it to me. I run it over my head, then down my arms and over my ugly chest.

I finish drying myself off and deposit the towel onto the bed. Elli hands me a glass of water. I drink it as fast as I can. I let out a huge breath causing me to start panting again; at least it's for a better reason than a nightmare. After I catch my breath, there is a silence between us that is unsettling, to say the least. Once again, I know that Elli wants me to talk about what happened, but I don't want to.

"I k-k-know you w… want me to talk about it," I say, looking down at my hands, "but… I… I can't, okay. N-n-not yet." He sighs and rubs his eye.

"I hate what that asshole did to you." Elli gets closer to me and places our foreheads together. "I want the old Percival back, the one that wouldn't take shit from anyone. The one I stood up for in high school. I miss him."

That hit me pretty hard; not gonna lie. Elliot misses me, but I'm right here. At the same time, I understand; I would love to go back and be the guy he's talking about. But, unfortunately, all that's left now is the ruins of the man I used to be. I sniff slightly, and I feel Elli's hand stroke my cheek and rub away the tears. He sits closer, and I slip my head down to his chest.

At this point, I should mention that Elli only ever sleeps in his underwear, so until my head hit his chest, I had completely forgotten that he was only in his underwear. It's a good thing that I decided to close my eyes too; that would have been an eyeful. Elli is still rubbing my back when I raise my head again.

"Percival, I think there is something I should tell you." I lean back slightly, worried about what he is about to say. I don't say anything, but I motion him on. He runs a hand through my hair and finishes on my jaw. He wipes off some of my remaining tears and takes a breath. "You need a haircut."

My jaw drops; out of all the things he could have possibly said, that one did not come to mind. I thought he was going to continue talking about the old me. The one that stood up for himself until he was forced into submission. Another thought that I had was him asking about the rubber on the floor in my old bedroom. Not up for explaining that right now. He is right, though. I really do need a haircut. Looking at the clock, I see it's only three a.m.; no chance I'm getting one right now. I manage to not laugh, but I nod, showing that I agree with him. He smiles and tells me that he'll take me to a good barber tomorrow morning.

I shake my head, thinking about what just happened; I glance at Elli once more, who is smiling. He's probably thrilled at his 'joke'. I kick him lightly with my left foot. He laughs and climbs in next to me, then wraps his arms around me. Suddenly I feel a whole lot safer than before, the image of Elli in the tank appears in my mind's eye, and I flinch. My fear subsides quickly, though, as Elli runs his fingers through my hair. I hear him mumble something just as I fall back into the land of Morpheus… That's sleep for those who don't know their Greek gods.

When I wake up, Elli is still holding me, so I cuddle into him a little more in an attempt to keep warm. Apparently, though, it was enough to wake him up. I hear a groan from behind me, and his arms loosen, then readjust around me. He lets out a content sigh and nuzzles me, something I am not used to but not opposed to either. It's nice to actually be… cared for again. So, with that in mind:

"Elli. W-we have to g-get up." He groans in protest and wraps me up a little tighter being careful of my chest. "Weren't y-y-you the one who said I n-n-n… needed a haircut?" Once again, he groans but lets go of me to get dressed. I stay in bed a little longer, knowing he is in his underwear, and once I know he has at least got something on his bottom half, I get up and grab the oversized hoodie that Elli gave me and walk behind him to the kitchen. **He has such a great butt.** <u>Yes, it is perfectly formed.</u> I've never… Oh, my gods, he really does have a good butt. How have I never noticed before? <u>A lot of reasons. Mostly involving an idiot and six years of isolation.</u> Meaning? **You forgot how good a butt he has and your opinion on it.** Oh.

It's been about a week since I moved in; this is the first time Elli has noticed my nightmares. Usually, I manage to keep quiet. I feel I've gotten comfortable here, and Elli says I've stopped walking around like I'm walking on eggshells, and yes, I have mostly been sleeping in Elliot's bed. I usually fall asleep on the sofa in my defence, and he just takes me through there. Actually, being here with Elliot again is strange and… I don't know. I keep feeling like I'm forgetting something. <u>You are, but we are not helping you.</u> Gee, thanks, guys.

I sit at the dining table; gods know why he got this. When we have had people over, we've been seated on the sofas. Looking at the table and the chairs, he definitely impulse bought something here, what though I'm not sure. <u>Not yet.</u> Yes, I will find out what it was he purchased… I mean, he probably bought all of this but still. Elli brings over two bowls of something; when he places it in front of me, I see that it is cereal, one of my old favourites.

"I… I h-haven't had th-these in ages!" I exclaim as I start digging into the cereal. Elli sits across from me, eating the same. They taste the same as they always did. I have been eating here, but I've been sleeping till almost noon most days, so I skip breakfast. This is only the second time I've had breakfast in the past week, the last time Sammy came over and made French toast.

"I started getting them after you moved out and broke contact; it was a good way to feel close to you again… then I started to like them, so no stopping having them now." He takes a spoonful. "When did you have them last?" he asks, I just shrug and continue to eat them, they taste too good to respond.

After I wolf down my food Elli takes the bowl away from me; he's finished too. That's when the bad stuff starts to happen again; I realise I've overeaten, and my body isn't happy about it. I quickly cover my mouth and run to the bathroom, where I throw up into the toilet. *Well, there goes the breakfast he made for you.* Shut up; it was still good. *Both times?* Obviously not, bitch. A hand touches my back, and I flinch away, spinning around to defend myself fist clenched. Only to see Elli standing with his hands up, showing me that it's just him. I calm down almost instantly and then throw up in the toilet again. Elli starts to rub my back to soothe me, and unfortunately, it makes me throw up again. For the last time, though, which is good.

Elliot rubbing my back reminds me of my mum; she used to rub my back whenever I was sick like this. I'm surprised it still brings me comfort and that Elli remembers it. To my knowledge, he was only ever ill at ours once. His parents couldn't come to get him, so he spent the day on our couch. Whenever he threw up, Mum was there to rub his back and give him some water. Whatever he had had subsided by the time his parents turned up. He was still off school for a few days to make sure he wouldn't infect anyone. Afterwards, I visited him to give him his homework and talk to him. He enjoyed my visits, except when I gave him assignments. I spit down the toilet and back away from it.

"Better?" Elli asks; I just nod. Throwing up is exhausting. I hate that. "Still feel like going out?"

"J-just need some w-w-w-water or something s… similar. I'll b-be fine," I manage to say. Elli nods and leaves the bathroom; I assume to get the water. *Imagine how he must feel? He makes you breakfast, and you throw up.* "This isn't his f-f…

fault; it's mine. I got t-t-too excited," I mumble to myself. He returns moments later with a glass of water; I drink it slowly – one mouthful at a time and breaths in between.

Eventually, my energy returns to me enough so that I can stand up with Elli's help. He walks me to his bedroom to give me my T-shirt and the trousers I was wearing the previous day. While I put on my T-shirt, he grabs some shoes for me. It gives me time to pull socks and underwear on, which I am thankful for.

I manage to pull my shoes on without Elli's help. I say without, but the truth is I stopped him from helping. Although my foot has been getting better, I'm still wearing the brace and putting things on, like socks and shoes, still hurts. If I'm getting hurt, I should be the one that causes it. I manage to get them on with very little pain, though, which is good. *That's what you say; I say differently.* What you say is bullshit.

Elli stands by the door with his keys; he smiles when he sees me, and I blush slightly… Why am I blushing? <u>Who knows?</u> **I'm sure you'll figure it out.** You two are the worst. I give Elli a faint smile in return and open the front door and step out. <u>Why have you stopped, Percival?</u> I… I haven't… this is wrong; I shouldn't be going out. He'll hurt me; he always hurts me. I have to go back inside. *Oh, yay, you're going to have a panic attack now.* Fuck that! I am not panicking. <u>Except you are.</u> Except I totally am. I can feel myself getting faint. This is so not how this day was going to—

My breathing suddenly steadies when I notice the arms wrap around me. Elliot. I quickly turn to face him and bury my head in his shoulder. I'm not crying, no tears left, I just need to… I need him. I need to be in his presence. **So close to the perfect sentence.** He starts to rub my back again, calming me down even more. I take a deep breath and let his scent overtake my senses.

<u>Well done, Percival.</u>

"Thank you," I mumble to both of them.

"Any time. I never expected you to get better overnight, you know. Things like this take time." I nod into his chest then lift away from it. I take a breath and turn towards the exit. I walk down three flights of stairs and out the front door, then my confidence wavers. Lucky for me Elli entwines our hands together and starts leading me away from the flats. I thought we were going to take the car, I guess not. It's probably a good thing because I need to do more walking anyway. He is still holding my hand; I always thought my hands were clammy or sweaty, but here he is willingly holding it and the smile on his face tells me that he is enjoying it.

We are walking for a good few minutes before Elli stops in front of a barber. He gives me a reassuring look and opens the door for me. I walk in ahead of him, but I shuffle closer as soon as he stands next to me. I'm trying, deliberately, to make myself look as small as possible. Elli seems to know everyone here and is really friendly with them all. I can barely remember a time when I was like that. Well, I can; I just don't think I could be again.

"Percival. How do you want your hair cut?" Elli asks me.

"Undercut. Number three and four," I say automatically. He seems surprised that I was so quick to reply. I've given it a lot of thought. I've also thought about dying my hair, but I think that's a step too far at the moment. Sighing, Elli manoeuvres me over to one of the chairs and sits me down. A black thing is thrown over me and fastened around my neck. Elli is still holding my hand as the barber starts to cut away all my hair.

She started with an electric razor which was a pretty excellent way to get rid of my hair. She begins with the number four on the side of my head. It's probably weird that I feel lighter; it's nice to have less hair. Once the initial cut is over, she starts on the sides with the number three, then a number two for my sideburns and the back of my head. She then takes zero to shape my hair more. She finishes off by shaping the rest of my hair with scissors. Ensuring that it's all of an equal length.

To be honest, as fun as this is, having someone I don't know playing with my hair isn't as good as having Elli play with it. I know she is just making sure there are no loose hairs on my head, but it still feels weird. The barber suddenly takes a broad brush to my neck and starts blowing on it too. I shiver at her, the touch of her breath against my skin. As soon as the cloak is lifted from my neck, I jump up and move away from the seat. Elli apologises for my strange behaviour and pays for my haircut.

On the way back, I keep running my hand through my hair. She really did a good job, even if I... I forgot to thank her. But, man, now I feel horrible, and Elli is friends with them, so it reflects poorly on him.

"You okay?" Elli asks, taking my hand; I don't mind it so much now.

"I... I forgot to t-t-thank her," I mumble to him.

"I'm sure she understands, buddy, I warned them that you weren't good around people. So they won't have taken it personally."

"S-still I should h-have r... remembered my m-manners." I take a slight step closer to Elli in the hopes it'll make me feel better. It doesn't.

"Would it make you feel better if we went back and thanked her?" he asks; I just shrug. I realise it doesn't really matter; they'll think I'm a weirdo already. If there is one thing I have learned about humanity, they make up their mind about someone very quickly. Elli stops me and cups my face, so I'm basically forced to look at him. **Not that you mind.** It's a lovely face. "They won't mind, Percival. Trust me," he tells me, and I do. I trust him. I nod, and he retakes my hand; I feel a little better about the situation, but not great.

"Home n-now?" I ask.

"We have one more stop to make," Elli says, turning a corner. So we walk for a little longer until we reach a small store where we both stop. When I look at the store, it seems really unassuming, but when we enter... oh boy, was I wrong. It's a comic book store, and it's filled to the brim with nerdy stuff. I know I could spend way too much money in here, for a fact. But, I also know that I'd have stars around my head in sheer excitement.

"You can look around, you know; we don't have to stand in the doorway," Elli tells me.

With that, I smile wildly and start running around the store to browse as much as possible.

A Total Nerd

I feel like a kid in a candy store. That's probably how Elli will describe me to the others, and I won't mind 'cause it's true. I keep finding old comics I owned when I lived with my parents; even new ones I didn't even know existed like Super-sons. They didn't exist when I was in high school, but I knew that Bruce Wayne had a son, and he was now Robin. Then apparently, Super-boy turns up as the son of another Superman, and then their kids teamed up. Looks fantastic, and I may have to get the first volume. OH, look at all those collectables! I could spend all day in this section; there's Assassin's Creed, Star Trek, Star Wars, and many, many Pokémon, and I mean a lot. There's a Mewtwo plush… I'm getting it.

I briefly glance at their manga section and see a few older manga that I recognise but don't care for. Some of the newer ones get my attention, though. Like one called My Hero Academia, I could buy it, but something else catches my eye. Assassination Classroom, I watched the anime and cried at the end; it was superb. I knew it had a manga, and now that I've found it, I'll have to buy it one day. I unwillingly pass by them and move onto the pops… whatever those are. They look funny but no. Why do they need to have a bobblehead too, it's unnecessary and… is that Minecraft Lego? I run over to the end of the shelf line and see that I'm fucking right! Minecraft Lego. I did not expect that, not gonna lie.

I have to remember that I'm paying for a wedding; otherwise, I will spend way too much money catching up on comics that I missed and plushies and merch. But... I still bought something else really cool; it was a graphic novel collection. I'd seen it on Amazon for way too much money, but now I've found it in this store. Which is awesome. Elli insists he buys the plushie and the comics for me, but I get there before him. What? Did you think I left without my wallet? I haven't been out of the world for that long.

I can barely contain my excitement on the walk home. I just want to read my new comics. I used to love going to the comic book store, Mum was always the one who took me, and when I started dating Jay, he came along. Sometimes we'd meet at the store, we'd always sneak kisses; it was the second-best thing I'd do that day. Comics came first, not sorry about that. Jay understood and agreed with me. Once while in our local comic book store, we found this awesome comic that we both wanted. One problem, there was only one copy. So we started fighting over who was going to get it. The only reason I wanted it was because I was going to give it to Jay for his next birthday; I remember thinking that we might not make it there.

Before we had left for the comic book store, things had gotten very heated back at mine, and I know we were both really close before we were called, so using that to my advantage, I kissed Jay hard on the lips startling him enough to let go of the comic. He started to kiss back as I stopped the kiss. I thanked him, kissed his cheek, and paid for the comic. As you can imagine, he was stunned and annoyed two months later when he got the comic for his birthday; I got a good laugh out of it. One of many that day, if I remember it right.

I miss chatting to him; he sounded weird, mainly because he

sounded like an Englishman in Scotland. Thinking about it, he was a bit of a perfectionist, little ser perfect. Makes it strange that he ended up cumming all over me once. Neither of us expected it, for the record. I didn't mind looking back. I wouldn't want to do that again. **Wait, what?** No comment. **You can't say that, tell me what you mean!** Don't think I will. **Oh, you are so gonna get overly horny for the next few hours, so good luck.** I've been horny since I left the hospital; this won't be anything new.

Halfway home, Elli wraps his arm around my waist. I don't stop him because I need help. I started to limp after leaving the comic book store; I tried very hard to ignore it. Eventually, I think Elli was tired of watching me suffer and lent me his support. I have to stop him from picking me up; I do not need to turn red in public, or worse, get a hard-on. I won't be able to cover that up for very long. After another ten minutes of walking, Elli lifts me up and starts carrying me; this time, I don't object; my leg is killing me. I rest my head on his shoulder and close my eyes slightly, taking in his presence and scent. I'm not weird, okay. It's just comforting to recognise a smell, like Elli. Also, I may have fallen asleep on him again. How do I know? Well, I'm very aware that he is now opening the door. I wake up fully when he places me on the sofa. I gently grab his arm, stopping him from going anywhere and mumble out a thank you. He comes back, kisses my forehead, and tells me it was nothing and that I should get some sleep. I nod and turn over, then pass out.

After a week, I finally adjusted to my new haircut; I'll admit she did a good job. We did actually go back the next day and thank them, and I apologise for my strange behaviour the previous day. They were really understanding. Turns out they get a lot of neurodivergent kids and adults in for haircuts, so it's not unusual for someone to spring out of the chair.

During the week, I played Minecraft, ignored all my horny thoughts and even finished my comics. Currently, I am re-reading the Super-sons comic I bought. I think I'm going to look on Amazon for the next one, but there might be more that I'm not aware of. I need Jay; he'd probably know about them.

It's Friday afternoon, and Elli is home keeping an eye on me. I don't mind, but every time he leaves the room, I know that he is walking quickly back to the living room to make sure I am okay. It's annoying. What's also annoying is that I can feel myself getting pretty sleepy and I'd rather read my comic. After my episodes last week and a few days ago, I really don't want to fall asleep, so I may have been lying to Elli about how much sleep I'm getting. But I think it's too late now; I can feel my eyes drifting shut, and... yup, I'm not opening them any time soon.

During my sleep, I'm briefly aware of someone stroking my head, telling me that I'm safe and that nothing will hurt me. It works, but I can't be sure it was a dream or reality. After that, though I start to have a really great dream, well, it feels great. We are at the wedding and Elli, and I, stand by the altar with Sammy and Abigail. Abigail is wearing her wedding dress minus her shoes. Sammy is just in his suit without the waistcoat or jacket, which still suits him. Although I'm not sure about the shorts. Skye and someone else I don't recognise; they both are wearing floral shirts, different colours, obviously.

Skye smiles at me when our eyes meet, then he nods his head to the right. I cock my head in confusion; he makes a silent sigh and basically mimes that I should look at Elliot. I finally look at Elli and see that he is wearing a pink floral shirt; he looks outstanding in it. I guess they decided to make us wear something a little more heat appropriate. I can't hear what the priest says now that I've noticed him; I'm more focused on Elli. Why is it that all I'm thinking about is how good he looks? I look down and see his hand is very close to mine; it would be easy for him to take my hand. I get the sense that he is nervous about public displays of affection in a foreign country. I'm not wild about PDA in general, but… seems like everyone knows us. I take the leap and slip my hand into his, and he holds it lightly; I watch as the smile on his face doubles in size. After that, the scene fades.

The next thing I know, Elli and I are making out on the way up to our shared room. I can't help but moan his name; I forgot how good a kisser he is. I'm the one to open up our room while I have him pinned against the door, kissing him very passionately; I didn't think I could get this way again. I finally get the door and push him to the bed. I straddle him and kiss him even more. The door closes, and I wake up. I'm kinda startled away as a door is closed. I look up and see Elli coming into the living room. He must have been worried about the look on my face because he drops his bags and runs over, and kneels next to me.

"Are you okay? Was it a nightmare? Do you need something?" he asks rapidly.

"N-no, it w-wasn't a nightm-mare. A drink would b-b-be nice," I tell him; he gets up, grabs a can of cream soda from one of the bags, opens it, and hands it to me. I take a few sips and place them on the table. I rub my face forcing myself to wake up.

"What scared you then if it wasn't a nightmare?" he asks.

"It w-was the door. There w-was one in my dream that sh-shut at the same time as the f-front door," I explain.

"Oh… was it a good dream? You seemed pretty happy when I left; of course, I had to calm you down slightly, but you had this smile on your face after that. It's not one I've seen on you in a while." Suddenly I remember the dream I had and start to blush.

You did this, Horny, didn't you? **No comment.** Fuck you, you spiteful disembodied voice. A hand is on my forehead. "Hmm, you seem warmer now; are you feeling okay?" I blush harder.

"Y-yes, I'm f-fine. J-j-just h-hungry. I'm g-g-gonna go p-p-p." Fucking, fuck you P.

"Okay, go pee," he responds and gets up to put away his shopping; I get up and run to the bathroom. At least my foot doesn't hurt right now. I shut the door behind me and cover my face; what the fuck is happening to me? The last time Elli turned me on was when we made out in the confession booth. That may have been fun, but Elli is like my brother, and it would be bizarre if we had sex. Not that I want to have sex with him because I do. DON'T! I don't want to have sex with Elli. Oh, and fuck you big time, Horny, you caused this. **I can neither confirm nor deny these accusations.** But, ugh, well, I can guarantee something for you.

Looking down, I can feel the hard dick in my shorts. Why don't I wear underwear on the regular? Makes things far too obvious. Ugh, I don't even need to pee; I need to take care of my boner. So I lock the door and strip out of my clothes. I grab a towel and place it over the closed, cold toilet seat, and I sit down. I lean back and hiss at the cold tank, I try again, and this time I stay there revelling at its cool touch. Speaking of touching…

I look down at my rock-hard member and take it in one hand; I haven't wanked solo in almost two months, so let's take things slowly, shall we? I start pulling back my foreskin and pushing it back over the head in slow motion. I whimper at my own touch and begin to speed up. Suddenly I'm aware that I don't really want Elli knowing that I'm doing this, so I place a hand over my mouth to stop myself from moaning too loudly, which I usually can't do. I start working my head slightly, causing me to shiver, and now I want more. So, I get it. I can feel my balls hitting softly against the toilet seat. It's kinda helping; the towel is very soft. Suddenly I get that good feeling rising up from the pit of my stomach. I know what that means. I stop working my head and go back to stroking the entire length of my dick until… I release over the bathroom floor and moan into my hand.

That felt good, not as good as it did when I used my toys but good nonetheless. I take a few breaths and remember I have to clean up. I grab some toilet paper and start to wipe up my cum, throw them down the toilet and quickly get dressed again. I flush and wash my hands, then leave the bathroom. I didn't enjoy being quiet, but I really needed to get that out of my system.

"Have fun in there?" As I re-enter the living room, Elli says I turn and see him on the sofa looking at me the same way I looked at him after I caught him wanking in our first shared flat.

"I h-hate you," I tell him and sit next to him, grabbing the cream soda can and trying really hard not to blush.

"You don't have to be embarrassed, you know. I figured it would happen eventually, just not so soon."

"I'm f-fine, Elli."

"Percival, you really aren't. You were abused, I'm doing my best to keep this to myself, but you really don't act like you have been through all of it. You have nightmares you don't tell me about, and you haven't been sleeping. And don't say you haven't 'cause I know you stay up."

"I *am* fine, Elli." I get up and start pacing. "I'm better than I've been in years! You don't know how often I wanted to get out of there and just go to a comic store, a shop or literally fucking anything to get away from that flat for a few hours. That asshole took fucking everything away from me except my computer and memories of you, and finally, I'm home, with you and I… I never want to leave you again. I can't; I would break if I ever lost you." I rub the tears away from my face. "I never thought I would see you again even after everything that's happened; I still feel like you..." I stop the thought halfway through and just start crying. Elli is quick to get up and bundle me into his arms. He rubs my back and lets me cry into his shirt quietly. I'm gripping his shirt, hoping that I can just hide from all the pain; I know I won't be able to.

"I'm sorry, I didn't mean to upset you," he tells me, and I shake my head.

"T-the truth is. I know I'm n-not fine. I d-d-don't think I'll ever b-be fine. He r... raped me so much, Elli. I feel so... so unclean and... I don't t-think my body can take much mm-more of anything." Elli runs his hand through my shorts and kisses my forehead.

We both stare at each other for a moment. I don't know what's about to happen, but without thinking, I grip Elli's shirt and pull him into a kiss.

Torn

Fuck, I can't believe I'm doing this, I'm kissing Elli, and he's kissing me back. Why am I kissing him? Why did I kiss him? Don't get me wrong, it's fucking amazing, but… do I want this? Do I even deserve this? Do I… do I want this? Fuck yeah, I do want this. I want this with Elliot. All the time, I want him. I so want him. I so… I so… what the fuck am I doing? I am so *not* ready for this. Stop the kiss then, idiot. I take some deep breaths. I think Elliot is saying something. His arms are around me. Can't breathe. Can't… Fuck, fuck, fuck. Fuck. Fuck. He has to let me go! Let me go! Fuck, fuck, fuck! I have to scream. Do not scream. I have to scream! Run. Run? RUN! Running. Pillow! Grab it and scream. Crying. Fuck fuck fuck. I am not ready for anything. Fuck fuck. F… u… c… k.

What? What happened? You had a panic attack, scared the fuck out of Elliot too. He has been tending to you, but I think he's worried that he caused this. What! No, he could never. It was all… Where is he? How should I know? I am in your head. Fine, I'll do it myself. Time to get up, I open my eyes to the dull light of Elli's bedroom. I give my eyes a quick rub, pull off the covers and walk right… into the bathroom, where I proceed to throw up the contents of my stomach.

"Percival?" I hear Elli say. He catches on quickly and is now rubbing my back, causing me to throw up a little more. I spit down the toilet and sit back; Elli hands me a drink. I accept, it's just water, so I spit it out down the toilet again. I take a few breaths and nurse my water. I feel that Elli wants to say something, but I think he's nervous about triggering another panic attack. I'd be lying if I said it wasn't a possibility. When I finish my drink, he finally speaks:

"You really scared me, Per." I don't reply, but I nod. To be honest, I'm not sure I can even speak right now. "What happened?"

"I…" I hear my voice, and I was right; I sound like a frog. So I clear my throat and try again. "P… p-panic attack."

"Oh, wow, you don't say," he says sarcastically; he takes a breath. Oh… he must be distraught; he never takes a breath unless he is angry. "Why did it happen? Did… did I do that?"

"What? NO! I did that." I crawl over to him and hold him, and he starts crying for a change. "I got myself too w-worked up when I… when I kissed you. I… I'm broken, Elli, more than I thought. It… it's not gonna be easy. T-to get back t-to who I w-was… if h-he even e-e-exists." I sniff out, he wraps his arms around my waist and holds me gently but close, and it's really… calming, actually. Hey, at least I can speak. He takes a deep breath, wipes his face and smiles at me. I give him a soft kiss on the cheek, letting him know I'm okay.

Suddenly I'm swept off my feet, and I'm flying through to the living room, and I land in Elli's lap. In the living room where the TV is showing a film. It's the first Pokémon film. I get comfortable and enjoy the popcorn that has appeared on the table. A glass of cream soda is passed to me, and I accept it, drinking from it. Apparently, vomiting can make you thirsty… also, the taste in my mouth is nasty. But, wait… where did that drink come from if I'm in Elli's lap? That's when I notice that everyone is here; Skye, Abi and Sammy. I turn to Elli and try to hide my now red face.

"W… when did t-they g-g-get here?" I whisper to him.

"Oh, sorry. I should have warned you; they arrived after your attack. I needed help calming you down," he quietly replies; his phone pings, so he answers it. "Oh, I have a surprise for you, here take this." He hands me my Mewtwo plush and slides me off his lap just as someone knocks at the door. I fold my arms around my plush, and I hear someone laugh, so I stick my tongue out to all of them; I don't care who laughed. I like this plush. The movie is paused suddenly, and I look around the room to the source.

"Are you okay, Percival?" Abi asks me.

"D-define okay?" I respond.

"He's fine, dear, that's a regular Perry response."

"And you're still annoying, Samuel," I shoot back, Skye starts laughing at my insult. I face the TV waiting for it to continue the film.

"Yeah, doesn't seem like he has changed at all," a new voice says. I spin to look to the door and see him. It's Jay. I stand up and face him; I never thought that he would be anywhere near me again. I watch Elli sneak past him and come over to me.

"Surprise," he tells me, wrapping his arms around my shoulders. Jay steps further into the room towards me, then I sort of break out of Elliot's hug and dive forward to hug the blond idiot in front of me. He hugs me back.

"I m-m-miss you, ya i-idiot." I laugh, so does he. I break the hug and step back. "How ll-long are you s-staying?" Elli resumes his position around my shoulders.

"Typical Percival insults me then asks when I'm leaving." He laughs. "I'm here for as long as you want me to be. So with that in mind, are you going to introduce me to your friends?" I nod, then Elli starts to introduce everyone.

"This is Abigail and Sammy, our university friends. Well, Sammy is, Abigail showed up and managed to tie him down. We love her, though." I can see that Abi is annoyed at Elli, but she's smiling, so she may be okay with his comment. Jay shakes their hands, and Elli continues. "And the loner in the chair is Skye. The doctor of the group. He keeps an eye on Percival."

Jay turns to face him, and Skye stands up to greet him; they both pause for a second. They shake hands and say hi. It's loaded with sexual tension.

"Talk about sexual tension." Almost instantly, the two men separate and blush.

"Come on, Elliot, that's not fair," Abigail says.

"Why do you think it was me? I didn't say anything!" he exclaims.

"Then, who?" Sammy asks, so I raise my hand slightly.

"YOU!" everyone shouts, minus Elli. I jump slightly and start to hide behind him.

"Okay, everyone, let's calm down, sexual tension… or not, we don't need to scare the guy with anxiety issues," Skye says, sitting back down and taking a deep breath, trying to calm down. Elli is next, and he pulls me into his lap again; I don't object. I'm still a little worried that everyone is upset with me. I grab the plush and wrap my arms around it; Elli wraps his arms around me and whispers that he liked my comment. I smile and blush but thank him.

Someone turns off the film, and we all start chatting, Jay sits in front of Skye, and both keep stealing glances at each other. They are *not* subtle. Elli gave me the bowl of popcorn which I keep munching on quietly. I should definitely be having something more substantial, but this is fine. I'm used to not eating much and being quiet. I'm used to both because *he* thought I was a loud chewer, so I got used to being quiet. I get so engrossed in eating that I barely notice Elli holding a drink in front of me, which I take and sip from. When he tries to take it away from me, I stop him.

"You okay?" he asks me while the others chat. I nod and smile at him. "Is that the… prevailing opinion?" I look at him for a second before I understand what he means.

"Oh, y-yeah. All q-quiet."

"What's all quiet?" Skye asks. Both of us turn to look at the staring faces of our friends; I've just noticed that they are very chill that Elli and I are so close.

"Oh, it's nothing important. A personal thing between us," Elli tells them, hoping, I think, that they will drop the subject. But Jay is here, and he never lets anything go, believe me.

"Yes, because it can't be any more personal than sitting in your best friend's lap. You two have always been close, but this feels new to even you, Elliot," Jay starts.

"What do you mean?" Abi asks; I give her a small death stare, which I don't think she sees… mainly because I can't do that kind of stare. I just look 'too cute' according to Elli… not sure that he still thinks that, though. **I think he does.** How would you know…? That's what I thought.

"When we were dating, I'd notice that Percival would sometimes talk to himself. It was never anything bad. I only caught him doing it twice; once, he was far more logical than normal during a study session. Another time was just before I got to his room. He seemed to be complaining about something; I can't remember what. It got me thinking about why, I just forgot it until now."

"Trust me, if I'd wanted to talk about it, then I would have;

it's still strange talking about it. I really thought that it was nothing until a few years ago. Now I would really like it if we dropped this subject and moved onto another one," I tell them all.

I remember both the situations that Jay is talking about. One of the subjects I hated was English, and I could never figure that shit out, so Logic would help me out. This was before Jay and I were dating. At the time, he was over, and we were working together. I couldn't figure the question out and replied to Logic when she answered my questions; I just didn't realise I'd said it out loud. The other time was just before he arrived. As he said, I was a little horny, and he was still a new voice for me to listen to, and Horny wanted me to see how far I could go with Jay. I tried to talk him down from it and complained, then Jay walked in when I started to get hard.

"I'd listen to him, Jay," Skye tells him, pulling me out of my thoughts. Jay looks back at Skye as if to say, 'you're a doctor; how can you not be intrigued?' but he surprisingly listens. But now I know that Skye is going to question me. So, I sigh and look at Elli.

"You know I'm on your side no matter what; this is your choice," he tells me.

"Fine, I'll explain what Elliot meant, only 'cause neither of you will get off my back about this." I point at Jay and Skye, then take a breath. "I hear voices in my head, have all my life. Elli only found out two weeks ago, and that's why I said it's all quiet. The 'voices' are not talking to me. They are probably as tired as I am. There's only three of them, Horny, Logic and… well, she doesn't have a name, but basically, she encourages me to self-harm, calls me worthless, shit like that. I dislike her the most. But she has been reticent the last few days, didn't even get a peep out of her when I had my attack." I take another breath, then lean back into Elli, who cuddles me, telling me to breathe. I'm not going to have an attack, but that could change as quickly.

"That… well, that explains so much," Sammy says.

"What?" I speak. Is he okay with it too?

"Yeah, actually, that answers a lot of my questions. In the hospital, you would talk to yourself sometimes, even when you were asleep," Skye explains. Jay nods; I think he feels bad 'cause he forced it out of me. The truth is I was going to have to tell Skye; eventually, this is at least on my terms. It's better than getting an appointment with him, the talking myself out of telling him beforehand. A sort of silence falls over the whole group. I don't know if it's awkward or not, but my eyes are darting around the room, looking for someone to do something, and I really hope someone picks up on it.

"So, who wants to order food?" Abi suggests, picking up her phone. Yes! Go Abi! "Any ideas, Sam?"

"Oh! What about a chippy?" he suggests.

"It's the middle of the day, Sammy," Elli retorts.

"So, what about Subway?" Skye suggests, everyone seems to like that idea, and we start ordering the food. We all chip in, sending Abi our cuts; shockingly, Jay says he'll pay for my lunch as a way of saying sorry. Oh… I must have slept the night. Is it still Saturday? I swear I have no clue what day it is any more. All I do is sleep and… Well, sleep. Elli rubs my arm, getting my attention.

"You okay? You look… Pensive," he speaks.

"Ha! Look at the man with the big words," Abi yells, making everyone laugh. Including me, which I think makes everyone smile more.

"I'm f-f-f-fine; it's just…" I drift off and start thinking again.

"You can ask anything, Per," Skye tells me.

"What day is it?" I ask.

"Oh. It's Sunday. Easter break started for Elliot yesterday. He didn't tell you?" Abi tells me. "Don't you remember the days I gave you for the wedding?" I shake my head.

"Elli filled out t-th-the dates, I just p... p... p-paid," I explain. Which explains a lot why Elli seemed happier that he wasn't working. "S-so, when are we going?"

"The wedding is on Wednesday," Elli tells me. "We leave Tuesday morning. I packed for you already, so don't worry."

"Anything else I've missed?" I ask everyone. No one says anything, and they all look at each other. They are keeping something from me. "What is it!" I raise my voice, Skye is the one to answer, but he takes a breath beforehand.

"You have to understand that we are just looking out for you, Percival. That's why we didn't tell you that. The trial was yesterday... he... he almost got away with it. But... you would be surprised how good a lawyer Abigail is. She presented the evidence that you gave to Sammy, and the jury was swayed almost instantly. In fact, afterwards, the press said they couldn't show the trial due to the explicit nature of the evidence. We kept you asleep during the day because, well, firstly, you were waking up and freaking out about everything, and second, people kept coming to the door to ask you questions."

"Woah, Per, are you okay?" Elli says to me suddenly, I don't understand why until I notice that I'm crying, and it's not bad for once, I smile at them all.

"He's gone. He has actually gone to jail." I hug Elliot. "Oh gods, he's actually gone!" I start crying more, and I'm laughing. It's really, very confusing. Then, slowly, I feel more arms wrap around me, and I know I'm safe.

I'm finally safe.

A Good Friend

I bring my hand to my eyes to clear my vision of all the tears and see everyone is hugging me; I embrace some of them back, but Skye was the only one I missed. Jay didn't join in; now that I think about it, he doesn't know what's happened the last few years. Finally, Abi and Sammy let go; I beckon Skye over and pull him into a hug, which he gladly accepts. Once I break the hug, I punch his arm as hard as possible, which probably isn't much.

"Ouch! Hey, what was that for?" he cries.

"W-who else can s-s-sedate me?" I respond. "I'm n-not h-happy about it, but if it's w-was the safest thing to d-do, I guess I can't be m-mad."

"It was all we could do to calm you down, Per. You would wake up and scream if anyone was touching you. Luckily you were passed out by the time that Skye arrived to put you under." Elli explains to me. I notice he is close to crying, so I settle back into his arms; I'm beginning to like this a lot more. **Just wait until something else is in you.** Shut up, Horny, it's not like that yet. **You know that I have a name, right, and I'm not a guy?** Wait… are you a girl? **Nah, man, I'm messing with you; I identify as a dude, like you.** So, what's your name? **I go by Nemesis, I don't know why, but I like it.** I respect your choices. What about you, Logic? Do you have a name? <u>I do not have a name, but I would like to have one.</u> I'm sure I can help with that.

What about Logan? I identify as a non-binary, Percival; Logan will not suffice. Ah, sure, that's a good point; I didn't want to assume—

"You okay, Percival? You've been in your head and mumbling for a while," Abi asks me, pulling me from my thoughts.

"Hmm? Oh, Nemesis told me his name, so now I'm thinking of one for Logic," I explain.

"Isn't Nemesis a girl's name? Like the Greek goddess of balance and vengeance?" Jay chirps in. **Tell that bisexual disaster that I don't care!**

"Oh." I snigger. "I was told to tell you that he doesn't care; sounds gender-neutral to me." **You forgot the bisexual disaster bit.** No, I didn't; having said that, everyone is laughing anyway.

"Anyway, what about Logic? Any ideas, what are we working with here?" Sammy asks.

"Well, they identify as non-binary, so that narrows it down to every name ever. Other than that, I have no clue." Suddenly the room drops into silence as everyone starts to think.

"Avery?" Skye suggests. Unfortunately, elves do not exist in this world, nor would I be their ruler. I shake my head.

"River?" Elli asks. I am not a body of water. I laugh at their comment but shake my head.

"Hunter!" Jay shouts, accidentally, I assume, since he starts to blush. I am of Logic, not the hunt.

"Panha?" Abi suggests. Hmm… this one is close but, I do not like it.

"I think that's a no," I tell her. "I have one, not sure where I've heard it, though." I am now listening. "Skylar," I say aloud. I remember it from that show Heroes, but I liked the sound of it. "It's gender-neutral and means noble scholar," I say to them, and they all nod at the name.

"It's a great name, Per," Elli tells me, dusting my face with red. What do you think? It is… a great name; I love it. From now on, I am Skylar.

"T-they love it," I tell them all, and there are smiles all around.

We continue talking for another hour about nothing in particular. Sammy and Abi swap with Skye and Jay so that they can sit next to each other. I am still in Elli's lap. He doesn't seem to mind; I know I don't. During our talks about the best Assassin's Creed characters, Jay gets up and moves to the other side of the coffee table and sits down, I watch Skye's face drop, and I can tell he is upset, so I tickle him with my foot, which gets a smile out of him and the conversation continues. We are interrupted half an hour later by a knock at the door; Sammy gets up to answer it.

"Percival, I notice you got a haircut; it looks much better than the unkempt look you had before," Skye compliments me. I unintentionally run a hand through my shorter hair and smile at him. Reply dummy. OH!

"Thank you," I blurt out, "Elli m-made me g-g-get it. I a-agreed." Skye nods.

"I should think about getting one myself; I was also thinking of dying my hair. I haven't done that since high school," he says.

"Have you always lived in Scotland?" Elli asks.

"Yeah, I used to live in Stranraer. Loved it there, but it's hard to get anything done in a town without a training hospital. So I moved here at the start of my course. What about you two?" Sammy comes back and starts handing out the food.

"Both of us are Scottish. We lived in Alloa 'til I moved to Edinburgh. Per moved a year later to start his teacher training and moved in with me. I was in uni but wasn't sure what I would do until the year before I lost Percival. I met Sammy during fresher's week, Although I'd heard of another first-year who was locked in his room studying already," he laughs and starts eating his food.

"Oh, fuck, I remember that guy!" Sammy says, sitting next to his fiancé. "Weren't you going to go knock on his door to get him to come out?" Elli nods then swallows as quickly as he can.

"I did, man! You know what happened?" Sammy shakes his head.

"He shouted back to you that he's bisexual and to leave him alone?" Skye interjects.

"How do you know about that?" Both men look very confused; I was too until it clocked. <u>Oh, I understand why.</u> Yeah, and oh, fuck.

"Y-Y-you were in their y-year. You w-were the s-studying g-g-guy," I clarify. Then it clicks for everyone else.

"Yup, for the record, I used to laugh about that with my classmates. I was invited but didn't go to freshers' night because that was the first-year party, and I was in my third year. Also, I was reading up about neurosurgery; I thought it might be a good field to get into," Skye tells us.

"Why didn't you?" Jay asks. Skye bursts out laughing.

"On my first test, I almost killed the dummy. My lecturer said I needed studier hands. I tried to steady them, but after sixteen failed attempts, she suggested I change my field."

"What did you go into?" Abi asks.

"I do general surgeries. But I also consult for GPs, a bit of everything, far more fun working with everyone. Including the surgeries. You get to see and help more people; I helped a woman with a broken foot the other day. She thanked me with a mint humbug, I hate mint, but it's the thought that counts." He laughs. "Speaking of, I'm gonna have to grab my lunch and go, I've got a shift in—" he checks his watch "—about an hour. I'm glad you're getting better, Per, I'll come to check up on you before your flight." He gives me a quick hug, grabs his lunch and with that, is gone.

"Who would have thought that, eh?" Sammy says. "Doctor Skye, living in our building. How didn't we notice?"

"I have no idea." Elli sighs.

"Well, you idiots probably didn't notice because you were too busy drinking. Or realise that doctoral students don't have a social life," Abi says, hitting Sammy's head lightly, I hope. I still flinch slightly and lean my head on Elli's shoulder while quietly chewing on my sandwich.

"And lawyers do?" Elli retorts.

"I helped your boyfriend out, didn't I?" she says; it takes me a second to realise who she is talking about. When it does click that it's me she is talking about, I blush, what I can only assume is an intense red. I look at Elli and see that he is also blushing but a lot lighter than me. I think I hear him let out an apology to Abi, then he wraps his arms around my waist. We all jump when a phone starts ringing.

"Oh, that's me," Jay says. "I have to get this excuse me," he gets up and goes into the spare room… I assume.

"And then there were four," I mumble; Elli smiles at me. Then, I sigh. "We're g-g-g-gonna have to t-t-talk sometime," I say quietly.

"I know, but can we leave it 'til everyone is gone?"

"W-when else c-c-could we do it?" I ask; Elli ponders this, then nods his head to the side, accepting my answer. Suddenly we hear shouting from the next room.

"WELL, IT'S NOT MY FAULT THAT THE CAT GOT RUN OVER!" Jay suddenly yells. He has a cat? <u>Had one, it seems.</u> "I DON'T EVEN OWN A CAR, YOU BITCH! MY PARENTS DIDN'T GET ME ONE, AND YOU WANT ME IN YOUR SIGHTS AT ALL TIMES. WHEN WOULD I EVER USE IT?" There's a tense pause, then nothing.

"I wonder what happened?" Elli asks. I hit his chest, telling him to shut up. Jay storms back into the room and retakes his seat. Nothing is said; I get up and walk over to him.

He looks at me; I see the anger in his eyes. Then I see the unhappiness of his life. I knew that his parents wouldn't let him do anything dangerous, explaining the lack of a car. Also, why we never went over to his when we were together. From the rumours, I heard they were wildly homophobic. I place a hand on his shoulder and pull him into a hug, and almost instantly, he breaks down crying. He hugs me back. I say nothing, just rub circles on his back; it's been soothing me when I've been crying, so why won't it work here. Eventually, I'm not sure how long, his sobs quieten down, and he sniffs a few times then breaks the hugs. He rubs his nose with the heel of his hand, then takes a breath.

"Th… thanks, Percival. Guess I n… needed that," he tells me.

"N-no problem." I pat his shoulder, then return to Elli's lap and kiss his cheek lightly.

"Do you… never mind. Actually, I don't want to be a burden." Jay suddenly changes his mind.

"Yes, you can crash here tonight. Despite the room being for him, Per has used the spare room for a total of… once."

"You didn't put me in there during my last attack?" I ask.

"You ran into my room, and we couldn't move you," he

explains. Guess that shows where my head is at.

"Thank you for letting me stay here. I'll be gone by the morning; it's my place she is staying at anyway," Jay explains.

"How did you meet her?"

"Actually... we went to school together." He rubs the back of his neck.

"Oh yeah, I remember... Wait... you don't mean. N-n-not Lisa? Please tell m-me it wasn't your ex," I beg him.

"Sorry, dude, it was her. We met again at university; she was totally awesome and seemed really carefree. It was only last year that I realised that I didn't really love the relationship any more. Then it clicked that she was actually very abusive to me. I've been trying to get her to break up with me for months. I guess she gave me a good excuse today." He laughs at the last part.

"Hey, you're f-f-free now, you c-c-can do what you like. If I r-r-remember, correctly, you were a v-very disastrous bisexual." I tell him. **Thank the gods, and thank you, Percival.**

"Yeah, that's a fair assessment. I was single for about a year before I met Lisa. There was a lot of cute guys in Dundee. Girls too..." he explains.

"Now, you can go have as much sex as you want with whoever you want," Elli cuts in. There is a pause, then everyone starts to laugh.

"Okay, you three, it's been fun, but I have a wedding to continue planning, and I've got to drag Sammy along too," Abi tells the room after we stop laughing.

"You're dragging me to the South of France? How romantic," Sammy replies, giving his future wife a look I never want to see from him again.

"You're going to France tonight?" Elli asks them.

"Yes, we have a liaison that is going to help us set up the

beach to get everything organised. Which reminds me. We need to head home and finish packing," Abi tells Sammy.

"Oh yeah, need to get the boys' shirts sorted out. Catch you guys in France," Sammy says, and with that, they both leave. I look around the room; I wonder what happened to my sandwich? <u>You finished it while Jay was in the other room.</u> Aww, man, that was a delicious sandwich.

"W... What's for d-d-d-diner?" I ask.

"You never used to eat this much, I swear," Elli tells me.

"I was out for a day. Can you blame me?" I stare at him.

"I can't?" Jay says, raising his hand; it looks kinda cute. "I can pay for food if you'd let me."

"Thank you, but we've been eating out way too much as of late. I've got something healthy and fulfilling that Percival will love."

"W-w-what is it?" I ask.

"Vegan spaghetti carbonara. No milk at all, so safe for your lactose intolerance."

"Vegan kind of gave you away there," Jay says.

"Why don't you two get reacquainted while I get to making it?" Elli suggests, slipping me off his lap and heading to the kitchen. Hey, I'm not complaining; I get to stare at his ass now. **And I thought I was the horny one.** You've seen his ass, haven't you? **I have, and you are right to want to stare.** Jay starts snapping his fingers to get my attention, and it works, much to my dismay.

"What are you looking at there?" he asks.

"Oh, n-n-n-nothing. So, L-L-Lisa, any g-g-good in the s-s-sack?" <u>What the hell was that?</u> I don't know; it just slipped out. I don't think Jay minded; he's laughing. I sigh, and we start talking while Elliot cooks us dinner.

"Oh my god, you really have it bad for him, don't you?" Jay realises after a minute of talking.

"I d… don't know w-what you're t-t-talking about." <u>Yes, 'cause this will end well.</u>

"Oh, my gods, you're totally in love with Elliot!" he says a bit too loud.

"Shout it louder, why don't you?" I take a breath. "Look, I do have deep feelings for Elliot, but what you don't know is that I got out of an incredibly abusive relationship almost two months ago. Things are still pretty raw. Elli has been there for me every step of the way. So have the others, but yeah, we haven't talked about it yet. I don't even know where we're going." I see Elli turn his head slightly; <u>he must be listening in.</u> Yeah, I just thought that. We'll talk about it later; he's got nothing to worry about.

"But what do you want, Percival? Do you want to date him?" Jay asks; I think for a second. **Oh, come on!** <u>Yes, please do not start this again.</u>

"I don't know… maybe?" Then I smile, then nod towards Jay, who smiles and squeals quietly to himself.

"Yes, I was rooting for you before we started dating. Now finally, my ship will sail!" I watch him roll on the floor for a bit, smiling to myself and then glancing at Elli and knowing that I am blushing. I don't think I care any more.

But first, we need to talk.

Nervous

An hour after we had dinner, Jay went to bed, so Elliot and I followed into his (our?) bedroom. Can I really call it his bedroom any more? I've slept there more than in my actual room. <u>You have fallen asleep on him quite a few times to be fair.</u> **Not that you mind**. Yes, I've slept on him a lot, no, I don't mind, now go to sleep, you two. I'm currently in the bathroom brushing my teeth, trying very hard not to reply to Nemesis and Skylar and get toothpaste everywhere. I know Elliot is waiting for me to finish so he can get into the bathroom. Jay apparently already did his.

I finish off, spitting down the sink, then heading to the bedroom. I pass Elliot in the hall, who is ready for bed… I keep forgetting that he sleeps in his underwear, which is what he's wearing. I blush and stare at his butt as he goes into the bathroom. **Gayyyyyy!** Oh, shut up you. I quickly strip myself of the hoodie I'm wearing, then sit cross-legged on the bed waiting for Elliot. I should mention that he told me how I ended up in my shorts and hoodie. Elliot changed me after my first attack. He wanted me to be in more comfortable clothing for when I got up. Although Elliot mentioned that afterwards, I woke up and screamed again until I passed out. He called Skye immediately after that.

I hear the door shut, pulling me from my thoughts of the day's events. Elliot standing in the doorway in his underwear and fading green hair. He rubs his arm and sits across from me.

"Oh… is it that time?" he asks, and I nod.

"What are we, Elliot? I have to know, you know why. I just..." I pause. "I can't start another anything without knowing that it's not gonna end the same way." I can feel myself fighting back the tears.

"Can I admit something to you?" I nod. "Have you ever noticed that I've never dated anyone? I don't actually have a sex life because it is basically one night stands with guys who want a quick fuck and a cream filling." I go to talk, but he stops me. "Wait, please, I'm... I'm not done. The reason I have never had a relationship is not that I don't want one. It's because I've been waiting for the right one. That's you, Percival. It's..." He takes a breath. "It's always been you. But every time I was going to ask you out, someone else got in my way. Like Jay or... well, you basically dropping out of my life for five years kinda stopped me too. If I'm honest, I was about ready to move on that day in the hospital, and then I saw you. And it all came flooding back to me: the way your smile makes me feel, how when you explain something, you never stutter, the way your brow creases when you can't understand something, and even the way think you can hide in your hoodie. By Hades, I even find your stutter incredibly cute. I am so in love with you, Percival, and it kills me that you haven't had me for the last five years. You say you can't lose me again, but I... I can't lose *you* again. I think it would kill me. But, gods, I don't know if you even feel the same way. I so want the flirting we've been doing to be more." I watch his tears slowly fall; I had no idea that was how he felt.

Suddenly everything comes back to me, every little thing he did for me. He would help me with my homework more than Skylar ever did. He stood up for me whenever someone made fun of my stutter. He was the only boy that my parents liked when I brought them home; they tolerated Jay. I remember birthdays; it didn't matter who I invited. It was always Elli that I would play with. Every birthday for the past six years felt empty without him. If I could go back and change anything, I'd go to the day I met my ex and slap myself; I'd make myself realise everything. Elli is my biggest regret. The one who almost got away. Elli is… oh, my gods! I am such an idiot.

"I love you too," I say. Elli's head snaps up, and he notices that, once again, I'm crying. "I can't believe it took me this fucking long. Oh, gods, I'm such an asshole. I love you so much. I think I must have forgotten? Fuck, I can't believe I forgot this feeling!" He looks so confused, I get up onto my knees. "I think… yes! That day when I was ten, I was coming over to tell you exactly that! So you can guess why I didn't. All this time searching for the one who can make me feel complete, and you've been beside me the entire time. I am so sorry, Elli; how can I make this up to you? I have to make this up to you!" I'm still crying; in fact, we both are. Finally, Elli comes forward, places his forehead against mine, and kisses my face before gently kissing my lips; I kiss back.

"Be mine. Be mine always, and I'll forgive you," Elliot whispers to me.

"Promise?" I ask.

"Promise." He laughs, and he pulls us under the covers. "Is that like our thing?"

"Our thing?" I ask.

"Yeah. Like in *The Fault in Our Stars*. They have the 'Okay? Okay', bit. We make promises instead." Like a proper weirdo, I laugh and tell him yes, I guess it is our own version of it. After that, we share a brief kiss, and I fall asleep in his arms. Happy for the first time in years.

Waking up next to Elli is the best thing in the world, hands down. Nothing will ever beat this feeling. **I know something that might.** You know what? You're happy, admit it, Nemesis. **Gods yes. You know how long I've been sitting on those feelings?** It has been a long time. Yes, I figured it would be. I sit up, leaning on my hands as the new day's light sneaks through the curtains. I look down at Elliot and see his bed head, very sexy. I smile, and lay back down gently and just stare at him for a while. Okay, that's not the only thing I do; I play with his hair too. This gets me his usual response of a gentle satisfied moan, but he doesn't wake up. I gently trace my fingers over his face, running over his cheekbone and down to his lips. He has very kissable lips. Only took fourteen years for me to finally call this hot piece of ass my boyfriend. Slowly Elli stirs and opens his eyes, and his soft blue eyes land on me. Instantly he smiles, causing me to smile too.

"Morning, sunshine," he mumbles out.

"Morning, greenie," I reply. Hang on... "Why, sunshine?" I ask.

"The sun is perfectly shining on you. Makes you look like the sun. Not to mention the way you light up my world." That causes me to blush. "Also, son of Apollo much?"

"That is so cheesy and not going away anytime soon, is it?" I ask.

"Nope." He pokes my cheek, then I grab his hand and gently kiss his palm, working my way to his wrist before laying his hand on my face. He strokes my cheek with his thumb then pulls me into a cuddle which I graciously accept. I rest my head on his chest and listen to his heartbeat. "Can I ask... what's a ship?" he asks suddenly.

"It's a big boat that goes on the ocean, usually carries people but sometimes its cargo," I respond, laughing as he nudges his entire body into me.

"That's not what I meant, sunshine. Jay said it last night; he said he was rooting for us and 'finally his ship can set sail'. What did he mean?" Damn, he was listening to that, okay, how to explain... oh, I got it.

"Do you remember the Percy Jackson book where Will and Nico finally got together? You were really happy, same with Percy and Annabeth in The Last Olympian?" He nods. "But we kinda fell out because I thought it would have been more interesting for Percy to be bi and end up with Nico."

"There are four years between them; it makes no sense!"

"Calm down, my point is. Those are ships. Percy and Annabeth, Nico and Will and Percy and Nico. That's a ship; it's literally just a pairing between two people. Usually, it's the ones who don't get together that cause the most fuss."

"Oh! Is that why you were mumbling that Pernico is much better than Percabeth?"

"Yeah, those are their ship names. Although, thinking about it, we sound a lot like pirates."

"So, what would our ship name be?" he asks; I have no idea how to answer this. It was only last night that I admitted I was in love with him, and he thinks I've had time to think of a ship name.

"PERLLIOT!" Jay shouts from the other room.

"Yes. Thank you, Jay!" Elliot replies. I roll my eyes at the two of them. Then mumble that Pernico is still better than Percabeth because it is. Unfortunately, Elli hears me, and he starts tickling me. I squeal and try to escape, which I manage to get away and run to the living room. I look for a place to hide, but I don't find one. Suddenly I am lifted up, and there my boyfriend tickles my stomach lightly, 'til I tell him to stop 'cause he's pressing on my stitches. I forgot about them, not gonna lie. He apologises, places me down at the table, and starts bringing over breakfast food, including some lactose-free milk that he must have gotten the other day. I grab some cereal and begin to eat. Jay tiptoes through to the living room, hoping that he isn't cutting in on anything. He knows he's not when Elli sits next to me smiling.

"Wait… did you guys get together last night?" Jay asks.

"Why did you think we were talking about ship names this morning?" Elliot asks, digging into his porridge.

"I assumed you were getting together this morning! I can't believe I missed it. Ugh!" He sits down opposite us and sulks. I laugh at his child-like attitude but continue eating my food.

Elli points out that there is regular milk but that he prefers oat milk, I've never tried oat milk, so I don't know if it's made with lactose or not. If it's not, that will save us some money. It's annoying getting two kinds of milk. I mean, I don't really know that, to be sure. I haven't been shopping outside since… well, since before I moved out. Makes me a little nervous just thinking about it. <u>Do not freak out; just focus on your cereal.</u> Thanks, Skylar. I take a breath and continue eating. Elli notices my discomfort and starts rubbing my leg to let me know I'm okay. It helps.

"Right, I'm going to get dressed and head back to Dundee; you're heading to France on Wednesday morning, right?" he asks.

"Yes, you know if you wanted to come with us, I'm sure you could get a ticket," I suggest. Jay just got out of a relationship; sue me if I think he should get out there some more.

"Nah, I've got a ton of work to do before the end of this week. I've got to finish my animation portfolio by then; going anywhere right now is out of the question."

"How is it coming?" I ask him.

"Meh, it's okay. I'm just stuck on the last few frames on the animated video."

"Always a perfectionist," I tell him; he smiles and agrees with me. It's another ten minutes before he leaves, then we are finally alone... and still in our PJs. Or, in Elli's case, his underwear, it's really turning me on, so I excuse myself to check my computer.

I haven't booted it up since I played Minecraft. Since then, so much has happened; I got a boyfriend, had three panic attacks, cut myself too many times, and did I mention that I got myself a proper boyfriend who actually cares about me! Once my computer has booted up, I open up my emails and sift through them to find a job. I'm gonna need some money since I just paid for part of a wedding. But, hang on, what's this? It's from the hospital.

Dear Mister Grace,

No words can tell you how sorry I am that we overlooked your situation sooner. There were rumours around the hospital that someone was abusing their partner. But, unfortunately, there was never anything concrete to go on. In retrospect, I should have just looked for the nurse who was stealing supplies.

Thank you for your work on upgrading our systems; I'm aware that you didn't finish the job, and I am extending an invitation to return when you are ready to complete the work. If you feel that you cannot return here, I would completely understand, and I will start to look for someone who can. In any case, I shall be increasing the payment by one hundred pounds to make up for your trauma. I feel it is, in part, my fault.

> *I assume since your now ex-boyfriend is, I hope, now in jail that the total amount should be made out to you and you alone. Once the work is complete, I would like to meet you in person. My office door will be open.*
> Sincerely yours,
> The medical chief

I can't read the signature that came with this, frankly lovely, email from the hospital chief. It must have been challenging for him to find out that one of his nurses was not only stealing supplies but abusing someone to the degree that I ended up in a coma for a month. I quickly write a reply letting him know that I should have no problem completing the work at the end of next week. I'm hoping that I can either have Skye or Elli come with me so that someone knows how to calm me down is close by. I should get the work down pretty quickly now that I know *he* isn't there.

After replying to that email, I got to where I left off, the actual hospital contract. The next job was a simple retrieval job, so I quickly sent the client a message asking if they still needed help. They didn't, but they wanted help making their computer child friendly. So first, I taught them how to put child locks on specific keywords and sites. Then, I showed them how to lift the restrictions once their kid reaches puberty. They said they wouldn't be raising the lock, but I reminded them that their child would find a way around the limits anyway, and it's best to just lift them. That's when they agreed with me and paid me for the hour it took.

Next was another easy job, but it took a little longer; I was lucky they were still interested in my help. The job was to help set up a flower shop website and connect the stock in the back room with the computer on the shop floor. Again, easy, but since I'm not there, it took longer to set it up with me typing out what to do. I guess it's lucky that he had done a bit of research and had set up the network with a range extender. He just didn't know how to set it up. Luckily, I did. After that, it was just a case of me setting up his website, getting his approval, then making it live. I didn't even realise it was two o'clock by the time I was finished.

"I swear it was just nine," I say aloud.

"You've been working non-stop since eight, sunshine," Elli tells me, bringing food with him. Yay food. I carefully take the plate away from him and place it on the desk. I am about to dig in, but instead, my chair is turned towards my boyfriend, who kisses my nose. "You're cute when you're working, you know that?" he tells me. I smile at him and kiss his cheek.

"You okay? I realise I've kinda just left you alone for six hours," I ask.

"It's fine. It's your job. Make much money?"

"Enough to go sight-seeing and get room service," I tell him. He kisses me again. This time he doesn't stop, and neither do I. In fact, I manage to wrap my legs around his waist so he can pick me up.

"What about food?" he asks, breaking the kiss.

"Later, let's just…" I stop hoping he'll know where I'm going with it.

"Tell me if it gets too much." I kiss him again.

"Elli… I'm nervous I haven't done this with anyone else, really."

"It's okay, sunshine." He kisses me gently and starts towards the bedroom. "We'll take things nice and slow."

Taking Things Slow

Elliot carefully lays me down on our bed, still kissing me slowly; my hands are gripped to his back carefully. I don't want to hurt him. He pulls away from the kiss and trails kisses down the side of my face making his way to my collar bone, where he nibbles on it. A soft moan escapes my lips and I quickly cover my mouth in shock. Elli laughs, then takes my hand away from my mouth and kisses my palm. He moves back to my neck, but this time goes to the other side, sucking gently on my neck, causing me to let out yet another moan; only this time, I don't cover my mouth. Elli tugs at my shirt and looks at me; he's asking for permission to remove it. I nod and sit up slightly for him to move the shirt off of me. Once my T-shirt is removed, Elli kisses my upper chest, down to my nipples which he sucks lightly. I've never had that done to me, so I was surprised at how good it was.

Elli stops suddenly, I look down at him, and he is running his thumb over some old scars. He traces each of them with one finger, finds more on the other side, and does the same. His feather touches make me want to squirm, but I manage to stop myself, but I do blurt out an apology.

"Why are you apologising?" he asks me, still tracing one of my deeper cuts.

"Look at me, Elli; I'm not exactly a pretty sight." I can feel the tears prick at my eyes until Elli kisses the scars making me jump.

"Don't be sorry, Percival. I think all of you is beautiful, scars and all. I don't care about them. I just care to make sure that they won't happen again." He kisses all of the cuts on my chest, then picks up my arm and kisses all of the scars on my left arm; he does the same for the right.

He sits up and crosses his legs, moving mine to either side of his hips. He runs his hands up my legs and up to my knees, then kisses both of them. He seems to contemplate something for a second before coming down to my face and kissing me again. I return the favour by gently running my hands through his thick fading green hair. I feel his hands slide under me and wrap around my back; he's remembered my scar, so he's cautious with my back. He lifts me up, I help, so now I'm sitting in his lap, in a far more compromising position than last night. I can also feel his stiff member pressing against my thigh through his underwear. Elli continues kissing me and works over my shoulders too. I just sit there, letting him do it, then he stops.

"What's wrong?" he asks.

"I mean um... I... last time I d-did this was with J-Jay, so I'm out of p... p-practice... I also was a switch w-when I d-d-dated him." I explain. Elli lowers his head and shakes it, I'm about to say something, but he interrupts me.

"Kiss me, right here," he tells me, tapping to a spot just below his right collar bone. I frown but obey and start kissing where he said to me too, then he starts to moan. So, I keep going; I start sucking on it just like he did to my neck, and he starts to swear! This gives me an idea. I stop kissing his right collar bone and move over to his left, kissing as I go. I don't kiss him particularly hard until I reach the same spot as before on the opposite side. It doesn't quite get the same reaction as before. I start moving up his neck, sucking as much as I can on the way up. When I reach his neck, I suck where it meets his shoulders, and that's when I get the best reaction out of him. I feel his entire body shiver as he moans my name in a way I never thought I'd hear. Pure lust. That causes me to break away very quickly.

"What's wrong? You were doing great, sunshine!" he exclaims. I can see the happiness in his eyes, so I kiss him gently, and I think he gets the picture. "Ah, okay, got you. I didn't even know about that spot, so thanks, I guess." He laughs, making me smile. He kisses me then gently lays me down again; he then moves back to my legs. I remember I'm still wearing my shorts, so he asks if he can take them off. I nod at him.

He gently pulls the waistband of my shorts over my... I should mention that my ass is pretty big; all those years riding dildos was good for something, I guess. Anyway, Elliot pulls off my shorts, exposing my stiffening cock to the room's colder air. It's quite pleasant, actually. Although I can feel myself blush, Elli smiles at me then takes his own boxers off.

"Now we're both naked. Together this time." He takes my hand and squeezes it gently. "Tell me if I go too far." I nod once again, too horny at this point to care about talking. Anything I say should be a string of moans, swears and Elliot's name in varying orders. He crawls up my body, kissing from my belly button all the way up to my neck, which gets another suck, making me moan his name. He kisses me gently on the lips and reaches over to his bedside table. He opens a drawer taking out some lube. I grab his hand.

"It's for me; if you wanted me in your ass today, then this would help, but I'm not going to do that to you now." I make an 'o' with my mouth and let go of his arm. He doesn't lube himself up yet but starts working his way down my body, kissing every bit he can; my neck, my collar bone, my nipples, my ribs. He avoids my bandage, then moves on to my stomach then under my belly button. My breath starts to quicken as he slows and gets closer to my member; I can feel his breath on the small amount of hair on my crotch. I should shave my body again. I suck in a breath as I prepare myself for Elli to take me in his mouth, but it never comes. Instead, he bypasses it and kisses my thighs.

He looks up at me and sees my confusion, then rolls his eyes. His hands roam up my legs to my belly then to my chest. They then transverse back down towards my cock, this time, he cups my balls in one hand and strokes his finger up my shaft towards my head, where he scoops some of the pre-cum that has been lingering there since he removed my shorts. Elli brings his finger up to his face to inspect it, or so I thought. Suddenly his finger dives into his mouth, sucking away the pre. My eyes widen at his actions, making him laugh. He returns his hand to my cock, pulling lightly at my foreskin. He pulls it back, revealing my throbbing head, then rolls it back over. I let out a low moan.

A memory flashes in my mind, it's too quick for me to remember what, but it scares me into sitting up. I shock Elli, and he instantly places his hands on my shoulders, getting me to focus on him. I put my head in my hands, and Elli hugs me telling me it's okay. I'm not crying or panicking, surprisingly. Whatever flashed in my mind scared me, though. I take a breath and lift my head. Elli smiles at me, and I kiss him letting him know I'm okay.

"Are you sure you want to continue?" he asks me.

"Yeah, I do. Just… I don't know, maybe leave my dick alone for the moment?"

"Hmmm. Well, you know that only leaves me with one other option. I'm not putting my dick in you, even I know that's too soon." I agree because it *is* too soon. So, I take his hand and hold it in front of us.

"You can use this," I tell him.

"What else am I gonna use? If you're not clean, I'm stopping though, agreed?" he tells me, and I agree. He grabs the lube and squirts some onto his finger, then he slips his hand between my legs and finds my hole. He rubs the lube over it, and I slide my legs apart so that he has better access. He massages my hole, gently slipping the tip of his finger in and out, getting the muscle to relax. Now, yes, I know it has been a whole month since I last cleaned out and stretched my ass. It's safe to say that Elli could possibly get at least two fingers inside me quickly because I've been stretching since I was fourteen. Don't ask how I managed to get them.

As I predicted, his first finger slides in without much resistance, I moan slightly despite this not being the main event. He's just checking I'm clean. I'll admit, though, I miss the feeling of something being inside of me. Elli pulls his finger out of my ass and inspects it; it's clean. I will still need to shave my ass and use a douche to clean the inside out if we eventually have sex. Satisfied that I am clean, Elli squirts more lube on his fingers. He then moves to better view my hole and the rest of me by kneeling by my feet. I raise my knees, and Elli gets in close. Slowly he inserts both fingers. The only reason I know is that I feel a little fuller than before. I also feel the resistance coming from my ass as he carefully slides inside me.

I have *so* missed the feeling of something I actually want in my ass, moving in and out. I'm not moaning loudly, just every so often. Elli inserts his fingers deeper and starts roaming the inside of my ass, I can feel it all, and it feels really nice. Then I get that good feeling again; it's only for a second, but it's enough. I quickly tell Elli to do that again, and he obeys and then the feeling returns in force. I remember what this is! This is my G-spot; this is my pleasure spot. I should mention that every guy has this; I will never know why it's in our ass, though. But now, I'm moaning every time Elli's fingers push against it. Elli speeds up, and I think it's on my request, but I'm enjoying this too much to care if it was or wasn't. I can feel my body shivering as he hits my spot. I tell Elliot that I love him, and he replies that he loves me.

Suddenly I moan really loudly, and I feel something land on my chest. Elli carefully removes his fingers, and I whimper at the lack of filling; I open my eyes and look down and see that I came. Elli didn't touch my dick once, but I still came. That makes two, I suppose.

"Nemesis will be happy," I mumble. **I very much am!**

"That was unexpected. Fucking hot and very welcome, but still unexpected. I didn't realise you'd been working your prostate this much."

"To be fair, my ass is probably… really sensitive now. As for hands-free, that's only the second time it's happened." I had to take a really awkward breath during that. What? Cumming makes me tired. I watch Elli jump off the bed and bend over. I turn my head and smile at the view; he shaves his ass too. Very perky. He turns back to me, towel in hand and looks around him. Now his dick is in full view. I cannot complain about that.

"What?" he asks. I just keep smiling. Although I've seen him naked, I should note that this is the first time I'm getting a good look at his dick. It's cut, which I knew. I remember the day he was told that he'd have to have an operation on it. He honestly thought they would cut it all off; not just the skin around the head. It was my dad who told him that everything would be okay. I think it looks attractive cut, to be honest. I can tell he shaves his pubes, but I can also see it's been a few days since he last shaved because the hair looks quite stubby. He's cold too 'cause his balls are not hanging loose but are close to his pelvis, but length wise he is about… I don't know how big he is, but I'd say seven and a half inches, at a guess, and quite thick. He is also rock hard right now. I'm stunned he's kept that monster from me; I like it, though. "Why are you smiling?" he asks again. I keep smiling.

"You bent over. I saw your very shaved and perky ass," I tell him. I don't know if he is blushing or not…

"You know what? Just for that…" He throws the towel away. "*I'm* cleaning this up." I have no idea what he means by that, but suddenly his face is sucking on my belly, licking up all of my cum, and I'm blushing like crazy. I did not think that's what he meant. Suddenly my dick is in his mouth, and I don't mind. It's only for a few seconds anyway as he cleans my tip… at least the cum is all gone now. Satisfied that I am, Elli collapses next to me and kisses my lips. I can taste my cum on his lips; I don't taste too bad.

"Umm, are you gonna deal with your dick?" I ask.

"Why? Do you want to help a guy out?" He wiggles his eyebrows at me. I give him a hard stare then stand up. I watch him move to the centre of the bed and go to grab the lube. But I am quicker. I snatch the lube and kneel over his legs. He looks confused and turned on at the same time; it's very erotic. I squirt some lube into my hand, place the lube beside me, then coat Elli's member. He starts moaning immediately. I begin slowly stroking his full-length, I'm smaller than him, and the extra length is kind of throwing me off. I keep thinking I have less room. I feel Elli's hands stroke my knees telling me that I'm doing a great job. To be honest, I'm used to pleasing my boyfriend, but this feels very different. It's like… I've never actually had this kind of validation before, and Elli didn't force me to jack him off. I chose to.

I speed my pace up, throwing Elli off. I know because he swears at the new rate; he likes it at least. I hear his breathing increase and his shoulders tense up. He mumbles that he's close, so I slow down. He whines at my now much slower pace. I wait until I can see he's gonna beg me, then I increase the speed again. Then he starts moaning loudly, telling me how close he is. Suddenly he's whining that he's cumming. The white liquid shoots out of his dick and all over my hand and his chest; Elli lets out an intense, satisfying breath. I move my hand up over his shaft, making him flinch. I let his dick flop onto his chest and finally get off him. I pass the towel to him, then stand in the corner. Elli notices and quickly cleans up and comes over to me, taking me into his arms.

"You okay?" he asks; I nod then shrug. "You did really well, sunshine, that move at the end was actually really nice, even though I flinched." He breaks the hug and lifts my head to look into my eyes. "Hey, I love you. If I didn't enjoy it, I would have told you. I was surprised you even did it. That's a big leap for you." I nod again then take a breath.

"I... I n-never did it for *him*. He would like just... f-force his... thing d-d-down my throat. I didn't think I w-w-was gonna do that either." He takes me into his arms again as I cry softly.

"Oh, sunshine. I'm sorry I didn't come to get you sooner." Elli strokes my head. I shake it and look up at him.

"I'm the one at fault. I was a stupid horny teen; I should have just gone home with you that night." I lean my head back on his chest, placing my hands on his pecs.

"I know." He kisses my forehead. "Okay. How about a bath?" he asks, and I nod. "I'll get it started. But, first, why don't you go eat."

"Yeah, 'cause you already ate," I mumble, smiling to myself.

"Oh, you cheeky bugger," he laughs at me. He squeezes me gently, then lets me go. As he walks past me, I slap his ass gently, shocking the hell out of him in the process. He shakes his head and rolls his eyes.

Ten minutes later, both of us are in the bath laughing at an old memory that he brought up. Coincidentally it's his circumcision story. I wasn't really helping the situation; I wasn't sure what was happening, so I thought it would be funny to fuel his fears. Mum was the one that told me to stop and explained the situation to me, then made me fix the damage I'd done. This was actually after we went on holiday that year; Elliot's parents had taken off to Egypt and didn't tell anyone when they would be back and sort of just dumped Elli at our door the day they left.

"Was it before or after we went to the campsite?" Elli asks as he washes my back. Yes, we remembered to take my bandages off this time. Skye left more, so even if we had forgotten, it wouldn't have mattered.

"It was after you got that infection from the beach. You were all itchy and swollen when we got back and were too scared to talk to Dad about it. The only reason you told him was that it got too sore," I remember.

"Oh yeah, now I remember. To this day, I have no idea how I even got that infection."

"Might have been the skinny dipping you decided you had to do two days before we left." I turn to face him, giving him a smirk knowing that that is his seeking answer.

"Yeah…" He turns around and hands me the loofah. I start cleaning his back. "Oh, by the way, sorry for what you're gonna see in the mirror," he continues. That was confusing, so I don't bother replying. I just continue cleaning his back.

Covered!

After I finished cleaning his back, Elli shaved his dick, balls and butt. I helped with his butt. Which was great fun because I kept teasing him about it. He was annoyed, but I think he enjoyed it. It felt like nothing's changed. After I finished, he got out and started shaving his face; he doesn't shave more than that. Once he was out, he handed me a razor, one he bought without telling me. Next, I get started on shaving my body. I guess I'm lucky that I was blessed with a lack of chest hair, it just doesn't grow. I still give it a once over, but there is basically nothing there anyway. Then it's on to my arms, which I start at my wrists working my way up to my shoulder, where I then soap up my armpit and shave *that* forest away. Next is my legs which I stand up to do and expertly remove all the hair. Finally, it's my crotch, which isn't terrible for a month's growth, but it's too much; I soap up and get to shaving.

When I first started shaving my dick, I researched how to do it safely. I learned that stretching the skin and putting zero pressure on the razor was suggested. It's right, but I've found that a bit of pressure is better. The stretching tip was the best I've seen. Although the worst part is my balls because there is always one bit I seem to miss. Also, I'm just gonna say this now, although it's possible to shave your ass without a mirror, having someone do it for you is way better. This is why I ask Elli to help me out once he finishes shaving his face. Of course, he takes it as an opportunity to tease and compliment me on my 'amazing ass'. I don't reply. Just let him carefully shave me while I'm on all fours in the bath. He finishes pretty quickly. Now I've just gotta do my face, and I put my bandage back on.

I step out of the bath, Elli handing me a towel, and look at myself in the mirror. My face isn't too bad, actually. Why is that? I should have like... a fucking bush on my face. Elli is still in the bathroom; I guess he's keeping an eye on me. I don't mind. I don't exactly trust myself with the razor, and it gives me a chance to ask about my face.

"Hey, I've been wondering, Why did I have less hair on my face when I was discharged? I didn't have to shave until last week," I wonder aloud, knowing that he will reply.

"Hmm? Oh yeah, I shaved you like... the day before you woke up in the hospital. And after Skye put you under. I think I did a pretty good job considering I hadn't shaved at all that month." He must have been distracted; I know he was staring at my back.

"Oh yeah... You did have a lot of hair on your face. I honestly didn't notice."

"In my defence, I was too anxious about the cute guy in front of me to care about my own hygiene." I blush at that and keep shaving. "Are you blushing under that foam, sunshine?"

"What? N-no, I'm not. You're t-talking c-crazy," I say. My face is blushing more; please don't let him notice.

"You are, aww, Per. It's cute when you blush." He comes over and wraps his hands around my belly, then kisses my shoulder. I shiver. "Too much?" he asks, loosening his grip.

"N-no. Last time someone k-k-kissed my b-back it was..."

"Well, I don't have to kiss your back if you don't want me to."

"I don't know. Which is an-annoying me. I just don't w-want you to look at my back; it's pretty hideous," I explain. He rests his head against my shoulder, kissing it gently. Then, he lifts his head and looks at my back. I feel his finger trace down my spine, or rather the scar that has probably appeared. I try to continue shaving. Which isn't easy when someone is feeling you up.

"It's still pretty raw, you know. Skye did a great job with the stitching. You could barely see them," he tells me.

"I never saw it; I just know it hurt like a bitch. I needed a transfusion afterwards… then I hacked into the hospital. I forgot about that." <u>You chose to omit that information from everyone. You did not 'just forget'.</u> Well, he doesn't need to know that.

"Why? How? Also, why?" Elli asks. I finish up shaving, wipe off the excess foam then put some moisturiser on before I bother to reply to him. Once I'm done, I take his hand and pull him through to the living room, where Skye left the bandage. I lay down on the couch, and Elli gets the idea.

"I was in the hospital because I was doing some work for them. Upgrading their security and finding anything that could be upgraded. Which I did. It was weird though, that morning I came in, someone had literally pulled the plug on all the servers, people were freaking out, and none of them thought to just go check the plug. Once I'd found that out, Skye insisted that I show him my back, so I did, and he noticed that there was too much blood. So he took me to his office and checked my back before I passed out, then he started the transfusion with a really nice nurse, Lindsay. That was her name. She was actually really nice to me. Didn't mind my 'drunk' mind comments," I tell him. Elli listened intently as he cleaned around my surgery wound before wiping it with a dry cloth and carefully applying the bandage.

"I dread to think what you said, especially if yesterday is any indication." He looks up at me, and I blush.

"It wasn't anything bad... I just called him hot, ouch!" I shout. Elli accidentally pressed on the stitches.

"Ah, shit! Sorry, sunshine, I didn't think that I pressed that hard. You're all done now, though." He sits back on his legs, hanging his head; he looks like a puppy that's been told off. I carefully sit up, sigh at Elli and notice that he is upset; I carefully pull his head into my chest.

"It hurt, but I'm fine, not bad for the son of Athena," I joke; he pulls his head out of my chest.

"Says the son of Apollo, which thinking about it now isn't too hard to believe," he tells me.

"What a pair we are, huh? Hey, at least you're not scared of spiders... what's that?" I ask, pressing on his collar bone; it looks like a bruise. Oh, there's another one on his neck.

"Percival, I think you should go look in the mirror properly," he tells me. So, I get up and head back into the bathroom, look in the mirror, and there they are.

"WHAT THE FUCK!" I stomp back through to the living room to find Elli as far away from me as he can be. "I'm covered in hickeys, you jackass!" I walk towards him, but he dodges and runs towards the bedroom.

"In my defence... you seemed to enjoy them," he counters. I get to the bedroom and shut the door with my good foot. He runs to the other side of the bed and is as far away from the door as possible.

"Just because they felt... okay, they felt fucking amazing. That doesn't mean you hide that I've gotten them from you! I just want to know how you did them so well... and how long these fuckers will last!"

"Well, my record is a month, but the guy literally asked me

not to stop for like ten minutes. So these won't last that long." I ponder over what he's saying. But... am I really that mad? At least he told me, and they did feel amazing when I was getting them. I motion my boyfriend over, and carefully he moves over, still wearing his towel, me too actually, we should get dressed. Once he is close enough, I wrap my arms around his chest and rest my head on his shoulder. I can feel him smiling and let out a sigh as he wraps his arms around my back.

I lift my head and gently kiss his lips; he kisses back, of course, and when I break it, I look at him, and I can't help but smile. I suggest that we get changed before we end up cumming again. He asks if that would be so bad, and I don't respond, just drop my towel in the door as I go and get some clothes. I hear Elli groan as I do, which makes me laugh, an evil one at that. One I haven't used in quite some time. I pull my shorts and T-shirt back on just as Elliot comes in and pulls on his Camp Jupiter T. He then goes back into his bedside table and pulls something out. I watch him do so in confusion. He pulls out two necklaces. Placing one on the bed, Elliot unhooks one and puts it around his neck. Once he's done, he picks up the other one and brings it over to me.

"I got this for your birthday just before... Before I lost you, then got one bead for every year you weren't home, so there are six." He hands it over to me, and I hold the beads in my hands. "I got the last one custom made." He scratches his cheek. He's nervous; I can tell why.

He got me a Camp Half-Blood bead necklace; the first five represent the first five Percy Jackson books, the sixth one is a sun. It's Apollo's Greek symbol; his Roman one is a lyre. I hold the beads in my hand, then quickly unclasp and put the necklace on. I jump into Elli's arms after that, telling him how much I love it. I wonder where he got it from, there isn't an official one, so this must be custom made. It's awesome! I really need to re-read the books. Apparently, there is even a new series out; I think it is called Trials of Apollo. Okay, I need to stop now before I have a full-on geek out. I get off Elli, and we head through to the living room and start watching a movie. Specifically, the Pokémon film we didn't finish yesterday. It was annoying to me that we didn't finish it.

We get cuddled up on the couch with a blanket, some popcorn and drinks and enjoy the film cuddling up with each other. When we last did this, I was sixteen, if I remember correctly, it was just after Elli left high school, like the day after. We sat cuddled up on his bed watching *Wrath of the Titans*; we really are hardcore into the whole Greek mythology thing. During the film, I sat next to Elli with my legs over his; he said, get comfy, so I did, but I got the feeling that he wanted to tell me something. He never did, though. I suppose he might not have said anything because I was dating Jay at the time. I still wonder what he was gonna tell me.

"Hey, wise boy, the last time we did this, was there something you wanted to tell me?" I ask.

"Wise boy?" he asks in return.

"Just trying it, felt wrong. Answer my question," I tell him, and he sighs.

"Yeah, I was gonna tell you something." I wait and look at him, trying to get him to continue. "Oh! You wanna know what it was? I was… Okay, I was gonna tell you that I was, am, in love with you, didn't have the guts to tell you then." I turn around and kiss his neck.

"Well, I love you too." He smiles and kisses me. "Only took you eight years." I laugh; he pulls me into his lap, making us both laugh. We start cuddling while watching the film.

The first Pokémon film is just as good as I remember it. Both of us are crying when Ash is turned to stone, I manage to grab us some tissues to clean them up, but we are still crying by the end of the film. Once Elli turns off the DVD player, someone knocks at the door. I say I'll go answer it; he nods and goes to grab the disc. I take one last sniff and head to the door. I open it up and see a very tired-looking Skye leaning against the door frame. As soon as he sees me, his entire demeanour changes from tired to protective. I know that look well enough by now. Before he can say anything, I tell him that I was crying from a film and they are hickeys; he lets out a relieved breath and asks if he can come in. I tell him yes; he greets Elli and collapses onto the single seat. I return to Elli's lap.

"Everything okay, Doc?" Elliot asks him. Skye suddenly jumps at his name being said, then looks for the source.

"Yeah, just… this is me just off today, well… I got sent home by the chief," he explains.

"What did you do this time?" I ask, exasperated, I know how hard he works.

"Nothing… Okay, I may have had back-to-back surgeries and not slept at all during my shift while I did; then, the chief told me he's retiring and wants me to help choose his replacement. Oh, and his top choice was me."

"WHAT?" both of us shout.

"What? He said that he's retiring in the next few years. Something about his family. I stopped paying attention."

"That's huge, Skye. Are you gonna take it?" Elli asks.

"What? Hell no! I have not been a doctor for that long. There are definitely better candidates, like the cardiothoracic surgeon or the head obstetrician. Both have been doctors for over fifteen years. They are way more qualified than me, a guy who hasn't actually finished his residency."

"How far into it are you?" I ask. Elli looks at me weirdly. "What? Do you not think I've watched *Grey's Anatomy*? It's fucking fantastic."

"He's right. It's got decent accuracy. But, I'm coming up to the end of my fourth year." He folds his arms over his chest. "Maybe in another five or ten years, I'll consider saying yes, but right now? No way am I ready."

"Sounds like the chief wants someone he can trust, and if he trusts you, you can use that to your advantage. Help him choose the next chief, then you have the reputation of being close to the chief. After that, who knows," Elli suggests.

"Is that Athena speaking or you?" Skye asks.

"That was one hundred per cent me. Wanna crash here tonight, man?" Elli asks. Skye nods and thanks us. He explains that he is also heading to France Tuesday night; like us. After searching a little bit for his boarding pass, it turns out we are even on the same flight and strangely in the same row. Elli puts on another film and starts to make food for us all.

"Do you like Percy Jackson then?" I ask.

"Hmm? Yeah, I've been waiting for the last Trials of Apollo book to be released."

"Who's your godly?" Elli asks.

"Odin." I look at him, shocked. "Shocking, I know it makes me a half-born, not a half-blood. I've always preferred Norse mythology to Greek. What about you, Percival?"

"Apollo, I used to be a lot brighter than I am now, not sure I'd still get him if I did the quiz again. But, I don't want to find out; I always prefer Apollo as a god anyway." Skye smiles at me and tells me he can see it.

"Hey, sunshine, you okay with me using my oat milk in the mac 'n' cheese?"

"I'd prefer some nectar but sure." Both men laugh at me.

Suddenly Skye sits up.

"Sunshine? You guys got together?" he asks.

"Yeah, last night." I smile and blush.

"Gods, I must be tired. Of course, you guys are together; who else would willingly get hickeys." I laugh at his tired state.

"Hey, not like it wasn't gonna happen eventually. Plus... Elli's really sweet with me."

Skye laughs, the life seemingly coming back into him; I smile and get up to grab him a glass and pour him a drink of something fizzy to wake him up. We talk while we are waiting for food, and Skye tells us that he'll grab his suitcase tomorrow morning and come back so we can just head from here together. We all agree that that is the best idea.

Whatever we are watching is so dumb, so I get up and change it to the original *Ghostbuster*s. I retake my seat on the couch just in time for Elli to hand me a bowl of mac 'n' cheese. He sits next to me, and I can tell immediately that he likes my choice of film. Elliot has a thing about classic movies, like *Ghostbusters*, *Good Morning Vietnam* or *Sister Act*. There is nothing classical about them, but he says that films from the sixties to the nineties are the best, but he has a soft spot for the Marvel cinematic universe.

Skye practically inhales his food then falls asleep on the armchair. Elliot and I laugh at him but take our time with our food, mainly 'cause if I go too fast, I *will* throw up. The good thing is that I'm putting on some weight, I'm not wild about it, but I know that I have to eat more. Weird to think that this time tomorrow, we'll be getting ready to go to France. Gods, things really are looking up for me.

Going to France

Waking up next to Elli? Fun but annoying. Waking up next to Elli as my boyfriend? Fucking amazing. He woke up first this morning and woke me up by kissing my forehead; I knew he was doing it. I was pretending to sleep. I'd woken up after the first kiss. I'm a light sleeper. He was kissing me for a good ten minutes until I finally decided to open my eyes, and he couldn't stop smiling. Neither could I; I kissed him, said good morning, then we cuddled again. We only got up after hearing the front door unlock and close. Elli gets up first, still in his underwear; I watch him leave our bedroom. I at least have the sense to sleep in an oversized T-shirt and boxers, so he has to work to see my ass.

Elli made us pancakes for breakfast. How he has the time to cook, work and look after me is beyond my understanding. I can't complain about the pancakes though, they are delicious. So, I asked him where he got the recipe.

"Where'd you learn to cook like this? It's amazing," I ask, taking a bite.

"Do you not remember?" I shake my head, confused. "Sammy is a chef; he cooked all the time in the flat we shared. He taught me after you left because I was... I was in a bad place. Not as bad as you mind, but bad," he explains. I sit closer to him, taking his hands and checking his wrists. There is nothing there. Thankfully, I didn't want him to be like me.

"Never do it," I tell him holding my exposed, scarred wrist next to his clean one. "I hate that he encouraged it, but... I thought I deserved it, still, do if I'm honest," I admit.

"I'd never even thought about cutting, but I was in a dark place. I knew that I'd get an earful if I did anything stupid. Abi recommended I talk to her doctor friend, Skye, who suggested I go to therapy. I ignored it for a while and thought about getting into fights. Specifically going after assholes like your ex." He takes my hand. "Then after a nasty fight where the police had to get involved, I started using a sharpy instead of taking my anger out on strangers." I pull him into a quick hug then punch him.

"Don't you *dare* do that again!" I tell him.

"Okay, I won't," he huffs, turning away from me. I grab his face and make him look at me, wishing he could see the pain in my face.

"You already know what it would do to me if I lost you again. I would do anything to make sure you lived. Just as you would do the same for me. So, don't cut, don't lie and don't get into however many fights before you realise there is a better way." I think I shed a few tears during that, not sure, but it gets through to Elli, which is the point, and I get a hug out of it because I got myself a little too worked up, and I think I was heading towards a panic attack. After I calm down, I go back to my pancakes. We go quiet for a while before Elli talks again.

"I should probably tell you how many guys I slept with then, shouldn't I?"

"And the girls," I say between bites.

"What? No, I'm not into girls."

"What? You told Sammy you were bi, didn't you?"

"No, I've always been gay. Have you forgotten what I told you the other night? That it's always been you? I never wanted anyone but you, so yeah gay, not bi," he explains.

"But that night six years ago. That was a girl you were

making out with... wasn't it?"

"Nah, that was just a guy with like, really long hair, terrible kisser actually. I'm so glad I never saw him again," he tells me, we hear the door open, and Skye enters with his bags. I'm still processing what I've just heard.

"Hey, guys," he says, shutting the front door and walking to the fridge. I wasn't watching, but it looked like he put in three drinks, two sandwiches and a wrap.

"Hey, Skye," we say together; I smile at it. Then get focused again.

"Oh, pancakes." He shuts the door and plates up a few for himself. "So, what are we talking about?" He sits across from us.

"Elli's gay, and I thought he was bi."

"Is there anyone in this group who isn't LGBT?" Skye laughs.

"I mean Sammy and Abi," Elli tells us. "But back to me, yeah, I'm gay, who told you I was bi?"

"I don't know; guess I had it in my head that you were. Although, that guy you were making out with was very feminine."

"He told me he was a fem-boy while we were making out. Not the greatest turn on for me. I'm glad I was too out of it to care." Elli finishes his pancakes and asks if I'm gonna finish my breakfast, but I shake my head. The truth is I feel a bit sick, too much to eat. I'm willing to stay down.

"Lay on the couch on your right side; you'll feel better. Trust me, I'm the doctor."

"How long have you been waiting to say that." I laugh out.

"Oh, fucking ages. But seriously, go lay down." He continues eating his pancakes while I go towards the sofa. Once I lay down on my right, as suggested, I start to feel better. Elli brings over a blanket for my legs and offers his lap as a pillow, which I can't say no to.

The rest of the day is spent talking, reading comics and watching TV. I finally got Elli into *Grey's Anatomy*, and we end up watching most of the first season before Skye suggests we get some sleep. Our flight is at nine in the morning from Edinburgh airport; it's not a direct flight. We have a three-hour layover in London. No point really going sightseeing there, doesn't mean we can't get lunch. It'll probably be lovely either way. I guess Skye's food is for the journey if we get hungry, or it was all for him. Elli starts going over the plan for the following day. We'll be getting up at four a.m. to get to the airport just after half-past, then there is security and finding the gate, easy stuff. Once we get to London, he suggests getting food and then finding the gate. We all agree, and then at eight o'clock, we all go to bed, alarm set for half three to get up for four. I hate it, but it's for the best.

I am rudely awoken six hours later by Elli's alarm; I turn over and accidentally hit him. I jump, and he wakes up; not the best wake up, but at least he is up; he's always been bad at getting up. We groggily get dressed and make sure Skye is up. When we tell him it's time, he sits up like a vampire and mumbles something like, who has woken me from my slumber? I don't really pay attention as I'm still half asleep next to Elli, who has to shake me awake again. After Skye gets dressed, we grab the food that he bought us while he was out; he puts them in his travel bag while Elli calls a taxi.

I grab all of our passports and the boarding passes, keeping them in the safest part of my bag. I'm lucky that you can renew your passports online now. Thankfully had the sense to keep it updated while I was with the asshole. I got a new one last year, so I've got plenty of time left before I have to replace it again. Before the taxi arrives, we do the last of our checks. When we hear the driver buzz the flat, we head down to meet him. I almost forgot something, but I quickly ran into the bedroom to get it; it's the necklaces that Elli got for me. I slide it into my bag and then head down to the street.

It's so fucking cold! Although I'm wearing my most oversized hoodie, I'm still freezing, even after wrapping myself in my hoodie. I may be exaggerating, but the wind, that's making it worse. Once we are in the taxi, I warm up slowly. I want to lean into Elli to warm up, but I don't trust this driver, so I decide to leave it.

We arrive at the airport; I almost don't want to leave the car, it's so warm. But at the same time, I know I would have fallen asleep if I had. We still have four hours before our flight which is plenty of time to get through security and find the departure gate. I have to admit, Edinburgh airport is really nice. It could be a lot better, too, like… cleaner, but I think that might be my OCD coming out.

There aren't many people around, so Elli manages to hold my hand; I love it, don't get me wrong, but I'm really nervous that someone will see us. I don't think Elli cares, but I do, so I let go of his hand and put them in my pocket. He seems upset, but I see Skye mutter something to him, and he cheers up slightly. I don't want to hurt him, but this is literally the first time I've been out in public. Not to mention he's really the first proper boyfriend I've had in years. Also, I don't know how tolerant people are. Once we find the gate, we all sit down and wait; Elli suggests that I get some sleep, only because I was rubbing my eyes to get them to stay open. In my delirious state, I nod and rest my head on his shoulder, then pass out.

Skye wakes me up with an hour to go before our flight; he also has to wake up Elli, who fell asleep on me while I slept. It's shocking how easily we can rest in each other's arms. Elli doesn't wake up when Skye tries, so I give it a go. Nothing normal works, so I try one last thing, I manage to expose the part of his neck that still has my mark on it, and I start to suck. That gets him moaning then; he realises what's happening and jolts up. One of his hands covers his neck; Skye and I sit at our seats, giggling like madmen at his response. I pass him his backpack and tell him it's time to go; he nods, still a little dazed.

While we walk to the gate, Skye gives me a bag and tells me that it's for the flight since I probably won't sleep once we are in the air. Elli laughs and comments that I can sleep anywhere; nothing can keep me from my sleep. He's right; I open the bag. He's gotten me a set of purple Skullcandy earphones so I can listen to my music. I thank him with a hug and open them immediately.

An hour later, we are on the plane, and I'm resting my head on Elli's shoulder, not really sleeping. While I rest, I hear Elli and Skye start talking, I don't want to listen to them at first, but I quickly realise that they are talking about me.

"I know Percival trusts you, but I still think that you are going far too fast. Slow down, please, for his sake," Skye tells him.

"I know you are a doctor, and I value your opinion. I *am* going slow with him. I've made sure he is comfortable before I do anything with him. I've stopped when he got uncomfortable, and actually, I do a good job praising him when he does a good job. Surely that's a good thing?" Elli reasons.

"True. I still think you should hold off from anything… sexual," Skye reasons; I deliberately stir at that but make it seem like I am still sleeping. Both men pause for a minute before they continue.

"We already did stuff the other day. Nothing he didn't want, and I was fair with him. I told him that I wouldn't have sex with him. I did... finger him, but if he wasn't clean, I would have stopped. I'm not an idiot, Skye. I work with kids who can be more challenging than Percival."

"As long as he didn't freak out, then he has to be improving with you."

"I mean, he was a little freaked when I moaned too much and when he made me flinch. But I told him everything was okay, and he calmed down. I wouldn't lie to him like that." Elli rubs my hair, and I instinctively lean into it and let out a little moan.

"He does seem to have improved immensely in your care. However, I'd still recommend caution; we don't want him to relapse."

"I agree, and *I* will make sure that doesn't happen." After that, they don't say any more, but I do hear one of them snoring softly. I carefully 'wake' up, pretending like I was asleep. Turns out Elli is the one who is still awake. "Feel better for sleeping, sunshine?" he asks; I nod, rubbing my eye.

"I've missed actually getting a decent night's sleep," I joke, then I realise that's not really a joke. "Sorry, that wasn't funny."

"Not really. Hey, why don't we sort out a music playlist for you?" Elli asks. I smile at the idea. I pull out my phone and get started on a list because I don't have the internet on the plane.

The rest of the flight to London Elli and I compose a playlist. On the list, we start with Sabaton, of course, Jamie Cullum, my favourite Jazz artist and the *Hairspray* soundtrack. After that, it gets a little tricky. I added a few more musicals like *Be More Chill*, *Wicked*, and *The Greatest Showman*. Elliot suggests some

Disney songs, so I add a few that I recognise, for example: 'Make a Man Out of You', 'Almost There', 'Won't Say I'm In Love', and 'I'm Still Here'. We are only in the air another half hour before we get the fasten your seatbelt sign. We wake up Skye, and I get this strange feeling in my gut.

"What's wrong?" my friends ask.

"I… there is a strange feeling in my belly. It's not bad, though," I tell them.

"Explain it exactly," Skye tells me.

"I feel… jittery, and I really want to be moving and see the sights; I think I want to smile, more than normal anyway," I tell them.

"There's nothing wrong with you," Skye says, leaning back with a smile on his face.

"Sunshine, you're just excited. Try and not worry; we'll be landing in London soon."

When was the last time I felt like this? Was it… I'm not even sure. But I like it. I can't wait to land now; in fact, here it is. Now I'm smiling and bouncing impatiently in my seat. Elli places his hand on my leg, and it calms me down slightly. I'm forced to wait for the last ten excruciating minutes before we can actually be let off the plane. Once the doors open, we try to get off as quickly as possible, but we fail miserably. We have to wait until someone lets us get into the stream of people. Which is no one, so we just wait till the end of the line and then join it.

Again, Elli grabs my hand; this time, I don't stop him. He doesn't want to lose me; I get that. Then I see the crowds in the airport, and my excitement dims slightly, and I move in close to Elli. He tells me that we'll be out soon and that I shouldn't worry. The airport is fantastic, and there are so many shops. This is the furthest place I've gone to in years, so that asshole can suck it!

"Sunshine, maybe calm down," Elli tells me, gently squeezing my hand. I blush, realising that I said it all aloud, but the truth is I can't stop smiling. My blush dims quickly as I realise I am one more flight away from my best friend's wedding. Not bad for a holiday, let's be honest. I can't wait.

Excited

Skye motions us towards the bulk of the airport. I can feel myself start to get a little more panicky; there are too many people, you can't exactly blame me. Both men seem to tell how uncomfortable I am and start searching for a place to sit down and eat something until the gate is ready. Elliot points out a Wetherspoons bar and restaurant, and we unanimously agree to get some seats. I'll be honest I start paying less and less attention to them because I'm flinching when I get too close to people, and I try to move in closer to Elli.

Finally, I get so distracted that he has to tell me to sit down just to get my attention again. Skye orders us some drinks using their app. They are really over advertising it though, it's above the bar and from what I can see on every table too. Speaking of the tables, it's really tightly cramped here, it's a wonder the staff can move. He then pulls out the food he got us yesterday and places them on the table. I instantly notice a lactose-free wrap.

"You okay, sunshine?" Elli asks me; I grab the wrap and nod. "We ordered you a Pepsi since there isn't any cream soda." I nod again, opening the wrap, pulling one out, and biting into it. "And I'm going to strip naked for everyone to see and make out with Skye," he says.

"Okay," I reply… wait, what? My head shoots up to him. "What?"

"Oh, so you are listening."

"Ah. Sorry, guess I'm really distracted," I explain; Elli moves his chair closer to me, takes one of my hands, and then kisses my knuckles.

"I know it's a lot of people, but I'm right here. So you have nothing to worry about. Skye's here too, and whatever."

"Hey, I'm his friend too, ya know," Skye says. These two are a dangerous combination. They are gonna make me laugh way too much. When the drinks arrive, we thank the poor waiter, and the boys start eating their food while I slowly eat my wrap. It's nice, but I've tasted better. While eating, I start making a playlist on my Spotify, adding the songs from my list, some I forgot to put on earlier. Like: *Miss Saigon*, McFly and P!nk. What? They're awesome. Once I finish with the wrap and my playlist, I connect the earphones and pull them up through my shirt, letting them hang over my chest.

I fold my rubbish, I realise we've sat in relative silence for most of our lunch. I say quiet; the airport is way too loud with chatter. I might not even hear the guys if they try and ask me something. I decide to jump on my phone and check out some newer musicals. I found a few new Disney musicals that have been released. One that catches my eye is called *Frozen*. It sounds dumb, but it got a second film, so maybe it was good. I check out the most popular song called 'Let it Go'. Terrible music, and just because you stop hiding in fear doesn't mean the fear isn't still there. The second film seems to have similar-sounding songs; I click on 'Into the Unknown' and by Apollo, this song is fantastic! Now, this is a good song about finding out who you are; I bet that's the second film's plot.

"Oh no. He found *Frozen*," Skye says to Elli.

"That's a bad thing? The movies were terrible, yes, but it's bad because?"

"Because 'Into the Unknown' is amazing!" I tell them.

"There's a Panic! At the Disco version," Elli tells me.

"Dude!"

"Hell yes!" I say, instantly looking it up and adding it to my playlist, along with the original version.

"You are a bad influence. You know that, Elliot," Skye tells him before finishing off his drink.

"Oh yeah, always have been. Hasn't Percival told you the story of his first wank?" Elli tells him, that catches my attention.

"No one, and I mean no one, needs to know that story," I tell Elli, trying to sound threatening. I don't think it worked.

"Go on then. Tell me." Skye teases me.

"No, please don't."

"So, it was in his fourth year at high school, and I could tell something had been bothering him all day, and I'd noticed that he was rearranging his dick quite often during the day. So, I had my suspicions. Unfortunately, we didn't walk home together that day; I can't remember what you were doing. Anyway, when he got home, I knew he would go straight to his room. So, once he was home, I went straight to his room, and he covered up just as I walked in. He was naked under those covers, and we both knew I knew. What I didn't expect is that as soon as I sat down, he would cum." Elli and Skye start to laugh to themselves, and I sit red in the face hoping that I can just disappear. That's not even the story of my first time. That was, however, my first time taking my new dildo all the way in. So, when Elli sat on the bed, it… well, it felt amazing, and I was already super close to cumming, and well I did. The first time he made me cum, though, so that's a plus.

"I hate you so much right now. You are gonna pay for that." I mumble towards Elli; I hear Skye giggling as he takes a bite out of his sandwich then looks at his watch.

"Hmm, we need to get going soon." He is swift to grab his bag, as is Elli to grab both his and my bags before moving his chair back to where it was before, then holding his hand out for me to take it. I smile at him, then quickly pocket my phone and pull out the single earphone I had in. He leads me out of the bar; it wasn't good, to be honest. Look nice enough but... I wouldn't go there again.

I walk beside Elli with Skye on his other side. There seem to be fewer people than before... wait, a stream of people is coming towards us. Oh, fuck, they are just off a plane. I take a step closer to Elli to make sure none of them hit me, not looking forward to that. A few of them get close to me, but they avoid me easily. They are all wearing some kind of suit, a few are wearing regular clothes like us, probably on their holidays too since there are kids among them. Suddenly someone hits into me—

"Slut," they say, and they seem to rush away again... and... and...

Now I can't get focused. I can't concentrate. Now all I can hear is that damn word over and over and over again. *He* used to call me that. He called me that 'cause that's what he thought I was, and he was wrong – he... music. I need my music. I stop, grab my phone, put my headphones in, turn on my new playlist, and turn the volume up. All I can hear are the lyrics. I close my eyes and stand there motionless, letting the beat course through my veins. I feel the song touch my soul and calm it. My head clears, almost; I hear that asshole again speaking that word. I feel a hand slip into my own, snapping me back to reality. It's Elli. He smiles and nods; I shake my head in return. Understanding instantly, he starts leading me to the gate.

We can't find seats, so we stand waiting for the gate to open.

My hand is still in Elli's, but I take my backpack away from him. He objects, but I can't hear him, so I assume he complains to Skye about it. I feel kinda bad for not paying attention to him, but I need this. I need something else to focus on. Suddenly I hear an unfamiliar voice sing 'Into the Unknown'. It's upbeat; it brings a smile to my face. I let my eyes drift closed, and I bob my head to the blaring drum beat. I'm not sure why I relate to this song so much, but I love that I do. I don't usually link with music. It's usually characters in books or musicals I relate to. To be fair, I do not relate to Alex Fierro in any way, but Evan from *Dear Evan Hansen?* Now he is someone I can relate to. The idea of feeling like you go through life like no one notices you and that you could just disappear without a trace, yeah, I get that. Also, Ben Platt, now that is one good looking guy! The song finishes, and I open my eyes in time to see the gate open. My focus must have been elsewhere because I don't remember cutting it close to our boarding time. I pause my music and pocket my phone and headphones.

"You feeling better now? You had us worried for a while there?" Skye asks, looking into my eyes. I keep avoiding his gaze, so he grabs my face to make me look at him, making me a little uncomfortable. So, I hold his hand with my free one to pull them away.

"I'm g… good. J-just an ass h-hole is all," I tell him. Elli and Skye share a look but say nothing. Elli brings our hands up to his lips and kisses the back of my hand. I smile at him and remember how much I love this man and how long I *have* loved him. All of my life, it's always been him. He was the one I was… stopping now 'cause it's beginning to sound familiar. I place one hand behind Elli's head and pull him into a light kiss. I mumble that I love him, he kisses me again and says he loved me too.

Our group is called onto the plane, so we all make our way over the catwalk towards the aircraft: man, two planes in one day. Never would have thought I could do that again. Had you told me last year that I would be flying to the south of France, I probably would have told you to piss off, mainly because I can't... couldn't even leave my flat, and that really bugged me.

"Hey, I've been thinking," I start.

"Dangerous," Elli interrupts. I give him a hard stare. "I'm sorry, go on." He giggles.

"I was thinking that maybe once we get back, we could think about, maybe, getting a house?" Elli says nothing, just stares at me with this perplexed look on his face; it's adorable but off-putting. "Never mind, it's a stupid idea." I find our seats and move right to the window. I place my bag between my legs, then I sit and look out the window and sigh to myself. I'm so pathetic. Why did I have to say that? I couldn't just keep it to myself a little longer? We've only been together a few days, moving in together? What am I thinking? I feel Elli sit next to me and take my hand.

"Percival," he says, I do nothing. <u>Why?</u> He doesn't want to get a house with me; the conversation is over. <u>Turn around, you dummy.</u> Okay, but this won't go our way. I face him.

"Sorry, I shouldn't have—" Elli cuts me off with a kiss which... I can't help but accept; he breaks the kiss and looks at me.

"I would love to look at houses with you. The only reason I haven't gotten a house yet is that it would only be me. But, now it's you *and* me, and I would love to get a place." I smile at him and pull him into a deep hug, then kiss his face. Then suddenly, I make a very unattractive sound. Yawning. "Get some sleep, sunshine, I'll wake you up before we get there." I nod and rest my head on Elli's shoulder and quickly fall into unconsciousness.

When I come to, I'm being carried by someone, I hate it, but at least I know it's Elli. I open my eyes and rub them. After adjusting to the lights, I look up and see my now faded, green-haired boyfriend. Next to him is my doctor, who is carrying both his bag and mine. I snuggle my head into Elli's chest and listen to his heartbeat. I keep my eyes open; I really don't need to fall asleep again. I've been sleeping too much recently; I can bet Skye would say it's something to do with the surgery. I mean, I did have lung surgery, so I can't say I'm too surprised that my body is getting tired quicker than average, but even after a month and a half, you'd think that maybe it would be better. Guess I just need to exercise more to make my lung stronger. I feel someone kiss my forehead, and I look up to see Elli smiling at me.

"Hey there, sleepyhead," he whispers.

"I'll kill you if you call me that again," I mumble back, which just makes him laugh; it may be an empty threat, but still…

"Sorry, I am kinda worried you're sleeping too much. Are you okay? Nothing hurting or pinching."

"With Percival's anxiety attacks, lung surgery, and not to mention the walking and travelling we've done today, you're gonna find he will want to sleep more. Nothing wrong with that. I have tricks to increase your lung capacity, but just getting out and doing these sorts of things will help a lot," Skye tells me; I just nod. In fact, I suddenly remember that we are in another country, and I silently giggle to myself.

Just look at me now asshole, never gonna get out again my ass, I'll go wherever I please. Looking towards where we are going, I notice that we seem to be following someone, and they seem to have a car. I tap Elli's arm, and he stops and lets me down; I wobble slightly and balance on him. My dizziness passes quickly, and I walk without support.

I don't have to walk far before we reach the car. After that, it's just getting into the back where I sit down next to Elli. He pulls out his phone and starts doing things; I don't know what because I am not a peeping tom. I pull out my own phone and start looking through some more songs, but I get bored quickly and jump on Facebook, where I find I have a message from Jay. Unfortunately, I have to download messenger before I can reply. Once it does finish downloading, I respond instantly:

Percival Grace
>Hey, we just arrived in Nice.
>*Jay changed his nickname to Jay*

Jay
>No worries, glad you got there safely. How was it?
>*Percival changed his nickname to Per*

Per
>Well... I slept through the whole flight, so I have no idea. But some weirdo called me a slut when we were changing planes. Almost had a panic attack, shockingly my new music helped a bunch and managed to calm me down.

Jay
>Hmm, that's weird. Wonder why.

Per
>Well... he saw me travelling with 2 guys, one of whom I can't keep my hands off of.

Yeah, I'm gonna assume he thought I was either cheating on one of them or I was dating both of them. Which is just weird.

Jay

Do you mean polyamorous? Yeah, bit confusing to me.

I might be willing to try it, though. Never liked 2 people tho, so it's unlikely.

Per

Not for me; I'm a one-man guy.

Jay

Oh, hey, that's a book… and a song.

Per

It is? Link me the book real quick seems like we are arriving. Speak once we get in, man.

Jay

K.

Jay sent you a link

I smile and put my phone away as we pull up to the biggest looking hotel I've seen in… well, in six years. Standing at the entrance are Abi, Sammy, and I assume the other two are Abi's parents too. We all step out, and Abi comes over to give us hugs. When she hugs me, she warns me that her dad is a bit of a homophobe. I thank her, and then Sammy comes to embrace Elli and me. Then Abi's parents come over; Abi's mum, a short woman with similar hair to Abi. Her eyes are almost an amber colour. She gives us all a hug but seems to provide me with the biggest one. She breaks the hug and holds my face.

"You must be Percival. Thank you so much for helping with the wedding. I'm not sure how we'll ever repay you," she tells me. I don't respond at first. I'm kinda freaked at the way she is touching me.

"Mum, remember I told you Per doesn't like unnecessary touching," Abi tells her, pulling her away.

"Yes, of course, dear, I am sorry. I was just so excited to meet you and your friends. Now, Elliot, I've met, but who is this fine young man?"

"Skye," I speak out, finally. "He's my friend and doctor."

"Ah yes," her dad finally says. "The one who reset my future son-in-law's leg. Nice to meet you, son." He extends a hand to Skye, who doesn't take it.

"I'm not your son, now if you don't mind, we have been travelling all day, and I would very much like to clean up and check on Percival's bandages." He faces Abi's mum. "It's nice to meet you both." Skye moves past the hulking man that is Abi's dad and towards reception.

"Sorry about him; he must be tired," Elliot says.

"These gays are all the same, overly dramatic," he speaks; his voice is annoyingly deep.

"You should be careful what you say; you piss off more people than you'll want," I tell him, then I take Elli's hand and basically pull him to reception. When we get there, I kiss his cheek and ask for our key. Yes, that was just to piss off Abi's butthead dad. I see Elli blush in the corner of my eye, I smile at him, and then we both start trying to stifle our laughter. I'm given our room key and told where to go, so we head to the lift. On our way over, two women come over to us; they seem familiar.

"Excuse me, are you Percival?" the taller one asks me. Then,

I notice that they are holding hands like Elli and I are; that's when it clicks.

"You must be Sammy's parents," I say. Oh that's right. Sammy's mother is a priest and married to a woman. You don't see that too often.

"I don't know that we must be, but we are. I am Emma, and this is my wife, Lauren."

"It's lovely to meet you both," Elliot says; we all hug quickly. I feel a little uncomfortable hugging Emma since she is a pastor and the same one who caught me making out with Elli. I'm not sure she's going to forgive us for that so easily; also, 'cause it's unnecessary touching.

"Have you just arrived?" Lauren asks us, carefully directing us towards the lift.

"Yeah. Just now, actually," I reply.

"Ah, so you have met the brute that is Bill then?"

"Oh yes, we have encountered him," Skye mumbles.

"Believe me. I think knowing that there are two 'gay' couples here will drive him mad," Lauren says.

"Not that we really care about labels," Emma butts in. "God loves us no matter who we love; that is the truth all people must learn."

"I agree, although I don't personally believe in the existence of a single god, nor does Percival," Elli explains.

"To which god do you subscribe to then?" Emma asks us as we step into the lift; I glance back at the doors where we see Abi's dad yelling at no one in particular, probably about us. I almost crack at that scene.

"We prefer the old Greek gods. They had a god for… almost anything including homosexual love since the idea of same-sex relations is not a new concept and was widely practised until the introduction of Christianity," Elli explains. I forgot how passionate he was about Greek mythology.

"Well, I respect your choice. However, it is not for me to change your mind. Heaven is what we make it, would you agree, Percival?"

"Hmm? Oh yeah, your beliefs definitely shape your ideas of the afterlife. Personally, I am aiming for the Isle of the Blessed."

The lift stops, and the ladies leave, saying they will see us at dinner. I'm not sure how to interpret the theological discussion we just had, but no one is upset, and both parties seem to respect the other's choices, so I guess this is a good outcome… but now all I can think about is Bill's reaction. Of course, as soon as the doors close, I snort then we all start laughing.

"Oh man, that was too funny. I can't believe you said it," Elli says, still laughing.

"I'm just as surprised as you that it even came out at all!" Skye laughs out, wiping away a tear.

"Did neither of you see Bill before we got on the lift? He was blowing up," I manage to get out. But, of course, my comment gets even more laughs out of us.

Suddenly I start coughing, which gets Skye worried, and he instantly stops laughing to check on me. He touches my back and chest gently, but as I do, I get a pain in my chest; I slap a hand into my stitches to try to stop the pain, but it just makes things worse and makes me groan in pain.

"Okay, we need to get him to your room," Skye tells Elli, who grabs me away from Skye and starts to carry me just as the lift comes to our floor. I mumble out our room number and give Skye the key. It turns out we are pretty close to the elevator anyway and probably right next to Abi or, knowing our luck, next to her dad. Skye opens the door after some sort of kerfuffle with the key, I'm unsure what happens, but he is clearly annoyed with the key and the door. When we finally get into the room, Elli lays me down on the bed. He peels off my hoodie and T-shirt. As he does, I notice the blood on my shirt.

"Damn," I say. "That was my favourite shirt," I tell the men, who shake their heads at my comment. Skye is quick to get a first aid kit out of his bag. He cleans my wound and butterfly stitches the part of the incision that opened up again. Lucky for me, most of it has healed by now, but here I thought it would be a good idea not to wear my gauze. Skye bandages up the wound with a smaller gauze than before; he then mumbles something to himself and is about to leave without a word. "Hey!" I stop him.

"Percival, I have to get to my room," he tells me.

"Without a see you later? Nice try, mister. Come here," I tell him, I stand up, and he stands in front of me. I look him in the eye, then give him a hug. He stands there motionless for a moment before, gently, hugging back. That's when I let him go; he smiles and leave, probably to sleep. I move back to the bed and lay down, taking a breath.

"And just when I thought we could relax. We get 'mister, it isn't proper'. Reckon we'll ever catch a break?" Elli asks me, joining me on the bed; I turn over and face him, giving him a light kiss.

"Probably. Once we get that house we talked about, and you've been looking for." He looks at me confused. "I may have peeked at your phone while we were in the car." He shakes his head but kisses me; he opens his phone to the last house he was looking at. I cuddle into him and look with him.

"No more surprises," I say. "Promise?"

"Promise."

Insulted

So apparently, we both fell asleep within ten minutes of lying down because the next thing we know, Sammy is banging the door, telling us to open up. When we finally get up, we find him carrying shirts for us both, saying that we will be late for the rehearsal dinner. Lucky for us, we had only been sleeping for an hour. The shirts Sammy gave us were white and had a pocket on the left side; I decided it would be best to put something underneath if my makeshift stitches broke again. At least the shirt would be okay... for a bit, at least. I'm just glad I packed a white T-shirt and not my fireflies one; I was... Aw, man, I was wearing that one. Damn it, it is so hard to get blood out of a white shirt. Believe me, I've done it; I'd wear red, but I do *not* look good in it.

Anyway, we are both quick to get dressed. Elli helps me a little with my shoes since I can't really bend over right now; I objected, but he gave me his shut-up look, and I listened. **Simp.** It's a convincing look! Once we are dressed, we all head down to the restaurant, picking up a sharp-looking Skye along the way. Who insists that I do not laugh too much during dinner and eat as much as I can handle but push myself if I can. I swear I thought I was putting weight on? <u>You are, just slowly.</u> Too slowly, apparently.

We are, unsurprisingly, the last to arrive, and we are sat almost instantly next to the happy couple, on Sammy's right, of course, since we are his friends. Skye sits next to Abi, however. They exchange some words, and apparently, he is happy to do something, and there was something about a girl called Samantha? Who's that?

Although Sammy asks about a baby Katy sleeping upstairs, there are fourteen of us in total, so I guess that makes fifteen guests total. The table is nothing like I thought it would be; I feel like I could be at a family reunion. But of course, the one person I don't want to be close to is Abi's dad, and he is sitting right across from me. Fortunately, both my parents were only children, so no aunts or uncles. Sammy beckons Elli and me closer so he can talk to us without others hearing:

"I want you guys to know that you are my new favourite people; Bill would not stop going on about how outrageous it was that I invited you." He suppresses a laugh and continues, "When I told Michael, he almost woke up Katy." I got lost in that, but I know who Bill is; he's the guy giving me daggers from across the table.

"Question," I whisper, and Sammy nods. "Who is Michael?"

"Michael? He's my older brother. Haven't I told you about him?" We both shake our heads. "I suppose you did go right to bed when you arrived. I'd guess you know maybe five or six people here. And I doubt you could point out my parents," Sammy jokes, well, I can prove him wrong.

"Course I can. She's the blond one wearing the pastor's outfit whispering into her wife's ear, Lauren." Sammy's face drops. "Don't look so surprised we met in the lobby. Who else is here?"

"Well, across from you is Bill and Amanda, Abi's folks. Next to Bill is Lily and Ben, Abi's aunt and uncle. Samantha is next to Amanda; she's Abi's not so identical twin, so I've got that to look forward to." We both laugh at that. "Right across from us is Brendan and his dad, my annoying big brother, Michael. They almost didn't make it; Brendan got into some trouble at school. Turns out he was just acting out 'cause Michael was too distant. They sorted it out, though. It's been hard for them since Thalia died in childbirth last year."

"So, why do I get the feeling… Bill wants to kill us?" I ask.

"Oh, is it because we are gay? 'Cause I'll kill him if he lays a finger on Percival," Elli butts in.

"Don't worry about him, he talks big, but Abi tells me he's basically harmless. I wasn't sure, but when I asked him if I could marry Abi, I thought he'd kill me, but I was wrong. He was just glad she was marrying such a stand-up man." Suddenly Sammy is called to his other side by his future wife, leaving Elli and me to talk.

"This is a lot of people," I mumble to myself.

"Are you going to be okay? You know that as one of Sammy's groomsmen, you have to stand up in front of them all," Elli asks, taking a spoon full of soup. I do the same, letting the warm liquid cascade down my throat, warming my chest up.

"Yeah, not like I'm saying anything when I'm up there," I joke, but that gets Elli thinking.

"Can I ask… would you ever want to be married?"

"I mean…" What do I mean? Do I want to get married? "I honestly don't know. I never thought I would live to see that day, if I'm honest."

"I'm not asking you to marry me. You realise that right," Elli says suddenly, making me laugh softly.

"Yeah, I know that. I guess—"

"I'm sorry, you two cannot be talking about your own marriage at my daughter's wedding. I won't have it!" Bill interrupts us, clearly someone who has gotten half a conversation.

"Dad, not now," Abi says.

"No, Abigail, I don't think it's very polite for these two… faggots to be discussing their marriage at yours. This is *your* day, not some man-slut who likes it up the ass."

Suddenly the room gets very… deafening. I can fucking hear everything, plates being stacked in the corner, the clatter of cutlery against the dishes and my heart in my ear… I have to go. I… I'm getting out of here. I apologise quickly and run from the room; even as I do, I hear people yelling. Why does everyone have to yell? I have to cover my ears. I make my way outside and down to the road. I see a sign for the beach, so I run that way.

Why is life so loud! Cars make too much noise with their honking and engine revving and the indicators; birds are dumb too, they can all just… Just—

"SHUT THE FUCK UP!" I suddenly yell. I cover my mouth, shocked at my own outburst. Then I collapse onto the sand… oh. I made it to the beach. Listening to the waves helps. I try to just focus on them, but it's not easy. I can still hear all the birds and people talking loudly to each other. I look over, and I see that they are setting up for the wedding; oh fuck, the ceremony is tomorrow, isn't it? Ugh, do they have to be so loud? I wish I had my music, and… my headphones are dangling in front of me? I follow them up and find Elli looking down at me. He says hi and kisses my cheek handing me my headphones and phone. I quickly plug in and turn my music on. I keep one earphone out just in case Elli wants to ask questions. Nothing is said as I wrap my arm in his, intertwining our fingers and leaning my head on his shoulder. Surprisingly Sabaton is good music for calming me down since it's so loud.

"What's on?" Elli asks; I hold up the spare headphone, which he puts in and nods approvingly. He doesn't take it out; instead, we look out over the sea at sunset. Eventually, I stop the music and take in the scenery and the warm breeze running over the beach. I take a breath.

"I don't like him," I mumble.

"Ha, don't think anyone does after we explained. Nothing in-depth; I just said you had a problem with anxiety, and confrontation doesn't help. Also, the right hook I gave Bill might have set the point across."

"Damn... I wanted to hit him." I smile up at Elli, and we lean in for a kiss, but just as we do...

"YO, PERCIVAL!" Sammy shouts from across the beach, my head dips in annoyance, and I look over to see him arriving with Abi and Skye in tow. We wait patiently for them to come over and sit down around us.

"So, Skye mentioned you both have news for us?" Abi starts, looking between us.

"Oh? Do we have news, sunshine?" Elli asks, playing the fool... why not?

"Not that I can recall, hun. Is there something we're missing?"

"Could it be that little thing that happened?"

"Do you mean when Skye didn't call Jay? Or that we are... Nah, it can't be that, can it?"

"Cut the crap, you two." Sammy laughs.

"But we're having fun." Elli pouts. I look at my boyfriend. "Fine, you tell them."

"Look, it's not a big deal anyway," I start. "But we did get to talking, and well, we are together now."

"Are you kidding? This is huge!" Sammy yells. I flinch somewhat but not enough for anyone to notice.

"Turns out I actually scared him into forgetting a few things when we were younger. He remembered them, though, so it's all good," Elli continues for me.

"What did you forget, Per?" Abi asks me softly. I pause for

a moment, take a breath then tell them.

"I've been in love with Elli for fourteen years. The day I told you about, that started my questioning, scared me into forgetting the real reason I was going to see this idiot that day."

"So, you two could have been together and married already if it wasn't for the wanking idiot next to you?" Skye asks; I nod. There is a silence that falls over us. It's peaceful, just the waves hitting the sand. Until Sammy starts laughing, then Abi, and eventually I do too. This is nice, though, peaceful.

"So, were you really discussing your own marriage at my rehearsal dinner?" Abi asks us.

"Not the greatest place to discuss it, I'll admit, but I was curious if we were going to at some point," Elli explains, and I think I finally have my answer.

"I... I wouldn't be opposed to the idea. Not now though, let's cement our relationship first before we go there," I tell him.

"Hey." He lifts my head to look in his eyes. "We can go as slow as we need; I'm not leaving you again." He kisses me, then pulls me in between his legs and wraps his arms carefully around my belly. I smile and blush slightly.

"So, to clarify, you're going slow... but you're looking at houses?" Skye asks, which makes everyone start debating whether house hunting is too fast for our relationship or if it's the right speed since we basically already live together. I need someone to look after me anyway. I take issue with that but, at the same time, I can't argue since Elli literally tied my shoes earlier today.

After another hour on the beach, we all walk barefoot, back to the hotel hand in hand with our significant other, except for Skye. Apparently, he is taking Samantha's place in the wedding as Abi's maid of honour. She got really annoyed that she had no say in the new nuptials and quit. Her loss. Now Skye just has to get Abi down to the beach tomorrow afternoon. We all head our separate ways after we get in. Sammy and Abi have to talk down her dad, Skye has to go with them as maid of honour, and we decide to go to bed. Anxiety attacks are not fun, and they are tiring. So, Elli and I head right up to bed.

I change out of my shirt and nice clothes and into my oversized hoodie, which I take off within two minutes of putting on 'cause it's too damned hot. So now I'm in my underwear in the bathroom, scared to leave 'cause of the scars on my stomach and chest that I keep tracing. Eventually, there is a knock at the door, which is locked.

"Sunshine? You okay?" Elli asks.

"I… I know you don't like my scars, and I want to cover them up, but it's too hot for my hoodie, so I'm not sure what to do." I rush out.

"Sunshine, I don't care about your scars, just come out and come to bed. If you really want, I can turn the lights off." He barters. I say nothing in return, but I do get closer to the door. "I'm worried about you, Percival, please open the door."

I open the door, and Elli is sitting on the bed, also in his underwear, his hands fidgeting with each other; I clear my throat, and he looks up. He's not crying, but he does smile when he sees me, I cover my stomach and chest and walk into the room. He meets me halfway, wrapping himself around me. My hands drop from my chest and belly and find their way around him. I smile to myself, this is real love, this. Patience, acceptance and just a touch of PDA. Okay, a lot. We separate, and Elli leads me to the bed and motions me to lay down. Which I do, when I do, I find him wrapping his arms around me again, pulling me in close. Then I close my eyes and fall into yet another dreamless sleep.

Having Sex?

When I wake up, I find that Elli and I stopped cuddling during the night; I'm not complaining, though. I have to pee. I quietly remove the covers and step out of bed. I'm tiptoeing towards the bathroom when I see my bag from the corner of my eye. I hesitate before grabbing it and finally heading into the bathroom, which I lock quietly. I don't want to wake Elli up.

Why did I grab my bag? Well, I kinda figured that I would have some kind of panic attack and want to clean. Since it's not a good idea to clean hotel rooms, cleaning myself would be the next best thing. So I brought my toothbrush, razors, shaving foam, aftershave, and my anal douche with that in mind. Now I'll be honest, I didn't think I would be using a douche for a long time, but... yeah.

I've been feeling kinda backed up, and when I found it while I was packing, I thought, why not? So I quietly place everything where it needs to be; razors in the shower and by the sink, along with the toothbrush, shaving foam and aftershave. I also grab the small bottle of lube that I brought just if I decided to use it.

I strip myself of my underwear and turn on the hot tap waiting for it to heat up. Once it does, I fill up my douche and screw on the top. I apply a generous amount of lube to the nozzle and then some more to my ass. I drop down to my knees, then carefully insert the douche into my hole, making sure it's all in before I squeeze the water into me. It feels bizarre. I haven't done this in about two months; it feels like I'm out of practice. Should

I have brought along a dildo? Oh, wait, I couldn't, I don't have any anymore.

After waiting for nearly ten minutes, and shaking my hips, I'm finally on the loo. It's over quite quickly, but I feel loads better already, and I got to pee. I debated having another one, but it did the job I wanted, so another one is just pushing my luck. I turn on the shower, and while I wait for it to heat up, I clean the douche out and brush my teeth. I check the heat, happy with it. I remove the bandages on my arm and lower chest and step into the heat.

I enjoy showering. The heat is excellent on your muscles. It's not as relaxing as a bath, but that's not the point of a shower. I run my hair under the water, and it flattens down over my head, almost covering my eyes, so I force it back then start cleaning. There is a loofah in the shower; I grab it, coat it in shower gel and begin to scrub my body. I don't mean to, but I tend to cleanse my body too hard, not enough to break my scars but enough that my skin starts to feel a little raw. Once I'm satisfied I'm clean, I wash off the soap then grab my razor. I shave away the tiny amount of hair that has grown since my last shave. I consider myself kind of lucky that I don't really grow hair on my chest, one less thing to worry about hair-wise.

I double-check myself and use the loofah again to make sure there is no hair left. Once I'm satisfied, I place the razor down. I clean my hair relatively quickly. I always think the hair on my head is the easiest to clean. After all, you are basically giving yourself a head massage, so by the time you are actually done, you don't realise 'cause you're more relaxed than before. I wash out the soap, then stand under the showerhead for a few minutes before turning it off and step out, wrapping a towel around my waist. The good thing about hotels is that they keep the towels in the bathroom, so you don't have to remember to bring them in.

Oh, lucky me, the mirror over the sink is one of those anti-steam mirrors, so it hasn't fogged up. So, smiling to myself, I grab my shaving foam and get started on my face. Of course, there isn't that much hair but still, not having it.

I remember the first time I shaved; Dad walked me through it. Bought me everything I needed, even taught Elli simultaneously, although his parents had to buy his stuff for him. Dad loves Elli, but he felt that his parents should be paying for personal grooming equipment, not him. So there we were in the bathroom with my dad telling us how to apply the shaving foam. Once we finished using it, he told us to wash our hands and pick up the razors. Next, he mentioned that we should fill the sink with some warm water to remove any hairs that come away. After that, it was up to us to start. I remember Elli and me looking at each other in the mirror, willing the other to go first. In the end, I went first and ended up cutting a bit of my face, that part just beside the ear. Dad stopped immediately to check it, wiping off the shaving foam. Then took me to his study, where he had to stitch up the cut. I still have a small white mark.

Dad admitted it was his fault, that he should have walked us through it a bit more than he did. I told him it was okay to learn, but this wouldn't stop me from shaving. We returned to the bathroom, where Elli waited patiently, and Dad talked him through it step by step. Elli nicked himself a few times, but nothing like my cut. When I got back to shaving after I healed, Dad walked me through the process again, and I didn't cut myself at all. Elli was jealous, so he had to mention the cut I got the first time I *actually* shaved. I think he still does; it's been a while. I finish shaving just as there is a knock at the door.

"Hey, sunshine, you in there?" Elli asks, sounding worried.

"No," I reply, suppressing my laughter.

"Oh, okay, sorry I... hey! I know it's you!" he yells back, and I burst out laughing.

"Sorry I couldn't help myself." I wipe my face and start applying some aftershave.

"Everything okay in there? You've been in a while," he asks.

"Yeah, I was just cleaning. Myself before you think I'm cleaning the bathroom." I wash and dry my hands, then unlock the door causing Elli to jump back.

"Oh..." He looks down. Seeing me in only a towel makes him blush, then I blush because I didn't even mean to leave without my underwear on.

"I'll... I'll get dressed," I say, backing into the bathroom again.

"NO!" Elli clears his throat. "No. It's fine, just unexpected." He smiles at me and then goes over to the bed; he pats the side I slept on twice. I hesitate, really wanting to put my boxers back on, but I decide to just go sit. Elli won't do anything I don't want him to do. To be honest, I'd be surprised if he wouldn't strip naked if I asked him... **Let's try it.** We shouldn't, but yeah, let's. I sit down and deliberately start acting awkward.

"So, what are... What are we gonna do today?" I ask, deliberately pausing.

"Well, the wedding isn't until one, and it's seven now, so I was thinking breakfast then see what the hotel has to offer," he replies, looking at me.

"Cool... Cool, cool." I shuffle slightly, and I hear him sigh.

"Okay. What's wrong?" he asks, facing me.

"It's nothing. I'm... I'm just very aware that I'm naked and you're not." I scratch the back of my head and try not to look at him. Why did you talk me into this? **I didn't; you talked**

yourself into it; I just agreed. Once again, Elli sighs and then I feel his underwear hit my head, blinding my vision.

"There, are you happy now?" he says, getting under the covers. I smile and nod at him. "Good, now get that towel off and come over for cuddles," he tells me, and I smile even more. I drop the towel away, and I slip under the covers to start cuddling Elli. Perfect.

Although. I can't help noticing the tent that has appeared under the covers around Elli's dick. I'm trying not to stare but the hard on I'm sporting isn't helping. I quickly readjust myself, so it's not poking him, but I think it was too late. He doesn't say anything. He just keeps looking at his phone, me too but to a lesser degree. Elli puts down his phone and kisses my forehead gently, making me look up at him making us kiss. I deepen the kiss and run my hand over his toned stomach. His hands wander all over my back, tracing a few of my scars. It, shockingly, doesn't make me that uncomfortable. I break the kiss then straddle him, wrapping my legs around his back so I can kiss him more.

I have no idea what's gotten into me, but I am enjoying this. Elli separates his legs, and I slip down between him, our rock-hard cocks brushing up against one another. Elli breaks the kiss this time, then reaches over and produces some lube for us. I hold out my hand for some lube, which he gives me. I take it and coat his throbbing member; he whimpers deeply as I touch him. I start to kiss his neck, making sure to suck at his sweet spot. While I do that, I slowly pump his cut member from top to bottom, working the head more and more. When he tells me to stop, I do, then use the remaining lube on my hand and start playing with his nipple. We get back to kissing.

As we kiss, Elli's hand wanders down to my own cock, and

he starts stroking it. Just like me, he goes slowly. He lifts me up with his other hand, crossing his legs, basically propping up my ass. His hand disappears for a moment, but he starts massaging a cold liquid onto my hole when he returns. I flinch, and he breaks the kiss and stops everything. He moves a hand around my back, supporting me looking into my eyes. I look back at him, nodding at him, letting him know that I'll be okay. He knows I'll tell him to stop if it's too much for me. He nods, then starts kissing my neck and nipples as he massages my hole, slipping the tip of his finger every so often. He sucks on my nipples as I moan softly, gripping onto him. Not for dear life; I just don't want him to stop.

He works his way back up my neck, and we start kissing again, but this time Elli slips his full finger into my hole. It feels foreign, but it also feels nice having something in there again… am I addicted to anal play? Possibly, but right now, I feel too good to care. I pinch Elli's nipple again, making him wince, and in retaliation, he slides another finger into my clean hole. I can't help but moan loudly as his second finger slides into me. I love it; I *want* more. I start kissing him more, gently rocking on his fingers. I may as well beg for his cock 'cause, let's face it, I want it right now, and I really didn't think I would be having this soon.

"Elli… hhnnngg, p-please," I moan out as I rock on his fingers.

"Please what, sunshine?" he asks seductively. I shiver as his fingers move in and out of me.

"I want you inside me. I… I want your cock," I moan, but the only reason I'm surprised right now is that I never say cock. Elli comes closer to me and kisses my neck; he asks if I'm sure, and I nod. Then when he gets to my ear, he breaths on it lightly, shooting shivers all over my body.

"Say please," he whispers, it's enough effort to not just force him into me, but I refrain and say please.

His fingers leave my hole, and he recoats his dick in a thick helping of lube, then lines himself up. He looks worried, so I reach a hand back and take his dick in my hand, helping him to line up. It just reassures him that I want this. He kisses me lightly as he slowly guide himself into my expanding hole, I moan the entire way down his shaft, and when I get as far as I can, I take a few breaths. Once again, Elli asks if I'm okay. I nod. Then he tells me to open my eyes and look at him. I hadn't realised they were closed. Still, I do listen and open my eyes. He smiles at me, and he's sweaty all over, but I realise that this is different. This isn't just a quick fuck, or rape even. This is a man who truly loves me and wants me to feel as good as he does. I kiss him deeply and start to bounce on his still throbbing member.

A few times, as I was enjoying the feeling of Elli being deep inside me, he would try and stroke me off, but after the third time and him slipping out, we both agreed that I could wait to cum. Besides the position we're in is perfect and is hitting the best spot in the world. My prostate. I think I'll need to go faster to get close to cumming. I look at Elli, and he kisses me lightly then grips my hips. That's when he takes over, he starts slamming his cock right against my prostate! I can't help but scream in pleasure. Fuck! This feels incredible, and with all the foreplay we were doing, I think we are both close to finishing.

"Ahh! Sunshine... I think... I'm..." Suddenly, with one last thrust, I can tell that Elli finishes off inside me, and as he does, he strokes my cock just enough that I cum all over him and moan out in pure ecstasy. I lean forwards and feel Elli's deflating meat exit my hole, and I end up collapsing on his chest, covering us both in my cum. We both breathe deeply into the other body, eyes closed, wishing we had a drink. I turn my head and look at the time. Half eight, we were at it for almost an hour and a half.

"Best hour and a half I've ever spent," I mumble to him. Told you I'd get hands free sex, Nemesis. **That you did, consider me satisfied.**

"I don't know about you, but I think we need to shower," Elli suggests.

"Yeah…" I sit up and look at him. "And the day is still young," I say suggestively.

"Oh my, Mister Grace," he says, surprised. I carefully get up, taking him by the hand and leading him to the bathroom.

"Can you blame me? You are the best I've ever had." I turn around, exposing my ass to him, and all he can do is moan and follow me into the shower.

Embarrassed

We may have ended up having sex twice more before we got close to leaving our bedroom. Can't say I blame us; in reality, we have probably been waiting to have sex with each other since I first caught Elli wanking all of fourteen years ago. I managed to actually cum hands-free when we were in the shower, satisfying Nemesis even more. And my gods, do I love the way Elli and I have sex. He is the best I've ever had; I wasn't just saying that to entice him.

When we finally get dressed, we walk down to the lobby hand in hand. We look out for our friends and find them at a five-person table. Two seats are waiting for us, and as the perfect gentleman, Elli holds out my chair for me, and I graciously take it. Instantly our friends can tell that something is up with us. First, I watch them all stare at us, wondering what has changed, then I think it is Skye who finally clicks to it.

"I cannot believe you two!" he whisper-shouts; he seems pretty horrified.

"What?" I ask, drinking the water from my glass.

"You had sex even though—"

"I'm gonna stop you right there," I interrupt him, "everything we did in our room is between us, and I consented to it."

"Three times," Elli mentions, causing me to blush and giggle at the same time.

"Damn... didn't think you had it in you, Elliot. Good job," Abi says, slapping his back. Skye, having given up telling us off, decided he wants in on the action too.

"So, who was on top?" He starts on his food that had just arrived. We order our own breakfast before answering him.

"I was, never saw Per as much of a top," Elli says.

"What is this? Embarrass Percival morning?" I mumble trying, and failing, to hide my blush.

"In fairness, not only am I correct. I did find all your dildos when you moved in with me."

"You did!" I shout a little too loud.

"In his defence, I found them and asked about them." Sammy perks up, I groan, and my head hits the table. Elli rubs my back and then slides down to rub my lower back, I look at him, and he knows not to go any further. When I sit back up, I pull my chair closer to Elli and lean on his shoulder. Then from behind, I hear a gruff cough, signifying that someone wants my attention. I don't listen to it at first, but I turn around when he does it again.

Before me stand Bill and his wife, who nudges her husband to start talking. He doesn't say anything at first, but when Elli stands up and stares him down, that's when he starts talking. The man flinches slightly at Elli, and I notice that he has a slight black eye that must be from where Elli hit him last night. Hopefully, it knocked some sense into him. At the moment, he is wearing casual clothes but still manages to look smart; I pull Elli back onto his chair before Bill starts to talk:

"I was told my words at dinner last night could be considered... offensive. So, I am sorry for my crude words."

"Are you?" I ask; he seems startled at my response. "Sorry, I mean? 'Cause people have been saying that a lot to me, and I'm starting to believe it less and less." Of course, that last part is a half-lie, but Bill doesn't need to know that. But I can see him ponder his reason behind apologising.

"What did you say your name was again?"

"Percival Grace."

"Hmm, yes, I read about your situation in the news. I'll admit, had I realised the extent of your PTSD, I might have stayed quiet... but you are right; I am not sorry for what I said. You should *not* have been discussing getting married at my daughter's wedding."

"Nor were we. Elliot was simply asking if it was a possibility. Which I couldn't answer at the time."

"Hmm, in that case, I apologise for overstepping. I hope you will accept." I ponder Bill's apology, deliberately as I can see my food coming over. Once it is close enough, I accept his apology and shake the hand he offers. We all say goodbye, and I finally get to have my food. I hear the two adults mumble as they leave for their own table, probably, and I'm pretty sure I hear Bill say he respected me. Amanda jokes and says that I'm the only gay he respects, after that they are out of ear shot. So, you know, that makes me feel a little better. Everyone seems really surprised at my attitude towards Bill, but no one says anything.

Pancakes are my favourite hot breakfast; no joke. They are excellent; it's a shame that they make them with milk, and I can't have them. I thought about having something else, but I'm not really focusing on the ingredients. It wasn't until Skye started kicking up a fuss when I realised what was happening. For the record, I did *not* have an allergic reaction, almost did, though. I wasn't really even paying attention, almost like someone keeps forgetting I'm lactose intolerant...

Anyway, Skye marches into the kitchen and demands

someone makes some milk-free pancakes. Of course, it makes Elli a little jealous, but I calmed him down, mentioning that he is the one that gets to take me home tonight, I wiggle my eyebrows at him, and he fully understands what I mean. But, unfortunately, so do Sammy and Abi.

"Man, you guys really want to get at it," Sammy casually mentions.

"I think it's cute," Abi says, finishing her orange juice.

"Hey, I've missed six years of good sex; I'm making up for the time I've lost," I say, leaning over to kiss him.

"You wanna make up some time right now?" Elli offers; I shake my head.

"I think my doctor has other plans." I nod towards Skye, who comes over with, quite frankly, a massive plate of pancakes.

"I know there is a lot, but there isn't any milk in any of them. I was vigilant."

"Skye, Percival will never be able to eat all that," Abi says. I keep staring at the pancakes. I'm not used to getting so much food. I slowly start on the pancakes while Abi and Skye debate what I need. Meanwhile, Elli encourages me to keep eating and is doing a better job than the other two. They argue at my table so much, they don't notice I finish the whole plate until I burp loudly. Nothing is said until I suggest that we all go and get ready for the wedding since it is almost half eleven. Everyone agrees. I take Elli's hand, and we walk back up to our room. Where yes… we have sex again. With protection this time. Elli finished me off after he came, but it was still amazing.

Once we finished fooling around, there was a knock at the door. It's Sammy; he asks if we are done, making me blush as Elli opens the door. Turns out Skye was with him. He looks annoyed that I just had sex again, I know he's my doctor, but really this is good for me... right? Apparently sensing the awkward atmosphere between us, Elli claps his hands together and suggests we get Sammy ready for the wedding. We all shove a naked Sammy into the shower, because he really does stink. Then we start to sort out our hair. Elli is unsurprisingly good with my hair and manages to tame it into my old undercut look, although I suppose it's usual for him.

Once Sammy gets out of the shower, Elli jumps in, saying he has a surprise for us. He then proceeds to lock the door and not tell us what he is doing. While he does his thing, I help Sammy get ready with his hair and suit. Although I can't find it, I grab some smarter shorts in the bag labelled 'For the Groom and His Men' for some reason, though all that's in there are four pairs of shorts and rather tight undershirts. We all pull them on and laugh at how dumb we look.

Just then, Elli steps out of the shower in underwear. The other guys look away, but I can't help but stare at the package beneath those shorts. **Yum.** Elliot's package was so distracting that I almost missed him pulling out four floral shirts that Sammy had obviously not picked out. Elli seems to have picked out our favourite colours too; pink, blue, green and purple. Can't say I'm complaining since I get the green shirt, Sammy gets a dark blue, Skye the purple, and Elli gets the pink. Then I notice that he is wearing a towel on his head. He pulls it off as I'm about to ask about it, revealing his rejuvenated green hair that matches the floral shirt I just got. Way to be subtle, love, and I'm blushing again. I sigh and pull on the shirt.

Once we are all ready, excluding our shoes for obvious reasons, we all start towards the beach. It's about half twelve, and Emma will not be happy if we make Sammy late for his own wedding. He was let off easy the last time, from what he has told us. As we walk towards the beach, Elli whispers that we could have dyed my hair pink to match his shirt, so I reply that we can do it when we get back up to the room. He smiles instantly. Gods, I love that smile. When we make it to the end of the aisle, where Emma and Sammy are waiting. I realise that Skye has left, probably to check on the bride.

We wait a little bit before the music starts, and we all move into our positions. Elli has to help me. Since I wasn't in the first ceremony, I had nowhere to stand, but next to my boyfriend seems appropriate for this one. From what I can gather, too, this is very different from the last one. Before, they went for a traditional wedding where the groom's men walk up with the bridesmaids, but I guess they are forgoing that tradition since there are only two of them.

What they aren't missing is Brendan and his baby sister walking up the aisle. I thought he was the ring bearer, not his sis… oh, wait, they had an issue with Katy. Once Katy is with her dad, Brendan comes over and joins us, standing a little in front of us. Finally, here comes the blushing bride walking down the aisle by her father. Skye, following close behind. Wow does she look good, I know I saw the dress when I was in the hospital but the lighting was terrible. Here she looks amazing, truly. Bill and Abi make it to the altar and Bill kisses her cheek. He passes her hand to Sammy, and they exchange a few words. Mainly along the lines of don't ever hurt her. Then the ceremony begins.

"Welcome friends and families of Sammy and Abigail. Perhaps this time, we won't have any accidents." The crowd laughs. "We are gathered here at the site of this white sandy beach, and Our Lord God to join these two people in holy matrimony. I know for a fact that you have both prepared your own vows since I wouldn't perform the wedding without them.

Without further ado, Samuel."

"Really, Ma?" Sammy says, shaking his head, then he clears his throat and takes Abi's hands. "Abi, four years ago, while searching for my best friend, we ran into each other, and since then, I can no longer imagine a day without you. You are brilliant, intelligent. You don't take my shit, or anyone else's for that matter, and you never once stopped supporting me in everything. Then last month, during that car crash, the one thing I never thought possible happened. I know the risk of me dying was almost zero, but, and I'll be honest, it's great to have you back, Per, but I couldn't stop thinking about you, Abi. You are the love of my life; I don't think I could ever love anyone more than I love you. Except for maybe one other person." Suddenly they both giggle, and she slaps him lightly on the arm. "Ouch... I hope you will take me as I am. I love you." He hugs her, but they are separated by his mother. I wonder what that was about? <u>Should we tell him?</u> **No, he should figure it out himself.** You guys are no fun.

"All right, we'll get to that soon. Abigail, your turn," Emma says. Abi takes a deep breath and looks at Sammy.

"I never saw the need to write vows. I thought they were... kinda dumb, but now, standing here, I finally understand why they are important. Four years ago, you were more worried about your lost friend than me. Or so I thought, I found I was wrong. You were kind and attentive even when you had so much more going on. And the day you proposed, I was almost going to say no. What changed my mind was when I realised how much I loved you. You were still there with me, even with Percival missing, and now he's back. You still love me, and I love you. I don't want anyone else but you."

"Who has the ring?" Emma asks. Besides me, Brendan

jumps slightly at getting called on but steps forward confidently and holds out the rings. I manage to sneak him a quick thumbs up which makes him smile. Abi and Sammy take the rings, and they hold them in their hands. "Abigail, do you promise yourself to Samuel, to love and to cherish, to have and to hold as long as you both shall live?" Emma asks, and Abi says: I do. "Then repeat after me…"

"I, Abigail, take thee, Sammy, to be my lawful wedded husband, in sickness and in health as long as we both shall live, and with this ring, I thee wed," Abi repeats. Emma then asks Sammy the same question and to repeat after her.

"I, Sammy, take thee, Abigail, to be my lawful wedded wife, in sickness and in health as long as we both shall live, and with this ring, I thee wed."

"It is on this day that Samuel and Abigail consent to love each other and by the power invested in me by the—"

"Oh, shut up, Pastor!" someone shouts. I don't bother looking. I'm too pissed. They were *this* close to being married, and some idiot has brought it to a stop. I paid for a lot of this, so yeah, it may not be my day, but I have a right to be pissed.

"With all due respect, you have no authority here."

"Oh really. Maybe this will change your mind." I hear a gun load, and my head springs up. Oh fuck. Why is he here? He can't be here. He's in jail. How the fuck did he get out? "Now, let's try this shit again. Stop the wedding, and give me what I want."

<u>Son of a godsdamn bitch!</u>

Stolen

How can he be here? He should be back in Scotland in a jail cell, hopefully getting beaten up by some overly buff gay man who he called a faggot or some shit like that. That would have made me really happy to hear, actually. But, instead, he's here and has a fucking gun, and he wants me! I… I don't think I'll be getting out of this one. I look at Elli and take his hand from behind him; I'm not leaving him. But, I can also tell I'm not going anywhere based on the pressure he exerts on my hand. He must be pissed enough that he is hurting me a little. I rub the back of his hand a little, and he calms down.

"Just who the hell do you think you are interrupting this wedding?" Wait, that was Bill asking that. What is he doing? I look over to him, and our eyes connect. He smiles at me and winks. What does that mean? Am I supposed to know why he's winked at me?

"Stay out of this, old man. I just want what's mine." He raises the gun to Bill; Bill seems unfazed by the gun pointing at him.

"I cannot see anything here that could possibly be yours. Did you pay for this wedding? No, you didn't. All you've done so far is stop my daughter from getting married. So, do us all a favour and—"

I hear a scream from the seats, and Bill is on the floor… bleeding. HOLY SHIT, HE SHOT HIM. <u>Calm, Percival, he will</u>

<u>not kill you, you know this.</u> Then there's only one thing I can do. Suddenly I'm moving, and I've jumped into the aisle to protect Bill.

"S-stop, w-what are you d-d-doing?" I stutter out, raising my hands in an attempt to stop him from shooting anyone else.

"Baby, there you are! Come on, we're leaving," he tells me.

"N… n-no. I'm here f-f-for this w-wedding, and I w-will s-see it through."

"You've seen enough. Now come on, I won't tell you again." He motions me towards him with his gun.

"NO! Fuck you. Percival isn't going anywhere," Elli yells. <u>He *will* get shot if you do not stop him.</u>

"Elli s-stop." I stand in front of him, my hands on his chest. I can feel my tears welling up already; I don't have a choice. If Elliot dies, then so do I. "I won't l-let you g-g-get hurt because of m-m-me."

"No! Sunshine, please… I-I can't lose you again," he whispers, "please just…" I wipe a tear away from his eye. Oh wait, he can find me! Oh shit! Before I did all that cleaning, I reactivated the tracker on my phone but changed things to activate only if the password is correct. I just have to make sure that Elliot can guess the password. I pull him into a kiss and hug him, placing my lips next to his ear.

"I'm sorry, Elli. You can stop him, just watch the sun fade, and think of me." I break the hug and turn away from him, willing myself not to cry. I take a breath and walk towards my ex to save everyone. That is the next right thing. One life for fourteen. My life for theirs. I watch *him* pull me into an overly tight hug. I feel like I'm just along for the ride now. I hear him yell… something, then he's grabbing my arm and pulling me away from the wedding. Skye can handle Bill; he's probably dealt with similar... although there aren't many gunshot wounds in Scotland. All I can really hope right now is that Elli got my message. If he gets it, then he can save me, and I will be saved. I just have to hang on until they find me again.

He pushes me against a car, and I hit my head against the window. I rub my head annoyed but not really wanting to piss him off. He walks around to the other side of the car and opens the driver's side. How the fuck did he get his car all the way to the south of France, he would have to know exactly where I was going to be. He tells me to get in, and I do. When I sit down, I notice that there is someone in the back seat.

"JAY!" I reach back to try to undo the gag and ropes he is tied up in. But, before I can get close, I'm pulled away from him and held in the passenger seat.

"I see you two have met. Well, your little friend here has been beneficial in telling me where you were going to be, and he was just itching for my cock. I barely needed to persuade him. But, of course, he got furious when he found out who I was. So now he's going to shut up forever." He points the gun at Jay's head, and Jay starts to whimper in fear.

"S... stop, y-you d-don't need to k-kill him," I force out, grabbing his free arm trying to pull the gun away from Jay's face. My eyes connect with Jay's for a moment, I can tell he is terrified. He also can't quite believe that *this* was the guy I dated after him. Unfortunately, I can also know that he will do anything to stay alive. "Y-you... y-you could u-u-use both of us," I suggest, his gun drops slightly. He turns all the way around and starts the engine. I quickly jump into the back seats and buckle Jay and myself up. He doesn't seem to mind. Once we get going, I carefully pull Jay's gag down and tell him to be quiet.

"This fucker is your ex?" he mouths. I roll my eyes and nod.

"You slept with him too?" I mouth back. He huffs and shakes his head and mouths the one thing I really was hoping he wouldn't.

"Rape." I sigh.

"What's going on back there?" *he* asks; I quickly replace the gag in Jay's mouth despite his objections and answer.

"N-nothing, just making s-sure he c-can't g-get out." I really hope he buys that; he doesn't respond, so I can only hope. Looking out the window, I notice that we are staying along the coast, which confuses me. Logically speaking, using a boat to escape is the best way not to be found by local law enforcement. Thank you for that, Skylar. "W-why are w-we sticking to the c-c-coast?"

"Only way I'll be able to get out of this godforsaken county is over international water, now shut up!" he tells me.

I don't dare risk talking or taking Jay's gag out again while we drive for the next hour. Any input, Nemesis? **Oh, dude, our emotions are all over the place; best not to ask me.** Wait... I thought you were just my horny thoughts, not my emotional thoughts? **Well... you thought wrong; honestly, he's known us for twenty years and still doesn't know why we exist.** You are extensions of my consciousness, the parts that allow me to understand my emotions or complex social situations. Seems he does know, Nemesis. **Shut up, nerd.** I smile to myself. What would I do without these two?

"Get out. We're here," *he* says. I unbuckle myself and Jay only to find that I am being pulled out of the car and Jay has been left behind. I protest, trying to run back to the car to get him. Instead, the back of my ex's hand is smacked against my head, and I fall into a daze. He pulls me into a hotel. I can tell it's small and definitely off the map. From my dazed state I barely manage to read the name. I mean, should be easy to find with the tracking, hardly anything is off modern maps. He asks for a room for him and his husband. I internally gag at that. The receptionist looks like he wants to ask questions. I force my head to slouch, making my… kidnapper catch me before I fall to the floor. In doing this, I grab the receptionist's eyes, making sure mine scream for his help.

"Iz everything all right, sir? Your partner lookz unwell," the girl asks; I can hear her heavy French accent.

"Oh him? He's fine." He leans in closer and whispers the next part; I can still hear, though. "He's a schizophrenic and has had a bit too much to drink. He'll say the voices made him do it." He leans away again, and the receptionist looks at me. I… I think I manage to shake my head, but she does nothing about it, just hands over the keys to the room. He throws me over his shoulder and starts walking towards our room. While we walk up the stairs, I hear the phone ring, I manage to see her look at me once more before her eyes widen with fear, and she moves out of my vision.

The one thing I never understood about this asshat is that despite the fact he likes seeing me bleeding, bruised and in pain, he can be incredibly gentle with me like right now. He almost hits my head on the door, and when he realises that, he sits me down on the bed and checks over my head, even giving me a few kisses that I don't reciprocate. Once he realises I'm okay, though, he gets up and goes into the bathroom and starts to talk about the last time we saw each other… I think.

"You shouldn't have run away, Percival, because now I have to punish you. And you know what happens to bad boys." He grabs my arm, and I see the flash of his knife. He stabs it into my forearm, and I scream in pain, only for him to cover my mouth to muffle the sound. He tuts at me, shaking his head. "Be quiet, or I'll forget to be nice." He starts to unbutton my shirt, exposing my bare, freshly shaven chest to the cold air of the hotel aircon. He expertly navigates around the knife, but I hear the sleeve rip slightly. The knife… It went right through my arm.

He forces me down and takes off my slip-on shoes, then my trousers and finally my underwear. I know what is going to happen. *Come on, Percival, fight back. This cannot be how it ends for you!* What? A… a new voice, who are you? *I am Daphnae, now grab the knife!* Now I get it, okay. I hold the blade still embedded in my arm and slowly start to pull it out. He turns his back and moves towards the door to make sure no one is coming, that's when I pull hard, and the knife slides out of my arm. I stand up shakily and tiptoe towards *him*. I get close enough, and I raise the blade to stab his back, but he turns around and grabs my wrist stopping me. I continue to push the knife towards him, however little that is. *Find a weakness and exploit it, bare feet!* I stomp on his foot hard, and the knife flies into his shoulder. He then forces me back, and the knife slips from my hands.

"Oh, you really shouldn't have done that." From my position on the floor, I watch him pull the knife out of his shoulder like it's nothing. "Now I have to punish you even more. I don't want to do this, but you must learn your place." He walks over to me, grabs my neck and lifts me up. He throws me onto the bed and holds me down; he smiles as he licks the bloody knife and stabs it into the headrest. He smiles at me sadistically and somehow manages to flip me over, and when did he get naked? *You need to fight, Percival. What resources do you have?* Just the knife. <u>If he tries to go for it, he will either lose it or use it against him.</u> So, my opt—

Oh, fuck, he's pushing into me! I try to move away from him, but he pushes down on my back, and I can't move. I reach my hand up and grab the top of the headrest, but he's entirely in me. I can feel him penetrating my ass, and it hurts. So much, I can't do this. *Yes, you can, Percival, you just have to get away from him. Run back to Elliot.* I look up and see the knife, I grab it, and then he is there grabbing my wrist.

"That's not for you," he says right next to my ear. He pulls my hand off the knife and takes it himself, then I feel him push it and his slimy member into my body. I can't help but scream, why me? Why can't I have my happy ending? Why did this mistake ruin so many lives; Why am I lying here taking this? *Fight, Percival.* <u>Fight, Percival.</u> **Fight, Percival.**

<u>Fight, Percival!</u> I spin my body around my hand, balled into a fist, but before I can even hit him, his hand connects with the side of my face, and I hit the pillow. I feel a needle prick my arm, and I fall limp, then the darkness overruns my mind.

Not Okay

My head hurts. My body hurts. I'm hurt but alive, I guess. I'm not tied down; that's a plus, but this bed is very uncomfortable. Wait, what's that? I can hear someone else breathing. It's light, not heavy like *his* breathing. I peel open my eyes, and the sun that is streaming in blinds me momentarily. I carefully try again, and they adjust to the new light. I look at the person in the bed with me. They are also, probably, naked, and their hair is… it's Jay. I carefully lay my hand on his shoulder, making him flinch. When he sees me, he calms down; I offer him a cuddle that he graciously takes, placing his head on my chest and arms around my waist. I return the hug and carefully rub his back which also has fresh bandages on it. Seems he had his way with both of us; I was hoping that he'd leave Jay alone, clearly not.

"H-he didn't even untie me. Just fucked me, and…"

"H-he used me again t-then untied you, t-to use y-y-you again." Takes all that is left in me not to cry. I guess I have my new friend to help with the support. *That you do.*

"He patched you up after he was done. I didn't… I couldn't stop him."

"It's f-fine. We are gonna get out of h-here." Jay laughs.

"It's not, but your stutter is back."

I don't make a comment on that. Yes, I am fully aware that my stutter had finally seemed to stop in the last few weeks. I didn't want to mention it in case it decided to return. Doesn't matter now, I suppose. It's back, and I think it's here to stay. **Not sure if this will help, but you didn't cum once last night.** How is that supposed to help? **It helps that you weren't enjoying it… and that I made sure you wouldn't.** That… is the nicest thing you've done for me. Like you said, we are a part of you. We may seem like we have different personalities. *But we are you.* I'm happy to have you all, even if you sound a bit like the other asshole voice who told me to hurt myself. *We are similar but different. I am your will to live and keep going.* She was the part of me that didn't want to live, the piece of me that was suicidal. She is still within you. She will never go away, but at least for now, she is suppressed, and Daphnae is in control.

In hearing that, I feel somewhat renewed. I take a breath and shakily get up, looking for my trousers. They are right where he left them, on the floor. I swing my legs over the side of the bed despite my body's protests; I quietly pray to Apollo for help and strength. I used to do this when I was younger; I haven't done it much recently, you can probably guess why. I slide down to the floor and grab my trousers; my underwear isn't in them, but they are close by, and I manage to grasp them. I pull them on and stand up then I start to fall. I get ready to hit the floor only to have someone grab my hips, keeping me standing. I see Jay holding me. I also see his still perky, if a little bruised, bare ass. I manage to sit back down on the bed with Jay's help. I reach into my trousers and pull out my phone – one new notification, asking me if I still want Elliot's phone to track me. I hear a car door close from outside. Shit! It might be him, be quick. I unlock my phone and accept the tracking, and I even send my location to him for good measure. I manage to put the device back in my pocket before throwing them to the floor. *He* enters the room moments later and sees me sitting up. He smiles. Gods, I hate that smile.

"Good, you're up. Need help getting dressed, baby?" he asks me in a sickly-sweet voice. Gods, why did I ever date this asshat. I manage to shake my head and pick my trousers back up, and carefully pull them on. I see Jay doing the same, although he is standing. I manage to pull my ripped shirt on and button it up, all the while he is watching the both of us. I spy my socks by the nightstand and grab them. It's hell pulling them on. I deliberately left my brace off as it was too bulky with the shoes. Now I'm paying for it. Fuck the other sock, my foot needs support. I painfully manage to get my sock on taking a breath, while I can I take the other sock and wrap it tightly around my ankle and the arch of my foot for support.

I don't care if I look like an idiot now. It's helping. I manage to get both my shoes on, one easier than the other, as you can imagine, and I stand up to look him down. Gonna need your strength here, Daphnae. *You have it, brother.* I smile inwardly at the way she speaks. He takes my arm gently then looks over to Jay. He has a sad sort of smile over his face. Suddenly he raises the gun. He gets to his peak quicker than I can stop him, and the gun fires. Jay falls to the floor, then a second later, I do too. With a pain in my cheek.

"You bitch! Great, now we have to go!" I look over to Jay from under the bed. His eyes are open in fear. He has a hand in his mouth suppressing his pain and another around his leg. *Ha! The asshole missed.* I am ripped unceremoniously from the floor and pulled out of the room. I smile inwardly to myself as I'm dragged to the car. I just saved Jay's life. I didn't mean to get him shot, but I saved him, and he only had one shot 'cause now the police will—

"Freeze!" Oh… speak of the devil. There are three cop cars outside the hotel and five officers, all pointing guns at us, but no

Elliot. I'm pulled in close to my idiot of an ex. He's using me as a human shield. Great. Maybe not! I feel the still-hot barrel of his gun being placed against my head, and just like that, all the cops lower their weapons.

"Now here's how this is going down; I'm getting in my car and driving away. If anyone of you follows us, this one takes the quick route to meet the devil." *The asshole holding a hostage is the only one meeting the devil today; talk about cowardly.* Not now, Daphnae.

He moves us towards the car and forces me into the driver's seat... oh fuck, it's been ages since I've driven. Oh, fuck, why am I... Why is he making me do this? I don't *want* to help him. Skylar, can you take over and drive for me? That is not how we work. Worth a shot at least. I start the engine, and suddenly it all comes back to me. It really is just like riding a bike. A three-tonne one at that, but still.

I remember the first time I drove was with my dad when I was fifteen. We were on holiday; Elliot came with us and started his lessons at the end of the year. Thanks to Dad, he already had his provisional licence sorted out. All he was waiting for now was to actually start. After that, Dad promised both of us that we could have our first drive in his car when we were on holiday. I called dibs and got to go first.

We used to go to the same place every year; Dad's workmate's father owned a farm in west Scotland. So, we got an excellent discount for the campsite, whenever we went away. Which was always at strange times, but never during the school year. Whenever we went away, which was always at strange times. But never during the school year. Since it was private land, we were allowed to practice. As promised, I got to go first, and when I sat at the wheel, I almost panicked when he told me to start the car. Noticing my panicked state, he walked me through it. He'd adapted his style of teaching after my shaving accident. Once I was actually driving, though, I found it relatively easy. Although I used the brake too much, Dad seemed to think I was a master at reversing, if I remember correctly. Annoyingly he got me to reverse the car back into its spot before he let me stop, and driving backwards is hard enough without a hill to contend with. Having said that I was successful.

Elliot did just as well as I did. But when it came to the reversing, Dad had to shout at him to stop before he ran into our caravan. When they came in for lunch, Mum and I couldn't stop laughing at Dad and Elliot's faces. By the end of the day, it became quite the joke between the four of us. I wonder if that story still holds its merit now that… that Mum has passed away?

I shake the memory from my head and reverse out of the hotel car park, surprising everyone around us. Mum always said I could be a race car driver if I wanted to be. I don't. Far too dangerous… That's a dumb thing to say since I've currently got a gun to my head. He tells me to drive a specific way, and I listen. I hope to all the gods that Elliot will find me. I manage to sneak a glance at the hotel, and I see two officers running into the building. At least Jay is in safe hands. I focus back on the road and increase our speed slightly. I notice that he tenses up. *It seems our big bully is scared of a bit of speed.* It would seem so; let's have some fun, shall we? I swerve through the next exit and speed up again once we are back on a straight stretch. I take another corner and another. All done with some sort of expert precision, something I really need an answer to.

Eventually, I pull back onto the road that we were on previously. I start driving along the road like I haven't just wasted five minutes to make sure the police can get the information out of Jay as to where we are going. I'm so glad he managed to spill his plan to me.

"WHAT the fuck was that, Percival?" he suddenly asks me.

"W-what was w-what?" I ask, acting innocent.

"Don't play the idiot. You taking that exit and driving like a fucking maniac!"

"Oh, that? It was n-n-nothing," I say with fake confidence. Then, to enforce it, I 'relax' a little more, trying to make it seem like being held at gunpoint happens to me all the time. "Man, I r-really n-n-need to drive more. I forgot h-how much f-fun it c-can be."

"After this, I'm never letting you go anywhere. If I have to lock you up in my basement, so be it."

I stay quiet when he says that. **What is this? Some sort of '80s drama movie?** Is that all you can think of right now? **What?** I roll my eyes and wonder how far it is to this dock he is taking us to. Hopefully, it's not much farther. Actually, I hope it's really far away. I hope Bill is all right and, most of all, I hope Elliot finds me. Gods, I miss him. But… after this, I don't know if I'll ever want to have sex again. I think the only reason I am still functioning right now is because of all the adrenaline running through my body. If that is the case, then I am definitely gonna collapse soon.

"Pull over now," he says calmly. I do as he says, and I stop the car for him. He gets out, but I don't. I need to wait for the tracker to catch up. "Get out," he tells me.

"No. This is where you leave," I tell him. I don't look at him.

"Not funny; get out now." He motions me out with the gun.

"No. This is when I leave you. This is the part of my life where I take control." I face him. "And you are never going to be a part of my life again!" I hit the accelerator, but a shot is fired before I do. I know he shot out my tire. I stop myself from driving off. Even he knows that driving with a flat is dangerous.

"I won't tell you again." Then, he points the gun at me. "Get out of the fucking car!"

Shaking, I take the keys out of the ignition and step out of the car. I move around the front. I'm ambling, not deliberately. I'm kinda just in shock about this whole thing. There are only two ways out of this, aren't there? <u>I can only foresee two outcomes, yes.</u> *Our time has been short, my brother, but we fought until the end. I, too, can only see two results.* **I miss Elliot; he made us feel complete.** That he did, I wish I could see him once more before the end. I take a breath as he grabs my arm and holds the gun to my head once again.

"I said not to follow me!" he yells. My head snaps up, and I see a cop car in front of us. Three men step out of the car, but I don't get a good look before pulling away down onto the docks. There is only one boat docked. Of course it is his. I've spun back around, and I see him, Elliot! He came for me!

"Elli!" I yell involuntarily, the gun is pressed harder into my head.

"Shut it, fag," he mumbles into my ear.

"Let him go. You've got nowhere to go!" Sammy shouts. "If you let him go now, maybe we can work something out."

"I am *not* going back to prison! I just want what's mine. Now I have it. I can disappear with it."

"He! Not it. Do you even realise that you have a person there? Not an object?" Sammy yells back. He is stepping closer.

"I said stay back!" He points the gun at Sammy, who stops and raises his hands. Shit, I can feel my adrenaline starting to wear down and my fear starting to rise. Keep it together, people.

"Hey, Perry, you, okay?" Sammy asks me. I manage to shake

my head. "You're gonna be fine, you hear me?" My kidnapper grips me tighter and seems to growl; I still nod, hoping to the gods that he is right.

"We are getting on this boat, and you better not try and stop us!"

"Give us Percival, and you can. That's all we want," Sammy says calmly. I do not remember Sammy being this good at negotiations, not bad for a chef. And he is married to a lawyer; he probably picked up a few things. <u>Ah, so you did see the ring.</u> It's glinting in the sun. It's hard not to notice it; I bet they finished the ceremony once… anyway.

"He's mine. Not yours! No one but me can have him."

"Too late for that," I mumble, his grip loosens, and he pushes me away.

"W… what? No, no, no, no, no! You're mine. No one can have you. NO ONE! WHO HAD YOU!"

"I did." Elli finally steps forwards. Suddenly, the gun is pointed at him. Elli has this cocky look about him. It makes me think of when we were younger. In fact, the last time we were in a situation where he was standing up for me, he also had green hair and looked this cocky. What's he planning?

"You," the bastard says. "Now my toy is tainted because of you."

"He was never yours! He was always mine. I have always loved him, and he has always loved me. If you take him away, I won't ever stop looking for him. Even if you kill me, someone will keep looking for him. You won't ever get rest. Can't you understand that?" I have no idea what is happening right now.

"No, no, no, he's ruined. You broke him. You broke my toy!" he yells, pointing the gun at the two men. I can feel my fear of him start to stir. Come on, guys, we have to stay calm. Elli and

Sammy have this. *I think I have an idea, when I say, stamp on his foot like you did last night.* <u>Preferably with the foot that you did not wrap with a sock.</u> **Please listen to the nerd. You do not want any more pain running through your body.** I can second that since I can barely feel my ass, and my leg is incredibly sore. I really should have taken it easy while I was driving.

"Elliot didn't break him," Sammy starts, "you broke him. You forced him to do things he didn't want to do. You cut him; you scare him. Look at him, look at Percival." He hesitates but looks at me. I plaster the fear over my face even more than I mean to, but it's enough to get me away from him and towards the water. I can jump in if needs be. Suddenly I'm being pulled back into his embrace with the gun to my head.

"NO! You broke him!" he screams. *Now, Percival!* I quickly stamp on his foot and break free of his grip, and the gun fires.

Alive

The next few months go by in a... blur, really. I'm not even sure I know who's been looking after me. I mean, I remember the gunshot. Then waking up in the hospital and a few times at home. Other than that, though... I draw a blank. That is until this morning when someone dunked a bucket of water over my head, partially breaking me from my shock. Whoever it is, is forcing me into the shower. They told me to get dressed in a set of clothes they provided. Then, they walk out of my room before I can see who it is.

I've mostly been sleeping in Elliot's room, I think; his bed seems to keep me calm when I have panic attacks. The only reason I know I've had them is because they, being my friends, keep marking it on the calendar when I do and don't have attacks. They seem pretty random to me, but Skye is the only person I know who could make sense of them. But he seems to be very busy these days.

Once I shower and am dressed, I am escorted out of my flat and into a car. Like I said, I've been in a bit of a daze for months, so I'm not even sure I know who's driving or if anyone else is... in... the... car. I feel myself start to hyperventilate. Why the fuck am I outside? I can't do this! He tried to kill my family just because I hit him. He shot Jay! Now I'm in a car going gods know where and I can't – a hood is pulled over my face and over my nose. They tell me to take deep breaths, and I manage to. I recognise the scent. It's Elliot's hoodie and calms me down almost instantly; hang on, I know this hoodie. Elliot told me that he got it during his time looking for me. He said it helped him keep his arms covered and not be tempted to cut them. Elliot effectively gave it to me after my first attack. I don't remember when he told me that, though, probably during the last night we were all together; I was wearing it then.

'...And in recent historical news, archaeologists in Norway have discovered an ancient artefact in the mountains, the exhibition leader has declined to comment on what has been found. He has, however, informed us that the artefact was at one point shaped like a spear, and once the runes on the side have been deciphered, they will know for sure what the artefact is...'

The car stops, jolting me from my thoughts, and the two of us get out. I leave my hood up, and I keep sniffing my hoodie. I really don't think I should be outside. Outside is dangerous; outside, he can find me. He *did* find me in France. He can find me anywhere! I feel my body stop moving; I look at where we are, and I see it's the hospital where Skye works. I do *not* want to be here. The person standing next to me gently places their hand on my back and starts directing me into the building. Reluctantly I let them.

When we enter, I try and shrink further into my hoodie. The last time I was here, everyone was under investigation for neglect. I wonder what became of it? Looking around, I see the nurse, Lindsay, that helped me when my back was injured. She gives me a sad smile, and I nod at her and give her a limp wave. She is quickly pulled away by another nurse asking for help, I assume. We pass another doctor who isn't paying attention and runs right into me. I stop after they hit me. I look at the floor and do nothing; I think the doctor is about to shout at me. Good, I deserve it. I wait for it, but it doesn't come. Instead, a hand is placed on my shoulder, and I'm told to start walking again. I don't, but I do turn around.

I look at the doctor and see it's the same one that caused a panic attack the first time I was here. I look down at my feet and mumble that I'm sorry. I quickly spin around and start walking. I have no idea where I'm going so, I'm grateful when my 'guide' redirects me towards the elevator. We get off on the top floor and head straight down the hallway. We pass a lot of offices; one has Skye's name on it. This can't be where we went, his office was on the first floor. I wasn't paying attention the first time. I stop in front of the door, thinking he might be in today, but I shake my head and keep walking. He'll probably be swamped.

We reach the end of the hall, and I see we are at the chief's office. Head of the whole hospital, the man I was talking to. Why am I trembling? I'm nervous but… Excited? My guide knocks on the door, and we enter. I am standing in front of the desk. The doctor before me has his back to me and is looking out the window. The position reminds me of someone, I can't place who.

"You caused me a lot of trouble, Mister Grace. Not that I wasn't expecting a bit of drama." I lower my head at his comments. He walks away from his desk and towards my guide. I know because I watch his feet. They exchange words. "Your friends are nice. Very supportive, even against my better judgement. I thought you would do better in a psychiatric ward, but they thought you'd do better at your flat. Gods know why I listened to them. Don't let them go, mind you. Everyone needs a good support system." I hear the door open and close. Now I'm alone with this man. Why? "Mine was my wife and my son. Of course I haven't seen him properly in… about eight years now, no explanation, just poof. No contact, a text here and there for a few years, then nothing. I saw him once, though, thinner than I remember and…"

"Trembling?" I mumble. It occurs to me that I might know who this is. But I don't think I'll be able to bear it if I'm correct. **We lost everything in France; I won't let us lose any more if I can help it.**

"Yes. Why do you look down, Percival?" he asks.

"I… I'm not s-sure I'll be a… a…" I can feel the tears falling.

"Visualise the word. You'll get it."

"Able," I get out. "Able to hh-handle what I f-find."

"From what I've heard, you can handle a lot more than you let on."

"NO!" I yell. Shocking myself. "I lost everything! I lost who I was! Then I finally started getting better, and it was taken from me. Again! I will not be hurt by anyone ever again. If you are who I think you are. Then… then…"

"Then what?" He pulls down my hood and turns me around, gently gripping my shoulders.

"Then I'll have to admit that she won't be there to comfort me. That no one can help me."

"What makes you think your old dad can't help you?" he asks.

Fuck it. I look up and staring back at me with the same eyes I see when I look in the mirror, still taller than me, my father hasn't changed. His hair is a little grey, but it's still him. My dam quickly breaks, and I am crying into his chest loudly. He is stroking my back and manages to calm me down. I sniff and break the hug, but I stay close to his chest. I take a few breaths and try to steady my voice.

"Hey, Dad." I laugh and smile at him; his hand comes to my

face and wipes away my tears.

"My beautiful baby boy. How I have missed you." He pulls me into a hug, and this time I can tell that he is crying too. Which makes me cry even more. For a long time, we just stay hugging in his office. I can't quite believe it's him, I assumed he was back in Alloa, but I am glad he is here. Eventually, we stop, and he sits us down and grabs some tissues for the both of us, and we clean up our faces and laugh when we see each other.

"Percival, I am so sorry I have stayed away for so long." He tells me.

"I'm not m-mad if that's w-what you t-think. It wasn't all your fault."

"I know. My hope was that the situation would resolve itself. But when Skye told me about what he found out, I knew I had to do something to get you at least out of the house, and it worked. Although I'll admit, having Young Elliot in the ER was a stroke of luck. Without him, I fear it would have taken a lot longer to get you away from—"

"I would p... p-prefer if we didn't m-mention *his* name," I interrupt him. Dad has a thing about people interrupting him, but I think this time he won't mind.

"No. I don't suppose you would like to hear it." He pauses; I can tell that he's choosing his words carefully. If he doesn't say it, though, I will. I'm not sure I can but, I have to at least admit it. If not for Dad, then for me. "You should know that the other male nurses that were associated with him and…"

"Abused me," I finish for him.

"Yes, that. Well, those men were fired, arrested and put on the sex offenders list, not necessarily in that order. But, still, they won't be coming anywhere near you ever again. Without… *him* they have no power, and I have made sure they will never be near you again."

"Thank you. I w-was worried some of the n-n-nurses hated me." With that, he laughs. I look at him and tilt my head in confusion.

"Oh, my boy. They don't hate you. Half of them are mothers themselves and basically became the Percival Protection Squad. One of them wanted to get T-shirts. I think it was my new head nurse, Lindsay, who led the charge in finding those who had hurt you. Six of them in total were arrested, including a doctor. The head of general surgeries, can you believe it? Lucky, I had just the man for the job once it became free."

"Skye? I w-was wondering why his of-office was up here." My dad simply nods. Then I start thinking about what he's told me. "Sorry, I'm about to r-ramble. To clarify, you would have let my situation resolve on its own, but after Mum's funeral, you changed your mind. I would guess you asked Skye to get close to my ex so that he could come over at some point to check on me or in the hopes that we would become friends. I'd guess you didn't count on the fact that we were already friends, thanks to social media. But after that, you had to actually get me out of the flat, so you came up with the upgrade scheme and seemed to make sure Skye was the one that would show me around and essentially keep me safe. So, you changed the code in the CT scanner, and you unplugged the servers. Did you even tell the staff? How many people were involved in this? Did you plan on that bitch doctor to give me a panic attack?" I take quite a few deep breaths after that. I am not sure when I had time to breathe during that. After I catch my breath, my dad sighs, turns his chair then leans back.

"Yes, I did do all that – however, most of the doctors were in on the… ruse. Even the head of general, naturally, he told your ex. I thought my plan was ruined when he showed up while you were fixing the CT scanner; luckily, it wasn't. After that, I felt I couldn't trust my senior staff, so I only trusted Skye. No, I did not mean her to give you an attack, but she apologised for an hour to me afterwards. She is actually very nice."

We talked for another hour about what happened when I was helping with their computer issues. Even that Elliot and I finally got together. He was thrilled to hear that, admitted though that he assumed it was Elliot when he caught me with a boy in my bed. Turns out he and Mum had a bet going to see how long it would take us to get together. Her stake was when we're at uni, his was at the end of high school, then after Elliot finished uni. Guess they were both wrong, not that I mind. I'm just glad to have my dad back. Something about talking this through with him makes me feel loads better.

"I was sorry to hear about France, though. You should know that other than Jay and Bill, no one was injured seriously. Well, there was one fatality, as you know." My head snaps up at that.

"Someone died? Who?"

"You don't know? Percival, you've been back for three months. What have you been doing?"

"I have no clue. I remember the gun going off, the hospital in France. Then basically nothing until this morning. I was kinda aware of people looking after me, but... ugh, I don't know. I honestly can't even remember coming home," I admit to Dad. He gives me a sad smile; he looks as though he might tell me something, but there is a knock at the door, and he stops himself. The door opens, and I recognise, finally, my guide. Skye, my personal protector.

"Sorry, sir, but it's five. I've gotta get Percival home before you go into surgery," he tells him. He smiles at me.

"Ah yes. Can't miss that, I'm afraid." He stands up and grabs a business card. I watch him flip it over and write something on the back, then he holds it to me. "This is my number and new address in Edinburgh, too many memories in the old place. I hope you can understand. And yes, I still have all your comics." I stand up and force him into another hug which he doesn't deny, but he does whisper to me that I shouldn't worry about France: "I'm sure you'll figure it out," he tells me.

"T-thanks." I walk towards Skye, then I turn back to him. "Love you, Dad." I say, smiling at him, like a genuine smile.

"Love you too, son. Now get yourself home. You'll need to get some food in you." He sends us off, and Skye starts escorting me back to his car. Nothing is really said between us. That is until we get outside. Now I know I'm used to holding grudges, less so in the last six years. But really, this is something I cannot just let go of. So, I turn around and punch Skye's arm… again.

"Ouch! Hey, what the hell?" He rubs his arm, then is forced to catch up to me.

"You k-k-know what that w-was for."

"For keeping your dad away from you? Or the thing this morning?" I give him a knowing look, "That wasn't my idea. Promise."

"I d-don't care. You st-still did it." I smile at him, and he starts to laugh.

I'm not sure what happened to me in the hospital. Maybe I just needed to see my dad, give myself… a factory reset to put it one way. I'm not saying I feel better. I'm definitely not ready to do anything… sexual. Just the thought makes me shiver. I'm sure that Dad can get me into therapy, so I can at least, I can at least call him and ask now. I really have missed him, although I'm pissed. He had to use such an elaborate plan just to get me out of that flat. I can't really argue with the results, though.

Skye has to shake me slightly to jolt me back to reality when we arrive at the flat. At least this time, it works. I can only imagine how much everyone has been worrying about me. Three months in a coma-like state, I'd be concerned too. This time Skye doesn't get out of the car. He just hands me my keys and tells me that he'll see me later. I thank him for everything, but I understand that he has things to do other than look after me. Once he leaves, I walk up to the door and open it.

I think about taking the lift, but I remember there isn't one. I walk up three flights of stairs and stand in front of the door. Home alone? Good idea or not? Why didn't I ask Skye to come up with me? Guess I should get used to the idea of being alone, at least… Why's the door open? I take the handle and push the door the rest of the way. I notice that the lights are dimmed, and there is a faint light emanating from the living room. Who is in my flat? I close the door, place my keys where they usually go, and cautiously walk towards the light source. When I enter the living room, I see the silhouette of someone in the kitchen. A naked someone at that, partially anyway, they are wearing an apron. They are cooking something, it smells excellent… smells like a meal Elliot made for us in uni. What was it again?

"It's home-made chicken kiev with a lactose-free garlic and herb sauce, fresh veg and, of course, potato wedges," the voice says, making me stop in my tracks. The silhouette brings two plates to the table, which has candles and a bottle of cream soda on ice. I look around the room and see that there are candles everywhere. I'm gonna fucking cry again, but I don't. Not at that anyway. Finally, the man's face comes into view, and I run over to his stupid face and kiss it. All over and over and over again. I mumble how stupid he is. All he can really do is laugh and kiss me back.

"You are s… such an idiot," I mumble and sniff once I finish kissing him.

"Yeah, I know. But I love you. I'd do anything for my sunshine." He kisses me gently.

"I love you too, Elli."

"I love you too, don't leave me again. Promise?" he asks.

"Promise."

Five Years Later

Better

Things are good. Like really good. Not that I have time to talk about them, it's Sammy and Abi's fifth anniversary. Elli is driving us; his hair is dyed, again. This time a dark blue. We don't want to scare the kids that will be there with Elliot's flamboyant hair colours. Over the last five years, he hasn't slowed down with the hair dye. He dyed his hair pink just to cheer me up on one of my worst days. I'll admit it worked; I couldn't help but smile every time I saw it. He explained what happened on the port five years ago.

So apparently, after I hit my ex's foot, I knocked myself out; that's why I don't remember anything after the gun was fired. But it wasn't *his* gun that was fired; it was the cop's. Only the officer didn't fire it. Elliot did; while we were all distracted with the idiots screaming. Elli managed to slip the officer's gun from its holder, and the moment it was necessary, he fired it at my ex. The officer commended him on his aim but took him into custody then deported him; now, he's not allowed back in France ever again. After we got back to the hotel, I was left in my room. Apparently, I was shaking so much that Skye had to sedate me once again, and he then got pissed and said he wanted to shoot my ex. Seems that the love of my life did kill him, just like he said he would. I don't know if it's romantic or not, but... it's a fantastic thought.

Five years travels fast, not gonna lie. I wouldn't have thought

I'd be here after five years. However, Elli and I did move in to a new house after about a year of living in the flat together. After everything that happened, we agreed it was best to keep things the same for my sake. Dad lives close by and is now retired, and I am still running my web design and repair business although I got back into teaching now. I'm a secondary computing teacher. I make no comment on the matter, but Elli argues better than the others. I also double as the engineering teacher when it's called for.

Finally! We pull up outside Abi and Sammy's, quite frankly, stunning house. I swear Abi is one of the only decent lawyers out there, but she still makes a fuck tonne of money. We exit the car, and Elli, ever the gentleman, waits for me and slips his hand in mine as we walk up to the open door. As we enter, I notice the swarm of people, and I grip Elli's hand tighter. I'm nervous. It's been a while since I've been to a party. Or a large gathering in general.

"Uncle Perry!" a child yells; I watch as this five-year-old child runs up to me. I instantly bend down, catch her and pull her up into my arms.

"Hey Chrissy, and h-how have you b-been?" I'm going to say this now, I hate being called Perry, but she hates being called Chrissy, so we agreed. She gets to call me Perry. I can call her Chrissy. Anyone else who tries is met with no response.

"I's good. How you?" Chrissy says with her broken English. It's cute.

"Oh s… same old." I turn her to face Elliot. "Look who c-came with me."

"Uncle Elliot!" She suddenly reaches over to him to give him a cuddle, I have to follow her, but Elli just takes her from me. I'm not complaining. My arms are kinda sore today.

"Christine, what have I told you about attacking your uncles?" Sammy says, coming over to greet us.

"To not to. But dis is a party, dat is different wight?" She looks at both of us for support. She doesn't need it, though. She definitely inherited her mother's negotiation skills.

"Well, she's got you there, honey," a very pregnant Abi says.

"Mummy!" She jumps off Elliot and runs over to her. "Look who came!"

"I see them, sweetie. Hello, you two." She hugs both of us. "Just you two?"

"Yeah, can't stay long, though. Early morning tomorrow," Elliot tells them.

"School?" Sammy asks, motioning us into the house. We follow.

"Yeah, I've gotta see which of the new students will need additional support and make sure our files are up to date. Last year was a fiasco with the information I had." The two men go off chatting about Elli's new work. I smile at my boyfriend. He is so passionate about his job.

"Look at that. A genuine Percival smile, where's my camera." Abi teases me.

"S-shut up. W-when's the baby due?" I ask, changing the subject, even if she is right.

"Babies, actually. Two months. Skye is more worried about it than I am. He's making sure that I'm getting the best care, nurses and… well basically everything," she explains and sits on the couch; I join her. Chrissy sits between us, playing with her mother's hand.

"Can you b-blame him after the last t-time? Y-you had her in my old flat, b-because you couldn't make it to the hospital, and she w-was a preemie."

"That won't happen this time. Skye has made very sure of that." She laughs, handing Chrissy a teddy, seemingly out of nowhere, to play with instead of her hand. The bear is thrown away, and she plops herself on my lap, and I give her my hands to play with. No, I don't know what her fascination is with hands. I look up, and I see just the man we were talking about.

"Speak of the d-devil," I say as he comes over, along with his date. Skye's date doesn't join us but goes to talk to Sammy and Elli.

"Percival. Good to see you. How's your dad?" Skye asks, taking a seat on the footrest.

"He's g-g-good, not enjoying re… retirement at all. Keeps asking if h-he can get his old job b-back." We all laugh. "So w-when were you two th-thinking of telling m-me?" I ask, pointing to the brunette that has just sat next to Skye.

"I texted you last week," he tells me.

"Percival changed his number three weeks ago, silly," Abi tells them. Making Skye very embarrassed.

"Sorry." He pauses. "Well, I suppose now is a better time than any. Percival, I'm dating your ex, Jay."

"Well, yes, I g-gathered that much." I smile at the two of them. The two kiss, making Chrissy gag. I laugh at her antics. "I wanna know w-when."

"I'll tell him," Jay says quickly. "He was around a lot during my recovery. And we remained friends, but then he kinda forced me to get therapy after an incident with a knife."

"I did not force you. I gave you an ultimatum."

"Yeah, as I said, forced. Get therapy or go on a date with you!" I clear my throat.

"But you are d-dating?"

"Oh… good point, that would be because I asked him out once I agreed to therapy," Jay admits, blushing hard.

"You two are hopeless. What about the knife?" Abi says to them.

"Oh, he accidentally cut his hand while cooking but was

laughing like a maniac as he almost bled out," Skye tells us. There is a stunned silence that Abi breaks:

"Right, little miss, time to go to bed."

"Aww, but I wanna stay up with Uncle Perry," she complains.

"Come on now, we agreed you could stay up to see them arrive, but you would go to bed when you were told," she reminds her.

"I'll take her, Abi," I offer, not just because Chrissy will want to be carried, but 'cause she's pregnant and walking up those stairs won't be fun. Abi agrees, as does the little girl that is now attached to my back.

I deliberately walk all over the place, moaning and groaning, to make it seem like she is too heavy for me. All the adults at the party look at me like I'm crazy, but they cannot deny the results of the giggling girl on my back. She giggles so much that she almost falls off. She grabs onto me so quickly that I worry she's hurt herself. Luckily, she hasn't, so I walk properly up the stairs and towards her room.

Her room isn't what you'd expect for a girl of her age. We should avoid conforming to gender stereotypes, so naturally, her room is filled with space-related things. She loves *Star Trek*, so there are posters of the Enterprise on her wall. She managed to get her parents to agree to buy her an astronomy magazine subscription. Some of which are scattered over the floor. I'd say she is spoiled, but she isn't; in fact, she is pretty down to earth for a girl with her head in the stars.

I groan as I deposit her on her bed. She giggles as I drop her, but it comes to a stop as I look for her PJs. Chrissy tends to be dropped off at weekends, so I'm used to getting her ready for bed. Thanks to this, I'm used to some of her mannerisms. For example, when she goes quiet like this, she usually carefully questions me in her head. Any second now, she'll get it and ask.

"Uncle Perry?" Right on cue.

"Yes?"

"Why aren't you and Uncle Elliot married yet?" I spin around to look at her. When did... where did? Huh... actually, that is a good question. I grab some PJs for her then sit on her bed. As she changes, I think of my answer.

"Hmmm, well. Y-you, see I haven't b-been well. F-for a long time, Elliot c-couldn't even touch me. Marriage w-wasn't really on our minds, not to say that we w-w-wont," I explain to her.

"Oh. You're okay now, though, right?" The little girl before me looks so hopeful. I smile at her and start to tuck her into her bed.

"It's n-not the type of illness t-that goes away. I have g-good days and bad d-days, mostly g-g-good with you, though."

"Hmm, okay. I don't think I understand, though." I kiss her forehead and stand up.

"You'll understand w-when you're older. Night, night, Chrissy." She replies, and I quietly shut the bedroom door.

I hate it when she asks questions like that. Makes me feel like I'm lying to her. I mean, I'm not, but I am keeping the cause of my depression from her. Honestly, seeing her made me feel a little better. I wasn't looking forward to coming tonight. The idea of leaving the house to go to a place full of people who don't know me wasn't settling well with me. I sigh and turn around to head back downstairs just as Elli comes up; he sees me and very quickly pulls me into a hug. He starts apologising to me, saying we shouldn't have come. I shake my head.

"No, it's fine, just—" Suddenly, my phone starts ringing, and I pick it up instantly. "Blair, is everything okay?" I hear nothing but heavy panicked breathing and yelling. "I'll be right there. Keep your breathing steady, okay, buddy."

"Is Blair okay?" Elli asks. I shake my head and run downstairs to find Abi. When I see her, still on the couch, I tell her that we have to go. I tell her there's a problem at home, she nods, and I run out to Elli, who is waiting with the car running.

While driving, I keep thinking that I want to drive because I'd be going quicker than him. He is so slow. I'm not driving because he won't let me, something about the reckless driving in France. He wasn't even there; I don't know why he is complaining. Elli turns the corner to our street, and I immediately see the source of Blair's panic. Before the car even stops, I am walking up to the man on my lawn yelling at the house. He sees me coming, but I still manage to punch him and hear the satisfying snap of his nose breaking.

"Get the fuck off my property!" I yell. I knew leaving Blair alone was a bad idea. I should have asked Dad to come over, but no, I had to leave my trans son alone in a house when his birth father wants him back so he can keep abusing him. I knew he was in the area, but I didn't think he'd find us, idiot Percival.

"You fucking ass!" he yells at me; he stinks of alcohol is all I can think. "Give me my daughter back!"

"There are no women in our house, only men," Elli yells at him, standing beside me. I hear another car pull up, but I'm too focused to care. The man drunkenly stands up and turns to face the house.

"I know you're in there, Marion! Get the fuck out here!" he yells, then he starts to walk towards the opening door. Instantly I am in his way.

"I won't ask again." I hold my hand out to stop him, and my other hand faces towards the door, telling whoever is opening it to stay put, but I have a feeling I know who it is. "Get off my property, or I will call the police."

"What's a faggot like you gonna do to a real man like me." I move around him and bend down to his level. He takes a swing at me, but he misses, so I grab his arm and throw him to the ground knocking the wind out of him.

"There is a lot more I can do." I pause. "Here's how this is gonna work. You leave, never return, or I call the police and say you violated the terms of the restraining order again. Sound good? Good." I don't give him a chance to answer before I run into the house and see someone hiding under Blair's bedsheets behind the sofa. I sigh and head over to them, carefully pulling the covers away from them. Under the sheets, I find both my kids holding on to each other for dear life. I pull the sheet away and pull them into a hug; I never should have left them alone. The youngest, Evan, is the first to latch onto me. Blair is a little more hesitant, understandably so.

"Percival! Are they…" Elli says, running in. "Oh, thank the gods." He comes over to us, gives our youngest a kiss, and holds his hand out to Blair. He takes it, but let's go just as quickly. I sigh.

"Okay, Blair, you stay here. We are gonna talk; I'm gonna take your brother upstairs. Okay?" I tell him, he nods, but I can tell he's not really paying attention. I rub his leg and scoop up the little boy attached to me, rubbing his back gently to calm him down. "Who was outside?" I ask Elli as we head to the hall.

"Everyone. I'm gonna tell them we're all okay. Sammy has called the police anyway; I'll make sure they get that asshole." I nod and kiss him as he steps outside. I bounce Evan a little, which gets him smiling then I head upstairs. No one will ever hurt my family. Yeah, things have changed.

Things are definitely better now.

A Dad

Evan doesn't seem to want to let go of me; I can't say I'm surprised, it's been a strange night. I wouldn't want to let go of him either. I spend the next few minutes bouncing him gently, telling him that things will be okay. We only adopted Evan two years ago, but he started calling us his dads as soon as he started talking; he adapted quicker than Blair, saying that it feels like we've had Evan since birth. He is a bundle of energy, and I have no idea how to keep up with him. He loves being carried and cuddled, not that I'm complaining; he is a great cuddler. When I finally feel Evan's grip loosen, I gently deposit him on his bed and tuck him in. Only to have him grab my trouser leg, I turn around and kneel next to his bed.

"What is it, sweetie?" I ask, stroking his thick blond hair.

"Is someone gonna take me away, Daddy?"

"Oh, baby, no. No one is ever going to take you away from us. You're our little ball of energy."

"But that bad man said… said that Blair is his. And, and, and said he is a girl, but Blair is a boy, right?" I laugh at his broken speech.

"Yes, Blair is a boy. Your big brother, nothing anyone says can change that. Now get some sleep, or I'll sell all your toys." I kiss his head again as he giggles.

"Night, Daddy," he says.

"Good night, Evan." I carefully close the door and walk downstairs to find Elli and Blair now sitting on the sofa. When

Elli sees me, he gets up and walks over to me.

I hate seeing Blair like this; it was after my own incident when we first found him. Actually, it was almost four months afterwards, we both found him running from someone. He was eight at the time. Both of us were confused but persuaded him to come to our place and get cleaned up. We would have kept him a secret, but we agreed that we had to call social services. When they arrived, he hid in our spare room and kicked up such a fuss that the officer gave up and said they would return when he was calm. That left us with a scared eight-year-old who we could barely stop from having panic attacks.

We managed to calm him down after a week of him staying with us. During that time, we realised that he was transgender. We didn't say anything to him at first as we wanted him to tell us. Of course, that didn't stop us from getting a name out of him, but he kept saying that he couldn't decide on one.

"What do you mean you can't decide?" Elli asked him. He didn't reply at first, just made a lot of hemming and mumbling before telling him to calm down and not worry about telling us. We continued eating the lunch I'd prepared. When he finally decided to talk, it had been about an hour since we all finished the food.

"I can't decide because I'm transgender," he told us, but he closed his eyes and seemed to be waiting for something. I decided to ask him.

"Are you w-waiting for s-something?"

"Well… you're gonna kick me out now, aren't you?" He slowly opened his eyes to finally see that Elliot and I were smiling, and we burst out laughing. I felt sorry for Blair at the time because he didn't understand why we were laughing. Thankfully he asked, "What's so funny?"

"Buddy, you do realise we are both gay, right? I know some LGBT plus people disagree with transgender members. But, we are not those types of people," Elli explained. I get up and kneel next to him, gently taking his hands.

"We accept you. For w-who you are, whether that's a b-boy, girl or even great big d-d-dragon. It's who y-you are." After that, he started crying, and that was the first time he hugged me. It took another week to find the perfect name for him, with our help. Once he had his name, it was easy to adopt him since his asshole of a dad basically gave him up and missed the trial. Since then, though, he hasn't stopped trying to find Blair. It's why we had to move. The restraining order helped for a while, but I'm not sure what we can do after tonight.

I tell Elli that I'll join him in bed later, but I have to talk to Blair now. Elli kisses my cheek, telling me that he is gonna say goodnight to Evan. He leaves us, and I look at Blair. His hair is short like mine, and he's a lot buffer than when we first took him in, and his voice is deeper too. It's been breaking a lot since he started on his T-shots. He started feeling a lot better once he started taking them, more like himself. I look at him and sigh. I grab his covers and wrap us both in then, sitting next to him, I place my arm around his back, and he slowly falls into my shoulder, and I enclose him in a hug. We say nothing.

"Why can't I be happy?" he mumbles into my chest. How can I even begin to answer that? I guess it *is* time I tell him what happened to me.

"You know, we almost didn't take you in. Not because we didn't want you or because we didn't think we could look after you. It was because Elliot was worried that I was avoiding my own problems by bringing you in. However, I forgot to tell him I had already started therapy, so once I told him that, he agreed."

"You need therapy? Why?" He sits up and looks at me.

"I was abused, like you. Beaten, cut, raped, shot at. I even hear voices in my head, not so much now, but I know they are still there helping me when it's necessary. I do miss them, though." Blair doesn't say anything, but I can tell he is relaxing more.

"I don't really understand why you are telling me this," he finally says.

"I guess I thought you were old enough to understand. I sometimes forget that you are only thirteen. You seem so different from the little kid that ran into me five years ago. But you have to trust me when I say that I won't let anyone hurt you again."

"I do, though, I just. Ugh, I don't know what happened tonight. He turned up at the door. I thought it was you guys, that you'd just forgotten your keys. When I opened the door and saw him, I froze. Suddenly I was that little kid again who was being beaten by his... by him. Evan heard the yelling and came downstairs to check on me. I was terrified. He suggested hiding under my covers; it kinda helped." I hold him a little tighter. "But I can't get him out of my head. The way he screamed my deadname, I just. Gods, it terrified me to think I would be forced to go back to him."

"He never called for you, though. He called for someone that doesn't exist. You are Blair, my son. My son that's had a rough night and should go to bed." I let him go, and he stands up, taking his covers with him. As he goes, I look around the living room and see the picture we took when we went to the beach for Evan's birthday. "And Blair. You can be happy, you just... You need to find it. You know you can talk to me if you get upset or in a shit mood."

"I know. Thanks… Dad." He smiles and walks out of the room, leaving me stunned. He finally did it. He called me dad. Gods, I could just squish him now; I think he is finally going to settle in. I relax and lean back on my sofa, raising a fist in triumph. What a day it has been; I don't think anything could surprise me now. I stand up and decide to head to bed.

When I get there, I open the door to find Elliot lying on our bed in a very seductive position. Candles are lighting the room, and it makes my heart burst with anticipation. Elli pulled something like this last time after meeting with my dad for the first time in seven years. In seeing me, Elli springs up and brushes the wrinkles out of his shorts. He smiles at me, then comes over to me and pulls me a little further into our room, then he gets down on one knee. Fuck, it's happening.

"Percival Grace, I have loved you for as long as I can remember. When I got you back, I promised myself I'd never let you go again, then we had that issue in France, and I thought I would lose you again. Now tonight, I have never loved you more than when you were defending our family. With that in mind…" He pulls out a ring and holds it up to me. "Will you do me the exceptional honour of marrying me and being stuck with this hot piece of ass for the rest of your life?" I laugh at his speech. I drop down to the floor with him and kiss his face.

"Yes, I will happily marry you." Then I kiss him again and accept the ring, then there is a knock at the door, and a little voice comes from the other side.

"Daddies, can we come in now?" Evan asks.

"Yes, you both can," Elli tells them, our two boys come in, and both are excited to hear that we are finally tying the knot. Blair seems especially happy. Evan jumps into my arms, and, much like Chrissy, he observes my hands and admires the ring that I have been given.

Of course, I send them right to bed as soon as they are done, annoyed at Elli that he let them stay up so late. But he proposed to me so we finally, after five years, had sex. It was just as good with him as I remember. Much like when we first started dating, he kept asking if I was all right and if he was hurting me. Of course, he wasn't, and it was still amazing. We had to be quiet, but I could tell Blair knew what we had done the following morning. He said nothing but kept giving me knowing glances. I was driving him to school when he finally asked me about it.

"Did you two… have sex last night?" he asks. He's clearly nervous.

"Yes, we did," I tell him honestly. "First time in five years, I might add and well needed for both of us."

"So… how does it work? With two guys, I mean. I know how it works with… hetero couples."

"Well, it works a little differently, but the pleasure is the same." I pull up in front of the school. "I can explain it to you tonight. After Evan goes to bed, I'll tell you everything. Starting with my past, I didn't do a great job of explaining what happened last night."

"Okay, I'll meet you in your classroom after school?" I nod, and he starts getting out. "See ya later, Dad."

I can't help but smile again, its gonna take me a while to get used to him calling me dad. But I love it; it makes me feel like he trusts me. I shake myself out and step out of the car and start towards my classroom. The walk to my room is always the same. First, stop in the staff room, check my messages, and catch up with some teachers, including the annoying English teacher who thinks he can flirt with me. Course this time, one of my co-workers notices my engagement ring and starts gushing over every detail. When we are getting married, how he proposed, will one of us be wearing a dress? I'll admit I'm comfortable enough in my sexuality that I wouldn't mind wearing a skirt, but not enough to wear a wedding dress... or do drag. That much, I know, doesn't interest me.

After the fiasco in the staff room, I grab my bag and head towards my classroom with my messages. Not that I have many. Once I get there, I find some of the kids waiting outside for class to begin. It's the usual group of fifth-year kids who are on a double period. They are great kids, and to be honest, when I was first given the posting, I was sceptical about teaching secondary kids, but once I got started, I discovered that the kids I'm teaching want to be here and mostly listen to what I have to say.

Currently, they are working on the practical side of the final exam. They all have to create an 8-bit game that functions on a computer or a games console. I swear I didn't have to do this kind of thing when I was doing my exams... or I was just so good I did it without really thinking. I sit down at my desk and log into my computer to be greeted by a picture of me, Dad, and Blair at Blackpool tower. Thinking about it, this was right before we adopted Evan. The bell interrupts my thoughts, and the kids outside knock on my door. I motion them in, and they all take their seats once the door is open, of course. I wait until the second bell rings then I stand up in front of my class. I take a breath. I got this. <u>Yes, you do.</u> **And we'll be here with you** – *every step of the way.* I smile to myself and begin speaking.

"Good morning, class. Let's get started, shall we?"